Praise for
When in Vanuatu

"It's never easy to be a trailing spouse, as Nicki Chen so lovingly shows in *When in Vanuatu*. Whether in the Philippines or the South Pacific island of Vanuatu, both in times of political upheaval, Chen tells of the often unspoken hardships and heartbreaks of finding home and family in a new land."

—SUSAN BLUMBERG-KASON, author of *Good Chinese Wife*

"Nicki Chen has, once again, deftly created a story of an exotic world. In *When in Vanuatu*, you will meet a fascinating international community of men and women intent on contributing to global development despite significant obstacles, both at work and in the homes they endeavor to create in a distant land. Enlightening and captivating."

—SALLY STILES, author of *Plunge!* and *Like a Mask Dancing*

"Once again, author Nicki Chen demonstrates her mastery of writing place and characterization. Having been an expat living in foreign countries as a young wife, I resonated with many of the opportunities and challenges Chen portrays. Give yourself the gift of peeking into not only the life of the protagonist, Diana, but also her community of friends and the unique cultures of the Philippines and Vanuatu!"

—KIZZIE JONES, co-project manager for and contributor to *Writing In Place: Prose & Poetry from the Pacific Northwest*

"In *When in Vanuatu*, Nicki Chen explores exotic locales and universal struggles. In this moving, fast-flowing novel, Diana's experiences in the Philippines and Vanuatu illuminate challenges of friendship, marriage, identity, and family that so many women, at home and abroad, face. It's ideal for book clubs or anyone who would want to read a modern, feminist Graham Greene."

—TEGAN TIGANI, book buyer at Queene Anne Book Company

When in Vanuatu

When in Vanuatu

A Novel

Nicki Chen

SHE WRITES PRESS

Published 2021
Printed in the United States of America
Print ISBN: 978-1-64742-034-5
E-ISBN: 978-1-64742-035-2
Library of Congress Control Number: 2020914056

For information, address:
She Writes Press
1569 Solano Ave #546
Berkeley, CA 94707

Interior design by Tabitha Lahr

She Writes Press is a division of SparkPoint Studio, LLC.

For all the expatriate wives I've known
for their courage and enthusiasm
for all they gave up and all they gained
for their friendship and fun and the delicious food they served

Manila

1989

1

*D*iana was high on hope that morning. Energized. How else could you explain the pace of her speed-walking? Her long-legged husband could barely keep up.

"Hey!" Jay called after her. "What's the rush?"

She jogged in place a few beats waiting for him to catch up. Then she took off again. This time he stayed with her. Jay was not unathletic, but, like most expats in the Philippines—herself included—the tropical weather slowed him down.

The service road that ran between their apartment building and Roxas Boulevard wasn't your typical walking or jogging path. In fact, Diana had never seen anyone else use it for exercise. It was a road, after all. But it was convenient. And at seven o'clock on a Saturday morning, you didn't encounter many cars and jeepneys. Today the first car they met, a silver Toyota with kids bouncing in the back seat, was turning into the American Embassy compound, the guard waving it through.

"Only two more days," she reminded herself out loud.

"Two more days?" Jay wiped the sweat off his forehead and frowned.

"Our appointment with Dr. Feliciano."

"Oh, right. The test results."

They dodged to the right as a jeepney approached, blaring pop music and throwing flashes of reflected sunlight from the profusion of mirrors and silver horses on its hood. The passengers, three in a space meant for ten, stared across the aisle at each other, unseeing. Suddenly the jeepney's wheels hit a pothole and splashed muddy water on Diana's white socks and bare legs.

"Reminds me of school," she said, reaching down to brush the muddy water off her leg. "How nervous and at the same time eager I used to be waiting for test results."

"That's because your tests always came back with an 'A' scrawled across the top."

"Not always." Slowing her pace, she glanced at Jay. "Whatever these tests show, I'm ready for it." She gave a determined nod and took a deep breath of air that smelled of diesel fumes, sun-warmed grass, and seaweed. She was more than ready. After three and a half years of trying and waiting and trying again, finally she would know what was wrong with her. Two more days. After that, no matter what Dr. Feliciano prescribed, she'd do it. Gladly.

Jay gave her a half smile and kept walking. He didn't like to talk about "their problem."

About half a mile beyond the American Embassy compound on a narrow strip of unoccupied land, the usual little open-air Saturday market that sold bananas, papayas, and T-shirts had added a big display of *parols*. The colorful tissue paper-and-bamboo Christmas lanterns had doubled the market's size. It was still November, but lanterns, the quintessential symbol of Christmas in the Philippines, came out early.

"See a lantern you like?" Jay asked. "We can drive by this afternoon and buy one."

"Yes, let's do." A red, white, and green parol with a three-dimensional star in the middle and white-and-yellow cut-paper tails had caught Diana's eye. The past few years when she and Jay lived in a house in Makati, they'd hung a parol on either side of their front door. This year in the apartment they could hang one on the balcony.

By the time they reached the end of the service road, they were covered in sweat and slowing down. Like every good trail hike, their Saturday walk ended at a point of interest. Not a waterfall or a viewpoint—this walk ended at McDonald's.

They pushed open the door together and got in line. Diana couldn't help but notice the women on either side of them and behind the counter who were looking at Jay, some of them with a quick glance and a blush, others with a bold stare or even a flirty smile. Jay was good-looking in any country, but in the Philippines, where he was taller than average, he attracted more attention than he did back in the States.

"The usual?" he asked.

Diana nodded. Eggs and pancakes at McDonald's had become a habit. It had all started on their first walk after moving into the apartment. They'd walked two miles in Manila's perpetual heat, and they were hot and thirsty. Then, like an oasis in the desert, McDonald's came into view. They'd just go inside, she thought, soak up some air conditioning, have a Coke or some coffee. If Jay hadn't said he wanted eggs and pancakes, Diana might have been satisfied with a coffee. But now, every Saturday when Jay wasn't on mission, they came out in tennis shoes and shorts intending to exercise for their health while at the same time fully aware they would stop at McDonald's for eggs and pancakes with extra butter and syrup.

They got their pancakes and sat down across from each other in a red-seated booth by the window.

"I have to go to Korea on Thursday," Jay said, sliding a pat of butter between his pancakes and slapping another on top.

She caught her breath. "Thursday?!"

"Thursday morning." He peeled back the foil on a syrup container and poured the whole thing on his pancakes. "A car will pick me up," he said, reaching for another syrup.

"Honey." She straightened up, frowning. "Why didn't you tell me?"

"I just found out yesterday. Chang was supposed to go, but Sanjaya wanted him to take over the Bangladesh Cement Plant project instead."

Stabbing her egg, she watched the sticky golden yolk bleed into the white and then down the sides of her pancakes and onto the plastic plate. Didn't he remember that Thursday was supposed to be the start of her fertile period? "How long will you be gone?"

"Ten days. If I can speed it up, I'll be home in nine." He licked his finger and gave her an apologetic look. As though he would stay home if he could, for her sake. As though having a baby was all for her, not for both of them.

2

$\mathcal{J}$ay was the only man in the room. The blond expat flipping through a magazine was already pregnant, and the cute Filipina across from her was carrying a baby and giving instructions to a *yaya* who was watching her toddler. Both women were past the point of needing to bring their husbands to an appointment with Dr. Feliciano.

Diana squeezed Jay's hand.

"Hey," he whispered. "It's going to be all right. Calm down."

"I'm fine."

He tilted his head toward her and raised his eyebrows.

"Jay, I'm fine." She pressed her heels into the carpet and held her jiggling knees together with her hands. He knew she had this thing—this restless leg syndrome. "I'm not nervous." She gave him a mischievous look. "Are you?"

"Humph." He smiled and looked away.

"Let's go look at the fish," she suggested.

He glanced at the folder on his lap. Then, taking one last look, he snapped open his attaché case and slid it inside. "Sure. Let's look at the fish."

The huge tank of saltwater fish was the focal point of Dr. Feliciano's waiting room. Like everything else—the blue-gray carpet, the tasteful modern paintings—it added to the feeling of calm and confidence. The spot-on decorating choices showed that Dr. Feliciano had a sense of what worked—in interior design anyway.

As they walked past her, the Filipino woman raised her chin in greeting, and Diana raised her chin in reply. The pregnant expat glanced at Jay first. Women always did. The woman smiled at Diana, and she felt for a moment that they belonged to the same club of mothers-to-be. Or would, as soon as Diana finished her long, drawn-out initiation.

"We haven't gone snorkeling in a while," Jay said as they stood watching the fish flit and hover. There were bright yellow butterfly fish with long pointed noses, orange-and-white clown fish, angelfish, tangs, and little bright blue fish. "We should plan a beach trip for Christmas. Bamboo Beach or Anilao. See fish in their natural environment."

"Or Hundred Islands," she answered, still watching the fish. "Abby knows someone with a place there. We could all go together, all three families." It was true; they hadn't been on a trip with the Rahmans and the Dinhs in ages.

In the early days, when they were all new to the Philippines, every few weeks the three families would drive off to some vacation spot on the beach or in the mountains. But these past few years, with all the coup attempts following the People Power Revolution, the shine had come off the Philippines. Or maybe they'd just lost their enthusiasm.

"Hundred Islands." Jay put his arm around her waist. "Let's look into it."

"Let's do."

A fat-lipped white fish swam straight toward her, his translucent little fins spinning at his sides, his mouth pulsing. She did love to snorkel. But first they had to find out what Dr. Feliciano could do for them.

The short hallway leading to Dr. Feliciano's office was flanked by two corkboards covered with photos of babies—naked babies, swaddled babies, bald babies and babies with lots of hair, babies in cribs, and babies in the arms of their beaming mothers. An obstetrician's trophies.

The most prized trophy, though, was reserved for Dr. Feliciano's desk. Inside a filigreed pewter frame, the diminutive doctor and her husband posed with their five children, a stair-step array of boy, girl, boy, girl, boy. It was a graphic demonstration of what could be done if you knew how to make it work.

"Please, have a seat." Dr. Feliciano indicated two leather chairs angled toward her desk. Settling into her own chair, she nearly disappeared behind the oversized mahogany desk. "Now," she said, "let's see what we have here."

Diana, balancing on the edge of her chair, glanced quickly at Jay. The way he leaned back and spread his legs, you'd think he was getting ready to open a beer and watch TV. He raised his eyebrows and smiled a half smile.

"Hm." Dr. Feliciano leafed through the papers, pausing now and then and nodding, shuffling the papers and then pausing and nodding again.

Diana reached for Jay's hand and squeezed it.

Finally the doctor leaned on her elbows and folded her hands. "Based on these tests . . ." She spread the papers out, picked one up, and studied it. "No." She shook her head. "I can't see anything wrong with either of you."

"But, Doctor . . ." A cold flash shot up Diana's spine. There had to be *something*. She was counting on those tests to give her the answer. She was prepared to do whatever was necessary—medicine, shots, even surgery. As she shifted her weight, the damp skin behind her knees separated from the seat with a kissing sound. "But, Doctor, if there's nothing wrong, then why can't I get pregnant?" Her legs were as steady now as a couple of tree trunks, but her heart was pounding in her ears like woodpeckers on a log.

"I understand, Mrs. McIntosh." Dr. Feliciano's smile was cancelled out by the ice behind her dark brown eyes. "You're impatient. You'd like to start your family as soon as possible. But for women your age, it takes longer to conceive. A period of three or four years is not unheard of."

She turned to Jay. "Your sperm count is excellent, Mr. McIntosh, for a man of your age, but naturally it's lower than that of a younger man. And the motility and velocity is . . ."

"Yes. Yes, of course," he interrupted. "So, Doctor, under these circumstances, what do you recommend?"

"You need to keep your sperm cool: no hot baths, and wear boxers instead of briefs. Mrs. McIntosh, you should continue to monitor your fertile periods. Record your basal body temperature every morning without fail."

Diana nodded. "I'm doing that."

"Exercise daily, thirty minutes of moderate exercise."

Diana and Jay both nodded. The doctor continued down a memorized list that closely resembled the written instructions she'd given them during their first appointment: adequate sleep, lots of fruit and vegetables, limit their fat and sugar intake, take the multivitamins she recommended for each of them, and maintain the ideal weight for their height.

"Remember," she said, looking directly at Jay, "continue to practice missionary-style sex. And . . ." she paused for emphasis, "you should try to limit your business travel as much as possible." Jay must have rolled his eyes because the doctor tilted her head and added, "Every opportunity missed decreases your possibility of success."

Before they stood up to leave, she had one more piece of advice for them. "You must relax," she said. "Stress can impact every aspect of your health, including your ability to conceive. I've observed you here in my office, and you both show signs of stress. Especially you, Mrs. McIntosh. If you want to have a baby, you must find a way to relax."

3

*E*ach time Diana drove to Makati, the traffic on EDSA—all eight lanes of it—seemed more congested and the smog thicker than the time before. Everything was gray now: the sky, the ten-story–high blocks of office buildings, the sidewalks. Even the few remaining low buildings at the edge of the highway seemed uglier than before, more covered with dust. By the time she turned onto Ayala Avenue, she was driving too fast, dodging jeepneys and buses and a few pedestrians.

She pulled into Makati Commercial Center, parked, and jumped out. She'd agreed to meet Abby and Madeline at Dulcinea at two forty-five. She glanced at her watch and ran.

By the time she reached the bakery, she was hot and irritated and almost ten minutes late. She yanked on the heavy glass door and stepped into air-conditioned sweetness. In an instant, the stink of diesel, sweat, and roadside garbage disappeared, replaced by the fragrance of toasted sugar, melted butter, and coffee.

Abby was waving at her from a window table, jangling her bracelets to get Diana's attention. Even without her bracelets, with the sun turning her auburn hair full-toned-Irish-lass red, Abby was hard to miss. Madeline was there, too, smiling and fluttering her fingers in greeting.

"Hey," Abby said. "You made it."

A complaint about the horrendous traffic was on the tip of Diana's tongue until she looked at Madeline's sweet, unflappable face. You couldn't complain around Madeline. At least Diana couldn't. Not without thinking about all that Madeline had endured during the Vietnam War. Despite all the friends and family who'd been killed or left behind, every time Diana saw her, Madeline was smiling.

"Sorry I was late," Diana said. She pulled out the little wrought-iron chair, adjusted its lavender cushion, and sat down. "I was thinking about *churros con chocolate* all the way here." It was true, more or less. The thought of spending a pleasant hour with her friends, talking, and eating one of her favorite treats had kept her from spending the entire drive stewing over her appointment with Dr. Feliciano and dwelling on the slow progress of the smoke-belching traffic.

Dulcinea's churros were legendary. The Spanish bakery also had the best mango pies Diana had ever tasted, not to mention mouth-watering cream puffs, *leche flan, brazos de Mercedes,* and, of course, their fantastic *sans rival.* But now it was almost three o'clock in the afternoon, the hour when Dulcinea served fresh churros con chocolate. Every table was occupied with expat women and Filipino men and women, all of them waiting for the same thing. The baker would be in the back, squeezing loops of fresh dough into hot oil while his assistant prepared the thick Spanish-style cups of hot chocolate that went along with it.

Jangling her bracelets again, Abby waved at a passing waiter. "*Tatlong churros con chocolate*," she told him, throwing a little Tagalog in with the Spanish.

"Ah," Diana sighed. "This is great. We haven't been to Dulcinea in such a long time."

Abby and Madeline exchanged knowing grins.

"*You* haven't, luv," Abby said. "Since you moved to Roxas Boulevard, we hardly see you."

"And we miss you," Madeline added.

"I know. I miss you, too. It's just that I hate fighting the traffic."
There I go, she thought, *complaining about the traffic.*

"For the life of me, I can't comprehend why you moved there,"
Abby said. "No one lives on Roxas. Nothing happens there."

"Except our husbands' work." With Jay's office walking
distance from their new apartment, it had made a lot of sense to
move. What hadn't been reasonable was to keep paying the higher
rent for a large house with a yard in Makati when there were only
two of them. Sometimes Diana regretted being so susceptible to
arguments of reason.

"Please!" Abby raised her palms to fend off the thought.
"Please don't mention our husbands' jobs. I'm sick of hearing about
the Development Trust for Asia and the Pacific. It's all Saudur talks
about these days. D-TAP, D-TAP, D-TAP."

Madeline grinned. "Don't they all?"

"Not like this. Every evening Saudur goes round and round
grumbling about his boss. He's fed up to here." She grazed the top
of her auburn curls. "Banerjee keeps giving the fisheries projects to
some guy who knows nothing about fisheries and assigning Saudur
projects that don't match his expertise. He's bloody furious."

"Saudur?" Diana said. "You're kidding. I've never seen him
get even mildly angry, let alone furious." Abby's husband was a
brilliant Bangladeshi with a Cambridge accent and a ready smile.
He could get overly serious. But angry?

"That's just it. He's usually so mellow. This thing has been
simmering for a while, though. Some blokes simmer."

The waiter was already back. Balancing his tray in one hand,
he served them small cups of thick hot chocolate and plates of
churros sparkling with hot oil. Before leaving, he placed a fresh
sugar bowl and three spoons in the center of the table.

"I have a bad feeling." Abby sprinkled sugar on her churros.
Then she broke off a piece and dipped it in the hot chocolate. "I'm
afraid Saudur's going to do something stupid."

Madeline tilted her head to the side. "What stupid thing would he do?"

"I have no idea."

"You see," Diana said. "You can't even *imagine* Saudur doing something stupid."

Abby shrugged. "Listen, I'm sorry. I talk too much. How've you two been?"

"Fine. Always the same." Madeline blew on her hot chocolate and took a sip. "Cooking, shopping, accompanying the children to the park or swimming pool, playing mahjong."

On another expat woman's lips, Diana thought, the list might have been a complaint, a description of the boring insignificance of her life. Coming from Madeline, it sounded more like an accounting of her blessings.

"How about you, Diana?" Abby asked.

"I'm okay."

"Doesn't sound like it. What's the matter? Have you heard from your obstetrician about those tests you were taking?"

Diana pressed her finger into some stray grains of sugar and lifted them to her tongue. Then she cleared her throat and leaned across the table. "Tell me something. Do I seem stressed to you? Nervous?"

Abby chuckled. "Aren't we all?"

"I'm serious. I mean more than most people."

Abby took a bite of chocolate-dipped churro and licked her lips. "I don't know if you're stressed out, but you are bloody persistent."

"What do you mean?"

"You know. You don't let things go. You're kind of obsessive that way."

"Oh, my god!" Diana said under her breath. Why didn't people understand? What was she supposed to do, stop caring? Stop trying?

"Persistence is also a virtue." Madeline nodded as she spoke, as though to confirm her own words. "We all need it at some time in our lives. But, Diana, what is this all about? What did the doctor say?"

"Nothing. After all those lab tests and X-rays, she couldn't find a single reason why I'm not getting pregnant. Not unless you count being stressed as a reason."

"So . . ." Abby raised her eyebrows. "If she couldn't find anything wrong, that's good, isn't it? Just keep on trying. And if you don't get pregnant, that's all right, too."

What? How could Abby say that? It wasn't all right. It absolutely was not. Diana clenched her fists and tried to keep her voice steady. "Of course we'll keep on trying. But . . ." She pressed her lips together and turned away. "We've been trying for such a long time. Ever since the day we arrived in Manila."

"Oh," Abby said.

"I didn't tell you at first because . . ." She bit her lip. "It's such a personal thing. Besides, I thought it would only take a few months, and then once I was pregnant, I could tell you. You probably got pregnant right away."

They both nodded.

"*Too* fast," Abby said with a crooked half-smile.

"That's the way it should be, isn't it?" Diana said. "A woman should be able to get pregnant."

Madeline stirred her hot chocolate, watching intently as the thick dark liquid swirled around her spoon. And Abby—Abby who wasn't afraid of anything—seemed to have trouble meeting Diana's eyes.

Diana looked away and then back at her friends. She felt on the verge of tears, but she continued anyway. "After a couple years of trying, I decided there must be something wrong with me. Or with Jay. Wouldn't you think so, too?"

"I guess," Madeline said.

"And then I found this doctor, supposedly the best fertility doctor in Metro Manila, and I thought she'd be able to find a solution for us. This morning when I saw her scrawling something on her prescription pad, I was so hopeful." Diana sighed. "Until I saw it. 'Relax.' That was what she wrote. Just 'relax.' Some prescription, huh?"

There was a moment of silence between them. Suddenly Abby lifted her half-eaten churro in the air like a scepter. "Well, then," she said, "let us relax and eat and drink."

Diana picked up her churro and studied it—the crispy ridges all along the bow-shaped pastry, the shiny sprinkles of sugar. Well . . . if this was what she had to do, so be it. "Okay," she said, dipping her churro into the cup of hot chocolate. "I pledge to become the most relaxed person you know."

She bit into the chocolate-dipped churro. And it was delicious. She took another bite and another. Mmm! Crisp on the outside, soft and moist on the inside. Lifting her cup, she let the thick chocolate linger on her tongue and slide slowly down her throat. "Soo good!"

Abby raised her cup. "I'll drink to that," she said, waving her cup in the air.

"To chocolate," Madeline said, tapping Abby's cup and then Diana's. "It makes everything better."

Diana put her cup down and licked her lips. "Jay and I have been talking about a beach trip over Christmas for our three families."

"Brilliant idea!" Abby said.

"I told Jay you knew someone with a cottage at Hundred Islands."

"Well," Abby said, "to be more precise, I know someone who knows someone whose aunt has a cottage there. I'll get right on it."

"Before we met you and Quan," Diana said, touching Madeline's hand, "Abby and Saudur introduced us to the beaches here. We were still looking for a house when they dragged us off to Matabunkay."

Madeline laughed. "Quan and I would not have conceived of doing anything so frivolous until all our affairs were in order— house, maids, car, school . . . everything. We are such serious people."

"Or so you believed until you met us," Abby said.

"Coffee?" the waiter asked.

The women nodded, and the waiter, a slender young man in a crisp white shirt, bent smartly at the waist and served their coffee.

"*Salamat,*" they murmured. He raised his eyebrows in subtle acknowledgement and backed away.

"I got such a sunburn on that trip." Diana winced to think of it.

"Don't remind me." Abby poured cream up to the rim of her cup and stirred, sloshing it into her saucer. "We dodged the sun most of the next day, remember?"

On that trip, the men stayed outside under the trees, napping, talking, and drinking chilled sodas and beers while Abby and Diana remained inside under a fan blowing hot air across their even hotter skin. They snacked on salty potato chips and drank Coke and Sarsi. And they talked, starting with their lives since they arrived in the Philippines and moving onto the lives they'd left behind, a subject that, as if by mutual agreement, was seldom discussed among expatriate wives. You didn't need to know Abby long, though, to realize she paid scant attention to convention.

"All these colas are gonna rot our stomachs," she said, pulling a bottle of Chardonnay out of the little fridge.

They were on their second glasses when Abby draped her legs across the arm of a battered rattan chair and turned their conversation on its head. "Bloody Philippines!" She drained her glass and lay back, waiting for the last drop of Chardonnay to fall on her tongue. "I'll never get used to this heat. Oh lordy! What I wouldn't give for a foggy London morning, the buildings and trees soft and gray and fuzzy edged, and me hurrying to court in my high-heeled boots and leather gloves, a woolen muffler tucked around my neck."

Diana hoped she wouldn't go on. She wanted to like this life that she and Jay had stepped into. And so far she did. Her first inclination was to argue the other side with Abby: *We'll get used to the heat. By next year we'll be old hands.* But Abby was a lawyer—a *solicitor*, she called it—and anything Diana said would just elicit a stronger counterargument from her. So Diana sat back and listened.

Abby had wanted to stay in London. Her family lived nearby. She had been an immigration lawyer with her own practice.

"I adored the law," she said, swinging her bare feet down to the floor. "Justice. Advocating for the downtrodden. All that glorious rot." She ran her big toe back and forth on a bamboo slat. When she looked up, her eyes were sparkling with tears. "All those years of study, all that struggle getting established, finding clients—all of it wasted." She wiped her eyes with the back of her hand. "I knew that if we left the UK, we'd be gone for years. And if we ever went back, by then I'd be too old and out of touch."

Diana squeezed Abby's hand. She wanted to hug her new friend, but neither of them needed another degree of heat on their painful sunburns. "Did you tell Saudur how you felt?"

"Not straight out. How could I? He'd tried for months to get a job in his field. But no one in London wanted a Bangladeshi fisheries expert. When he got the offer from D-TAP, he was giddy. I argued with him a bit, pleaded my case. But I was just finishing up maternity leave, and a baby in each arm certainly complicated my argument." She coughed out a mirthless laugh. "London loved me," she said, pushing her hair away from her face, "but it bloody well failed Saudur. In the end, it was his future or mine. I stepped back, and we chose his career." She sighed. "So," she said. "How did Jay talk you into coming here?"

"Um . . ." Diana shrugged. "We both agreed."

"Oh?" Abby said, raising her eyebrows.

"Okay," Diana conceded. "Not at first. You know . . ." She bit her lip. "We had a nice life in Seattle—two jobs, a house, my mother nearby." She looked away, trying to remember how it happened.

"I guess . . . well . . ." She shrugged. "Jay was so enthusiastic about working at D-TAP. He called it his 'dream job.'"

Abby nodded knowingly.

"And then, I started thinking I should be more adventurous. Try something new." She looked down, her eyes falling out of focus. "I wanted a baby, but I think I also wanted something more out of life. I didn't know what . . . something."

"That elusive something," Abby said. She stood up, and for a moment there was an awkward silence between them. Then, she tottered to the sink and turned on the cold water. "Damn, it's hot in here," she said, sticking her head under the stream of water. She stayed there until her red hair was good and wet. Then she straightened up and shook her curls like a dog after a swim.

That day, Diana had sympathized with Abby. At the same time, though, she'd wanted to think of her own situation as quite different. True, she too had left her job behind, and she'd also worked all her life to build a successful career. But an accountant's job wasn't about justice or serving the downtrodden. All that mattered for an accountant was getting the numbers right. You couldn't cry over a job like that, could you? Back then, Diana believed she'd be able to return to her career later and that soon she would have a baby to care for.

It had seemed so easy in those early days. So certain. She lifted her cup and stared at the black, bitter coffee. Leaning closer, a partially formed reflection of her face took shape on its wavering surface—an under-the-nostril view of half her face. Ugly and incomplete. She quickly blew it away and took a sip.

"We'll have to bring large floppy hats and plenty of sunscreen on this trip," Abby said. "The twins will want to be in the water all day long."

That first beach trip had been Diana's introduction to snorkeling. Before then, none of them except Saudur had snorkeled. He had taught them all. "The snorkeling should be good at Hundred Islands," Diana said, imagining herself floating facedown in the warm sea, gazing at the fish and coral. Relaxed. Totally relaxed.

She wondered: Would a stress-free getaway really make any difference? Could Dr. Feliciano actually be right?

4

The parking lot at Cartimar was quiet. The housewives and maids who shopped early looking for the freshest fish and seafood, the choice cuts of meat, and the best selection of fruit and vegetables were long gone. Only the late and the lazy remained, and those shoppers like Diana who'd come for something else. Even the carry-your-bags boys seemed to be finished for the day.

The other regular at the Cartimar parking lot was a boy—a teenager really. He kept apart from the others, hiding in the shadows, waiting for the right moment. Then he'd sidle up to a lone shopper and pull aside his rags and expose his fingers and nose, eaten away by leprosy. Whenever he approached Diana, she gave him money. She wanted to help the poor boy. But it was hard to look at his sores. She was ashamed to admit that she was always relieved when he didn't show up.

Today she had just one errand to accomplish: pick up some orchid food at a little shop across from the wet market. The shops, which sold handicrafts, potted plants, birds, fish, and the occasional dog or cat, were separated from the main market by a road and a single strip of parking places. The little shop that sold orchid food was at the far end of them.

The nervousness didn't take hold of her until she'd finished buying the orchid food and was on her way back to the car. She felt it first as tightness in her shoulders and neck and the back of her head, then as a racing heart and an overwhelming hunger for air. It was that poor boy with leprosy. Every time he'd approached her, she'd been returning to her car. She tried to look normal and relaxed as she surreptitiously searched for him in the shadows between cars. Last time, though, she hadn't seen him until he was right there, at her shoulder. She fished in her purse so she'd have money ready in case he stopped her.

This was the leper's tragedy: the disgust people felt. The shunning. The fear. Knowing that leprosy wasn't as contagious as people used to think didn't help. She still felt sick to her stomach when she saw the boy's open sores.

Her car was waiting for her, baking in the sunshine. As she unlocked the door, she couldn't resist looking over her shoulder. She turned and waited a moment, half-hoping the boy would show up so she could give him something and half-hoping he wouldn't.

Once inside, her breathing returned to normal, but her muscles still felt tight. Was this what Dr. Feliciano meant about her showing signs of stress? She leaned back against the seat, letting its searing heat soak into her back and relieve the tension. Maybe she *was* an uptight person.

She closed her eyes, enjoying the warm, moist sauna-like air. Dr. Feliciano probably practiced yoga and believed in meditation and essential oils and the healing power of precious crystals. What Diana wanted from her, though, was science. Instead the doctor had given her a diet and some exercises and told her to keep track of her menstrual cycle and fertile periods. And now all the doctor had for them was her exhortation to relax. Where's the scientific precision in that?

She slid the key into the ignition and stopped.

What the heck?! As long as she was here, she might as well give the doctor's advice a try. What could be more relaxing to watch than the languid to and fro of her own fish?

A nasty smell drove her from the first pet shop, only to find herself at another dingy storefront. Gritting her teeth, she walked in the door and hurried past the snake cages and an obnoxious mynah bird with no table manners. The parakeets were lovely, though—dozens of them tweeting and fluffing their feathers in huge cages. She stopped to admire a parrot while nearby an elegant white cockatoo fanned his yellow crest.

In the back section, aquariums on three levels lined the walls, reflecting shades of blue and green back on each other. Walking between them, she was drawn to the large saltwater tanks with their endless variety of brightly patterned fish. They were too expensive, though, and presumably harder to care for. It would have to be freshwater fish. She moved among the tanks, standing and squatting, judging the fish for their beauty and swimming style. The darters were out. Whoever said watching fish was relaxing couldn't have been thinking of fish that moved more like pecking chickens than soaring eagles.

She gave the guppies, angelfish, barbs, and tetras due consideration. Her favorites, though, were the goldfish, especially those with long flowing tails. One beauty had a white tail and orange body. Another was gold all over.

She pointed them out to the man who conveniently appeared at her shoulder when she was ready. "Also this orange and white spotted one," she said. She moved on to the next tank where several goldfish wove past each other like scarf dancers auditioning for a part. "Those two," she said, pointing out the orange and gold long-tailed fish that looked like twins.

"How big is your tank?" the man asked.

"I haven't bought one yet."

"Oh," he said, drawing it out in an accusatory way. "You must buy the tank first. If you want five fancy goldfish, you must buy a big tank—fifty, sixty gallon. I will supply everything: filter, gravel, plants, fishnet, light, fish food."

"Mmm." It sounded expensive. "Can you take a check?" She threw out the question even though she knew what his answer would be.

"Cash only."

She always carried cash. She hoped today she'd have enough. She wanted to get started right away.

When he'd finished adding it all up and she'd bargained for a better price, the total was still slightly more than she had.

"You pay for fish later. Everything else, you pay now," he said, tapping on his calculator to get a new number.

She bristled a little. How did he know she was short?

"Fish must wait," he added. "One, two days. Maybe longer."

Diana frowned. "No. I'll come back this afternoon."

"Too soon. You must prepare the water first. If water is too fresh, fish will die." He held up a book the size of her hand. "Buy this book. Only fifteen pesos. You will learn best care for fish. Come back when water is right. Then you buy fish."

She sighed. "Okay. But you must save those five goldfish for me."

"No, ma'am. Is not possible. If other customer wants, what can I do?" He raised his palms and shrugged.

"You can show him other beautiful fish."

He looked unconvinced. "I will try, ma'am."

~

According to the little fish book, the aquarium shouldn't be placed near a window, which, according to Diana, would have been the very best location, right in front of the living room window. Then she would have been able to put her feet up on the footstool, relax, and watch her graceful goldfish swimming back and forth. The book warned against it, though. Sunshine encouraged algae growth. She had to find another spot.

"On the buffet?"

Clarita shook her head. "No, ma'am."

The maid was right, of course. They needed to keep the top of the buffet free for serving food to guests.

"Why don't you just put the tank down somewhere, Clarita, until we decide where to put it."

"It's not heavy, ma'am."

But it was heavy. Though Clarita was young and fit and taller than many Filipinas, she was still small. A hundred and ten pounds, Diana guessed, maybe a hundred fifteen. Diana and Jay hired her a few months ago when their first maid, Angelica, quit to take a job as a yaya for a Dutch family with a new baby. When Diana hired Angelica, she'd told her she liked caring for children. In fact, she only consented to work for them after Diana assured her they were planning on having children soon. After years of waiting, Angelica finally sent her cousin to take her place.

"I give up," Diana said after a quick tour of the bedroom. "There's no good place for this aquarium. I'll have to go back to Cartimar and buy a stand."

"Yes, ma'am." Clarita adjusted the aquarium an inch higher on her belly and then turned and hurried away toward the kitchen.

That evening when Jay got home, the tank was bubbling on its wrought iron stand, the light buzzing and the artfully arranged water plants growing out of the well-washed gravel.

Diana kissed him. Then she stepped aside, giving him an unobstructed view of the new aquarium.

"There's going to be a large anti-American demonstration tomorrow," he said, ignoring the bubbling sixty-gallon aquarium not ten feet away.

She shuffled closer to the aquarium, daring him to notice. "A demonstration, huh? I thought Filipinos loved Americans." She was teasing him, of course, trying to lighten his mood. But she was aware of the tensions that simmered below the surface related to the history of American colonialism and the huge US military bases on Philippine soil.

"It's a love-hate relationship," Jay insisted, "the most explosive kind. You'd better stay home. It could get rough."

It was just a march, she wanted to say. Besides, an anti-American demonstration did not a revolution make. You couldn't argue with Jay, though, about anything that had to do with her safety. He was crazy that way. "I'll be fine," she said.

"That's all? You'll be fine?" He set his attaché case down, closed his eyes in a long, slow blink, and sighed. "You'll be the death of me, Diana."

"I wouldn't want that to happen." She took his hand and smiled up at him. His hazel eyes had taken on a sea green tint.

"Then you'll stay here tomorrow, right?"

"Don't worry, honey. If I do go out, I won't go anywhere near the demonstration."

Seeing he was about to object, she put an arm around him and kissed his lips.

When was he going to get over this obsession with her safety? She had a life to live, things to do. Tomorrow she and two other women from the D-TAP Women's Club were scheduled to interview two dozen boys for scholarships to the technical and vocational training section of the Don Bosco Technical College in Mandaluyong. She couldn't back out. True, she might have to drive past the demonstration, but she certainly wouldn't be right in the middle of it. That wouldn't be good enough for him, though. She'd just have to get home before he did and hope he wouldn't call while she was away.

"What do you think of our new aquarium?" she asked, dragging him closer.

"Where are the fish?"

She laughed and hugged him. "You're as ignorant as I was. We have to wait a few days for the water to cycle. If we put the fish in immediately, they'll die."

"Hm."

"I bought it for relaxation. You remember Dr. Feliciano's part-ing words at our last appointment, right?"

He frowned. "Buy an aquarium?"

"No. She said if we wanted to get pregnant, we had to find a way to relax."

He stared at her as though his mind were elsewhere. "Oh," he said.

5

Diana and Madeline Dinh were leafing through the first few applications when Gerda Klein burst into the room. "That blasted demonstration. Ayala Avenue was blocked all the way from Rustans to the Makati Medical Center." Ignoring the drops of sweat trickling down her forehead and collecting on her eyebrows, Gerda glared at her watch. "Seven minutes late."

"Don't worry," Diana answered. "We're almost on time."

"I like to be punctual." Gerda found a chair at the head of the table, opened her folder and nodded at Brother Carlo. "Would you be so kind, Brother, as to send in the first candidate?"

According to his application, Rolando Matapang was the eldest of six children. He lived in Tarlac City, and he aspired to become an electrician.

"You may sit there, please." Gerda indicated a chair at the head of the table.

The boy edged into the chair and waited, straight and nervous as a schoolboy in the principal's office.

"Now," Gerda demanded in a voice that had all the warmth of a drill sergeant, "tell us about your marks in high school."

"Yes, sir," the young Matapang replied. "I mean, yes, ma'am." He dropped his head. "I . . . I finished with . . . um . . ." From his reluctance, one would have thought he had something to hide, but in fact his grades were more than adequate. After a few softball questions and comments from Diana and Madeline, he calmed down and was able to present himself as a smart, articulate young man.

Gerda gave him five minutes and then excused him and called the next boy. It didn't seem like much time, but with twenty-six candidates at five minutes each—Diana quickly did the math in her head—the interviews would take two hours and ten minutes. She checked her watch. It would be interesting to see if Gerda's precision would last.

The next boy was more confident, and the third candidate had an adorable smile. Sometimes he was so busy smiling, in fact, that he couldn't remember the questions.

Diana kept notes, jotting down the boys' answers and her impressions of each of them. In their clean white shirts, heads neatly barbered, smooth faces scrubbed, the boys reminded her not of her own college days but of how old she was. At seventeen and eighteen, they were roughly half her age. She could have been their mother. A handful of the candidates didn't look up to the task, but they were all so earnest and hopeful that she wished the Women's Club had allotted money for more than three scholarships.

Gerda did make a valiant effort to keep each interview to five minutes. But by the time they finished interviewing, eating the sandwiches one of the older students delivered, making their choices for the scholarships, and touring the facilities with Brother Carlo, it was already three o'clock—later than Diana had hoped, but she still had time to make it home before Jay got back from work.

She drove through the school gates, humming, enjoying the sense of satisfaction of a simple job well done. Yes. She'd almost forgotten how pleasant it was to have a job and colleagues.

Once she turned onto the highway, she forgot about the pleasures of work and concentrated on getting home on time. Epifanio de los Santos Highway, the highway with a name so long everyone just called it EDSA, flowed normally for a while.

Then, as they approached the intersection with Ayala Avenue, everything stopped, and out came the vendors of steamed peanuts, cooked quail eggs, *sampaguita* leis, Chiclets, and loose cigarettes. A young girl selling strings of fragrant sampaguita blossoms knocked on Diana's window. She was tempted. She would have loved to buy some to wear around her neck and hang on her rearview mirror. She couldn't, though, without having to tell Jay where she'd been, so she waved the girl away. A boy barely in his teens scuffed past smoking his own wares. "Philip Morris," he yelled, "Marlboro."

She peered down the street to her right and saw only the usual crush of traffic and crowds of people waiting for buses. A normal day on EDSA. She tapped her fingers on the steering wheel, wondering when the light would change. Who wouldn't be stressed with traffic like this?

At the next light she saw a few demonstrators carrying signs: No to US Bases and Junk VFA, even one that said, Stop the Rape of Our Women. They had finished marching, though. They were standing with their signs resting casually on their shoulders, waiting for the next bus.

~~~

She opened the door of their apartment with just enough time to change into shorts and a T-shirt and wash the sweat and grime off her face. When Jay walked in at five fifteen, she was out on the balcony watching the ebb and flow of life sixteen stories below—workers making their way home on the jeepney-clogged side streets, cars and taxis rushing down Roxas Boulevard, drivers lounging near resting cars, and brown-legged boys pedaling their bikes just inside the palm-lined boulevard.

What held Diana's attention, though, as it so often did, was the garden between their apartment and the twenty-story condo next door. The green of the garden was an oddity in this crowded, gray city. A silver-haired woman in wooden clogs strutted along its driveway, flinging her arms toward tasks to be accomplished, pantomiming her instructions. A gardener in an electric green T-shirt ran to her across the grass, only to be sent back for a different tool. Another gardener, smart in red shorts with white stripes, stood at attention, rake in hand, his young, firm legs and muscular shoulders impatient to be set in motion.

"What are you looking at?" Jay came up beside her, smelling of that familiar mix of floor wax, dusty reports, smoke, and stale sweat that she associated with his office.

"I was just watching the gardeners next door."

He shook his head. "Can you believe that place still exists? With a property that size, they could build another twenty-story condo."

"Thank goodness a developer hasn't got his hands on it yet."

He put his arm around her shoulder and joined her in contemplating the garden. One of the gardeners was pushing a hand mower, causing thick blades of grass to spray out like sprinkles of green water.

"So much green," Diana said.

Jay squeezed her shoulder.

Maybe he wouldn't mention the demonstrations. She nestled in closer and directed his attention to the red sun slipping away on the far side of Manila Bay.

He leaned down and kissed her forehead. "I'm glad you stayed home today, honey. I hear it was a huge demonstration."

How fast the body reacts! And how little control she had over it! Surely Jay could feel her racing heart pounding against his chest.

"So far," he said, "no reports of casualties, but . . ."

"It was just a demonstration, Jay. A peaceful demonstration." She pulled away from him.

"That's how things start, honey."

Why had he put her in this position? Because—damn it! It was his fault. It was his unwarranted worries about her safety that pushed her into a corner. She didn't want to lie to him or sneak around behind his back. If it were up to her, she'd share everything with him. Every thought, every step. That's the way it should be between a husband and wife, wasn't it? Still, she couldn't stay locked inside this apartment. She just couldn't.

He was looking at her. Waiting for a response. In the long dusky shadows, she couldn't read his expression.

"Are you thirsty?" she asked. And when he nodded, she kissed his cheek and hurried off to the kitchen to make some *calamansi* juice.

All through dinner she harbored the bitter taste of her anger. Whether it was anger at him or at herself, she couldn't say. Spooning chunks of Clarita's pork adobo over her rice, she half-listened to his long, convoluted account of some office politics. Akiyama, a Japanese director, wanted to ingratiate himself with the former prime minister of Japan by finding a position for his nephew. It was the kind of story Diana hated, even on a day when she wasn't nursing a grudge. D-TAP gossip detracted from her image of her husband's profession as a noble effort to help the poor in Asia. If he was going to talk about work, why couldn't he tell her about the people who would have clean water or more productive farms or jobs as a result of his projects?

Forcing down a few more bites of adobo and rice, her mind wandered, snapping back just in time to hear the crucial bit of information. The job Akiyama planned to give to the former prime minister's nephew was currently occupied by Abby's husband, Saudur. If Akiyama got his way, Saudur would be left high and dry. Jay went on to recount the tangled tale of how Eddie's secretary had used subterfuge to get access to the file that detailed Akiyama's plan.

"And that's how we found out," he declared, stabbing his plate so hard she was afraid he'd break it. "Akiyama doesn't care a whit that Saudur's an experienced officer and the nephew is an unknown quantity."

Diana stared at the adobo on her plate, the chunks of soy-sauce–darkened pork, the strips of fat. "What will Saudur do? He has a family. They can't go back to London, you know. Nobody wanted to hire him there."

Jay chuckled. "Who told you that? I'm sure he could've found a job in England, just not the one he wanted. Hey. Aren't you going to have some *pancit*?" He scooped up a forkful of rice noodles with shrimp, pork, and vegetables and stuffed it in his mouth. "Anyway," he said, pausing to chew, "Saudur has friends. Eddie and I joined forces and found something for him. A position that suits him even better than what he has now."

Diana let her breath out. "Thank goodness. Why didn't you tell me that in the first place? Which department?"

"It's in the regional office in Vanuatu."

"Vanuatu? You mean Abby and Saudur will have to move?" She wasn't even sure where Vanuatu was. Somewhere in the South Pacific, she thought. It didn't matter. One way or another, Abby would be gone.

"It's the perfect place for Saudur. In Vanuatu he'll finally have his fill of fisheries projects."

"What if Abby doesn't want to go?"

He shrugged. "She'll like it there. Everyone says Port Vila is the most beautiful town in the South Pacific. Here, let me give you some before it gets cold." Using the serving spoon and his fork, he pinched up a messy clump of pancit and dropped it on her plate. "Enough?"

She nodded. Men didn't need their friends the way women did.

She picked at the pancit while Jay described how he and Eddie Wu used their contacts to uncover the job in Vanuatu. "Saudur didn't know about Akiyama's machinations until today. We didn't want to worry him until we had something positive to offer. You remember Marshall and Carole Anne Charbonneau, don't you?"

"Yeah. Blond with a southern accent."

Jay frowned. "Oh, right. You mean Carole Anne. Anyway, I contacted Marshall, and he assured me he had a place in the Vanuatu office for Saudur." He paused for Clarita who was standing behind him, waiting for an opening.

"Finished, sir?"

"Yes. Thank you."

She took his plate and turned to Diana. "Ma'am? Was everything all right?"

"Yes. It was very good, Clarita. But . . ." Diana looked down at her plate, at the barely eaten rice noodles with their tiny shrimp and thinly sliced pork, cabbage, and onions. "I wasn't hungry tonight."

Clarita took their plates without comment and disappeared into the kitchen.

"I talk too much," Jay said when she was gone. "Sorry. How was your day?"

"My day? Um . . . it was good." She wished she could tell him about Brother Carlo and the scholarship candidates that she, Gerda, and Madeline had interviewed. She wanted to explain how dear those scrubbed young men were, how earnest in their hopes for making lives for themselves.

Clarita returned with a steaming bowl of rice pudding. She set it in the center of the table and looked at Diana for acknowledgment.

"Oh," Diana said. "The rice pudding." She dished some up for Jay and then for herself, a rich raisin-studded custard smelling of cinnamon and nutmeg—the fragrance of her childhood.

"You're crying," Jay said. "What's the matter?"

"Nothing. Nothing. The pudding reminded me of Mom, that's all. This is her recipe." She touched the corners of her eyes with two fingers. But the tears kept coming. She grabbed a paper napkin and wiped her face. Abby was her best friend. She didn't want to lose her.

She blew her nose. Okay. She was all right now, she thought, straightening her back. No more crying. She dipped her spoon into the rice pudding. It was perfect, the cinnamon-sweet custard, the soft rice and plump raisins. Cooking was the one thing her mom had still been able to do for her and Andrew after Daddy died, the one hope Diana had that her mother would someday recover and start taking care of them again. She swallowed, but an involuntary sob surprised her, and she sucked pudding into her windpipe.

Before she knew it, Jay was squeezing her diaphragm from behind and then slapping her back. "Hey," he said when she stopped coughing. "Are you all right?"

She wiped her eyes with the clean napkin he gave her, but the tears kept coming. By now she was so wound up she couldn't quit sobbing. "I don't know why I'm crying," she blubbered. She was a child abandoned by her father—a woman soon to be abandoned by her friend—a wife waiting for a child who may never materialize.

She had Jay, though.

He put his arms around her. "It's all right," he said.

But it wasn't all right. He and Saudur were arranging a move without consulting Abby. Jay was going off to Korea during Diana's fertile period. Worst of all, he treated her like a porcelain doll, and it was all because he wouldn't let go of what happened to Celeste. She took a big drink of water, shoved her chair back, and stood up. "I drove to Mandaluyong today," she said.

Jay's face looked blank for a moment. Then, beginning to comprehend, he pushed himself up from the table.

The anger on his face made her defiant. "They weren't demonstrating on the highway. I was perfectly safe."

"But why? Why did you lie to me?"

She bristled at the harshness of the word. "I didn't lie." She wiped her nose with the back of her finger. "It was a mental reservation."

"Here." He fished a handkerchief out of his pocket.

"I had to go," she said, taking the handkerchief. "They were expecting me." She blew her nose. "Gerda and Madeline Dinh and Brother Carlo. And all those boys, too. They were expecting me." She found a clean spot on the handkerchief and wiped her eyes.

"What are you talking about?"

"Scholarships for low-income youth," she said, sniffing. "So they can learn a trade at Don Bosco Technical College."

Jay closed his eyes and sighed.

"The boys came from all over the province. Some from even farther away." She blew her nose.

"On the day of an anti-American demonstration, you'd think they could have sent someone who wasn't an American."

It was on the tip of her tongue to mention all the dangerous places he'd traveled for work: the Khyber Pass and Southern Mindanao, the flooded countryside in Bangladesh. She stopped herself. Better to quit while she was ahead. "I'm sorry," she said.

"I worry about you, Diana."

"That's the problem. You worry too damned much about me. Come on. Let's get some air."

They stood on the balcony and watched the red-and-white lights from cars, trucks, and buses flowing in opposite directions along Roxas Boulevard and the rectangles of light and dark in the condo beyond the now-dark garden. When she thought enough time had passed, she told him about some of the boys they'd interviewed. She looked at him for a response, but he just stared into the night, as though he were the sole aggrieved party. "You know, Jay . . ." She pressed her lips together, ready to argue her side of the story. Then, stopping herself, she described in humorous detail how Gerda had scared the first applicant with her crisp commands. And Jay laughed. She leaned into him, and after a few awkward moments he put his arm loosely around her shoulder.

6

She shouldn't have told him about going to Mandaluyong, she thought as he disappeared into the bathroom. If she'd just kept her mouth shut, they wouldn't have this rift between them now.

She sat on the edge of the bed listening to the steady spray of water on the tiles and the uneven rattle of the air conditioner. Who was she kidding? Whether she opened her mouth or kept it zipped shut, Celeste would always be there between them.

She stood up again, unzipped her dress, lifted it over her head, and threw it over a chair. On the day he'd told her about Celeste, she'd been sympathetic. Nothing more.

It was their third date. They'd arranged to meet for a drink after work at a place near her office, the Emerald City Café. Looking in through the window as she walked to the entrance, she saw him sitting alone at a small window table, an amber-colored drink in his hand.

"Am I late?" she asked as she slid into the chair across from him.

"No, no. I came early. Thought I'd get a head start." He held up his glass and sniffed in an unsuccessful sort of laugh. "What would you like?"

She picked up the cocktail menu and skimmed the list, the vodkas and rums, the bourbons and tequilas, the exotic drinks with fruit and cream. An enormous, confusing list.

"Can I get you something?" The cocktail waitress paused in mid-stride and raised her eyebrows at Diana.

"Um. A glass of wine. Something red."

"Other side." The waitress pointed at the drinks menu and flipped her hand over to illustrate.

"Bring me a Chianti," Diana said. It was the first wine that popped into her head.

Jay swirled his ice and took a big swallow. "Another whiskey sour."

From the start, it was obvious to Diana that something was wrong. They'd hit it off so well before. Yet that day while they waited for her wine and Jay's whiskey, their conversation seemed stilted. She looked over her shoulder for the waitress. When she turned back, Jay was watching her.

He cleared his throat and dropped his gaze. "There's no easy way to say this," he said quietly. "I was married before."

"Oh."

He smiled. "That's all? Oh?"

She shrugged. "I'm shocked a little, I guess. I can't really be surprised," she added with a self-conscious little laugh. "You're a good-looking guy. Thirty years old. Plenty of time to be married and divorced."

"Chianti and whiskey sour," the waitress announced.

Jay nodded and waited, tapping his fingers softly on the table as she threw down the paper coasters and set their drinks in front of them.

"I'm not divorced," he said when she was gone.

"What?!" Now Diana really was shocked. Had she been dating a married man?

"My wife died."

"Oh!" She let out the excess air trapped in her lungs. Thank goodness he wasn't married. But still, why hadn't he told her? She told him about her dad.

"I lost her seven years ago," he said, looking out the window. "For a long time I didn't feel like dating. And then when I did start seeing women again, well . . . let's just say, it didn't always work out." He picked up his whiskey sour and took a big gulp.

"That's just the way dating works."

He shook his head. "No, there's something about having a deceased wife that scares women away. One woman told me she didn't want to compete with my dead-but-ever-present first love."

"You're kidding. That's what she said?"

"Yeah."

Diana lifted her wine glass and twisted the stem. Outside, the drizzle was too fine to be seen, visible only in the shimmering droplets on a woman's dark hair and the neon colors splashing across the wet sidewalks. She took a sip of Chianti and put the glass down. She was already more than halfway in love with Jay, and she had no intention of letting his unfortunate first wife spoil things. "What was her name?" she asked.

"Celeste." The name was soft as it slipped from his lips. Sibilant. "We went to high school together. Started dating in college."

Okay, she thought. That's quite enough. She did not want to know anything else about this woman he'd loved and married. Besides, he was obviously uncomfortable talking about her. So she should just let it go.

And yet . . . yet, she did want to know. "Jay," she said.

He reached across the table and took her hand.

"How did she die?"

The color drained from his face as his hand tightened around hers.

"It's all right," she said quickly. "I shouldn't have asked."

He shook his head. "On our first anniversary, we went to Mexico on vacation." He spoke in a flat voice, looking somewhere just over Diana's shoulder. "Puerto Vallarta. We stayed in a new hotel north of town." He paused and turned, gazing now at the people sitting around the room at scattered tables, men in suits and women in professional clothes, laughing, talking, ordering happy hour dishes to go with their drinks. "I chose the hotel," he said finally. Outside it was raining in earnest now. People were flipping up their hoods and opening their fold-up umbrellas. The fat raindrops clattered so hard on the awning outside their window that Diana could barely hear what he was saying.

"That's where . . ." He swallowed. "Puerto Vallarta. It's where she died. I was playing beach volleyball," he said, his voice rising from its studied flatness. "Playing with some guys I didn't even know. She wanted to go for a swim, and I said I'd join her in a few minutes. I didn't want to leave the game because the score was tied, and . . ." He pressed his lips together. "I wanted our team to win. Then, when we did win, the other side begged for a rematch." He stifled a sob and continued, his voice thick with sarcasm. "I could have said no, but I wanted to be a good sport."

The bloated blood vessels in his forehead scared Diana. She wrenched his glass away from him and squeezed both his hands.

"She went swimming without me. Searchers found her body the next morning three miles down the beach."

"Oh, Jay, I'm so sorry."

He pulled his hand free and took a gulp of whiskey. "She was pregnant with our first child."

~~~~~

Diana unhooked her bra and threw it on the bed. It had been years since that evening in the Seattle café, yet they'd never again talked about Celeste's death. Diana still didn't know where she was buried.

She walked into the steamy bathroom and opened the shower door. "May I join you?" she asked, stepping inside without waiting for an answer.

7

*H*er five fancy goldfish rode home from Cartimar in five plastic bags filled with water. Riding next to them in its own water-filled bag was an ugly catfish. The pet shop owner had insisted that a bottom feeder that ate algae was essential for the health of her aquarium. Fine. As long as the dark-spotted, prehistoric-looking creature rested quietly at the bottom of her tank, she'd try to ignore him.

She would have liked to dump the goldfish into her aquarium immediately. But there were rules for acclimating fish. Who knew this supposedly relaxing hobby would have so many meticulous requirements! First you had to take off the rubber bands, roll down the sides of the plastic bags and float them in the aquarium until the water in the bags was the same temperature as the water in the aquarium. Then you had to test the pH in both waters and add a little aquarium water to each bag every fifteen minutes until the two pH's were the same, or nearly so.

Two hours later the goldfish were swimming free in their new home. Diana pulled up a chair. They were like kids let out for recess. Up and down and around the tank they swam, propelling themselves forward by wiggling their fat bodies from side to side like legless bulldogs. Disappointed that they weren't as graceful as she remembered, she focused on their flowing tails and listened to the bubbling water filter.

The longer she sat still and tried to relax, the more everything annoyed her. The trucks rumbling by on the street below. The honking taxis. Clarita in the kitchen slapping something soft and wet onto the cutting board and then hitting it hard. Diana imagined a cleaver breaking through flesh and bone before thudding to a dull stop and then coming down again and again.

She shook her head to clear out the sounds. *Just watch the fish.*

Instead, she thought about Abby, wondering why her friend hadn't called. Hadn't Saudur told her yet about moving to Vanuatu? Or was Abby so upset she couldn't dial the phone?

Earlier, before driving to Cartimar to get the goldfish, Diana had spread the atlas out on the dining room table. She'd leaned low over the table and squinted, looking for Port Vila, Vanuatu's capital. She finally found it on an island so small that the words had to be written on the ocean. Port Vila was a town on an island that was nothing but a tiny dot in the middle of a huge ocean. Not the kind of place Abby would like.

Suddenly she was aware of her legs vibrating, shaking the chair. She squeezed her knees together and gritted her teeth. Then she crossed one leg over the other and rubbed it hard and fast. She'd never been bothered by this . . . this restless leg syndrome— not until Dr. Feliciano came along and accused her of being stressed. She glared at the ugly catfish, somnolent as a snake on a hot rock. Nothing restless about him. He flicked a whisker, expressing his disdain as he continued resting motionless at the bottom of the tank.

Damn! She jumped up and tromped across the room. How could this fish-watching help her relax? She was more nervous now than when she started.

"Sorry, fish," she whispered, circling back to the aquarium. "It's not your fault." She touched her fingertips to the glass. Maybe by tomorrow her beautiful long-tailed goldfish would have settled down. Maybe then she'd be able to sit still and watch them.

In the meantime, she needed to get out and move.

~~~

Clarita was standing over a pot staring out the window when Diana poked her head in the kitchen door. "I'm going for a swim at Seafront."

"Yes, ma'am."

The room smelled of onions and garlic. "Beef for dinner?" she asked.

"Yes, ma'am." Clarita put a lid on the pot. From the side, her usually animated face was expressionless.

"Smells good." Diana started to leave and turned back. "The goldfish are very active in their new tank now. You should take a look."

The elevator door opened to reveal . . . great! One of the yakuza soldiers and his girl. Diana stepped onto the elevator without looking at them and jabbed the already lit button for the lobby.

She'd ridden the elevator more than once with this gangster and his partner. There was no mistaking them. They dressed to stand out. You'd think yakuza would want to blend in, but obviously these two didn't care. Either they had friends in high places, or they didn't realize how tasteless their flashy clothes were. A Filipino would never step into public in brown and orange plaid pants, a purple shirt, and a shiny gold jacket. Why anyone would was a mystery.

This wasn't the first time Diana had seen one of them with a pretty young Filipina. If only she could warn the girl that the "good paying job in Tokyo" would turn into something else. These men weren't interested in singers; they were recruiting prostitutes.

After a slow drop from the sixteenth floor, the elevator came to rest at the first floor, and Diana stepped out into the lobby. The poor girl would enter Japan as an entertainer on a fake passport and visa. That's how they'd keep her there—that and the money she would owe for her airfare.

Diana knew these things now. These and many more. She wondered what her mom would think of the things she knew.

~

The swimming pool at Seafront was untouched, a perfect blue mirror image of a perfect blue sky. Diana left her bag and towel on a table and descended the ladder into the cool water. It was early afternoon. In another hour, the pool would be filled with children. Now there was only a toddler in the kiddie pool and a couple of babies sleeping in strollers while their mothers sipped sodas and chatted. The toddler's mother was daydreaming, watching the swirls of water around her bare feet as she sat on the edge of the kiddie pool kicking in slow motion. Diana sighed, closing her eyes as she lowered herself into the water. Mothers could be so blasé, as though the existence of their children were as ordinary as a glass of two-percent milk.

She pushed off, starting her laps, as always, with the freestyle. Ever since she was twelve, she'd followed the same routine, alternating between freestyle, breaststroke, backstroke, and sidestroke.

She did a flip turn and pushed off the wall, automatically changing to the breaststroke. Before her dad died, she didn't swim laps. In the months following his death though, she was too keyed up to stay in bed waiting for her alarm to go off. Eventually she realized the swim team started practice at five thirty. She could watch their practice and squeeze in a few laps of her own when they finished. By now, the routine she'd invented in seventh grade had become such a habit that she couldn't swim laps any other way. A habit now, but that first year swimming had been her salvation, a prescription for survival that she had written for herself. Her mom, deep in grief, had been in no condition to help her out.

She flipped and pushed off the other wall, changing back to freestyle. She'd taught herself not to remember scenes of Daddy in the hospital or—even worse—her last glimpse of his body in the coffin. But she couldn't forget those images of Mom, sitting at the kitchen table staring into a cup of cold coffee, her hair flat against her skull and frizzy on the ends. Day after day, she wore the same red-and-green plaid pajamas and navy-blue terrycloth robe, fuzzy slippers on her feet. She probably wasn't much older than Diana was now, but she'd looked old.

It had scared Diana, seeing her like that. When she walked into the kitchen after school, her mom wouldn't register her presence until she called out to her or touched her shoulder. Then, she'd force a pathetic smile and ask about school. An empty courtesy since she obviously was incapable of hearing what Diana needed to tell her. "Fine," Diana would say, even though being the object all day of her teachers' self-conscious sympathy and her classmates' whispered comments and curious looks was far from fine. She held back her tears because she was sure her mother would break into a thousand pieces if she cried.

Each day Diana had brought the mail in, but it remained unopened in the fruit bowl or on the counter or on top of the toaster oven. Once, Diana set a new stack on the table next to her mother's coffee cup. On top was a bill from the electric company. Surely, she'd thought, her mom would open that one.

Instead, she had given Diana a quick, apologetic glance and looked away. "Oh, honey," she said. "I know I ought to . . ." She let out a weary sigh that morphed into a sob. Then, clutching the table, she pulled herself up. "Maybe later."

Later? Diana had thought as her mother scuffed across the floor. *And when will that be?* She stared at the cracks in her mother's heels and the mottled white skin of her ankles. It wasn't fair, she thought, blinking hard in a vain attempt to stop her tears. *He was your husband, but he was my daddy. And I want him back.*

It hadn't been fair, Diana thought now as she rolled onto her back for her backstroke lap. Hadn't her mother known how frightening it would have been for her children if the lights and heat had been cut? And where was Andrew all this time? He'd been sixteen years old, for god's sake. Diana had mentioned the bills to him once, and he'd assured her with a shrug that Mom would take care of it. He might have been too busy with soccer and band practice and history homework to notice that Mom wasn't taking care of anything. But Diana suspected he just didn't want to admit that their mom had fallen apart and that until she recovered, she was incapable of taking care of her children. Whatever the reason, he shouldn't have left the family's finances in the hands of his twelve-year-old sister.

She remembered how helpless she'd felt that day, how all she'd wanted was for someone to hold her and comfort her and take care of her. But who? There was no one left. As far as she could tell, she had no choice but to squeeze back her tears and pay the bills herself. She gathered them up and stacked them on the kitchen table. Then she walked over to the wooden pencil holder her grandpa made and took out the beautiful brass letter opener. Her dad had taught her how to use it when she was nine years old. She used to love the feel of that shiny brass blade slicing through paper, and she'd loved sitting next to Daddy and helping—separating out the advertisements, licking the stamps and return address labels. He didn't teach her how to write a check until the year before he died. He was coughing a lot in those days, complaining that his cold wouldn't go away. No one knew yet that it was lung cancer.

Filling out and recording the checks was no problem. But what if Mom wouldn't sign them? Finding her lying on the couch, an afghan tucked under her chin, Diana opened the blinds and turned off the TV. "Here, Mom," she said, handing her a pen and a notebook to write on. "Could you sign these?"

If she thought her efforts would help her mom snap out of it, she was mistaken. Instead, they gave her an opportunity to sink deeper into her grief. "Oh, sweetheart," she'd said when she'd finished signing. She dropped the pen and fell back on the sofa cushion. "I don't know what I'd do without you. You're such a good girl."

By the time the life insurance check arrived, her mother seemed to have returned to normal. She became once again the lively, concerned parent she'd always been. But Daddy had always taken care of the finances. So when she saw the insurance check, she took one look at it, endorsed it, and handed it to Diana. "Such a lot of money," she sighed. "Sweetheart, can you figure out what to do with it?"

And that was how it all began. As long as Diana lived at home, her mom never paid another bill or made a financial decision. "I'm just a crazy artist," she'd tell people. "But my Diana, I tell you, she's a genius when it comes to money."

A genius? Ha. Diana did a flip turn and started another lap. It didn't take a genius to ask the bank manager for advice and then bring home the papers for a CD ladder for Mom to sign.

She swam another lap. And then another and another, swimming laps until all her thoughts and remembrances were washed away. By the time she climbed out of the pool, she was tired, but she felt calmer than she had for a long time. *Maybe if I swim laps every day*, she thought as she padded across the tiles, dripping water on the way to her towel, *maybe that will change something inside me. Maybe then . . .*

She left it like that, somewhere between a hazy thought and a hope. If she were to line up all the intermediate steps between swimming and holding a baby in her arms, the flaw in the plan might become clear. And she did so want to believe.

"Ma'am."

She was only halfway through the door when Clarita came running, wiping her hands on her apron. "Mrs. Rahman called when you were out, ma'am. Three times."

Diana sucked air through her teeth. Saudur must have told her about Vanuatu. "Thanks, Clarita. I'll call her."

"She sounded, um . . . not right, ma'am." Clarita pinched her eyebrows together. "Something not good."

"I'll call her right away."

Passing through the dining room, Diana grabbed a wine glass and an open bottle of merlot. This would not be an easy phone call.

She was holding the wine in her mouth, feeling its tingle and waiting for Abby to answer, when the doorbell rang.

"Damn! Damn! Damn!" Dispensing with hello, Abby marched past Diana and into the dining room, her flip-flops slapping against her heels, her red curls springing out at awkward angles. "I've been trying to call you."

"I know. I was just about to call *you*."

"Clarita told me you were swimming, but when I got to Seafront . . ." Her eyes were wet with hurt and accusation. "You were already gone."

"Oh!"

Diana held her arms out, and for a moment Abby collapsed against her. Then she pushed Diana away. "Don't. You'll make me cry."

"I'll get you a glass. I have an open bottle of merlot."

"Saudur acts as though my opinion doesn't matter. I'm just the little wife who will go along with whatever he decides. He didn't see fit to tell me anything until today at lunchtime." She swung around. "You and Jay already knew, didn't you?"

"Jay told me last night." She held out the glass of merlot, the wine such a deep red, it was almost black.

"You see." Abby accepted the glass and took a big swallow. "First I give up my job and my beautiful London for him. And now he expects me to pick up and move to some godforsaken village in the middle of nowhere."

"Has he accepted the job?"

"No, but he talked to Marshall Charbonneau this morning before I was up. Then he shaved in our bathroom and ate breakfast across the table from me like it was any other day. All the while he was planning to tear our lives apart. He couldn't tell me sooner, he said. He had to be certain the job offer was firm. Bloody hell! He couldn't talk to me before he had everything worked out? How does that make any sense?"

"He's worried, Abby. He doesn't want to lose his job and leave you and the boys high and dry." Diana was surprised to hear herself sounding like Saudur's apologist. She didn't like what he and Jay had done any more than Abby did.

"Right. The bloody breadwinner. The bloke who brings home the bacon."

"He told you about Akiyama, right?"

"Of course. All that shit about Akiyama scheming to give his job to the nephew of the former prime minister of Japan. So? All these men—your Jay among them—assume that Saudur has already lost before he starts fighting." She shook her head in disgust. "I tell you, Diana, if somebody tried to take my job away, they'd have a bloody big fight on their hands."

8

It was four o'clock, and Diana was in no mood for an early morning phone call. Not after last night and her run-in with the mad flying cockroach.

Cockroaches that stayed on the floor didn't bother her. They were huge—two inches long here in the Philippines—and disgusting, but they were harmless. At night when she spied one in the kitchen, it usually scurried away the moment she turned the light on. She'd been known to stomp on a cockroach that didn't move fast enough.

Last night was different, though. She wasn't in the kitchen; she was in the shower. And the cockroach wasn't scurrying away; he was flying, madly spinning and bouncing off walls. Worst of all, he landed on her neck. For a moment, his disgusting scratchy feet clung to her. She screamed, swatting at him, and ran out of the shower, grabbing a towel to wrap around her.

Snatching her robe from the hook, she shoved her arms into the sleeves while he buzzed around the bathroom like a drunken bomber pilot.

He was quiet just long enough for her to slide into some shoes and wrap a scarf around her neck. Then he started up again, darting first one way and then the other. He dived toward her, and she ducked. How the hell was she going to kill him when he was so fast and unpredictable?

She found a broom, a shoe, and a book. Her weapons. Then she opened the sliding glass door to the balcony, and for the next hour she chased him around the room. He'd light somewhere, and she'd swat at him with one weapon or another. Before her strike connected though, he'd spin away, up or down or—worst of all— straight at her. Sometimes he hid, and she waited.

When she finally saw him fly out the door, she didn't know whether to trust her eyes or not. She slammed and latched the door. Then she sat on the edge of the bed, her heart pounding. When she was finally satisfied he'd flown away, she finished her shower and got ready for bed. After fixing herself a cup of tea, she sat up in bed reading until midnight.

So when a jangling phone startled her out of an uneasy sleep, she was not happy. *Who the—?* She reached for the phone, cleared her throat, and squinted at the clock. *Four o'clock? Really?* "Hello," she croaked.

"Diana, hi. Eddie Wu here."

"Eddie, Jay's on mission."

"Yeah, I know. That's why I'm calling you. To warn you. There's a coup in progress."

"A coup? Again?" Hadn't there been six or seven already? There'd been a failed coup d'etat or two or three every year since Diana and Jay moved to the Philippines.

"This one's the real thing. Early this morning rebels took over Fort Bonifacio. They captured HQ and the Army Operations Center. Word has it the soldiers didn't put up any significant resistance."

"Oh," she mumbled. The mention of Fort Bonifacio woke her up. The fort was in Makati, not far from the houses of people she knew.

"My sources say the rebels have control of Villamor Air Base, the domestic airport, and two television stations."

She rubbed her eyes. Why was he telling her this now? What was she supposed to do about it?

"Minutes ago there was gunfire at the Ninoy Aquino International Airport."

He was loving this, Diana realized. A big news event with him smack in the middle of it. Eddie would always be the young reporter he'd been before joining D-TAP, the guy with sources and contacts all over Asia.

"You should be safe where you are," he said. "But, Diana, keep your head down. And if you have any questions, call me. I'll check back with you later."

"Thanks, Eddie."

Despite Eddie's breathless description of events, it was hard to take these coup attempts seriously. Like brown-outs and traffic and huge cockroaches, you had to accept coup attempts as a part of life in the Philippines. So far, most attempts to overthrow Cory Aquino's government had fizzled before they started or soon thereafter. The worst loss of life had been in 1987 when fifty-three people were killed, many of them bystanders, shot for daring to jeer at the rebels.

Diana hung up. She glanced again at the clock. It was only 4:10. Maybe she could go back to sleep.

She lay back on her pillow. But every time she tried to close her eyes, her eyelids resisted. It seemed that the time for sleep was past. Sitting up, she switched on the bedside lamp and reached for the remote. Eddie was right, channels two and four were off the air. She scrolled down to channel nine. Live coverage, but nothing was happening. The camera's view rested on men in camouflage conferring beside a tank, scanned a group of curious civilians, and returned to the men in camouflage.

Diana sighed and opened her side table drawer. She took out her thermometer and notebook. Every day since their first appointment with Dr. Feliciano, she'd recorded her morning temperature. When it rose by one degree, she circled that day in blue on her calendar to indicate ovulation. The first day of her period she circled in red. Her six-day fertility window was bright green—green for new life. She'd made the first fat green mark in this cycle on November thirtieth, yesterday. The day Jay left for Korea.

She slid the thermometer under her tongue. When enough time had passed, she read and recorded the result. The numbers were all there, neatly noted, making it perfectly clear that another month would be wasted, another opportunity lost.

The air conditioner rattled, almost blotting out the occasional grind and whir of early morning traffic down on the boulevard. A fuzzy-edged strip of yellowish light escaped through a crack in the curtains. Moonlight? All-night lights on balconies? She leaned back against the headboard and gazed at Jay's side of the bed, the covers unwrinkled and cold. How long would it be before he heard about the coup?

Returning the thermometer and notebook to the drawer, she noticed her new bottle of coral nail polish. She shrugged. In the absence of a better idea for passing the time during the early hours of a coup d'etat, she might as well polish her nails.

She was applying the base coat on her right hand when the phone rang again. "Diana. Sorry to get you up so early." It was Franz, another colleague and friend. She held the phone with her left hand and fanned the air with her right while he repeated more or less what Eddie had already told her.

"I'll be careful, Franz. Thanks so much for calling. Say hi to Anna and the girls." Diana blew on her wet fingernails, picturing Anna at the pool at Seafront with her adorable little daughters. Their smooth, suntanned arms and legs, their curls—one honey, the other the color of mahogany—almost eclipsing Anna's shapely, sophisticated beauty.

Between phone calls, Diana managed to polish her fingernails without much more than the usual number of smudges.

Diana was applying the top coat when President Aquino came on television. She was wearing a bright yellow dress, the color that had come to symbolize both her husband's assassination and the peaceful revolution that had brought her to power. Looking down at her paper, the president spoke in a gentle, womanly tone, assuring her people. "We shall smash this naked attempt once more," she said in a vain attempt to sound angry and strong. Diana loved Cory Aquino, but—and not for the first time—she wished Cory were able to project a stronger image to her fractious countrymen.

After breakfast, channel nine went off the air, and Diana switched off the TV. From her balcony, she gazed at women in bathrobes and men in T-shirts and shorts on balconies across the way. They'd dragged chairs out and were drinking coffee and combing their hair. When bombs exploded, they hung over their railings to see where they'd landed. Everyone likes a spectacle.

Three funny little planes that looked like old Japanese Zeros from World War II kept flying over. *Tora tora* planes, they called them on TV. It was hard to take this coup seriously if the rebels were going to use what looked like toy planes. Diana ran inside to get her sketch pad. The tora toras and the half-dressed people on their balconies were crying out to be turned into cartoons for her to send to Andrew.

She'd tried writing letters to her brother Andrew after she and Jay moved to the Philippines. But when she reread them, imagining how they must sound to him, she'd wanted to throw them away. Sometimes she did. Her life seemed so small. So insignificant. When she gave up her job to move here, she'd given up a big part of her identity. All she was left with were her dinner parties and charitable work, her women's club meetings, bazaars, and outings. And that wasn't her. She was living the life of a woman from another century. How could her brother, a Jesuit priest, be interested in her trips to the dressmaker or the trouble she had getting used to having a maid?

Finally she'd given up, and instead of letters, she'd started sending him little cartoons and doodles with funny comments or clever commentary below. Because Andrew taught history at Gonzaga University, she'd concentrated on subjects of historical significance. She'd never been able to compete with her older brother.

As she passed the aquarium, she paused for a moment to watch the fish. These past few days they'd begun to live up to their promise. She'd stopped forcing herself to sit and gaze at them, but every time she passed the aquarium, she would pause and enjoy their graceful movements. When she walked away, she always felt just a little bit more relaxed.

This time, though, when she paused, it looked like something was wrong.

It was the beautiful goldfish with the white tail. The others were chasing her, biting at her underside. Trying to get away, she twisted and turned and hid behind plants. But they wouldn't leave her alone. Diana leaned close and waved her hands. *Stop! Please, please stop!* she mouthed. What were they doing to her beautiful goldfish?

"Ma'am." Clarita came up behind her. "Ma'am, can we go up to the roof?"

"What?"

"The roof, ma'am. Everybody is up there."

"Why?"

"To see American planes and tora toras. Can we go up, ma'am?"

Diana turned away from the aquarium. "Why not." Surely it was more humane to watch a dogfight in the sky than to stay here and witness this mob execution in her own aquarium.

They took the stairs the two flights up to the roof. Pulling open the heavy door, they stepped out onto the grubby top of the building and looked around, blinking at their total exposure to the hot, white sky. It was as though a party had formed on the roof, a casual, impromptu party attended by neighbors, most of whom Diana had never met. They were gathered in clumps, laughing and talking and looking up. The big attractions were the comical little tora toras circling high like hawks and two sleek Phantom jet fighters shouting their deadly force to the entire city, leaving their roar echoing across the sky long after they were gone.

"American jets," people shouted, craning their necks. "F-5 Phantoms." In normal times these jets didn't fly over Manila. They stayed up north near Clark Air Base. Diana gazed at the sky until her neck cramped. Cory must have asked for help, she thought, rolling her neck to one side and then the other.

The rooftop "party" dragged on, but no one wanted to leave. People would disappear for a while and then return with folding chairs and beer and snacks. There was always something to watch: helicopters flying low over Manila Bay, jets zooming past too high to be seen through the cloud cover.

People here lived on political drama. They knew the actors and followed their opinions and their rise and fall from power. Expats who'd lived in the Philippines longer than Jay and Diana said that everyone had been starved for news, gossip, and drama during the fourteen-year dictatorship of Ferdinand Marcos. When he was chased out of the country and democracy restored, they couldn't get enough.

Diana and Jay had missed the country's most dramatic events by months. If they'd moved to the Philippines earlier that year, they might have arrived smack in the middle of the unrest caused by a rigged election or during the People Power Revolution with millions of people in the streets demanding Marcos step down.

But they hadn't.

People who'd lived through that upheaval always seemed to be expecting something almost as big to happen again. Revolutions, demonstrations, and coups were entertainment, all the more stimulating and fun because they were real and just a little bit dangerous. She had to admit, she understood the attraction.

Looking up now at the white sky and rubbing her neck, she noticed that the city had become quiet, not totally silent but quieter than usual. A car here, a jeepney there, a few people walking along the boulevard, a kid on a bicycle, an ice-cream cart ringing its bell, a rooster, a dog. Shadows from the boulevard's palm trees stretched across four lanes, leaving bouquets of shade on parked cars in front of their building. She glanced at her watch. Four o'clock.

"We should go down," she said, suddenly worried. She'd forgotten about Jay. If he'd called while she and Clarita were on the roof and no one answered, she wouldn't know how to explain their absence.

~~~~~

She didn't hear from him until the next morning, day two of the coup. She was sitting on the bed watching television, barefoot and bare-legged in her short shorts. A senator in an expensive *barong Tagalog* was pounding his fist on the desk in outrage that government planes had strafed and killed their own troops. "They nearly cut one soldier in half at the waist," he sputtered as the station switched to a video of the scene. Without warning, the camera moved in close to show bloody internal organs spilling grotesquely from the soldier's body.

Diana gagged and clicked it off, tossing the remote across the bed. The phone rang just as she was beginning to remember the gruesome images from the Vietnam War that had invaded their living room every night when she was a teenager.

"Diana."

It was Jay, his voice, rich and low and familiar. "Honey," she whispered, suddenly feeling a great load of tension and loneliness slip away.

"Thank goodness! I've been trying all night to get through. Are you all right?"

"All night?" Her eyes stung to think how much he loved her. "I'm fine, honey. Fine. You shouldn't have stayed up. You need your sleep."

"Don't worry, I napped. Listen, sweetheart, I'm trying to wrap things up here early. As soon as the Manila airport opens, I'll fly back."

She didn't ask how he could complete a mission that was sup-posed to take ten days in three or four. This time, when he insisted she stay inside and be careful, she didn't roll her eyes. Today it felt good to be loved and cared for and worried about.

"I'll call you again tonight. Gotta go."

And just like that, he was gone. The ceiling fan whirred over her head, going nowhere, stirring the stale air of their bedroom.

She turned off the TV and called Abby. She could always depend on Abby to add a note of levity. And she did. She made jokes about the coup and complained only briefly about Saudur's plan to move them to Vanuatu.

When they finished talking, she called Madeline Dinh. As she might have expected, Madeline wasn't impressed with the little coup playing out a couple of miles from her house. It must have seemed like nothing compared to what she'd experienced in Saigon during the early days of the Vietnam War.

"It does not affect us here in Urdaneta Village," she told Diana. "Only problem, some people worry too much. Elise's ballet teacher cancelled class. Now Elise has nothing to do. I have to give her a math assignment."

They talked for a while. And then, even though it wasn't quite noon, Madeline said she had to think about what to have for dinner. "I haven't been to the market for three days," she said. "I don't know what I can make without fresh basil and cilantro. Even my lemongrass is wilted."

"Quan is a lucky man, Madeline. You're such a good cook."

"Cooking is an important duty for Vietnamese wives."

"What if you didn't like to cook?"

Madeline laughed. "I can't imagine such a thing."

Diana felt a twinge of guilt. She did like to cook . . . more or less. Lately, though, she'd been spending less and less time preparing menus, teaching Clarita new recipes, or doing the cooking herself. The Asian women she knew never lost interest in cooking. They spoiled their families with delicious dinners every night of the week.

With Jay on mission, Diana realized, she was even less likely to cook. She should be paying more attention to food—the four servings of fruit, five servings of veggies, six of whole grains, and two or three of protein Dr. Feliciano recommended. And she would, starting today. But first she had to check on her goldfish. She'd been putting it off, afraid of finding the beautiful white-tailed goldfish floating belly up.

On first glance she was relieved. The goldfish were all swimming peacefully, turning and waving their long tails.

Then she looked more closely.

"Clarita," she shouted, running into the kitchen. "Where is she? The white-tailed goldfish."

Clarita looked up from the kitchen table where she was eating fish and rice. "She died, ma'am. I throw her away."

Diana pictured a bloated little fish floating in the toilet bowl, a flush sending it swirling down and away.

"Shall I fix your lunch now, ma'am?"

"What?" Diana blinked. "No. No. Just coffee and toast today. Thank you."

9

*C*licking off the TV, Diana watched the tangle of images and sounds shrink with an electronic *whoosh* to a single white dot and then disappear. What a total waste of time! She'd spent the better part of the morning sitting in a darkened room, glued to the TV. And the Philippines wasn't even her country.

She straightened the sheet, walked around the bed, and smoothed out the thin seashell beige cover. What now? She placed her hands on her hips and stared through the glass door at the brownish haze hanging over Manila Bay. Being cooped up in this barren wasteland of an apartment made her feel dry as sand.

As she turned away from the door, an image came to her unbidden of a woman, a foreigner, wandering across the sands of an Arabian desert.

Oh, lordy, she told herself. *Snap out of it.*

Lately she'd been having these little spells of expatriate ennui. They attacked her like a tickle in the throat that could easily go from bad to worse if she didn't hurry and take a sip of honey-and-lemon common sense and remind herself that no one had much control over the course of events, even in their own country. Besides, the coup was winding down. It wouldn't be long before it fizzled out like all the others.

After a shower, her wet hair smelling like an evergreen forest, she sat down at the desk in the guest room and took out a pen and some stationery. Every week since she and Jay moved to the Philippines, she'd written to Mom and made sketches for Andrew. It was a habit she'd begun out of a sense of responsibility but one she'd come to appreciate. Pulling together the events of the week gave her a chance to construct the story of her life—one version of it anyway—and to find some meaning and humor in it. That first year, her letters gushed with all the new and exciting and, yes, difficult experiences of living in a foreign country. Now, after three years, it was harder to find fascinating topics—though she always found something.

She clearly had to start that day's letter with the coup. It wouldn't be front-page news in the United States. In fact, her mother might not even have heard about it. By the time Diana's letter arrived, it would be old news. But she couldn't leave it out. She summarized the basic facts and assured her mother she'd been perfectly safe. It wasn't hard to come up with comical sketches and doodles for Andrew. The coup lent itself to humor—if you wanted to think of it that way. She was smiling and finishing up a sketch of a man in a singlet hanging over his balcony and looking at the sky, shaking his bottle of San Miguel beer at a pair of tora tora planes, when Eddie Wu called.

"Diana, have you heard?" His voice had the breathless tone of someone dashing up a steep Hong Kong hill.

"Heard what?" She stretched the phone cord to get as close to the window as possible. What now?

"This whole thing has blown up. The government troops had the rebels on the run, but they didn't bother to contain them. They allowed the insurgent troops who occupied Fort Bonifacio to retreat down McKinley Road and EDSA right into Makati, six or seven hundred of them. They're holed up in the hotels now."

As he ticked off the names of the luxury hotels in the financial district, the Mandarin, Intercontinental, Peninsula, Manila Nikko Garden, Diana's heart jumped to her throat. Eddie was right, this coup had suddenly become serious. Most of her friends lived in the residential areas surrounding those hotels.

But why, she wondered, was he calling her? Their apartment on Roxas Boulevard was a thirty-minute drive from Makati, longer than that for rebels on foot. She was safe here, wasn't she?

"Now they have hundreds, maybe thousands, of potential hostages," he said, "snipers on the roofs and leaning out the windows. They shot up the big supermarkets and department stores. They're crawling all over the villages—Bel Air, San Lorenzo, Urdaneta." His voice cracked. "You need to stay where you are, Diana."

"Your wife, Eddie, is she okay?"

"She's fine. So far they haven't invaded Dasmariñas. We're going to stay in a hotel here on Roxas tonight. She's packing a bag as we speak. I sent a car to pick her up."

"Good." Good for Eddie and his wife. Good for Diana. But what about Abby and Saudur in San Lorenzo Village, the Chatterjees, Browns and Yamamotos in Bel Air, and the Olsons and Dinhs in Urdaneta?

The Philippines' raucous politics, not to mention violent goings on all across Asia, were familiar topics at dinner parties. But Diana and Jay and their friends were usually observers, not participants. The D-TAP officers provided aid and assistance. Their wives played tennis and mahjong and took care of their children. They didn't get shot at the supermarket.

As soon as Eddie hung up, she dialed Abby's number. "Abby, are you all right?"

"Fine," Abby said, not sounding totally convincing. "I'm fine."

"But Eddie Wu said the rebels are in Makati now."

"So I hear."

"You've been hearing gunfire?"

"No." Abby's laugh sounded strained. "I mean I've heard the news. Don't worry about us, Diana. We'll be fine."

"Why don't you and Saudur and the boys move in with us. It's safer here on Roxas Boulevard."

Abby laughed again. "I don't think you want that. The twins would drive you and Jay up the walls."

Diana objected, but Abby held firm. "Listen," she said, "we'll be quite safe here in San Lorenzo Village."

They talked for a while, and then Diana spent most of the rest of the afternoon on the phone calling other friends and answering their calls. Each person had one more bit of information or piece of advice—or one more joke to ease the tension.

The sun was still up when she stepped out on her balcony. Two hundred feet away, in the building across the garden, a man was gazing at the bay from another balcony. Despite the clouds, his bare back looked golden as sunlight on a September afternoon. He ran his fingers through his dark hair, igniting red highlights. Then he turned toward Diana's building, and she became part of his view as he was of hers, anonymous people in buildings across the space of a large garden.

Neither of them looked away, but Diana was thinking about Eddie now. He'd called earlier to remind her that the US Marines were guarding the American Embassy, so she didn't need to worry about the rebels coming this way.

When the phone rang, she was expecting more breathless news from Eddie. Instead her brother's distinctive, always serious baritone cut through the long-distance crackle.

"Diana, are you and Jay all right?" Andrew was never one to waste time on small talk.

"Jay's in Korea. And, yes, I'm fine. I wrote you a letter this morning. Haven't had a chance to mail it yet." Was it only this morning? She flashed back to the light tone of the letters she'd written to Andrew and Mom, the funny cartoons she'd sketched. How quickly the situation had intensified! She'd need to add more up-to-date information to those letters. "Does Mom know?"

"She's probably just getting out of bed. But it's all over the news this morning—snipers on rooftops, tourists and expats getting shot."

"Will she call you?"

"You can bet on it. As soon as she hears."

"Just calm her down, Andrew. Tell her how safe I am. Remember, we don't live in Makati anymore. That's where it's all happening—the snipers, people getting shot. Just tell her I promise not to leave my *very safe* apartment. Tell her not to call. It's too expensive."

"I'm worried about you, Sis. Urban warfare is the most dangerous. With the rebels dug in, it could go on for weeks."

"Don't worry, Clarita and I have a big bag of rice, and meat and fish in the freezing compartment." She didn't tell him how little they kept in their tiny fridge. Like most people in the Philippines, they made frequent trips to the market. They liked their produce fresh.

Before hanging up, Andrew gave her his priestly blessing. He'd been a seminarian the first time he gave her his blessing, and it had been all she could do to keep from laughing. Her big brother playing priest? The closer he came to his ordination, the more annoyed she became. His new identity seemed to distance him from her and Mom. By now, though, he'd grown into his priesthood. It suited him. And she'd long since come to expect their conversations to end with him asking God to bless her.

She put the phone down. Andrew's mention of urban warfare was sobering. He was a historian. He knew what could happen and what *had* happened in other times and places. But he wasn't here. So far the government wasn't fighting the rebels; they were negotiating with them.

Diana walked across the room. Now what? She'd already talked to Abby and everyone else she could think of. She stood in front of the aquarium, watching the rhythmic opening and closing of the gills on the largest goldfish, the sheen of his body, the perfect design of his scales.

"Ma'am." Clarita stood in the kitchen doorway. "Was that sir?"

"No. It was my brother."

"Ma'am, when will sir come home?"

"Maybe tomorrow."

"I'm afraid, ma'am. They say many terrible things on the radio. Sir should be here."

Diana put her arm around Clarita's shoulders. "I know. He's trying. As soon as the airport opens, he will come. He promised. Now let's go make something tasty for dinner."

The two women worked together shelling shrimp, distracted from their worry by a friendly shrimp-shelling competition. Suddenly Clarita shook the shells off her hands. "I can make *ginataan* for dessert," she said. "My friend downstairs has jackfruit. And we have *kamote* and *sago,* two *saba* bananas, a coconut . . . Oh!" Her buoyancy suddenly collapsed. "No *ube.*"

Ube was just another yam, and they had yams already, but it was purple, and ginataan didn't have enough color without a few chunks of purple ube.

"Maybe my friend has some," Clarita said, regaining her good humor. She untied her apron and hurried out the door.

Nothing like the prospect of sweet, rich food to raise the spirits, Diana thought.

10

"Mummy. Mum-my!"

"Now what?" Abby groaned, pushing her chair back and giving Diana and Jay a wry sideways glance. "I told you you'd be sorry you invited us into your home."

"Mummy, Mummy, Mummy!" The twins' high-pitched cries bounced off the shiny apartment walls like sirens on a narrow city street.

"Si-mon, Jer-e-my." Abby sang their names, ending each on a high note as she strode down the hall toward the bathroom. "You were supposed to be brushing your teeth. They'd better be sparkling by the time I get there."

Diana exchanged glances with Jay, who returned her smile and then quickly took a drink of water as though he were afraid to acknowledge the sweetness of the little bedtime drama.

"Sorry," Saudur said, sliding his fork across his plate to capture a few stray grains of rice.

Diana shrugged. "For what? It's fun having you all here."

And it was—the everyday racket a family made, the homey way it filled the corners of the apartment. Earlier in the day she'd called Abby and invited her and Saudur and the boys to move in with them for a few days so they could escape the unsettled situation in Makati, but at first Abby had been determined to tough it out. "You worry too much," she'd told Diana. "Turn off the friggin' telly and relax." It wasn't until Jay got home and talked to Saudur that Abby gave in and packed their bags.

"You and Jay are great hosts," Saudur said, "but you're not used to the kind of hubbub four-year-old boys make. You couldn't possibly be enjoying it."

"But I am. The sound of children is a huge relief after the quiet of the past few days with Jay away and only Clarita and the goldfish for company."

Jay patted her hand. "You know I came as soon as I could."

"I know." Diana let her hand slip away from Jay's so she could start clearing away the dirty dishes. The airport had been closed. She knew that. It had been impossible for Jay to fly back from Korea. It wasn't his fault. But sometimes it seemed as though he was always away when she needed him. And the previous night had been one of those nights.

"Saudur!"

Diana turned to see Abby marching into the dining room with the twins in their matching Super Mario pajamas tripping along behind. "Did you tell them they could bring their swords?" She waved the short silvery swords for Saudur to see.

"They're just plastic, darling."

Jay rolled up his magazine and gave Saudur a conspiratorial wink. "Little men need their weapons," he said, striking a fighting pose.

"Men!" Abby rolled her eyes. Then she herded the boys into the living room where their sleeping bags were rolled out side by side on the carpet. "Okay, you two ruffians. Crawl into your sleep sacks. I'll keep the swords, and Auntie Diana will read you a story." She reached into her bag and pulled out *Wynken, Blynken, and Nod*. "I was going to save this for Christmas," she said, handing it to Diana. "But, what the hell, it's only three weeks away."

"En garde," Simon shouted, pointing an imaginary sword at Jeremy.

"En garde, you dirty pirate," Jeremy replied, slashing the air and dancing around his brother.

"Boys!" Abby pointed at their sleeping bags.

"Last one in is a rotten egg," Simon cried. He ran across the living room holding his nose and jumped on the sleeping bags. "Marco," he whooped.

"Polo." Jeremy was right behind him.

They were rolling around like a couple of puppies when Diana sat down on their sleeping bags. "Come and sit beside me," she said, patting spots on either side of her. They scared her, these two rambunctious boys. They might ignore her. What would she do then? Every time she thought about the baby she and Jay would have, it was a girl, small and sweet and helpless. In her imaginings, she was holding her and rocking her, feeding and comforting her, changing her diapers and loving her. She'd never questioned whether she would be a good mother.

Simon and Jeremy stopped rolling around and looked at her. She held up the book and smiled. And without further urging, they crawled over and snuggled up beside her.

"Wynken, Blynken, and Nod," she said, showing them the cover.

"Wynken," Jeremy giggled.

"Blynken," Simon sputtered.

"And Nod," they said together, laughing.

She read to them about three pajama-clad children sailing off in a wooden shoe and a talking moon and fish swimming through the sky. And they listened, sober faced. But every time she read, "Wynken, Blynken, and Nod," they dissolved into a fit of giggles.

By the end, they were snickering quietly and yawning.

"Time to sleep," Diana said, helping them into their sleeping bags. When she leaned over to kiss their soft cheeks, their eyes were already closing.

"How do they do that?" she asked Abby.

"You mean go from full speed ahead to sound asleep?" Abby shrugged. "It happens every night."

"Come and join us," Jay said. "We saved you some fruit salad."

"Thanks." She sat down and dished up chunks of mango, papaya, and banana. While the others talked about the coup, Diana ate the soft, sweet fruit and remembered the pleasure of feeling the twins' little bodies next to hers.

11

*U*sually, as part of the whirlwind routine of Jay's homecomings from his missions, he unpacked his suitcase right away. A quick kiss and hug, and then, while he tossed dirty clothes in the hamper and hung his suit and clean shirts in the closet, an explosion of talk—the people he met, the stories he heard, the exotic sights he saw, the business he conducted. Jay's business trips were adventures. Whether they lasted one week or three, he returned from them so wound up that all Diana could do was step aside and watch and listen.

Today had been different. He dropped his suitcase at the apartment door and ran to her, lifting her up and kissing her. No dirty clothes. No stories about Korea. After that he turned his attention to getting Abby and Saudur out of Makati. "You asked them to come?" he asked, incredulous. "No, no, no. In a case like this, you don't *invite* them to move in with us. You *insist*. It's like paying the bill in a restaurant. You don't offer, you grab the bill and corral the waiter with your money ready to go. I'll talk to Saudur. He'll see the logic of it."

And Saudur did. Within the hour, Diana opened their apartment door to find Abby, Saudur, and the twins standing in the hallway in a puddle of suitcases, sleeping bags, and favorite pillows.

"You may regret this," Abby said. But even she'd begun to worry about staying in Makati. Just before Jay called, she'd found a cross inside a circle scrawled on their gate. It was the symbol used by the rebels to identify American families who would later be used as hostages. "I ask you," Abby said, tossing her red curls, "do we look like Yanks? Do we sound like Yanks?"

Maybe not, but one way or another, Diana was glad to have them there, out of harm's way.

She closed the bedroom door behind her. It had been a hectic day, but now, with the twins sound asleep in the living room and Abby and Saudur in the guest bathroom preparing for bed, she'd finally have some time alone with Jay. "Well," she said, tilting the blinds for privacy. "Here we are."

He nodded. Then he turned his attention to the as-yet-unopened suitcase and swung it up on the bed. "I have something for you."

She'd almost forgotten about the gifts. They were another step in his normal whirlwind homecoming routine. No matter how hectic Jay's trips were, he always found time to buy something for her, and it was always something nice. Returning from past trips, he'd presented her with Swiss chocolate from Hong Kong, silk fabric and jade earrings from China, batik tablecloths and shadow puppets from Indonesia, lacquerware bowls from Vietnam, and even a carpet from Pakistan.

With this mission shortened from nine days to six, she was surprised he'd found time to shop. "You shouldn't have," she said.

He threw back the top of the suitcase and removed his toiletries bag, exposing a large lacquer box between his folded shirts and a stack of D-TAP files.

"Oh, my!" she said as he lifted out a burgundy-colored box decorated with mother of pearl storks. "It's beautiful." She ran her fingers over the storks' outstretched wings and the red full moon behind them.

"Open it," he said. "It's a jewelry box."

Inside, was a mirror and red velvet lining, spaces for rings and earrings on the top shelf, for necklaces and bracelets below. "It's exquisite, honey. Thank you."

"Wind it up. It's also a music box."

She reached underneath and turned the winding key. The tune was sweet, but nothing she recognized. She looked over at Jay for help.

Striking a dramatic pose, feet wide, chest high, one arm reaching out, he sang along with the tinkling melody in a haunting tenor. *"Arirang, arirang...."*

"Wow!" she said when he finished. "Is that the way they do karaoke in Korea?"

He laughed and nodded.

"What do the words mean?"

"It's an ancient song," he said as he lifted a stack of shirts out of the suitcase. "Something about a woman getting left behind when her lover crosses over Arirang Pass."

Diana waited for the sweet, sad tune to play itself out. Then she closed the lid and set the box on their shared chest of drawers. "Why don't you take the first shower," she said. She took the D-TAP files from him and set them next to the jewelry box. "I'll unpack for you. Go on. I'll take care of it."

"Okay."

He spent a long time in the bathroom, and when he came out, he was all steamy and fresh, his black hair combed back like a hero from an old-time movie.

"My turn," she said, giving him a quick kiss. "I'll be right out."

No flossing, no shampoo, no moisturizer. Just a fast brushing of her teeth and a lukewarm shower. She couldn't have been in the bathroom more than four or five minutes. She frowned. So why was Jay lying on top of the bedspread with his eyes closed?

"No, you don't," she whispered. He couldn't just fall asleep when tonight might be the last chance they'd get in the month of December. After tonight, 1989 would be gone. In another nine months and fifteen days, she would be thirty-five years old. She dropped her towel and climbed up beside him. "Honey?" She put her lips close to his ear. "Are you awake?"

"Mmm."

"I missed you," she said, caressing him. "Did you miss me?"

"Uh huh."

"Really?"

"Missed you," he mumbled.

She tried everything, but she couldn't get him to open his eyes. It didn't matter. He was awake enough to lift his head off the pillow and kiss her. Conscious enough to squeeze her buttock. Sufficiently awake to make love to her.

Afterward he rose up on one elbow, a perturbed look on his face. "Why did you ask if I missed you?" He smiled and shook his head. "If I didn't miss you, my love, then why the hell would I have fought so hard to get out of Seoul on the first plane headed to Manila? Getting and keeping a seat was no easy task. Every time I turned around, another reporter or photographer was trying to bump me. The airport was chock-full of them, reporters from the AP, UPI, *New York Times*, *Washington Post*, CNN, BBC, *The Guardian, Globe,* and *Mail, USA Today* . . . and every one of them desperate to get to Manila before the story cooled. If I told you how much a reporter from the *LA Times* offered me to give up my seat, well, then you'd appreciate how eager I was to get home to you."

She cuddled up next to him. She loved this man, baby or no baby.

Then she closed her eyes and sent off a silent prayer that this evening would bear fruit.

⁓

"Auntie Diana! Auntie Diana!"

How, she wondered, could the voices outside her door be so loud while still retaining the quality of a whisper?

"Auntie Diana, come quick." Little knuckles skittered against the bedroom door.

As though they didn't know how to knock properly, she thought, yawning and stretching herself awake. Wasn't it too early to get up? "Okay, boys," she said in a stage whisper. "I'll be right there." She slid out of bed and grabbed her robe, looking back at Jay who was making a soft sleepy sound halfway between a snore and a purr.

Opening the door, she saw two small dark figures in a dark hallway. The sun wouldn't be up for a while yet. "What's wrong?"

Simon grabbed her hand. "Quick! Come and look." He dragged her down the hall and into the dining room with Jeremy galloping along behind.

"Auntie Diana." Jeremy tugged on her robe and looked up at her with tears in his dark brown eyes. "Your fish stopped swimming."

Oh great! She groaned. She should have disposed of her poor sick fish before the twins arrived. She knew it was going to die . . . her beautiful gold and white goldfish.

"See," Simon said, pointing at the bloated fish floating sideways on the surface of the water. The twins' creamy brown faces looked ghostly in the aquarium's blue light.

Jeremy whimpered. "He's sick, isn't he?"

"He's dead," Simon said. "I told you he was dead. Isn't he, Auntie Diana."

They looked up at her for an answer. And she nodded. What else could she do? "Yes," she said. "It looks like the fish is dead. I'm so sorry, boys."

Jeremy started crying, a closed-mouth wind-up of a cry that threatened to explode. Quickly she knelt down and hugged him. She hoped this wasn't their first dead animal.

"Simon," she said, quickly pulling a plan together, "would you go to the kitchen and ask Clarita for two paper towels. We're going to have a funeral for the fish and bury him in the planter on the balcony."

Jeremy stopped crying. "Can I bury him?"

"Here's what you can do, sweetie. When Simon gets back, you can scoop up the fish with this net."

Jeremy took the net from her and stood at attention, the net across his chest like a little soldier with his sword.

Remembering animal funerals from her childhood, Diana presided over the solemn ceremony. Jeremy netted the dead fish and dumped it on Simon's paper towels. Then Diana invited Clarita to join them, and they all processed around the dining table and out onto the balcony singing "We Shall Overcome," which was probably as suitable as any other marching song. Clarita found a trowel, and Diana dug the hole. Then the boys wrapped "Goldie" in one of the paper towels and interred him in his planter grave under the pink bougainvillea bush.

"God bless our little fish," Diana prayed.

"Amen," the boys shouted. Then, having satisfied the ceremonial demands of death, they ran off to wake their parents.

Another fish down, Diana thought as she shoveled dirt into the hole and patted it down. If only she knew why "Goldie" died. She studied the three remaining fish. They seemed all right. For now. "Some source of relaxation you are," she whispered, shaking her head at the fish.

12

Two days later, although most of Metro Manila had already returned to normal, Makati was still a war zone. Rebels roamed its office buildings and residential neighborhoods. They looted and slept and posed for the TV cameras. When they were bored, they shot rats and cats and fat orange-green papayas. Their leaders had been captured or were in hiding, so they chose new ones to negotiate with the government.

"The Philippine army is useless." Abby swished her hand across the swimming pool and flicked water in the air for emphasis. "A bunch of ineffective twonks."

Diana opened her mouth to defend them. To be fair, you had to admit that the army had stopped the coup, and now they were negotiating for the rebels to surrender. So why sacrifice government troops when the rebels had snipers atop the Makati high rises and hundreds of potential hostages? Negotiation was a reasonable course of action. But then, she thought, slowly kicking her feet in the cool water, Abby wasn't in a reasonable mood. For the past two days, Abby and Saudur had been fighting. Out of courtesy, they'd kept their arguments behind the guest room's closed door. But with six people in one small apartment, it was obvious what was going on.

Diana gathered her long, wet hair together at the nape of her neck and twisted it, enjoying the coolness of the water as it dripped on her hot shoulders. They'd been at Seafront all afternoon, sitting in the shade when they could, slathering on sunscreen when they were out in the sun, and still her shoulders and back felt crisp. "How about one more swim?" It was almost dinnertime. The earlier crowd had dwindled to one old man swimming laps and two boys jumping off the diving board, pretending not to hear their mom shouting for them to get out.

Abby looked down at her freckled knees and sighed. "No, you go ahead. I don't feel like swimming."

Diana shrugged. "I'm fine here just kickin' my feet in the water with you." She reached over and patted Abby's knee. It was a small gesture of sympathy, but that was all it took to set her off.

"It's not fair," Abby said, snuffling and wiping her eyes. "Why should I always be the one to give in?" She threw her hands up and glared at Diana. "It's because I'm a woman. I fucking hate being a woman."

Diana's instinctive urge was to stand up for her gender. She liked being female. But she knew exactly what Abby meant. It was that power differential, the belief among both men and women that women were somehow inferior. She'd seen it back in Seattle with her colleagues and clients. But she'd never experienced the full extent of that power differential until they moved to Manila, where she and all the other expat wives struggled to find some relevance and a modicum of power.

Abby jabbed her chin in the air and continued. "I have to give in because Saudur's the one making the money. But why am I not earning money? Because I sacrificed my career for his. That's why not. And why did I do that? Because I'm a woman."

It was on the tip of Diana's tongue to say something mollifying. *You'll work it out.* Or, *I've heard that Vanuatu is beautiful.* Exactly the kind of things a woman is expected to say. As she kicked her feet in the clear blue water, the coral toenails she'd painted in bed on the first day of the coup rose and fell, briefly breaking the surface before sinking again.

"I may not be earning money," Abby continued, "but I have obligations here. Being president of the Makati International Nursery School is not a bridge party. Next week—if they ever march those bloody hooligans out of Makati—I'm scheduled to interview candidates for a new teacher for the three-year-olds. After that, I have an appointment with Mrs. Chang to explain that even though her two-year-old daughter is brilliant, we don't accept anyone who is less than thirty months old. Then there's the year-end party to plan and the new playground equipment to order. Damn it! Diana, I like being president of the nursery school. And I'm good at it. I damned well don't want that scatterbrained Jenny Littlejohn to take over."

"They wouldn't choose Jenny Littlejohn, would they?"

Abby sighed. "You never know."

The melancholy in her voice seemed to spread a haze of sadness over the water, slowing the strokes of the old man who was still swimming, his long, pale arms circling like slow-motion windmills. You make plans; you choose a career; you marry the man you love. And yet, you never know . . .

"Let's go get dressed," Abby said.

Only moments earlier, the sun had been sparkling on the water, the sky bright blue. Now the sky was muddled, streaks of lavender and peach bleeding into the quickly fading blue. The table where they'd left their bags and towels was already in full shade. Diana reached up, plucked a plumeria from one of the trees, and held it to her nose. Then she wrapped her towel around her shoulders, and she and Abby headed for the shower room.

In a city of crowded spaces, Seafront's shower room was an anomaly. An oasis of space and cleanliness—lockers and benches and white tile, individual showers and roomy toilet stalls. Everything clean and in working order. Today it felt different, sanitary and cold. Sinister. Diana placed the plumeria on a bench beside her bag, abandoning the small, fragment of nature to the room's unbendable surfaces.

She picked up the plumeria one more time, sniffed it, and put it down. Then she stepped into one of the shower stalls and turned on the water.

"I'm going to miss Jollybee," Abby shouted from the next stall, her voice echoing off the shiny tile.

"Jollybee?" Diana tossed her suit onto the divider beside Abby's—a turquoise one-piece next to a fuchsia bikini.

"They have this brilliant burger, the 'Amazing Aloha.' You should try it. Beef, bacon, lettuce, cheese, and a big juicy pineapple ring in a bun."

It was hard to keep up with Abby's moods, impossible to catalog the list of all the things she loved and hated. After living in the Philippines for more than three years, she must have a long list of things she'd miss if they moved to Vanuatu.

Diana used to keep a list like that, a mental list of the things she liked.

A dollop of foaming shampoo slid down her forehead, and she brushed it aside. When she was a child, her mother had advised her to always take note of beauty and to keep an invisible list of all the things she liked. For a while Diana faithfully kept that invisible list, adding to it almost every day.

When she emerged from the shower, wrapped in her towel, Abby was already in the communal area between the lockers, stepping into her underwear. "I don't know if you noticed," she said, glancing up at Diana, "but Saudur and I had a big fight last night." She pulled her pink flowered panties over her hip bones and snapped the elastic with her thumbs, sending a little jiggle through the delicate skin on her belly. "It was a battle for the title of most powerless."

"Most powerless?"

Abby laughed. "I know, it sounds crazy now, but at the time we were deadly serious." She hooked her bra and bent over to let her breasts fall into the cups. "It started with me complaining that he didn't even ask me if I wanted to move. His excuse was that it wouldn't have done any good. He had no choice in the matter. 'I'm powerless,' he said. And that's what set me off, his insistence that he was powerless, when I figured that I was the one who had no control over the direction of my life.

"I screamed at him, something about how much I hated being powerless. And all the frustration I'd been feeling came bursting out as tears, which just made me angrier. I do not cry."

"I know," Diana said. "I've never seen you cry."

"It's a skill I learned in law school. Never show weakness. Anyway, you'd think that at the very least, my tears would have earned me a modicum of sympathy." She took a rolled-up dress out of her bag and shook it. "But no. Saudur was more intent on pleading the case for his own powerlessness. His big brown eyes got all watery, and all I could think of was, no, don't do that. I'm the one who is powerless." She buttoned the last button on her sunny, button-up-the-front dress and looked up, smiling. "You must have heard the ruckus we were making."

"Yeah. We did hear something. But, you know, the air conditioners are so loud . . ."

"Did we keep you up?"

"No. Don't worry about it."

They stood in front of the mirror, Diana towel-drying her long hair, Abby fluffing out her auburn curls.

"I was furious. I jumped on top of him and pinned his arms to the bed." She gave Diana a look that was one more of pride than regret. "I haven't brawled like that since I was a kid," she said, snickering. "In those days I was a holy terror."

Diana dug a brush out of her bag and set to work brushing her hair straight back and catching it in her left hand. "Sounds like you enjoyed it."

"Damned right! You can't beat fighting for a good adrenaline rush." She gave her head a shake to set her hoop earrings swinging.

She slipped on some bangles and painted her lips red. Then she stood back and watched Diana pin her hair into a sideways French twist.

"You're such a classic beauty," she said when Diana had finished. "The kind of woman a prince would marry."

Diana gave her a wry smile. Not if the prince wants an heir to the throne, he wouldn't.

13

Makati had been back to normal for more than a week now. On the fifth day of the occupation, the government negotiated the departure by bus of 818 foreigners who'd been stranded in hotels and condos. The following day, December seventh, the rebels marched back to their barracks in Fort Bonifacio, and Abby, Saudur, and the boys returned to their house. The occupation of Makati had left ninety-nine people dead, fifty of them civilians. Now, a week after Makati's return to normal, no one knew whether the rebels would be punished. Most of the officers had simply slipped away.

Diana added a tag to Clarita's gift and set it under the tree. This year for the first time, the American Embassy had flown in fir trees from Washington State. Stepping back, she breathed in the sweet evergreen scent. It felt almost like Christmas.

Humming along with a carol on the radio, she could feel the coup beginning to fade into memory. In a few years, hardly anyone beyond the families of the ninety-nine victims would remember it. Historians like Andrew would say that it could have been much worse. She doubted that history would look kindly on the rebels, though. No one Diana and Jay knew sympathized with them. Jay derided them for their incompetence. Saudur blamed them for their continued loyalty to Marcos. Abby laughed and said they were motivated by a thirst for adventure and fame—which was certainly true of their leader, Honasan, who was widely viewed as a grandstander. Perhaps, though, history would look kindly on Cory Aquino. She seemed to be a good and honest person who had the bad luck to be elected president at an extremely difficult time.

Anyway, Diana hoped this would be the last coup attempt so that the Philippine government could get on with the business of governing, and the rest of them could get on with their lives.

She reached behind the tree and plugged in the lights. Then, singing along with Madonna to "Santa Baby," she stepped back again and admired the tree with all its shiny red and gold balls. Yes. It felt very much like Christmas.

When she was a child, Diana and her mom were known in the family as the master decorators of Christmas. They made wreaths and table decorations. They wrapped gifts in secret in Mom's studio and decorated the tree when Daddy was at work. Seeing it for the first time, he'd fall on the floor in amazement. "I've never seen anything like it," he'd swear. "Cross my heart and hope to die." On Christmas Eve, when it was his turn to open one of his gifts, he'd insist that he couldn't possibly open such a work of art.

"Open it," Diana and her mom would shout. "Open it. Open it."

He'd shake his head over and over until eventually he'd give in. Then he would remove the bow and paper ever so slowly, peeling off the Scotch tape and grimacing if he tore a bit of paper by mistake.

Some years the master decorators would make their own wrapping paper using watercolors and stencils and cut-out snow-flakes. Once they made silk-screened poinsettias and holly. Another year they made origami stars and reindeer and tied them on top of the packages.

After Daddy died, Diana and her mom stopped turning their Christmas gifts into works of art. Mom bought wrapping paper and ribbon at the supermarket, and Andrew wrapped his gifts in the Sunday comics. He was already a teenager by then and Diana would be soon. Santa Claus wasn't real, and over-the-top gift wrapping was just plain silly.

Reaching under the tree, Diana pulled out two large gifts wrapped in red and white Santa Claus paper, their misshapen forms hinting at the dump truck and bulldozer inside. Simon and Jeremy wouldn't appreciate a fancy bow, but they might like some origami reindeer.

She set the gifts on her desk and searched through the desk drawers for origami paper. In a bottom drawer, she found a thick stack of it, precision-cut paper in every shade of the rainbow. She separated out some midnight blue, brown, and moss green sheets. It had been years since she'd done origami. She wasn't sure she'd remember how to make a reindeer.

Once she got started, though, it all came back to her—the folding and creasing, opening up, and then folding again, the geometry of origami squares, rectangles, and triangles.

When she finished, "Carol of the Bells" was playing on the radio. *Ding dingy dong, ding dingy dong.* On the balcony, the tissue paper tails of the Christmas lanterns she and Jay had bought at the Saturday Market were fluttering in the breeze.

~

She hadn't been to Abby and Saudur's house since before the coup attempt. Today, entering San Lorenzo Village, driving past the guard post, everything looked the same as before. The only thing that had changed was her awareness of how close the village was to the high-rise buildings the rebels had occupied. If she looked straight ahead as she drove down San Lorenzo Drive, all she saw was the gracious tree-lined streets and two-story houses. When she tilted her chin back another inch or two, though, the hotels and condos towered over the tops of the trees.

She turned onto Apostol Street, parked in front of Abby's house, and walked up to the gate, a paper bag filled with Christmas gifts in each hand. Like all the houses in the Makati villages, Abby's was surrounded by a wall. Her wall was made of concrete blocks skim coated with cement and painted white.

Diana rang the bell, and something—was it the shrill sound of the bell?—stirred up a fluttering in her chest. A kind of butterfly of anticipation, as though she had something to tell her friend. She didn't, of course. She laughed. Being four days late wasn't the kind of thing you shared with a friend. No matter how much it meant to Diana, in reality, four days was just a late period.

"Good afternoon, ma'am," Abby's maid said as she swung the gate open. "Come inside. I'll call Mrs. Rahman."

"Auntie Diana, Auntie Diana!" The twins raced across the grass toward her, Simon sprinting ahead, his arms pumping, heels kicking up behind him, poor Jeremy struggling to keep up. It was amazing how different their running styles and skills were. From a distance you'd never guess they were identical twins.

"Auntie Diana." Simon tugged on one of her bags. "What's that?"

"Christmas presents."

"For me?" Jeremy peaked inside the other bag.

"The big presents are for you and Simon. The others are for your mom and dad."

The boys sprinted ahead looking over their shoulders to be sure she was following them into the house, through the entry, and into the living room where Simon performed the baseball maneuver of sliding to a stop with his forward foot under the Christmas tree. "Put 'em here," he instructed.

Jeremy stood in front of the tree, his arms spread wide like a small MC on a TV game show. "See our Christmas tree. It's the bestest ever." He raised his eyebrows, waiting for her confirmation.

For a moment Diana couldn't speak. The tree was far from perfect. Tinsel hung in globs reaching only half-way up. A paper chain began on one branch and petered out after a two-foot run. Construction paper stars and bells and candy canes decorated with stickers and crayon scribbles were scattered haphazardly among evenly spaced lights and balls.

"Yes. It's the bestest ever," she said, swallowing the lump in her throat. "I hope I can have a Christmas tree like this someday."

Behind her, a woman's footsteps started down the stairs and stopped. Diana turned around, and there was Abby, halfway down the stairs, looking like she'd been caught in a children's game of freeze.

"Diana, hi," she said, starting up again. She swept her hand over her T-shirt and shorts. "I meant to change into something more presentable." She frowned at the paper bags Diana brought. "What's all this?"

"Christmas presents. For us." Simon reached inside one of the bags and wrestled out a large gift.

"For our Christmas," Jeremy said, grabbing the gift from him and putting it under the tree.

"Hey! Let Auntie Diana take care of that. You boys go play."

"Oh!" They plodded away, feigning exhaustion.

"Mummy." Simon whipped back around. "Can I show Auntie Diana our bullet holes?"

"Later. Now go on." Abby flicked her wrists at them. "Scat."

"Whoa!" Diana raised her eyebrows. "You have bullet holes?"

"A couple in the perimeter wall. One in the side of the house. Let's go sit in the lanai. It's too hot in here."

Abby's lanai was a kind of screened porch, open to the living room and hall on two sides and screened on two others. It seemed cooler than it was because of all the plants. There were large potted palms and philodendrons on the floor and ferns and ivy and orchids hanging from the wrought iron grills. In one corner, green and yellow parakeets chirped and flitted around inside a large cage. The jungle-print cushions on the rattan chairs completed the illusion.

Abby's maid was right behind them with calamansi juice, cookies, and napkins. She set the tray on a glass-topped table and turned to leave.

"Could you bring us some wine, Lourdes, and a couple of wine glasses?" Abby asked. "There's a bottle cooling in the fridge." She glanced at Diana and just as quickly looked away.

Diana's heart sank. Something was wrong. Not that they never had wine at two in the afternoon, but, well . . . If her suspicion was correct, they were both going to need a drink.

For the past few days she'd been kidding herself. And why wouldn't she? Abby had been so convincing. She'd stamped her foot and vowed in no uncertain terms that she was not going to move to Vanuatu, and Saudur would just have to find another position here in D-TAP's Manila office. It was the day the rebels marched back to Fort Bonifacio. Jay and Saudur were at the office. The twins were watching cartoons. Diana and Abby were gathering things together for their return to Abby's house in Makati.

Diana was looking for stray toys when Abby made her announcement.

"I've decided."

"Decided what?"

Abby stuffed the boys' PJs into a suitcase and zipped it shut with a ferocity that left no question about her determination. "I will not move to Vanuatu."

Her face had been almost as fiery as her hair that day. This afternoon, though, all that ferocity was gone. Without her usual "Lady Danger" red lipstick, without any makeup at all, Abby looked pale, her eyelashes nearly invisible. She looked less like the confident Londoner of her adulthood and more like the freckle-faced Irish lass of her childhood. "Sorry," she said, "I haven't made any reservations for the beach trip we talked about."

For a split second, Diana felt a flash of relief. They weren't moving after all. Abby was just feeling bad about the beach trip.

The fan whirred and the parakeets chirped. Outside, the laugh of a neighbor's maid overlaid the ever-present distant hum of cars and buses and motorized tricycles.

Abby cleared her throat. "We won't have time to go to the beach. I'll be packing." She picked at a loose strip of rattan on the arm of the chair. "Saudur's taking the job in Vanuatu. Friday was his last chance to decide before they gave it to someone else."

"You're leaving." Diana hadn't meant for her words to come out that way. So soft, as though she were giving up on their friendship, assigning Abby to her Christmas card list.

Without looking at Diana, Abby walked across the room to the birdcage. "You and Jay might be able to get reservations on Borakay," she said, her voice breaking. "Or Matabunkay or La Playa del Norte."

"Abby, please," Diana jumped up. "Please don't worry about us." She put her arm around Abby's shoulder. For a moment they gazed at the parakeets, pretending Abby's sniffles were lost among the birds' chirps and warbles.

Abby pulled away and covered her face with her hands. "What can I do?"

"Get me a tissue. Better yet," Abby said as Lourdes made her entrance, wine glasses tinkling, flip-flops slapping against her heels. "Get me some of those paper napkins and a glass of chardonnay." Abby blew her nose on one of the napkins Diana brought and wiped her eyes on another. "I told him I wouldn't go," she said, stuffing the napkins in a back pocket.

Diana handed her the chardonnay, and they lifted their glasses in a silent toast. Oh, my gosh! Diana thought, suddenly remembering. I shouldn't be drinking today. She was only four days late, but late was late. She twirled the pedestal of her glass slowly between her fingers and thumb and watched the parakeets hop and preen and flutter their wings.

"I insisted I'd bloody well pack the kids up and move back to London." Abby took a big gulp of wine. "Said I'd get my old job back. Hire a nanny."

"What did he say?"

"Saudur? Ha. He looked worried for a minute. But, hey." She shrugged and took another drink. "He knew I'd give in. What the hell happened to me, Diana? I've become a typical expat wife. I don't have any life of my own."

"That's not true, Abby. You'll never be a typical anything."

"I don't know. I don't know what I am anymore." She emptied her glass and ran her fingers through her hair, letting it fall in a tumble. "I need some more chardonnay."

Diana followed her back to the low table where Lourdes had served the wine, juice, and cookies.

Abby held the bottle over Diana's glass. "Hey. What's this? Your glass is still full."

"I have to drive home."

Abby raised her eyebrows. "One small glass?"

"And . . . I'm starting to get a headache."

"Oh. I'm sorry." Abby filled her own glass and sat down. "Do you know there's not a single stoplight in Vanuatu? Not a bloomin' one. But then, why would they have a stoplight. The so-called downtown in the capital city only has one main street and two or three side streets. Can you believe it? Hey." She frowned at Diana. "Are you all right? You look almost as bad as I do." She pulled her T-shirt away from her body as proof.

"I'm fine. Just a little . . . I don't know."

"Here. Have a biscuit."

Yes, Diana thought as she scooped up a handful of shortbread cookies. Sugar! Yes!

By the time she stood up to go, all the cookies on the plate were gone. She could feel them puffing up her stomach as she walked to the car. She slid her car key into the lock and stopped. Then, with the fingers of her left hand—as though she knew it would be there—she touched the pimple blooming between her eyebrows.

14

The cramps didn't start until almost an hour after she left Abby's house. The first pain hit while she was riding the elevator up to their apartment. A dull ache low in her abdomen, nothing more. By the time she and Jay sat down to dinner, it had spread to her lower back. And by bedtime, all she could do was curl up with her knees pressed to her chest and wait for the Midol to take effect.

Maybe it was better this way, she thought. Better to feel in her body what she felt in her heart. Her body was discarding the very blood and tissue meant to cushion and nourish her baby. That shouldn't happen without pain.

"What's the matter, honey?" Trailing a stream of Irish Spring-scented steam from his shower, Jay padded across the floor to their bed.

"Mmm," she groaned. She shouldn't have to explain it to him, should she? Didn't he pay attention to the calendar? Why else would she be hugging her knees to her chest if she didn't have cramps?

He climbed up beside her, dripping water from his wet hair. "Cramps?"

"Yeah."

"I thought you were awfully quiet at dinner."

He'd noticed? She thought he'd been too involved in talking about his next project—something about livestock development in Pakistan.

"Here. Let me rub your back."

She straightened her knees and rolled onto her stomach. His warm, practiced hands knew exactly how much pressure she liked, how fast she wanted him to circle over her pelvis, one hand moving clockwise, the other counterclockwise. She took a deep, slow breath, and as she started to relax, the pain became more bearable. "I thought it was going to happen this time," she mumbled into the sheets. "I thought I was pregnant."

"But honey, how could you be? I was away."

"And then you came back."

His hands went still. "You mean the night I flew in from Korea?" He chuckled and went back to massaging her. "So that's why you woke me up."

"Hey!"

"You were all over me, my dear."

"I missed you. Not everything is about getting pregnant, you know."

"You sure about that?" He leaned over and kissed her neck.

"Yes. I'm sure."

After a week of Christmas parties and holiday preparation, Christmas Eve was quiet. Too quiet. Even Clarita was gone. She'd taken the week off and sailed away to her family's home on Masbate. She wouldn't be back until January.

Diana pushed the play button on the CD player and turned the volume up a smidgen. Maybe the familiar carols of the Mormon Tabernacle Choir would stir up some holiday spirit. "Have a seat," she told Jay. "I'll be the Christmas elf."

In Diana's family, the youngest child was given the honor of passing out the gifts. And since Diana was younger than Jay by two years and two months, this year and every year since they moved to Manila, she had been the elf. Jay didn't have any corresponding Christmas customs. He'd grown up overseas, moving from one country to the next each time his dad was reassigned. His family's was the kind of lifestyle that valued new experiences over family traditions. Now his father was stationed in Johannesburg, South Africa, and his sister Fiona was living in Paris.

"Ah," Diana said, taking a cylindrical box with no bow out from under the tree and squinting at the tag. "This one is for Mr. Jay McIntosh." She presented it to him with a flourish and twirled away. A dancing elf.

He gave the thinly disguised bottle a little shake. "I think I'm going to like this one."

He always played along with her, even though she suspected he thought the whole thing was just a little bit silly.

"And look at this one." She reached for a package, all bold colors and geometric shapes tied with twine. "I wonder where this came from." She winked at Jay. His mother always made good use of local materials and styles in her gift wrapping. Holding the gift over her head, Diana turned from side to side as though she were displaying it to a room full of people. "Oh, my goodness! This one's for me." She set the package on a side table and carried on in the same vein. If there was one lesson Diana had learned from her dad, it was that if you wanted to make an occasion special, you had to overdo it.

They kept up the ritual of good cheer all through the opening of the gifts. Afterwards, with the gifts unwrapped and the paper and ribbon thrown away or folded and saved for next year, Diana brought out a freshly baked apple pie and a carton of vanilla ice cream.

Santa didn't come during the night, but the next morning Diana woke up thinking about her childhood and her mother and Andrew. It was too early to call them, though. Mom would be in the middle of cooking—stirring the gravy, testing the turkey, placing lettuce leaves and squares of cranberry salad on small plates. Better to wait.

She kissed Jay softly behind the ear and tiptoed into the kitchen. When he joined her, she had an omelet with ham, mushrooms, and cheddar cheese ready to take out of the oven and a stack of Grandma's gingerbread pancakes on the table.

"Merry Christmas," she said, offering him a cup of coffee.

"Merry Christmas to you, my love." He took a sip and sat down. "I haven't seen pancakes like these since last Christmas."

"If you like them, we can make Grandma's pancakes a tradition in our house."

"I like them."

They took their time eating and cleaning up. Then they got dressed and drove to San Antonio for Christmas Mass. By the time they got home, it would be just about the right time to place a phone call. Twelve thirty in Manila, eight thirty yesterday evening on the US West Coast.

Diana dialed and waited. The rings sounded strangely hollow and high. But when Mom answered, she sounded fine, a little giggly maybe. "It's the eggnog," she said. "I love my Christmas eggnog. All that cream and nutmeg. Gary made it with bourbon this year instead of rum. And I tell you, honey, it's every bit as good. Maybe better. Have you opened your gifts yet?"

"Last night, Mom. It's Christmas afternoon here. Twelve thirty."

"I can never remember how much behind or ahead you are. Thank goodness you keep track of those things."

"Hi, Anne," Jay said from the phone in the bedroom. "Merry Christmas."

"Oh, Jay. Merry Christmas. Hey," she shouted, her voice only slightly muted. "Can you guys quiet down? I'm talking to Diana and Jay. Long distance. Andrew, get on the other line."

"Who all is there?" Diana wanted to picture them: Mom in her apron, Grandpa in the La-Z-Boy, his feet up, yelling at Grandma to stop fussing and sit down.

"The usual," Mom said. "Grandma and Grandpa, your Aunt Emily and Uncle Gary, Bonnie and Dennis and their kids. Little Jenny was our Christmas elf this year. She's only learning to read, so her brother Jake had to help with the names on the tags."

Mom talked about the turkey (too dry), Grandma's mincemeat pie ("We all took a sliver so we wouldn't hurt her feelings"), and the weather ("Aunt Em says she saw a few flakes of snow, but no one believes her"). Diana assured her that Manila's weather was still hot. Jay said that no, they wouldn't be calling his parents. They usually traveled on the Christmas holiday, and this year they were on safari in Zambia. Grandma and Grandpa got on the line to say hi. And then, since the call was expensive, everyone yelled "Merry Christmas," Andrew gave them a Christmas blessing, and they all said good-bye.

Diana stayed staring at the glasses lined up on the bar in front of her, her hand still resting on the phone. Coming up behind her, Jay rested his hands on her shoulders.

"I just can't believe Bonnie's kids are reading already," Diana said.

"Why?" Jay dropped his hands and stepped back. "How old are they?"

Diana turned around to face him. "That's not the point." She quickly wiped her eyes. "Bonnie is two years younger than I am. Two and a half. After my birthday we'll call it three. Damn it, Jay. I'm too old to be the Christmas elf."

Manila
1990

15

She awoke feeling suffocated by the sweaty, hot sheet and pillowcase, the thick blanket of sweltering, humid air pressing down on her. It was a miracle she'd been able to fall asleep sometime halfway through the night.

She started to stretch her legs and stopped just in time. Her calves were too tight, ripe for a charley horse. All she'd have to do would be point her toes and at least one of her legs would seize up.

She dropped them over the side of the bed and swung her feet like a child on a high stool. There. Better. If only it weren't so damned hot. She fanned her face with both hands. Then she lifted her hair off her neck, twisted it, and tied it in a sloppy knot at the back of her head. For a split second before the humidity closed in, the back of her neck felt almost cool. She glanced up at the ceiling fan, wishing it back to life. The electricity had been off for almost twenty-four hours. Surely it would come back soon. She threw on her short cotton robe, the merest nod to modesty in recognition of Clarita's presence in the apartment. Then, leaving her slippers behind, she went looking for Jay.

With the doors to both balconies open and no air conditioners to mask the sound, the roar of traffic on the boulevard below broke into their apartment like a gang of bungling, screeching cat burglars.

Diana walked past the study and into the dining room. Without power, the aquarium was dark and silent. Ever since the last goldfish died in January, she'd tried to ignore it. But there it was, the hideous black algae eater that was always lurking at the bottom of the tank when it wasn't darting after some little bit of food.

Jay was sitting at the dining table, looking very much as he did every weekday morning—his leather shoes shined, his black hair slicked back, and his pale blue cotton shirt ironed. She pulled out a chair and waited for him to look up from his *Asian Wall Street Journal.* If she were to touch his face now, so soon after his shave, it would feel as smooth and clean as a child's skin after a bath.

"Morning, honey," he said, turning the page of the paper and refolding it. In a few minutes he'd be sitting in his office, enjoying the air-conditioned coolness provided by D-TAP's backup generator.

"Morning," she said, returning his greeting minus the smile. She plopped down in her chair. Using her cloth napkin, she wiped her face and the back of her neck. It was hard to think straight when it was this hot. The tension in her shoulders and the pressure behind her eyes distracted her. She wasn't made for this kind of weather.

Today wouldn't be the last power failure they'd see this month. The electricity always went off in May. Wouldn't you know it— May. Manila's hottest month. It was every bit as hot as April, and more humid to boot. Already there was a hint of the coming rainy season. All day tall cumulus clouds would boil up like giant gods over Manila Bay. They'd hold their breath until, by late afternoon, they couldn't hold it any longer, and the rain would fall.

"I made an appointment with Dr. Feliciano," she said, throwing it out like a challenge.

"Dr. Feliciano?" He set his coffee cup down. "Why?"

"Why?" She looked at him sideways. "Maybe it's because another five months have gone by and I'm still not pregnant?" She heard the sarcasm in her voice and didn't like it, and yet she kept going. "Or because my thirty-fifth birthday is coming up?"

"Honey." He closed his newspaper and reached for her hand. "I just meant . . . I mean, I thought Dr. Feliciano said there was nothing wrong with us and we just had to be patient, follow her recommendations, and relax."

She pulled her hand back. "I called Dr. Feliciano because 'waiting and relaxing' . . ." She made air quotes around the words. ". . . isn't working. We need to try something else."

"Like what?"

"She's the doctor. She should be able to tell me."

He looked at the ceiling. Not exactly an eye roll, but she caught it.

"I just don't want you to get your hopes up." He looked at his watch. "Sorry. I've gotta go." He took one last gulp of coffee. Then he pushed his chair back and walked away, the *Asian Wall Street Journal* rolled up in one hand, his attaché case in the other.

She watched as his perfectly ironed blue shirt and slicked-back hair retreated into the hallway. She didn't fail to note that he closed the door behind him just a little harder than his mask of control should have allowed for.

"Ma'am." Clarita was standing a few steps back from the kitchen doorway, her gaze carefully fixed on the floor. "Do you want eggs, ma'am?"

"Ah." Diana pulled her robe together over her chest. Right. Breakfast. "Um . . . a scrambled egg would be fine. Thank you, Clarita." She wasn't sure she could eat anything right now. Maybe after some water. She lifted the glass to her lips, and . . . Ugh! She screwed up her face and put it down. The water was lukewarm. Of course. The ice in the freezing compartment would all be melted by now.

When Clarita came back with the scrambled egg, she didn't seem to know where to look. She slid the plate in front of Diana, backed away, and almost ran into the kitchen.

Oh my gosh! Diana's cheeks flashed hot with embarrassment. Clarita must have been standing in the kitchen listening to them.

Closing her eyes and fanning her face with her hands, Diana tried to play it back. It was all so private—her infertility and her distress, the way she'd talked to him. Had she shouted? Did they have a fight? She hated how out of control she'd sounded. She wiped her face and the back of her neck. It wasn't Jay's fault they had no power and the heat was making her crazy.

Grabbing a *pan de sal,* she nibbled on its soft crust and wondered how many fights between her and Jay had been averted because they had a maid who could hear them fighting. And was that a good thing? Shouldn't a husband and wife have a heated argument every now and then?

She looked down at the pure white center of the little bun. Pan de sal was the ultimate comfort food, way too simple and sweet to be healthy. She put it down and scooped up a forkful of scrambled eggs.

~

Sitting behind her enormous mahogany desk, Dr. Feliciano looked like Alice in Wonderland after downing the DRINK ME potion that helped her fit through the tiny door.

"Good afternoon," the diminutive doctor said. She motioned toward one of the armchairs. "How are you doing?"

"Fine." The doctor's sympathetic tone had caught Diana by surprise. "I'm fine." She blinked to head off a tear. "I'm still not pregnant, though." She cleared her throat.

"Well, then," the doctor said, "let's see what we can do about that." She rifled through some papers and pulled out what appeared to be the instructions she'd given Diana and Jay on their first appointment. "First, I'd like to review this page." She reached for the reading glasses she wore around her neck. "Have you kept your weight within the range we agreed upon?"

"Yes." Fortunately, gaining weight was one problem Diana hadn't had since they moved to the Philippines.

Dr. Feliciano leaned over her desk and squinted at Diana. "Are you sure? You look a little thin. Remember, if your body mass index falls below twenty, you won't have enough fat to metabolize the estrogens you need."

"I weighed myself this morning. I'm right at my goal."

"Good." Dr. Feliciano slid her finger down to the next item. "Daily morning measurement and recording of your temperature for the purpose of predicting the start of ovulation?"

"It's the first thing I do every morning."

"Good. Recording your temperature is a valuable tool. But it's only valuable insomuch as you put the knowledge to use." She removed her reading glasses and leaned forward. "Your husband travels a lot, I recall."

"Yes. It's part of his job."

"Hm." She let go of her glasses, allowing them to dangle on their silver chain. "Couldn't you go with him?"

"With him? On his business trips? He'd be busy working."

"I realize that. But still, you'd have your evenings together."

"I don't know," Diana said. "Maybe . . ." Could she? It didn't seem likely. As far as she knew, wives never went on mission with their husbands. And if she did, what would Jay think?

"Think about it." Dr. Feliciano moved her index finger down the list. Did Diana exercise regularly? Did she remember not to douche before sex or use a commercial lubricant? "If you focus on foreplay," she added, "you won't have any need for a lubricant."

Diana nodded. This was her fifth appointment with Dr. Feliciano, but she still wasn't comfortable talking about foreplay in clinical terms. Kissing and touching, whatever she and Jay did in the privacy of their bedroom, were more than a means of lubricating the vaginal canal. She was afraid that naming it too many times in a doctor's office would strip away, little by little, all that made lovemaking real and wonderful.

"Boxers not briefs for your husband," Dr. Feliciano continued, "and a multi-vitamin with folate. Is he still taking his vitamins?"

"Yes."

The doctor worked down the familiar list of recommendations. "Adequate sleep? A healthy diet?"

"Yes," Diana answered. "Yes." She and Jay had been observing every recommendation on the list for months. She knew them by heart. As she answered Dr. Feliciano's queries, her attention wandered to the items on the big mahogany desk: an orchid with creamy blossoms, a basket holding paper clips and push pins, a stack of Post-its, and an array of framed photos, some facing the doctor, others turned toward the patient. The doctor's family photo had been updated since Diana's last visit. In the previous picture the five children were arranged according to height. This one had the girls kneeling on the grass and the three boys standing behind them.

"And *do* continue to stick with the missionary style," Dr. Feliciano concluded. "You can experiment with other positions later." She tucked the paper back in the folder. "These are the basics."

Diana cleared her throat. "Doctor, uh, if we find that I still can't get pregnant . . . um . . . what about . . . I mean, could we look into something like . . . a test-tube baby?" She'd been keeping the idea in reserve. She hadn't said a word about it to Jay. He might think she was being obsessive and weird. Back in the late '70s, when people heard about the test-tube baby in England, they thought it was freaky. But now, more than ten years had passed. People would be getting used to it.

"You mean in vitro fertilization," Dr. Feliciano said, quick to provide the correct terminology. "It's a relatively new procedure. Experimental some might say. Even though it *has* gained a degree of popularity in several countries, it's not available here in the Philippines. Even if it were available, I don't think you would be a suitable candidate. From all that we have seen, you should be able to conceive without resorting to exceptional means. And you, my dear," she said with little sympathetic shakes of her head, "are still quite young."

"I'm almost thirty-five, Doctor."

"You're still well within the peak reproductive age range of twenty to thirty-eight." She opened the folder again. "Ah, yes. Relaxation. How is that going?"

Diana felt a flash of anger. "I've been trying, trying very hard." She looked down at her clenched fists. "But trying hard seems to defeat the purpose."

"Yes, yes. One must know *how* to relax." She grabbed a pen and scribbled on her prescription pad. "Here," she said, ripping the paper off and handing it to Diana. "Make an appointment with Marilu Reyes. She teaches yoga and meditation, and she counsels people with anxiety disorders, phobias, and panic attacks."

"But I don't . . ."

"She's very good. I think she will be able to help you." Dr. Feliciano closed the folder and pushed her chair back. "Come back in three or four months, and if you're not already pregnant, we'll see if something further needs to be explored."

Halfway to the door, Diana turned back. "You said the procedure used in England, in vitro . . ."

"In vitro fertilization."

"That it was becoming popular in several countries. Which countries would that be?"

Dr. Feliciano allowed herself a small sigh before naming them. "Australia and the United States were the first to follow England. Austria, Sweden, France, and Singapore were close behind. But as I said, I don't think IVF is for you."

Diana thanked her and hurried away.

Passing through the hallway and into the reception room, she looked straight ahead, focusing on the large blue aquarium at the far end of the room instead of the baby pictures on either side of her. In front of the tank, a small child swayed, turning his head slowly from side to side as though mesmerized by the lazy movements of the fish.

It may work for him, Diana thought as she hurried past the reception desk, but raising fish had been a total bust for her.

16

Marilu Reyes's Forbes Park house stretched deep into the property, almost disappearing in the shadows of fully grown acacias and fat blossom-laden kalachuchis. Its mossy carved posts hinted at respectability and old money. Diana clenched her fist as she followed the maid up the sidewalk and into the house. She was determined to take these lessons or sessions or whatever you called them seriously. What other choice did she have?

The studio was in the front of the house, just to the right of the entry. The woman who met her at the door was wearing lavender tights, robin-egg blue leg warmers, and a loose off-the-shoulder T-shirt. Her expression, though, was more Zen than *Flashdance*. She ushered Diana into a large air-conditioned room with buffed wooden floors and floor-to-ceiling mirrors cut across horizontally by waist-high handrails. "My mother teaches ballet here," she said in explanation. She raised her chin toward a pile of mats in the corner. "In a few weeks you'll be ready to join my yoga class and meditation sessions." In the meantime, it looked like it would be just the two of them in the big, empty, reflecting room.

They sat down in folding chairs angled toward each other in front of a bank of windows. The plants and orchids hanging in front of the windows broke the sunlight into thousands of soft-edge pieces. "We'll start with breathing," Marilu said. She described in detail for Diana the benefits of slow deep breathing and the dangers of shallow fast breathing. Then she laid her hands on Diana, one small hand on her chest and one on her belly. "Relax your shoulders," she said. "Breath in your tummy. In, out. Deep down. Slower. Remember, dear, this is not a foot race."

Until then, Diana had assumed Marilu Reyes was about her age. Maybe she was older, though. Or maybe she called everyone dear.

In the next exercise, Diana practiced relaxing, slowly, slowly, one muscle at a time, from the top of her head on down.

During the final fifteen minutes they tried some yoga poses— downward dog, bridge pose, and child's pose. By then, Diana's determination to take the class seriously was ebbing. As she caught sight of herself reflected in the wall of mirrors, she had to press her lips together to keep from giggling.

"I'll see you next week," Ms. Reyes said as she walked Diana to the door. "And remember, dear, practice, practice, practice."

"I will," Diana said, although the only thing on her mind as she walked to the car was the funny stories she would tell Abby about this first "class" with Marilu Reyes.

Slamming the car door shut, she exploded into a fit of laughter. It wasn't really that funny, she thought as she leaned over the steering wheel, coughing and trying to catch her breath. She fumbled for the box of tissues on the floor. She wiped her nose on her arm. Then she teased the box closer and grabbed a tissue. "What the hell am I doing?"

When she got home, the words she needed to tell a funny story to Abby were gone. The pictures remained though. In their study, with the air conditioner rattling out a stream of cool air, she found a sketch pad and set to work recreating exaggerated versions of the images of herself she'd seen reflected on the mirrored walls of Marilu Reyes's studio.

She'd completed two sketches and was starting a third when the electricity went off. She slammed her pencil down. Damn! She leaned back in her chair, and drummed her fingers on the desk. A brownout now and then was one thing, but every day . . .

She picked up the sketch pad and leafed back to the finished drawings. Not bad, she admitted, grinning at the floppy-eared spaniel she'd drawn. A pure fabrication. The dog sat cocking his head and smiling a doggy smile at a woman posing on all fours, her butt in the air and her hair in her face. *You call that downward dog?* the dog asks. In the other sketch, a woman is sitting on the floor in lotus position, her eyes closed, a hand on each knee. *How the hell do I relax my pancreas?* she asks in a bubble over her head.

Diana smiled. Abby would appreciate the humor. After adding some color, she would stuff the sketches in an envelope with her next letter.

Whew! Diana fanned herself with the sketch pad. After all these years in the Philippines, she was still amazed at how a room could turn hot and stuffy within minutes without the air conditioning. Before long she was going to need a cold shower.

The phone rang, and, as though it might be something important or hopeful or . . . purely out of habit, she hurried into the dining room to answer it.

"Hey." It was Jay. "Can you meet me for lunch at the office?"

He didn't have to ask twice. The air conditioning at his office would be more than welcome. "Sure," she said. "I'll be there."

~/

The D-TAP lobby was a spacious, high-ceilinged area designed to accommodate large gatherings and to display gifts from various Asian and South Pacific countries. It was meant to impress visitors, Diana thought as she pushed open the heavy glass door and stepped inside. The lobby was alive with men crisscrossing its floor, shaking hands, patting backs, or hurrying off to meet someone at a favorite restaurant. In the midst of all the motion, only Jay was still, illuminated by the invisible spotlight of their connection.

She'd been with him only hours before, but from across the room, she was aware of how good-looking he was.

He saw her, smiled, and strode across the great marble floor to her side. "Marshall Charbonneau wants to see you," he said, giving her a quick kiss on the cheek.

"Why?"

"He wants to give you something. He didn't say what." He put his hand on her back. "Let's go. He's waiting for us in the Executive Dining Room."

Every time Diana had lunch with Jay in the Executive Dining Room, she was struck by how nice it was—white tablecloths, filtered sunlight, silent air conditioning—and by how the men chatting, laughing, and eating there didn't seem to notice.

She didn't recognize Marshall Charbonneau until he waved them over. He had an enormous bald spot on the back of his head now, and when he turned around, all she could see was the mustache. Eddie Wu was sitting across from him.

"You remember Marshall, don't you?" Jay asked, pulling a chair out for Diana.

"Of course. How's Carole Anne?"

"Carole Anne?" Marshall tilted his head like a dog catching the scent of a fox. "Oh, she's just fine. Busy with her garden and her riding lessons and whatever else it is she does while I'm hard at work."

Jay and Eddie chuckled, a kind of acknowledgment, Diana thought, that they all belonged to the same club, a club composed of hard-working men who supported women with nothing better to do than take riding lessons.

"So," Diana said, "What brings you to Manila?"

"Business," Marshall looked at his watch. "I have a meeting with the vice president as soon as we're done here."

Diana didn't know Marshall well. But seeing him now, she remembered that every time she saw him and Carole Anne at a dinner party hosted by mutual friends, he was always talking about himself. A few years ago, the Charbonneaus had moved to Vanuatu. Now Marshall was Saudur's boss.

Eddie raised his arm. "Pssst," he said to get the waiter's attention.

You could count on a good meal in the Executive Dining Room. Soup and salad, a main course, and dessert, all geared to the tastes of an international staff and served by well-trained waiters in white jackets.

"The usual for me," Eddie said before their waiter had a chance to announce the daily special.

"Yes sir."

"And, Rolly, I'm gonna need another San Miguel in a minute."

"Coming right up, sir."

The special that day, which the rest of them ordered, was *tom yum* soup, crystal noodles with prawns, Thai basil with chicken, and a scoop of mango ice cream for dessert.

"Hey, Diana." Marshall pulled an envelope out of his inside jacket pocket and dangled it over the table. "Got something for you."

She leaned across the table and took it. Scrawled across the front of the envelope in Abby's familiar bold handwriting was Diana's name. "Thanks," she said, slipping the letter into her purse.

"We rescued Diana from a brownout," Jay said.

Eddie groaned. "These brownouts! I'm sick of them." He tilted his head back and emptied his beer. "If Cory hadn't mothballed the Bataan Nuclear Power Plant," he said, handing the empty bottle to the waiter who'd just arrived with cold beers for the men and a coffee for Diana, "we'd have all the power we needed."

"That woman's way outa her depth," Marshall said, shaking his head and rolling his eyes.

Diana cleared her throat. "Excuse me. Cory wasn't the one who built a nuclear plant over a fault and within spitting distance of a very active volcano." Diana couldn't understand why people gave Cory Aquino such a hard time. After all those years under a dictator, you'd think they'd be happy to have a president who was at least trying to help the country.

Jay looked at her and bit his thumbnail. He and Diana had argued more than once about Cory Aquino, Jay criticizing her, Diana coming to her defense, neither of them admitting that their view had anything to do with Cory's gender . . . or theirs.

"She didn't have much choice," Jay said finally. "The public was scared stiff of anything nuclear so soon after the Chernobyl disaster."

"That's her problem," Marshall said. "She doesn't have the *cojones* to go against public opinion."

"As for me . . . Eddie fanned his face with his hand. "All I want is enough power to run my air conditioner. And . . ." He raised his beer. ". . . keep my San Miguel cold."

When their soup arrived, the men had moved on to office gossip. For the juiciest bits, they leaned over their bowls, slurping and lowering their voices. The juiciest gossip among D-TAP officers had nothing to do with sex. It was all about power. *McCarthy was angling for Yamamoto's job. Patel was spreading rumors about Torres, and they suspected Kapoor put him up to it.* Diana had never been a big gossip. Even if she had worked for D-TAP and known all the parties involved, she wouldn't have enjoyed the conversation.

Jay put his spoon down and smiled at her. "Do you like the soup?"

"Yeah. It's good."

After the main course arrived, the conversation shifted to D-TAP projects and missions. Every so often they'd remember Diana and tear themselves away from shop talk. Before long, though, they were back at it again. Their work was just too darn interesting. If D-TAP didn't have a policy against hiring spouses, Diana thought, she wouldn't mind working for them herself.

Twirling some crystal noodles around her chopsticks, she considered her old job. It wasn't the most exciting thing in the world to be an accountant, but when she worked, she'd had a sense of accomplishment at the end of the day. And she and her fellow accountants always had something to talk about at lunch. She was remembering some of those lunches when Marshall first mentioned Johnny Gamboa.

"Poor old Johnny," he said. "Looks like I'm gonna have to replace him. I don't think he's going to recover from that stroke."

The waiter brought their ice cream, and, almost in unison, they picked up their spoons and dug in. Magnolia's mango ice cream was irresistible—creamy with chunks of mango, and just the right consistency. With the sweet, creamy taste of mangoes in her mouth, Diana lost track of the plight of poor old Johnny Gamboa, the tragedy of his stroke, and the need to replace him.

17

Diana rolled onto her back and floated motionless, staring at the sky. Abby's letter and her own confused feelings about it fluttered at the edge of her consciousness.

By now, clouds would be billowing up over the bay. But here at the pool, the sky was pure blue, its simplicity broken only by a pair of dragonflies stuck together in a mating dance. Their iridescent wings flashed in the sunlight as they dipped and rose in their graceful tandem flight over the water.

The thought of finishing her laps made a brief appearance. Then it melted away. Instead she watched the dragonflies. They flew toward the tables and frangipani trees, and then, a minute later, swooped back. Finally, breaking apart, they zoomed off in opposite directions, as though they'd never met. As though one intercourse would be enough—which might be true for dragonflies. Considering their short lives, they would need to get it right the first time.

She stroked to the ladder and climbed out. At her table, she threw a towel around her shoulders and sat down. She didn't need to reach into the outside pocket of her bag. She'd already read Abby's letter. But here she was with the envelope in her hand. She slid the letter out and unfolded it.

Abby's first letters from Vanuatu were angry. Even her hand-writing had been angry. She'd shouted her complaints, the words landing with a smack on the page. *I've been exiled,* she wrote. *Like Napoleon. Only worse. Napoleon's Elba was only a few kilometers off the coast of Italy. This little speck of land is in the middle of the largest ocean on earth. A sitting duck for the next typhoon or tsunami.*

In those early letters, she made lists of the things Vanu-atu didn't have: *no cultural events, no movie theater, no newspaper deserving of the name, no shopping after noon on Saturday and all day Sunday, and,* she added again, *there isn't a single bloomin' stoplight on the whole bloody island. I should pack up the twins and move back to London. To civilization. Damn it!*

Her vehemence had worried Diana. Surely she would cool down before long. She shot off letters, encouraging Abby, telling her she would like Vanuatu eventually. "I know you," Diana wrote. "Before long you'll be right in the middle of all kinds of fascinating activities and projects."

And now she was. Only four months after moving to Vanuatu, Abby's life was full. She was volunteering at the twins' school, and she'd joined the Natural Science Society, a quirky organization with old colonial types as members. She was helping them organize a trip into the interior of the island to look for a rare orchid endemic to Vanuatu. There were parties and picnics, and everywhere Abby turned she ran into interesting people with exotic stories to tell—a British sailor straight out of a tale by Robert Lewis Stevenson, a beautiful dark-skinned woman who was said to be one of the many mixed-race children of the Frenchman in James Michener's *Tales of the South Pacific*, Aussie adventurers, and Chinese and Vietnamese businessmen whose great-grandparents had been brought to the island by the British and French.

In this letter, the one hand-carried by Marshall Charbonneau, Abby talked about planting papaya trees from seeds and banana plants from suckers. *Everything grows so fast here,* she wrote. *We'll be eating our own fruit in no time.*

That's when Diana had to stop reading. The words and enthusiasm reminded her of herself four years ago when they were new to the Philippines. *You can plant a broomstick, and it will grow here,* people used to tell her. And so it seemed. When she and Jay drove out of the city, they saw plants climbing all over each other in their enthusiasm for growth.

That first year everything Diana saw delighted her—the clouds of pink bougainvillea, the fat carabao mangoes, the fish and squid fresh from the sea laid out on market tables, the squids' ink spots still dancing under their thin, transparent skin. Everyone she met delighted her—the dressmaker who worked without a pattern, the boys who sold garlic-roasted peanuts on the highway, the beautiful old Filipino woman who owned three houses in Manila and a condo in Hawaii and lived in the oldest one, a house beside a stream that attracted snakes.

And the expats. Diana was delighted to have friends from all over the world, men and women whose ordinary conversations were peppered with hints of the exotic places and lives they'd seen and lived. No wonder Jay had been so eager to take a job with D-TAP and live overseas. Finally it made sense to her.

When he had sprung the idea on her back in Seattle, though, she'd balked.

They were eating breakfast when he found an ad for an Economic Development Specialist in the back pages of *The Economist.* "That's me," he shouted, jabbing the page with his index finger, his eyes shining. "I'm perfect for the job."

"Where is it?" she asked, crunching into her toast.

"Manila."

She put her toast down and licked the raspberry jam off her lips. "Jay," she said, frowning. "You already have a job. We already have jobs here."

"Not like this one." He pushed his chair back and stood, holding the magazine to his chest. "This is the kind of job I worked for all the way through graduate school, the kind of work I wrote about in my doctoral thesis." He circled the breakfast table, a dreamy look on his face.

That day, she'd had no intention of leaving behind the life they were building in Seattle. They both had good jobs: Jay teaching at the University of Washington, Diana as an accountant for the city. They had a beautiful house and a mortgage. They didn't have children yet, but they didn't need to move abroad to have a baby.

Jay was so happy, though, so enthusiastic that it was hard to tell him straight out how crazy she thought the idea was. So when he said there'd be lots of competition and he probably wouldn't get the job, she'd agreed that it couldn't hurt to apply. If he did get a job offer, they could decide then whether or not to accept it.

He didn't hear anything for a couple of months, so she'd nearly forgotten about it.

Then, one fine July afternoon, she pulled into the driveway and found him sitting on the top step of the porch grinning. It didn't enter her mind that his obvious glee had anything to do with a job offer that would upend their lives.

It was one of those long daylight-savings-time summer days when the sun hangs in the sky way past its bedtime. Jay was already in his shorts. He stood up and waited for her to get out of the car, never once losing his silly smile. "I got the job," he said when she was halfway up the sidewalk.

"What?" She skidded to a stop. "What job?"

"D-TAP."

"D-TAP? What's that?"

He was too caught up in his good news to slow down. "Development Trust for Asia and the Pacific. Remember?" He skipped the last two porch steps, landing with his feet apart and his arms spread wide. "They want me to start September thirtieth."

"Wait." The conversation they'd had months earlier came back to her in a rush. And suddenly she was scared.

"Come on. I'll tell you all about it."

She hesitated. She had a feeling that if she unglued her feet from the sidewalk, she was going to fall into a deep dark hole she couldn't climb back out of.

"Come on. Let's go inside."

She picked a stem of lavender and rubbed the flower between her fingers. When the sweet, piney fragrance dissipated, she crushed the sprig between her palms and let the bits and pieces scatter over the sidewalk and onto the shiny black toes of her high-heeled shoes. Then she brushed her hands together and followed Jay into the house.

He strode down the hall and into the kitchen. "It's a fantastic deal. A great salary and a very generous relocation allowance."

"Hey. Slow down." The kitchen still smelled of their breakfast bacon, she noted as she kicked off her shoes. "I thought you said your chances of getting the job were slim." Her feet were killing her. She leaned against the counter and lifted one foot to give it a good rub. She'd spent the last nine hours in shoes that were too new, too tight, and too high.

"They *were* slim. And yet, I got it."

She let go of her sore foot and straightened up. "But Jay, why would you want to work in Manila when we have perfectly good jobs here?"

He pushed away from the counter. "I have an *okay* job, Diana."

She stepped back, puzzled by his apparent anger.

"I have a dull pay-the-bills, soul-destroying job as opposed to this position in Manila, which is my dream job."

"What?!" She squinted at the man she'd been married to for the past two years. "I thought you liked teaching. You never said anything about a dream job."

He threw up his hands. "Teaching the Theory of International Development to college students is a pale facsimile of being out in the field and doing the work myself. You can see that, can't you?"

"Of course, but . . ." She felt him dragging her into it, proving his case as much by his fervor as by his arguments. She slid her hand over the countertop, grabbed a dishtowel, and rubbed at some fingerprints on the fridge. Every time she entered the kitchen, she congratulated herself on the paint colors she'd chosen. Ecru was just right for the molding, and she loved the way the sunflower yellow walls caught the morning light and held onto it for the rest of the day. She tossed the dishtowel over her shoulder and gazed at their lovely walls. "We just painted the kitchen and breakfast nook," she said, immediately aware of how foolish she sounded.

"If that's what's bothering you . . ." He gestured at the sunflower yellow walls.

"No, no. It's not just that." Where did she start? It was her job and her mom and brother. Andrew lived on the other side of the state. Who would look out for Mom? And what about their friends and neighbors? What about their house, the lovely old Wallingford house they'd saved for and repaired and painted?

He turned and walked away, hitting the backs of chairs with the flat of his hand. When he reached the French doors, he stopped and stared at the deck and the yard, the apple tree and the hydrangeas and rhodies. She was on her way to put a sympathetic arm around him when he opened the door and stepped outside.

She couldn't see his face, but the backs of his ears were red. He was leaning on the deck railing, his head down, elbows out, the muscles in his back and arms showing through his T-shirt. The pale skin on his arms and legs, even under all that black hair, always made Diana aware of his vulnerability. He was hurting. And she was the cause of it. But really! Moving to the Philippines? Wasn't that a crazy idea?

She poured a Pepsi for herself, grabbed a beer for him, and took them outside. For a while they sat in their wrought iron chairs, drinking and watching a squirrel steal seeds from the bird feeder.

By the time the squirrel had his fill and scurried away, Jay seemed to have calmed down. He put his beer on the table and looked at her sideways. "The salary is fifty-five percent more than what I'm making now," he said. "You wouldn't have to work." He raised his eyebrows. "And you'd have maids."

She chuckled. "Maids? What would I do with maids? I'm really sorry, honey. But I don't know why you thought I'd agree."

Above them, a small white cloud was breaking apart, the pieces floating away and dissolving into nothing.

"Think about it," Jay said, giving it what she thought was one last shot. "All that cosmopolitan culture, the parties, lots of time to take up new hobbies. My mom has always loved expat life."

"Jay." Diana shook her head. "Your mom and I are nothing alike. Another beer?" she asked, draining her Pepsi.

He shook his head.

"I'm sorry, honey." She thought it was over then. Picking up the bottle and empty can, she started through the door.

"Diana."

"Yeah?" She turned back around.

"Please. Just think about it. We don't have to decide for another couple of weeks."

She couldn't remember now what he'd said to convince her or whether she'd convinced herself. One way or the other, though, as the days passed, she came to believe it wouldn't be so bad after all to give up her job and their house. She started questioning whether she'd always played it too safe, wondering whether she actually did want a settled life with one day very much like the one before it.

She did remember that Jay was the one who brought up the baby. Earlier that year, she'd stopped using birth control, and they both assumed she would be pregnant soon. "If we move," he said, "you'd be able to take care of the baby. You wouldn't have to rely on daycare."

Maybe that was what convinced her: imagining what it would be like spending all that time with their baby. Or maybe it was just that the "dream job" at D-TAP seemed more important to him than their ordinary life in Seattle did to her.

That must have been it, she thought as she folded Abby's letter and slid it back in the envelope. She was leaning down to tuck it into the outside pocket of her bag when a kalachuchi blossom fell, brushing against her arm. She picked it up and held it to her nose, took a sniff, and tucked it behind her ear.

It was her fault, she supposed, the way she felt. She wanted to blame Jay for talking her into moving. She'd like to blame Jay's mother for deceiving him, for pretending she loved being an expat wife, that it fulfilled her to trail her husband around the world, filling her time with bridge games and tennis lessons and charity bazaars. But that wasn't the true picture of Diana's mother-in-law. Whether or not Linda McIntosh had chosen the unsettled life and her supportive role in it, she did make the most of it. She became an expert on the history and culture of every country they lived in. She had friends all over the globe and kept up with them. She initiated a small project to sell placemats hand woven by poor Ghanaian women.

Diana stared straight ahead, unmoved by the shimmering blue of the pool. Happiness was out there somewhere. Was it her own fault for not finding it?

A small group of school-age children was just entering the pool area, the boys whooping and running ahead while their mothers and one smug little girl in a ruffled pink and purple bathing suit tagged along behind. The lifeguard raised his megaphone and shouted at the boys, who switched to speed walking until they were close enough to the edge of the pool for a quick run and a leaping cannonball. Diana watched the little girl walk to the shallow end and ease herself into the pool, holding tight to the ladder. She hesitated before letting go. As she sank into the water, she gasped, eyes wide, as though the water and her immersion in it were a shock. Then, just as quickly, she gave her mom a big smile and a wave.

There must be millions of ways to be happy. But right now for Diana, there was only one.

18

*I*t sounded like one of those big open-air buses, the kind with rust bleeding into its multicolored paint job. Diana winced at the grinding of gears, a long painful effort that ended when it dropped into its normal baritone growl. The noise below rose and fell—jeepneys and trucks and motorized tricycles, each with its distinctive, irritating sound. You'd think all that racket would disperse a bit before reaching their fourteenth-floor apartment.

Squeezing her eyes tighter shut, Diana tried once more to empty her mind. Meditation was turning out to be a lot harder than she'd expected. Her mind kept jumping around, restless as a baby kangaroo escaping from its pouch. "Don't worry," Marilu Reyes had told her. "If your mind wanders, simply bring it gently back."

Rama, Diana chanted, silently repeating the mantra Marilu had given her. *Rama . . . Rama.* A bead of sweat rolled between her eyebrows and into her left eye. *Rama,* she recited, trying to ignore it. Her eye stung, though, a stinging itch that wouldn't stop. She couldn't resist wiping it away.

Below, someone laid on his horn, followed by the inevitable screeching of tires.

She was sitting in the study, the door closed so Clarita wouldn't interrupt her. The window was open, but even so, the room was stuffy. And noisy. The power was out again and had been since midmorning.

Settling back in her chair, Diana focused on her mantra for a few seconds before sliding away into thoughts and questions that clamored to be heard. What about Marilu? Why had she decided to teach yoga and meditation? And in her mother's house! Did she live there? Did she have her own children?

Diana jerked her mind back to her mantra. Why couldn't she do this? Was she incapable of meditating?

No. No no no. She wouldn't accept that. She gripped her knee to make her leg stop jiggling. She wasn't the problem. It was Manila. All this noise. And heat. And traffic. No wonder her mind kept jumping around.

In one of her early letters, even when Abby still hated Vanuatu, she'd said that Diana would like it. *It's so laid back*, she wrote, *you'd think everyone was stoned. Except they're not.* Ever since that letter, Diana had thought about Vanuatu, imagined what it would be like to live in the "most relaxing place on earth." Her mind wandered to the possibility of visiting Abby, soaking up South Pacific calm for a week or two.

Wait! Her eyes blinked open. What was it Marshall said at lunch yesterday? She'd been focusing on the sad news of Johnny Gamboa's stroke, blinded by an old "good girl" habit of selflessness from seeing the opportunity his misfortune presented. Damn! She was ashamed even now for making the connection. And yes, poor Johnny Gamboa. But Marshall didn't expect him to recover enough to come back to work, and if he didn't, Marshall would have to hire a replacement. Why not Jay?

⁓

She was in the kitchen helping Clarita with a recipe for curried cream of chicken soup, when she heard a series of small familiar sounds. She and Clarita glanced at each other, smiled, and looked away as the door closed and Jay's footsteps tapped across the hardwood floor.

"Hey!" he said, kissing her hot cheek. "It's stifling in here." He took her hand and led her into the dining room. "What do you say we head down to the Westin Plaza for dinner?"

"Ohhh!" she sighed. "That's the best idea I've heard all day. I'll tell Clarita. She can save tonight's dinner for tomorrow."

"If you hurry, we might be able to get a table in their Japanese restaurant. I'll give them a call."

Diana had become expert at taking a quick shower. Like most people in the tropics, she had plenty of practice. She dried off and grabbed her current favorite for eating out, a form-fitting cotton dress. She'd chosen the subtle blue, green, and lavender print for its relaxing quality.

"Zip me up?" she asked, anticipating the kiss Jay always gave the back of her neck when he finished. Then she put on her lipstick and earrings, stepped into her shoes, slung her purse over her shoulder, and off they went.

Walking between the potted bamboo and into the coolness of the Japanese restaurant was like stepping into a manmade miniature version of a park in springtime. Diana hadn't always appreciated the stark simplicity of the Japanese aesthetic, but tonight she understood. By subtracting the excess that cluttered the world, Japanese design allowed the mind to rest.

Jay put his arm around her while they waited. And for a moment she felt deeply content, as though this were enough, the two of them together.

A young man, who could have been Japanese but was probably Chinese, led them to a table. He pulled out her chair and placed heavy menus in their hands. The vase between them held a single iris and two sword-like leaves.

"I've already decided," Diana announced without opening the menu. "I'm going to have tempura."

Jay laughed. "You're so American."

"I love tempura. Nobody does deep frying like the Japanese."

"You do know they learned the technique from Portuguese missionaries in Nagasaki, don't you?"

She shook her finger at him. "Don't be so pedantic, Professor. I don't care where they learned it. The Japanese perfected the art of deep frying."

The restaurant was filling up fast. If the tourists living in the hotel didn't hurry, they'd have to try another restaurant or order room service. Jay turned and raised his chin at a couple with two children being seated not far from them. "It looks like we're not the only expats escaping hot, stuffy houses and apartments."

He was right. The family had "expats" written all over them, from the well-worn stuffed bunny their toddler was dragging to the particular kind of casual clothing they wore. Even though tourists wore shorts and sandals in the afternoon, they usually dressed up for dinner. Mainly, though, it was something elusive. The family had a we-belong-here way of interacting with the waiter and settling themselves in their chairs.

"Here's to my lovely wife," Jay said, raising his glass. "To us."

"So," Diana said after they'd clinked glasses, "how much longer will Marshall Charbonneau be here before he heads back to Vanuatu?"

"A couple more days."

"Hm." She watched a waiter glide across the floor, a large tray balanced on the flat of his hand. "We should invite him for dinner."

Jay looked puzzled. "I thought you didn't like him."

"Oh . . ." This was no time to remind Jay that Charbonneau was a fat, narcissistic New Yorker who got where he was through scheming and bullying. "It's just that . . ." She cleared her throat. "You know, he's been here for a while. He must be tired of hotel food and eating alone."

"I don't think we need to worry about Marshall Charbonneau being lonely." His eye roll said it all. Everyone knew about Marshall's reputation for hiring hookers when he traveled. "I'll ask him, though, if that's what you want."

Diana took another gulp of wine and looked away. She was already feeling a little woozy. The wine wasn't clouding her thinking, though. Instead it seemed to have cleared her mind, slowed it down enough that all the clatter and clutter and extravagant desires of her heart got swept away, leaving behind some inconvenient facts. The projects handled by the South Pacific office were small and inconsequential. Would Jay want to move to a regional office when he could stay at the headquarters and continue working on all those big important projects he cared so much about? She put her glass down and swallowed a sigh.

"We can take him to that Spanish restaurant in Malate," Jay said. "With the power so uncertain, we can't invite him to the apartment."

Diana nodded and looked away. For a moment, her crazy idea hung on refusing to die. Then the waiter arrived with their entrées. Jay's steak *teppanyaki* and her tempura.

"I hope you're hungry," Diana said.

"I'm always hungry for a good steak."

His enthusiasm for such large quantities of meat always puzzled Diana. You'd think he was a teenager, not a thirty-six-year-old man who'd reached his full height of six foot one almost two decades earlier.

While Diana was touching the tips of her chopsticks together, preparing to clasp a prawn between them, Jay, in the efficient manner of a man who loves steak, cut off a slice, cut again, and, without missing a beat, forked the meat into his mouth.

"Mmm. Perfect," he said. How he managed to utter the words without looking like a man talking with his mouth full, Diana couldn't say. "Does the tempura meet your expectations?" he asked.

"It's excellent."

"You know," he said, cocking his head and smiling, his knife paused in mid-cut, "I think you'd like eel. It's nothing like tempura, but I think you'd like its sweet, rich taste. They grill it, so it's crispy on the outside. I'll have to take you to Seoul sometime. They have great eel."

She placed one prawn's pretty pink tail on the edge of her plate and picked up another. During her last appointment, Dr. Feliciano had suggested that she go with Jay on his business trips so they wouldn't miss being together during her fertile periods. Maybe she was right. There was no reason Diana couldn't go along with him. She held her prawn in the air and caught his eye. "I'd like to go with you on your next mission."

He raised an eyebrow. "Not the next one, honey. You'd have nothing to do. Besides, my next mission is to Pakistan. It isn't safe there, especially where I'll be going."

"Where are you going?" Diana knew quite a few Pakistani ladies, fellow members of the D-TAP Women's Club. It couldn't be that dangerous. Most of them went back to Pakistan for home leave every couple of years.

"We'll be going into the tribal areas up near the Afghanistan border. Looking at a possible route for a proposed pipeline." His eyes lit up.

This was why he liked his job—the exotic locations, the whiff of danger, the projects that offered progress to developing countries. And this was why she hated to ask the man she loved to give it all up for her.

19

"When's it going to stop?" It wasn't the wetness that bothered her. It was the sense that they were locked in a garish watery cell, one that traveled with them wherever they went, blocking out the rest of the world. That and the sense that this was a waste of time since she'd dropped the idea of talking to Jay about Johnny Gamboa's looming medical retirement.

"Remember last year at this time," Jay said. "It rained for the biblical forty days and forty nights." He was driving, as he always did when they were together, even though she knew her way around Manila better than he did.

She winced at the whine of the windshield wipers as the car slowed to turn into the hotel. "I wish I hadn't suggested taking Marshall out for dinner. He's not my favorite person."

"He's not so bad." Jay pulled up under the hotel's canopy and stopped. "Besides, he's all alone in the hotel. He'll appreciate the company."

"He might appreciate our company, but I'm not sure I'm in the mood for his."

Jay patted her knee. "Smile. There he is." He raised his eyebrows. "Whoops! It appears he didn't need our company after all."

Diana affected a smile and waved. Next to Marshall's flabby bulk, the petite Filipina at his side looked like a Barbie, four-inch heels and all. She glanced back at Jay. His shrug seemed to indicate that they were supposed to pretend there was nothing strange about Marshall, who'd left his wife at home in Vanuatu, taking a pretty young Filipina out to dinner. Or rather, that she and Jay were taking them both out. Oh, well, she thought as she opened her door and stepped out to greet them. Maybe they were just friends.

"This is Liza." Marshall looked down at the girl and grinned. "Liza with a 'z.'"

"Not Lisa with an 's,'" the girl sang back up at him. Her smoky contralto wasn't a perfect imitation of Liza Minnelli, but it was close.

"You don't mind if she comes along, do you?"

"That's fine." Jay opened the back door, and Liza climbed in giggling at the assist Marshall gave to her small, tight butt.

"Jay and I were thinking of Casa Armas in Malate," Diana said over her shoulder once they were underway. The slick boulevard reflected back smudges of red from a double line of taillights that reached only to the edge of the curtain of rain.

"Yeah. Spanish food," Marshall said. "Liza and I can share a paella."

"And *flan de caramelo* for dessert," she purred.

"Sure thing, baby. Liza and I are old friends, you know."

"Really." This twenty-something girl wasn't exactly Diana's idea of an old friend.

"Yeah. Liza was the main attraction at my favorite nightclub in Hong Kong. Weren't you, babe? She sings like a bird . . . a bird who took singing lessons from Ella Fitzgerald and Barbra Streisand." He chuckled and did something that made her squeal. "It doesn't hurt that she has all the right curves."

Diana looked straight ahead and rolled her eyes.

"You're back in Manila now?" Jay asked Liza.

"Yes, sir. For now."

"Imagine my surprise," Marshall said, "when I found Liza sitting on the piano in the hotel lounge and singing my favorite song."

"Which song?"

"You know, babe, that one where you sing way low down and sexy."

It was going to be a long night. One consolation: The food at Casa Armas was top notch.

The place they'd chosen was an old-style Spanish restaurant. Diana didn't know whether to be surprised that, nine decades after the end of Spanish rule in the Philippines, their influence still remained, or whether to be surprised that there wasn't more of it. After all, the Philippines had been a Spanish colony for more than three hundred years.

Across from the receptionist, the would-be knight of La Mancha held his wooden lance at the ready.

"Oh! Don Quixote!" Liza exclaimed.

Marshall put an arm around her and patted the carving's shoulder. "Where, pray tell, is your squire, sir?" he asked.

Ignoring Marshall's little joke, the receptionist scooped up four menus and showed them to their table. No sooner had they pulled their heavy chairs out and sat down than Marshall swept his arm across the table and announced. "Paella for all."

"Sounds good to me," Jay said.

"We'll see." Diana opened her menu and glanced at the list of *aperitivos*. She *had* been thinking of paella, but . . . damn it! She could decide for herself. On the other hand, when Jay ordered a pitcher of sangria for the table without asking anyone, she gave him a big thumbs-up with only a momentary recognition of her hypocrisy. Everyone liked sangria, didn't they?

"So . . ." Liza licked her lips and leaned across the table. "Marshall, baby, have you ever tasted black paella?" The tabletop pushed her breasts up and pointed them straight at him.

"Sounds intriguing," he said as though he were simply flirting, not choosing what to eat.

"It's my favorite," she said in a little girl voice. "They make it with squid in its own ink. Let's share a dish for two. Okay?" How could he refuse?

Diana looked at Jay. "Paella Valenciana?"

"Sure thing."

When the flirting had run its course and the sangria had been poured, Jay and Marshall turned to their favorite topic, D-TAP. The thought of asking Marshall about Vanuatu crossed Diana's mind, but she bit down and dismissed it. No sense torturing herself. It wasn't going to happen. Instead she turned to Liza. "Good sangria."

"Yes."

And since sangria doesn't lend itself to small sips, they both raised their glasses high and let the fruity goodness flow over their tongues and down their throats.

Liza put her glass down and ran a finger around the rim.

"That's a lovely ring," Diana said, noting the sparkle on Liza's finger.

"Thank you."

They looked at each other and smiled, each waiting for the other one to think of something to say.

Breaking the silence, Liza raised her pretty eyebrows and asked: "Do you have children?"

Whoa! From the smallest of small talk to piercing Diana's heart and soul in a single step. "No," she said as evenly as she could manage. "Not yet."

"Why not?"

Diana took a breath and pressed her lips together, her mind racing to find an artful dodge. Why was this young woman, this stranger, this girl Marshall picked up in the bar, asking her such a personal question? *It's none of your business,* she wanted to say. Instead she answered truthfully: "I haven't been able to get pregnant yet."

Liza nodded and left it at that.

Diana took a breath and exhaled out the tension that had built up with Liza's questions. She'd said it plainly, her sadness, her failure. And now Liza understood. They sat for a long moment, gazing across the table at the men. Then they glanced at each other and smiled. "Did you like living in Hong Kong?" Diana asked.

"Are you kidding? I bloody loved it. It's the best place in the world for a singer. People in Hong Kong love Filipino musicians. My brother and his band are a big success there." It turned out that on the twin topics of Hong Kong and musicians, Liza had a lot to say. Her older brother was the one who'd brought her to Hong Kong. Seven years ago, he'd sent enough money for a one-way ticket. His reason: He and the guys in his band needed someone to cook for them. "He thought I was just his baby sister. Then one day he let me sing at one of his gigs, and . . ." She threw her arms out in a ta-da pose. "The people loved me. That's how I got my start."

Diana smiled and nodded. She was beginning to like Liza. "Will you go back to Hong Kong?"

"Yes, ma'am, when I save enough money."

Seeing how Liza slumped in her chair and stared at the table, Diana hesitated to ask the next obvious question. If Liza wanted to talk about her reason for leaving Hong Kong, she would.

"We sent money at first," Liza said softly. "For Mami's doctor." She picked at her nail polish and rocked like a child trying to sooth herself to sleep. "Our other brother in Saudi, he sent money, too. Auntie Paz was there to help out. Also the cousins. We thought she was gonna get well, so I stayed in Hong Kong. But she only got worse. Then I had to come back to the Philippines, to our town." Liza crossed herself. "God rest her soul."

"I'm so sorry," Diana said.

Liza cleared her throat and looked away.

Diana wanted to hug her, to say something comforting. But what? What can you say about death? She patted Liza's hand, and while she was still wondering what to say, the waiter arrived.

She had to suppress a gasp when she saw the black paella that

Marshall and Liza ordered. Their platter was piled high with rice, squid, and some unrecognizable vegetables, all of it stained blueish black by the squids' ink. The dish was saved from total gloom by the prawns scattered on top. In contrast, Jay and Diana's *Paella Valenciana* was a fiesta of colors and shapes—creamy white rice, green peas, pink-veined prawns, chorizo medallions, chicken legs, and mussels with their shells open like hungry mouths.

Marshall frowned at his paella. "This better be good," he said, wagging a finger at Liza.

She shot him a kissy-lips response, and placed two big scoops of paella on his plate. Then she delicately plucked two prawns up by their tails and artfully arranged them, tails up, on top of his paella.

"Okay, here goes." Marshall scooped up a forkful of paella and held it in the air a moment. The wrinkles between his eyebrows deepened as he opened his mouth and took a bite. "Hey!" he said, nodding and smiling as he chewed. "Not bad. I've gotta give it to this little girl here. She has a way of pushing me in new directions. Don't want to get stuck in a rut. Right, babe?"

"No way."

Diana couldn't help but smile. This was a new Marshall, all congenial and easygoing. It was too bad he had to be cheating on his wife before his fun side came out. She shared a glance with Jay as he dropped a mussel shell on their shared shell plate.

"So, when did you start singing?" Jay asked, his face all serious and bland as though she were a business associate and not a girl Marshall picked up in the hotel bar.

Liza sat up straight and raised her chin. "The day I was born."

"I told you," Marshall said. "She's a little nightingale. A real natural."

Jay nodded. "What kind of songs do you sing?"

"Every kind. Anything you like. I look at the people—their faces, clothes they wear, their talk. Then I choose a song for them. I know thousands of songs. Every kind."

"What song did you choose for Marshall?" Diana asked.

Liza chuckled. "First time I see him, I see his haircut, very short, and his tie, too skinny. And I see his baby blue eyes, so happy. So I think this man, he like old song, not too sad."

"What did you sing?"

"'Sweet Caroline.' You know, Neil Diamond."

Marshall put his fork down. "'Sweet Caroline,'" he sang, attracting head-turns at four or five tables. "'Da da da.'"

Diana clapped her hands. "Perfect. And what song would you sing for Jay?"

Liza leaned across the table and studied him. She took a long swallow of sangria and narrowed her eyes. "Song of Don Quixote," she said finally with a big satisfied grin. "'Impossible Dream.' If I sing it to him, he gonna cry."

"Me?" Jay asked with an embarrassed little laugh.

"Yes," Diana said. "Absolutely." She wondered if he remembered how years ago, when they were still dating, that very song had brought tears to his eyes during a performance of *Man of La Mancha*. She thought it was sweet then. She still did.

"Okay." Jay scooped up a bite of chorizo and rice. "What about Diana?"

A butterfly fluttered up from Diana's stomach to her throat. She wasn't sure she wanted to hear this. Opening herself up to Liza was too much like sitting down at a fortune teller's table and offering her palm. She pulled her hands back and clasped them together.

Liza squinted and pursed her lips. "Hm." She leaned closer to Diana. Then she looked up at the ceiling. "'Memory,'" she said, pouncing on the word like a cat on a mouse.

"What? You mean the song from *Cats*?" Diana was appalled.

"'Memory,'" Liza sang softly, "'all alone in the moonlight . . .'"

"But, Liza," Diana objected, "that's the song the elderly cat sings."

"Young, old. Doesn't matter. Feeling matters. You have big feelings in here." She tapped her chest. "But deep, very deep down. This song is right for you. I tell you, if I sing it to you, you gonna cry."

Why? Diana forced herself to smile. Why did Liza think she had deep hidden feelings? "It's a lovely song," she said, "but isn't it awfully sad?"

Liza straightened her back and frowned. "It's not a sad song," she said, grabbing Diana's wrist. "It's a song with feeling. Not the same thing."

Marshall drained the last of the sangria into his glass. "Hey, boss," he called to the waiter. "Another pitcher here."

While they ate, they talked more about music and Hong Kong, which led naturally into a favorite topic for D-TAP men: great restaurants in Asian capitals and favorite dishes they'd eaten there. By the time the second pitcher was empty, Diana was laughing at Marshall's jokes. Actually he could be quite the charmer. He was entertaining them now with stories about Vanuatu's quirky history.

"Back in the days of exploration and colonization . . ." He popped a bite of flan de caramelo into his mouth. ". . . the British, French, and Germans were picking off islands in the South Pacific." He licked the corner of his mouth and continued. "Fiji became a British colony; the French took Tahiti and New Caledonia; and Germany set its sights on Samoa. But who would get the New Hebrides?" He turned to Liza. "That's the old name for Vanuatu. Anyway, the Germans were coming up fast, and the Brits and the French didn't want Germany to get it, so, for the first time in their history, they decided to share. And that's how the New Hebrides became a French-English condominium."

"Condominium?" Liza's big brown eyes widened.

"I kid you not. That's why today in Vanuatu you can speak English in the morning and practice your French in the afternoon. And," he said, "that's why, even now, I have freshly baked French bread delivered to my doorstep every morning. I tell you—" he turned to Jay "—Vanuatu is an island paradise. You should come and see for yourself."

Yes, Diana thought. *Yes!*

"I could find you a job. I know the boss," he said, winking at Diana. "I tell you, you guys would love Vanuatu. Isn't that right, Diana?"

She wanted to climb across the table and kiss his fat lips. "I'm all in," she said. "We just have to convince Jay."

Jay gave her a look of open-mouthed astonishment.

"You see." Marshall wagged his finger at Jay. "Mark my words, Johnny Gamboa is not gonna recover from his stroke. His job will be yours for the taking."

Jay gave a nervous little smile and quickly changed the subject.

20

Jay pulled into the entrance of Marshall's hotel, and they all got out.

"Thanks for dinner." Marshall shook Jay's hand. Then he leaned over and, with a self-satisfied smile, placed his hands on Diana's shoulders, pulled her closer, and kissed her cheek. Stepping back, he nodded at Jay, put his arm around Liza and turned to go. "Think about it," he said over his shoulder. "You gotta keep the wife happy, you know." He turned back around and gave Liza an apologetic squeeze. "Wife *and* girlfriend. I expect Johnny Gamboa to give up and retire in a month or so," he shouted as he and Liza stepped into the revolving door.

Before Jay could say anything, Diana grabbed the keys out of his hand. "I'll drive," she said.

The rain had turned into a warm, thick drizzle that felt like sweat on her shoulders and arms. She flicked it off and slid into the driver's seat.

Jay slammed the passenger side door and reached for the seat belt. "What the hell were you thinking back there?" He snapped the seatbelt into place and glared at her. "I have no intention of transferring to the South Pacific office. Now Marshall's going to hassle me about it."

"I was thinking . . ." She shifted into gear and took off down the drive faster than was absolutely necessary. "I was thinking that I want to move to Vanuatu."

The standing water on the driveway rose up on either side of them like great spray flowers. Like waves crashing against rocks. Like the splashes and wakes Daddy's speedboat made in Big Lake the two summers before he died. She'd always loved those splashes, the bigger the better. She would hold onto the seat laughing while Daddy or Andrew sent the boat bouncing over a big wake. She'd lean over the side waiting to be splashed on a sharp turn. Finally, near the end of that second summer, Daddy gave her a turn at the wheel. And she loved it. For her, boating was all about the speed and the splashing and spray. She made a sharp turn onto Roxas Boulevard, sending the car into a small, satisfying skid.

"Hey!" Jay shouted. "What are you doing?"

Smiling, she moved into the fast lane and continued speeding down Roxas Boulevard, splashing the slower cars and buses while Jay sat helpless in the passenger seat.

"I meant what I said." Her voice was just loud enough to be heard over the now heavy rain pounding on the car's roof. "I want to move to Vanuatu."

He laughed. "You're not making sense, honey. We don't just pick up and move on a whim. I think you had too much sangria." He braced himself against the dashboard. "Now slow the hell down."

Instead, she forced a tricycle into the slow lane and kept going. "It's not a whim. I've been thinking about this for a while."

"I don't care how long you've been thinking about it. It's *my* job you're talking about."

"It may be your job," she shouted over the sound of rain and flapping wipers. "But it's my life, too." There was a strange catch in her voice. It stopped her for a moment. "Don't you see, Jay?" she went on more quietly. "This whole thing isn't working for me, and I feel like there's nothing I can do about it. It's as though you're saying I don't have a voice in what happens to us."

She slowed down, and for a while they rode on in silence. Then, as they turned into their apartment, he squeezed her knee. "I'm sorry, honey."

Maybe he supposed that was the end of it. Diana would park the car; they'd ride the elevator up to their apartment. Before bed, they'd talk about Marshall's wife and his girlfriend or catch some last-minute news on TV. Diana would tease him about his kinship with Don Quixote; he'd tease her about being an old cat. Then they'd wash up and go to bed. No hard feelings. Later, when Marshall contacted him, Jay would laugh and say Diana had been caught up in the moment, and no, he wasn't interested in transferring to Vanuatu. And that would be the end of it.

Well, if that's what he was thinking, he was wrong.

She'd broken through an old barrier, and she wasn't in the mood that night to build it back up again.

The apartment was quiet when they entered, full of blurry crisscrossing shadows. Diagonal beams, the nightlight and the balcony lights working at cross purposes, defined the shapes of walls and tables and chairs. Clarita's door was closed, the kitchen dark.

Jay flicked on the overhead light. He grabbed a glass drying on a towel, opened the fridge, and poured himself some chilled water. "Want some?" he asked, reaching for another glass.

She took the glass from his hand, filled it herself, and put the pitcher back in the fridge. Looking around the kitchen, she realized how ugly it was. Sterile and ugly. And it had nothing to do with her. The white walls had been chosen by the landlord not to offend anyone who rented it. The small white refrigerator with the freezing compartment above looked like something from someone else's past. The floor tiles were more suited to a bathroom.

"This place has bad *feng shui*," she said. Diana didn't know much about feng shui, but surely her kitchen in Seattle, with its sunflower yellow walls, its French doors leading out to a green fertile space brightened with flowers and an apple tree had good feng shui. "Everything about Manila is wrong for me. For us."

"So, now you believe in feng shui?"

Suddenly she felt weak and unbearably tired. "All I know is that everything here is bringing me down." She leaned back against the counter. "This city is gray and hot; it's noisy and crowded. No matter how hard I try, I can't relax here."

He let out a dramatic sigh. "You've been taking that doctor too seriously."

"Dr. Feliciano."

"Right. Dr. Feliciano. The good doctor and her phony prescription. Who ever heard of relaxation as a way to get pregnant?" He put a hand around her shoulder. "Come on. Let's go to bed. It's late."

She put her glass down and pulled away from him. It would have been easy to just give up. She glanced at the crack under Clarita's door. There wasn't any light, but that didn't mean she wasn't listening.

They turned out the light—the ugly fluorescent light—and made their way through the darkened rooms—the dining and living rooms and the hallway. They didn't turn a light on until they reached their bedroom.

Jay closed the door behind them. Diana turned on the air conditioning. (Thank goodness the power had come back.) Neither of them looked at the other. Jay made a point of removing his shoes and socks, socks in the hamper, shoes in the closet. Everything neat and precise. Diana kicked off her shoes and stood there, wondering what to do next while Jay unbuttoned his shirt and hung it up.

She sat down on the bed. Why couldn't he understand how much this meant to her? Didn't understand, or didn't care? He used to care about people. In fact, that was the first thing that attracted her to him, how much he cared about people. That and how good-looking he was. Still was. She watched him take his wallet out of his back pocket and set it on the nightstand.

The day she met him, she and her roommate had just returned from a two-day cycling trip to Victoria via Sidney, British Columbia.

They had loaded their bikes onto the bed of Jenn's pickup and climbed into the cab. When Jenn turned the key, though, nothing happened. The sun was just setting, and they were tired and dirty. They'd parked at the far edge of the Anacortes ferry terminal's lot. The cars that were still around all seemed to be hurrying out the exit. Jenn popped the hood. She leaned over and stared at the engine. "We need help," Diana said. "Do you have jumper cables?"

Turning around, she saw Jay and his friend approaching. Afterwards, she had no recollection of the friend. Only of Jay, striding toward them, concern turning his hazel eyes sea green in a departing car's headlights. "Do you need some help?" he asked, looking directly at Diana.

"We have a dead battery." In her memory, it was only her and Jay. Jenn and Jay's friend might as well have not existed.

Jay checked the connection. He was the one who tried again to start it, the one who found the jumper cables behind the seat, who ran back to get his car. He was the one who suggested they all have a bite to eat in downtown Anacortes. If she and Jenn hadn't been wearing sweatshirts and cutoff jeans, their hair in need of a good shampoo, Diana might have thought he was too smooth. Instead he came across as caring, even chivalrous, the kind of good-looking young man you have a bite with. And when you're done eating, you have no qualms about giving your phone number to such a kind and caring young man.

If she were going to be truthful, she'd have to admit he still cared about people. He even cared about her. But how much?

21

The birthday party was over, the boisterous little girls on their way home. Diana stood back and watched as Madeline escorted the last child and her mother to the gate, thanked them for coming, and waved good-bye. The latch clicked, and for a moment the reverberation of metal on metal hung in the air. Then there was nothing. Just the soft rustle of leaves overhead and a disquieting silence.

"It's so quiet," she said when Madeline joined her under an acacia tree.

"They were dreadfully noisy, weren't they?" Madeline smiled and shook her head. "Little girls in groups . . . Thank God Marie didn't invite boys. Can you imagine a bunch of six-year-old boys chasing the girls around the garden?"

"The girls screaming at the top of their lungs . . ." Diana smiled. "I can imagine it." The last time she'd been on a school playground was when she was a child herself. But she remembered how it felt, the giddy excitement of running away from boys. She touched Madeline's arm. "This was delightful," she said. "I'm so glad you invited me."

"No. Thank *you*. I needed moral support. I was so worried it would be raining again today. And the games. You never know if they'll work out. Do you think they were too old for the *calesa* rides?"

"No, no. They liked it. Did you see how they scrambled to climb up on the cart?" In a world too often gray, the brightly painted calesa and the girls in Easter-egg-colored dresses were a welcome sight, giggling, squeezing in, waving as the not-so-lively horse clip-clopped away down the street.

"They'll be too old next year," Madeline said as they strolled from one shady spot to another. "I'll have to think of something else." She grabbed the string of a pink balloon caught in the kala-chuchi tree and pulled it loose. "I'm tired," she said. "Let's sit down."

The child-sized wooden tables and chairs Madeline had rented were neatly stacked beside the driveway in a colorful low structure of red, blue, and yellow. One maid had crumpled the tablecloth from the long serving table and was carrying it into the house for washing. The scraps of pizza and spaghetti were gone. The remains of the cake with its Little Mermaid on top had been wrapped and brought inside.

The two women sighed and sank into a couple of wicker chairs on the patio. Madeline's sigh sounded like relief. Diana's was something else. The noise and excitement and nonstop young energy of the children had kept her from thinking about last night. But now it was back, the inescapable echo of angry words filling up the empty air space. "Where . . . ?" She cleared her throat, but it didn't get rid of the tight, scratchy feeling. "Where are Marie and Camille?"

"I told Marie she could open one gift before her bath. She's inside, probably shaking and measuring all the gifts to find the biggest and best one."

Diana stared out across the yard. But nothing, not the grass or the ivy-covered wall or the maid struggling to fold up the legs on the serving table, registered with her. She and Jay had both been so angry, so hurtful.

"Diana. Are you all right? Do you want something to drink?"

She tried to say she was fine. But she couldn't. "Jay and I had a fight last night."

Madeline sat up straighter, her eyes wide.

"Don't worry, he didn't hit me. I didn't throw dishes." She felt bruised, though, bruised and guilty. "I started it," she said. "I told Marshall Charbonneau I wanted to move to Vanuatu."

"Oh, no. Not you, too." Madeline clapped her hand over her mouth. "Sorry."

"We took Marshall and his girlfriend to dinner at Casa Armas."

"Girlfriend?" She covered her mouth again. "Sorry."

"I wasn't going to say anything because I knew Jay wanted to stay here. 'Where the action is,' as he says. But when Marshall started talking about Vanuatu being an island paradise and how much we'd love it, I just let it all out."

Madeline tilted her head, waiting, as though she didn't know what Diana meant.

"I told Marshall I wanted Jay to transfer to Vanuatu. Jay didn't say much then, but it was obvious he was not happy. As soon as we dropped Marshall at his hotel, he let me have it. I think he expected me to apologize."

Diana clenched her hands around the woven strands of Madeline's wicker chair. Despite the ceiling fan and the high roof over the patio, the air felt hot and sticky.

"You didn't apologize?" Madeline said.

"No." Diana shook her head. "I was so tired of keeping it all in. Do you ever feel trapped, like you have no control over what happens to you?"

Madeline nodded ever so slightly, but the faraway look in her eyes made Diana flush with embarrassment. Of course Madeline understood. When she was a teenager, she'd spent years in a refugee camp, trapped and helpless, waiting for someone else to decide her fate.

"It's not a good feeling," Madeline agreed.

Diana quickly blinked back tears and took a little tight breath in through her mouth.

"It must be frustrating. You've been trying to conceive a child for so long. Does that have something to do with it?"

Too choked up to speak, Diana nodded. She hadn't been able to find words to tell her friends—or even her mom and brother—how she felt. Not without sounding silly and self-centered. Not without sounding like a comfortable white woman complaining about her life when, within view of her apartment balcony, a jumble of squatters' shanties huddled on the reclaimed land of Manila Bay.

Madeline pulled a handkerchief out of her bra. "Here," she said. "Don't worry, it's clean."

It was a lovely, clean handkerchief, soft and fine with tiny pink roses embroidered along the borders. But who the hell keeps a handkerchief in her bra these days? Oh, yes. Madeline does. "Thank you." Diana lifted the hanky to her nose, still uncertain.

"Please, keep it. I have a drawer full of them."

If only Jay had been as understanding. If only he'd been as quick to see the connection between her continued failure to get pregnant and her desire to get out of Manila. Oh, how she wished he could appreciate how she'd been scrambling to find some meaning for her life, pinning all her hopes on a baby, and month after month being thwarted. Vanuatu may have been a pipe dream, but it was her pipe dream. And last night, driving down Roxas Boulevard in the rain, she'd been convinced it was all she had.

"My parents never fought," Diana said, dabbing at her eyes with Madeline's handkerchief. Her nose was dripping, but she hesitated to blow it on such a beautiful thing.

"You mean they never fought in your presence," Madeline said with a meaningful tilt of her head.

"I suppose." Diana blotted the end of her nose, and then she blew it, as gently as possible. "The trouble is, once you say something, it's there forever."

"Don't worry. You'll get through this."

Suddenly the back door burst open, and two little girls came running toward them, their black hair bouncing on their pale shoulders and their matching strawberry dresses. "Mommy,

Mommy," Marie shouted. She was holding up two colorful boxes and a large tablet. "Look."

"I want, I want," shouted Camille, opening and closing her little hands as she tried to edge around Marie.

"Let's see."

Marie dumped everything on Madeline's lap.

Art supplies. Diana felt her heart leap at the sight of them—thick white artist's paper, a box of what looked like expensive felt-tipped pens in twelve vibrant colors, and a box of watercolors and brushes. The exact kind of gift that had thrilled her when she was Marie's age.

"Did you keep the card?" Madeline asked.

"Yes. It's from Allison."

"Here." Madeline held the supplies up for her daughter. "Show this to Auntie Diana. She's an artist."

"Me?" Diana asked, her habitual denial.

"Yes, you." She patted Marie's shoulder. "Auntie Diana will show you how best to use these beautiful pens and paints. And don't forget to share with your sister."

"Yes, Mommy."

"Here, Camille. Come and sit on Mommy's lap."

Diana tucked the hanky into her bra and held her arms out to Marie. "Let's see what you have? Oh, my! This is very good watercolor paper. Now, we'll need a little bowl of water for the watercolors, and an apron to protect your pretty dress." She took Marie's hand, and as they started toward the house, her imagination took over. "We can paint anything you like, Marie, friends with balloons, a birthday cake with candles, a horse and calesa." She laughed. "We can make a rainbow with all these colors."

"Yes," Marie said with a little skip. "I want a rainbow."

Later, when Diana was leaving, Madeline took her hand. "We all fight with our husbands," she whispered. "The important thing is to make the fight count."

22

On the second day after their fight, Diana woke up with a feeling of heavy, confused determination. Jay was already up, out on the bedroom balcony. "It's cloudy but no rain yet," he said, stepping back into the bedroom and sliding the door shut. "Do you want to chance it?"

Chance what? she was about to ask before she remembered it was Saturday, the day they usually took a walk together before breakfast. "How cloudy?" she asked. Throwing back the sheet, she got up and reopened the sliding door so she could see for herself. The weak purplish light that found its way through a thick cloud cover wasn't very encouraging. But they'd missed their Saturday morning walks for the past three weeks because of rain.

Like a team, they stepped into their shorts and pulled T-shirts over their heads. They unfolded their socks and put them on, Diana balancing on one foot and then the other, Jay sitting on the edge of the bed. As soon as their tennis shoes were tied and Jay's wallet stuffed in a back pocket, they were ready to go.

Manila was never cool. But that morning, despite the humidity, it was cool enough for a nice walk. "So far, so good," Jay said, holding his palms up to the sky as they left the building.

They started off down the service road in the usual direction moving at a brisk pace. Their Saturday walks weren't meant to be leisurely strolls. They walked side by side, skipping around and over puddles left by the previous night's rain.

Already a day and a half had passed since their dinner with Marshall Charbonneau. A day and a half out of fourteen, and Jay hadn't budged. She had twelve and a half days left to convince him. Falling half a step behind, she took a quick glance at him, taking in the easy movement, the lean, smooth muscles in his arms and legs.

Twelve and a half days, she thought as she hurried to catch up to him. Or . . . She took a sudden gulp of air. She didn't want to think about how uncertain the time was. Johnny Gamboa could decide to retire sooner than Marshall expected, or he could hold on for weeks, hoping against hope that he would recover enough to go back to work. Either way, by then, Jay had to be willing to step into the vacant position.

When they reached McDonald's at the end of the service road, they were hot and sweaty. Diana paused at the door. A fat dark cloud overhead was daring them to dawdle. She was about to suggest they start back. But the force of habit was strong, and when Jay pushed the door open, she followed him in.

"The usual?" he asked, not bothering to look up at the menu above the row of cash registers.

"Yeah." Her mouth was already watering for her egg and pancakes, butter melting between the layers, shiny, sweet syrup dripping over the edge, hot dark coffee on the side.

Jay put his arm around her waist as they stood waiting for their order. When it came, he tried to put everything on one tray and carry it himself, which would have been fine any other day. But today she didn't feel like being the damsel in need of rescue. Grabbing their coffees, she hurried ahead of him and slid into a booth by the window. She couldn't deny it. She enjoyed being treated like "a lady." There was a downside of being on the receiving end of chivalry though. It was the wrong kind of symbolism for their relationship, especially now.

He sat down across from her. And as he unloaded the tray, she wondered how the hell she was going to make it clear to him that she didn't intend to back down. He needed to understand that where they lived was a decision for them to make together.

"I've been thinking . . ." Jay slipped a pat of butter between his pancakes. Then he put his knife and fork down, leaned his elbows on the table and looked into her eyes and grinned. "You've never been to Bali."

What? Where did that come from? She looked away, picked up a half-and-half packet, and peeled back the cover. "Uh, no. Have you?" She'd never heard of a D-TAP project in Bali.

"Yeah. When Dad was stationed in Jakarta, he took us on a Balinese vacation one summer." He paused, waiting to catch her eye again. "Yesterday I checked some weather stats. July and August are right smack in the middle of Bali's dry season. We could spend a few days there after I get back from Pakistan. Give you a break from all this rain." He smiled, obviously pleased with himself.

Great! She picked up a plastic spoon and stirred the cream into her coffee. A trip to Bali was the perfect temptation. He couldn't have chosen better. She took a deep breath and put the spoon down. "Right now, Jay, I'm not so interested in a break, as beautiful as Bali must be."

"What?" He reared back. "But honey, you'd love it—beaches and mountains, art, music, and dance everywhere you look."

She sliced her egg with the side of her fork and watched the yolk spilling out, thick and golden, the white jiggling ever so slightly. This time McDonald's got "sunny side up" right. "I'd love to go to Bali, honey. Really I would. Just not now. If Johnny Gamboa decides to retire . . ."

"Johnny Gamboa? Really? I told you . . ."

"I know, I know. But I told *you* I wanted to move."

"Oh, god!" He looked at the ceiling. "Not this again. I'm *not* transferring to Vanuatu. I tell you, Diana, Vanuatu is not the panacea you imagine. You think the Philippines is a third-world country? You should see Vanuatu."

"That's not the point."

"Then what *is* the point?" He slammed down his little plastic knife. "What the hell is the point?"

For a moment she couldn't think what it was. She just knew that her life wasn't working here, that a small South Pacific country she'd never seen before was exactly where she needed to be, that unless they lived there, she was never going to have the child she longed for. "The point is," she said, "you need to start listening to your heart . . . and to your wife."

Jay just shook his head and took a big bite of egg and pancake. *Listening to your heart.* What was wrong with her? That was a stupid thing to say. It was becoming all too evident that if Jay listened to his heart, it would tell him to hold onto his dream job. Diana and their future children would be somewhere farther down the list of his heart's desires. If she was going to convince him to see things her way, she'd need a better argument.

She stared at her plate. And if she was going to choke down a few bites of pancake, she'd need some lubricant. Picking up the sticky syrup bottle, she poured circular streams of fake maple syrup all over her pancakes and watched it soak in.

Half a dozen bites later, she had to stop before she gagged on all the sweetness. "Let's go," she said, taking a big gulp of coffee and standing up.

Jay looked from his empty plate to her half-eaten breakfast and quickly looked away.

She picked up her tray and headed for the waste bin. "We'd better hurry before the rain starts," she said over her shoulder.

They made it halfway home before it hit, a light rain at first and then a real downpour. They ran, splashing through puddles and soaking their shoes and socks. With less than a mile to go and dry clothes waiting for them in the apartment, a tropical rain was no big disaster. In fact, Diana found it strangely exhilarating—the cooling rain, her wet hair and clothes, the feeling of strength in her legs as she ran. She sprinted ahead of Jay, who quickly caught up and passed her. The rest of the way home was a close race, neither giving an inch until a jeepney driver laid on his horn behind them and they had to get over. Finally, as they neared the front steps of their building, Diana spurted ahead again. If the top step was the finish line, she won.

And if small victories are worth anything, why not enjoy them?

She opened the door with a flourish, and held it for Jay.

"Thanks," he said.

"No problem."

23

They had a corner table by the window. A private spot, separated from everything and everyone by poor lighting and the white noise of sounds canceling each other out. The clatter of dishes was muffled by the indistinct voices of other diners and muted by the constant background music of the rain outside. After sitting through a Stephen King thriller, the clatter around their corner table seemed almost calming.

"Talk about tense," Jay said. He picked up his spoon and stared at his *halo-halo especial.* "I'm still shaking."

Diana dug into the mango ice cream on top of her halo-halo. "Kathy Bates sure does a good crazy woman." Like all compelling villains, Bates's character was determined and smart—crazy smart. And she was utterly ruthless. Diana scooped up another spoonful of ice cream. "You've gotta love her single-minded devotion to Misery, even if Misery *was* a fictional character."

Jay shivered. "She started out looking so normal. That's what creeped me out." He looked down at his halo-halo as though he'd just remembered it was there and scooped off a big bite of ube ice cream. "Too bad we missed *Goodfellas.* Guns and gangsters are so much easier to take than a woman with a butcher knife and sledge hammer."

"You think so?" Diana stabbed her spoon down to the bottom of the glass and began lifting the sweet beans, *macapuno,* and *nata de coco* through the crushed ice and evaporated milk. "Remember the first time we had a halo-halo?" she asked, carefully mixing everything together.

"Yeah," Jay said. "Abby talked us into it."

Jay and Diana had been newcomers then, living in the same apartment-hotel as Abby and Saudur while both families looked for a house to rent. Together they discovered Manila. Halo-halos had been one of many finds. It seemed, Diana thought as she looked out at the rain, that when they went out together during those early months, the sun was always shining.

At this moment, though, the rain was just what she needed. A fluid screen. A mental barrier holding them inside, together. Because now it was time. Since their walk to McDonald's, they hadn't talked much about Vanuatu. She hadn't shouted or cried or argued her case. Not for lack of desire. Every time she saw him, she wanted to pepper him with pleas and complaints. It wasn't easy to restrain herself, but she knew that arguing and pleading all too easily morphed into nagging, and that was deadly. Nagging could only result in one thing: resistance. Sometimes she was tempted to stomp her feet and threaten to leave him. She'd never really considered leaving Jay, though. She loved him. She wanted to have a baby with him. The thought of saying out loud that she might leave him made her shiver.

So all week she'd forced herself to hold her tongue. She'd waited and considered what she could say to convince him. And now it was Saturday again. Another week gone. She had only five days left to make her case. If she even had five days. It was possible that she was already too late, that Johnny Gamboa had made his decision about a disability retirement faster than Marshall expected and by now they'd found someone else to take his place.

Her heart skipped to her throat. *Please, God,* she prayed, *don't let it be too late.*

She'd imagined making her plea to Jay in the quietest, most private place possible. But she was ready now. Their corner table would have to do. She stirred her cold, sweet treat and ate a few more bites. Then she put her spoon down and sat up straight. "I have something to say," she said.

Jay stopped eating. He frowned slightly and leaned away. All week he'd been the bandleader trying to cheer up a crowd of one with peppy music, the affectionate husband who would have brought home flowers and chocolate if he weren't afraid of looking guilty. He must have known his efforts weren't working this time.

"I wanted to say," she began, "that I really am proud of you for the work you do at D-TAP." Oh, shit! Already this was sounding like a prepared speech, boring, and stiff as a starched shirt. She cleared her throat and continued. "And I'm proud to support you. You've said before that D-TAP is your dream job. And I can see that it's exactly what you're meant to do with your life." Saying all this out loud, it was obvious that it was just a big buildup to the inevitable "but." She could hear it, and she assumed he could, too. Why else would he busy himself mixing his halo-halo, the spoon clinking like castanets against the glass?

"But," she said, "when we agreed to move to Manila, it was with the understanding that this would be a good move for both of us. We assumed that getting pregnant would be easy and that by now we'd have a couple of children." She bit her lip. The accelerated clinking and circling of his spoon flustered her. "But it's been nearly four years, Jay. We both know it's not working."

"What's not working?"

"Manila. My life here. Do you know what people ask me the first time we meet? They ask, where does your husband work? I like being your wife, but that's all I am here. I have no identity of my own."

He stopped stirring and leaned across to pat her hand. "Honey, that's not true. You're so much more than that."

She bit her lip and blinked back a tear. This wasn't going well. She had to get control of herself. "Like I said, I know how much you like your work, so I'm not asking you to quit and move back to Seattle. I am asking you, though, to transfer to Vanuatu."

"Vanuatu?" He sighed and shook his head. "I don't see how that would help."

"It would get us out of Manila, away from the brownouts and the unending heat and smog and traffic jams. The anti-American demonstrations and coup attempts. And just maybe, it would give me a chance to relax and have the baby we both want before I'm too old."

"Oh, Diana," he said softly in a way that might have meant he understood what she was trying to say and might not have.

Saying it out loud, her reasoning sounded thin to her. And yet, she knew in her heart that something had to change. Her life was ticking away, and she hadn't grabbed hold of it yet.

Taking a deep breath, she leaned her forearms on the table, and looked directly into his eyes. "I've decided that after four years of following your dream, now it's my turn. It's my turn," she said again with a decisive nod of her head. "And I choose Vanuatu."

He didn't move a muscle. Then, finally, in what Diana chose to interpret as a positive sign, he blinked, and he sat back and gave his ice a slow meditative stir.

Having said all she had to say, Diana picked up her spoon and ate her halo-halo, the sweet beans, saba bananas, and macapuno, the crushed ice and sweetened condensed milk, the jackfruit and nata de coco and tapioca. She ate it all, one cold, sweet spoonful after the other.

On the way home, Jay was quiet, commenting only on the traffic and the rain. Perhaps he was considering her words. At least she dared to hope he was. For a moment at the end, they'd seemed persuasive.

Later, though, when she looked back on her little speech, she wasn't sure she'd said much of anything at all.

On Sunday, neither of them brought the subject up. And by Monday, Diana was prickling with anxiety. More than once, she paused in front of the phone, considered calling him at work, and then walked away. Or she went so far as to pick the phone up, start dialing, and then, lacking a new winning argument to make, put it back in its cradle. If he couldn't understand or accept her rights in their relationship, what more could she say?

Stuffing her bathing suit and a towel in a bag, she headed for the door. "I'll be back before dinner," she called to Clarita on her way out.

At the Seafront restaurant and the embassy PX, people with umbrellas were coming and going. But the locker room where Diana changed was empty, the pool and the area around it deserted. Rain clattered on the metal umbrellas and purred on the surface of the water. She checked the sky for lightning and seeing none, dove into the pool and started swimming, back and forth, back and forth until she was thoroughly exhausted.

By the time she pulled into their spot in the underground parking, it was getting late. She checked her watch, and her heart skipped a beat. Jay would be home soon. It was time to confront him again. She climbed the single flight of stairs to the lobby and stood in front of the elevator's closed doors watching the numbers on the indicator light count backwards from fifteen. They paused on twelve and then again on nine before descending at regular intervals to eight, seven, six . . .

"Hey, lovely lady."

She turned around, and there was Jay, smiling, a sampaguita lei looped over his fingers. It was one of the fancy leis with a medallion of the tiny flowers.

"Hold still."

She ducked her head, and as he placed the lei around her neck, she breathed in the jasmine-like fragrance. "Thank you, honey. Where'd you get this?"

"A vendor was selling them outside the D-TAP gate."

Diana's mind was racing. The elevator arrived and a couple of Filipino men and one woman got out. The lei *was* nice, but sampaguita leis were sold everywhere—on the highway and in parking lots all over the city. *Why did he decide to buy one for her today?* she wondered as the elevator started moving up.

Jay lifted a lock of her wet hair and let it drop. "Looks like you got caught in the rain."

She fluffed her hair back from her temples. "I went swimming." Did he take her silence the past two days as a sign that she'd already given up hope of moving to Vanuatu? Was he just trying to soften her up with flowers?

The doors opened on the sixth floor and the man who'd been standing in front of them got out. The moment the doors closed again, Jay pulled Diana to him and gave her a quick kiss. "Alone at last."

"You're in high spirits."

He smiled. "You'll see."

She narrowed her eyes at him. What would she see? Had something happened at work to put him in such a good mood?

"Clarita," he called the moment they walked in the door. "Can you find my bottle of good scotch?"

Clarita wiped her hands on her apron and hustled off to fetch it.

"Neat?" he asked, taking out two glasses.

She wasn't sure how she took scotch, but she nodded anyway. What was going on? Did he get a raise? A promotion? Suddenly she remembered hearing him and Eddie Wu talk about the possibility of Tiongson being promoted to a director's job, leaving the manager's job wide open. If Jay had been promoted to manager, she thought as Clarita appeared with a bottle of scotch, Diana could kiss any Vanuatu plans good-bye.

"This one, sir?" Clarita asked, holding up the distinctive three-sided bottle of Haig Pinch.

"Yes, that's it. Thank you, Clarita."

Jay held the bottle up for Diana to see. "Twelve years old," he said proudly. He poured a generous two-finger shot into each glass and handed one to her. "Let's go into the other room and let Clarita cook in peace."

They walked through the dining room and living room and then stood for a moment watching the muted sunset through the rain-streaked sliding glass doors.

"So," Jay said, turning to her with a half smile. "I have some good news and some bad news." He tapped the side of his glass with one finger and licked his lips. "The bad news is, I didn't get the manager's job. They gave it to Hoffmann."

"Oh, honey. I'm sorry."

He shrugged. "It seems that Hoffmann had a family connection with a well-placed director."

"That's so unfair."

"Yeah. He wasn't a good choice. I'm afraid the department's work will suffer with him in charge."

Diana had met Hoffmann at parties, and her impression of the man was that he was insufferably arrogant and not very bright.

"That was the bad news," Jay said, a smile breaking through. "The good news is that I may not have to work for him."

"What?"

"I contacted Marshall today."

Behind the dark row of palm trees along the boulevard and the jumble of squatters' shanties, the flat expanse of newly reclaimed land and the gray-white waters of Manila Bay, the sun was slowly sinking. Even at the end of a rainy day, it had the power to throw a tangerine blush on the straight gray clouds and turn the low edge of the sky a glowing purplish pink. Diana squinted at the red half-disk of the sinking sun, trying to make sense of what he'd just said.

"I sent him an internet message, told him I'm interested in Johnny Gamboa's job."

"You did?"

"You look shocked."

"I am."

He winced. "I guess I deserve that." He put his arm around her shoulder as the sun flared and sank out of sight.

"Is this because of Hoffmann, because you didn't get the manager's job?"

"No. Although, yes, it would have been hard to turn down the manager's job. Maybe it's better I didn't get it. Yes." He nodded in agreement with himself. "I'm glad I didn't." He looked at her and paused. "I don't know if you noticed, but what you said after the movie . . . it really hit me hard."

"It did?"

"Yes." He sounded hurt. "I thought about it a lot—seriously thought about it. What a selfish SOB I've been!" He leaned down and kissed the top of her head. "You deserve to be happy, my love. And if you think moving to Vanuatu will make you happy, then by all means, let's do it. It's your turn to choose."

She threw her arms around him, bumping her glass against his back.

"To us," he said, stepping back and raising his glass.

She clinked her glass against his. "To us," she said, taking her first drink of the scotch. It burned all the way down her throat, but it settled warm and comfy in her chest.

"I should hear back from Marshall in a day or two," he said. "Nothing is certain. But I think our chances are good."

24

The apartment was a mess—boxes stacked against walls, drawers and cupboards left open, packing tape piled on end tables. A glorious mess. And Diana loved it—the hustle, the sense of purpose. It felt as though their once neat and somnolent apartment had come alive.

Humming, stepping around boxes in the dining room, she carried her grandmother's teapot from the china cabinet to the table. Without its ever-present embroidered cloth, the table looked naked. Stacks of old newspapers, a jumble of dishes, and a cardboard box, its flaps reaching out like four clumsy wings, replaced the bowl of fruit and the precisely arranged place settings.

"You know," Jay said. He was standing in the alcove behind the bar where he kept his tool box tucked between bottles of wine, whiskey, and assorted liqueurs. "You know," he said again, nodding, "you're braver than I am." He wrote something down, another item added to the list of tools he wanted to buy while they were still in Manila.

"Ha." She pushed a newspaper aside and set the teapot down. "What have I ever done that's brave? You're the one who jumped out of a plane."

"I was in the army. I had to jump."

"Still . . . sounds brave to me."

"You would have done it."

She chuckled. "I don't know about that."

"The thing is . . ." He stared at his pen. ". . . I was afraid . . ."

"Who wouldn't be?" She wadded up some newspaper and stuffed it inside the teapot.

"No, no. I mean . . . that too, but . . ."

She tried not to roll her eyes. Jay was so articulate most of the time. He could explain the ins and outs of providing safer drinking water in Bangladesh or setting up family planning clinics in Indonesia. But when it came to talking about his feelings, he tended to stumble around on a host of unlikely back roads and detours before he ever got around to what he wanted to say.

"I mean this whole thing." He cleared his throat, put his pen down, and picked up a wrench. "Trying to have a baby and . . . we get our hopes up . . ." He looked at the ceiling. "That's what scares me."

"I didn't know you felt that way." She had the crazy urge to run to him, as though she could calm his fears with a hug and a pat on the back. "We have to have faith, honey."

"You see. You're braver than I am. You don't give up."

"Of course not." She frowned. "Wait. You haven't given up, have you?"

Jay lowered his eyes. He turned the wrench over in his hand a couple of times. Then he returned it to the toolbox. "No. Not now. Maybe for a while I did. I don't know. I do know that I didn't want to think about it. I mean, every month we failed. And it hurt, you know." His voice cracked. He took a deep, ragged breath and continued. "I saw how much it hurt you, too. You tried not to show it, but I could tell."

She was caught unaware by gathering tears, pain clutching at her throat.

"After a while I think I was afraid to hope anymore," he said.

This was why they seldom talked about her failure to get pregnant. It was too painful. Looking down at her hands, Diana saw that they were still clutching a sheet of the *Manila Chronicle*. "Then why?" Her voice betrayed her with a squeak. "Why did you do this thing? Why did you go along with me about Vanuatu?"

"You crazy woman, because I love you." He smiled at her for a moment. Then he looked down and started fingering their stash of batteries as though he might have said too much. After a long silence, he spoke again. "What you said after the movie that day threw me for a loop. I've been so selfish. You came here to the Philippines for my sake. So now . . . well . . . I think you're right. It's your turn to set our course for a while." He picked up a hammer, swung it a few times in the air, and put it down. "No one knows whether this noble enterprise of ours is going to succeed." He smiled. "But maybe you're right and all we need is to get out of Manila and live in a quieter, more peaceful place."

"I sure hope so."

They looked at each other across the dining room table. The extended moment felt like a covenant, a hope they both shared and a promise of fulfillment.

"I wonder if they have a hardware store in Port Vila," he said.

She frowned. "They would, wouldn't they?"

"We'll see."

She wrapped a full sheet of the *Chronicle* around the teapot, carefully tucking it into the cavity and around the spout. Suddenly, as she placed the teapot in a box beside a stack of wrapped saucers, she felt a stab of uncertainty. What if Port Vila didn't have a hardware store? What if the path she'd chosen turned out to be wrong for them? She walked across to the china cabinet and took out a stack of dessert plates. Then she took a deep breath. This is what she wanted. She just had to believe that it would all work out.

It was happening so fast, though. They had to be in Port Vila, the capital of Vanuatu, on August fifteenth. Jay had contacted Marshall on July twenty-first and heard back from him the following day. Marshall said a doctor in Manila had already declared Johnny Gamboa eligible for disability retirement, and Gamboa had elected to take it. He hadn't been kidding when he said he wanted to hire Jay if the position opened up.

As soon as Jay heard the news, he'd called Diana from work to tell her. "Good news, honey," he said. "We're going to Vanuatu."

"Really?"

He'd laughed. "Yes, really. Marshall wants me there by August fifteenth. That's only three weeks away." She heard him suck in his breath. "You're going to have to take care of most of the packing. I've got so much to handle here before I go. Well," he'd said, rallying, "and so our adventure begins."

⁓

Preparations for moving involved a whole series of tasks and decisions. They needed to make airline and hotel reservations, sell their car, and borrow or rent one in Port Vila until they could get a new one. There were arrangements to be made with a moving company and extra boxes and wrapping paper to locate. And there were all those decisions about what to bring and what to give away and to whom. Then they had to pack up the small things and supervise the movers who would take care of the furniture. There was no room in Diana's head to think about what they were leaving behind.

Not until the night of the farewell party.

It was at Madeline and Quan's house, a dinner party for some of Diana and Jay's best friends. When she and Jay pulled up to the house, Diana was still preoccupied with packing details and decisions. Once they got out of the car, though, the whole world widened around her. She looked at the sky where a smattering of stars was trying in vain to compete with the bright lights in Madeline's windows, and a silent, serene moon kept watch above the treetops. Something—maybe it was the sound of laughter from inside or the scent of *damas de noche*—reminded her of their first dinner parties in the Philippines. How romantic they'd seemed then!

Quan met them at the front door. "Welcome," he said, kissing Diana on both cheeks and giving Jay a warm one-armed hug. Then he led them into the living room, a large space, filled to bursting with many of the friends they'd made over the past four years. Such an attractive group, Diana thought—the men looking smart and distinguished in their batik shirts and informal *barongs,* the women looking beautiful, each in her own way. Dark or fair, outgoing or quiet, they all had strength of personality. And they all looked lovely tonight, Sheila Chatterjee in a sari, Emily Brown and Gerda Klein in colorful dresses made from batik and Thai silk, fabric brought back from missions no doubt in their husband's suitcases. Diana, too, was wearing a dress made from fabric Jay brought back from a business trip, a sleeveless dress with a long straight skirt made from Malaysian batik.

"Hey." Madeline's slim arms wrapped around Diana from behind. "I'm going to miss you," she whispered in her ear.

"Me, too." Diana smiled, blinking away a tear.

Madeline squeezed her arm and stepped back. "Sorry. I need to get back to the kitchen. Luz is waiting for me to taste the soup. Quan will take care of you."

"Right. You two need some drinks. Mirasol. Please see what Mr. and Mrs. McIntosh would like to drink. Then . . ." Quan jingled his ice cubes. ". . . we men can retire to the lanai and leave the living room to the ladies."

The women smiled at their husbands and each other. No one really minded the separation. Their lives and their conversations were so different from their husbands'. Besides, they'd all get back together at the dinner table where the hostess would seat them man, woman, man, woman, with no spouses sitting together, of course. It was all very old-fashioned and at the same time elegant, Diana thought as she squeezed in on the sofa between Clare Campbell and Sheila Chatterjee.

For a while the talk among the women centered around food—Madeline's well-earned reputation for cooking amazing

Vietnamese dishes, Sheila's curries, the high price of fish and shrimp these days. There was some talk of children—Clare's new baby, birthday parties and summer school, and Emily Brown's son who would soon be leaving for college.

"Rhode Island is so far away," she moaned. "He could at least have chosen the West Coast. Not that I'd be able to help him out if he got in trouble there either." She covered her mouth as though stifling a sob. "I can't believe my baby is going to be so far away from me."

"Lucky him," Giulia Moretti mumbled under her breath.

Emily's mouth dropped open.

"I just wish *I* were going to Rhode Island along with him," Giulia added. "I'm fed up with Manila."

Diana felt rather than heard it, the slight collective gasp, the breath-hold that froze the air for a moment. They all had their ups and downs, their complaints and struggles. But when they were together in a group, they tried not to talk about them. It was like an unspoken creed, the "expat-wife rule": smile, share the small good things, joke about the problems, even if your jokes are sarcastic and mean. And if you must complain, let it be to your husband or best friend. Everyone knew that unhappiness could spread like an infestation of lice.

Giulia certainly had changed. When Diana first met her, she seemed to be genuinely happy and engaged with her life in the Philippines. She and Paolo were the most enthusiastic dancers at the D-TAP parties. When she and Diana volunteered at the free medical clinic on McKinley Road, Giulia never missed a day. She was the one who organized the Women's Club trip to Corregidor. But this past year, for some reason, Giulia's sparkle had disappeared. And expat-wife rule or no rule, she wasn't one to hide how she felt.

If she noticed the uncomfortable looks on her friends' faces, Giulia didn't let it stop her. "And now we can't even go to Baguio," she said, a lament spoken with both hands beating the air like an orchestral conductor building up to a crescendo. "We had our trip all planned. And . . . wouldn't you know it, a natural disaster." She dropped her hands and looked around the room as though suddenly realizing how unseemly it was to compare the disruption of her vacation plans with the disaster of last week's earthquake.

In the interlude of silence that followed, Clare reached for some peanuts, Sheila Chatterjee recrossed her legs, and Emily took a sip of rum and coke. They may have wanted to go back to talking about food or children, but once the earthquake was mentioned, they couldn't look away. Even in Manila, they'd all felt the tremors. But up in the mountain city of Baguio, five thousand feet above sea level, the quake had been much worse. It had hit 7.7 on the Richter scale. Buildings collapsed; landslides closed all the roads leading to Baguio and damaged the runway; and, from all they'd been able to find out, more than a thousand people had been killed, maybe more. Diana and her friends had all vacationed in Baguio at one time or another. They knew its roads and shops and hotels.

"I keep thinking about the Hyatt Terraces," Emily said. She sucked in her breath. "We stayed there last year."

"It's terrible," Clare said. "All those people trapped under the rubble, survivors sleeping in the park."

Giulia shook her head. "This country! If it's not an earthquake, it's a typhoon, and if it isn't a typhoon, it's a coup or a bus drivers' strike."

They all fell silent again, feeling perhaps they'd gone too far down a dark road. The bus and jeepney drivers' strike was still going on. They'd undoubtedly heard about the burned buses and the strikers and bystanders who'd been shot, but no one said anything. Enough bad news for one day. And it *was* a party.

"It was a lovely party," Diana said as she and Jay walked to the car, pleasantly full after the magnificent dinner Madeline had served. The delicate flavors of fresh basil, cilantro, and mint were still with them. And yes, it *had* been a lovely party, Giulia's complaints in the living room easily swept away amidst all the good cheer over dinner. "Mmm." Diana raised her arms and breathed in the flower-scented air. "I love damas de noche."

"Careful, honey," Jay warned, steadying her as she wobbled on her high heels. "Looks like someone had too much wine."

She shrugged. "You never know until you try to walk in high heels. I have no idea how much I drank. Quan never let my glass go dry."

"That's his way. Quan's an attentive host."

"Yeah." Diana sighed. "I'm going to miss them, all of them."

"Don't worry. We'll be back."

"I guess so." The future seemed too uncertain to think that far ahead. But he was right, she'd only asked for a couple of years in Vanuatu. He must have taken that timeline seriously and arranged with headquarters for a limited stay in the South Pacific office. Still, she wasn't ready to think about coming back to Manila.

They got in the car and drove down the quiet streets of Urdaneta Village and out onto Makati's main avenues where the crush of the buses, jeepneys, and cars taking people to and from work was well over.

"Do you realize," Diana said as they turned onto the highway, "that all the men at the party work for D-TAP?"

"Sure."

"I mean, we do know other people, but most of our good friends are associated with the same organization."

"It's a large outfit."

"I know." They were quiet for a while. On another occasion months ago when Giulia was just beginning to turn against her life in the Philippines, she'd complained about being tired of being identified as a D-TAP spouse. "I have my own identity," she'd insisted, her eyes on fire. "I'm me, Giulia Moretti." They all felt that way. But it was unavoidable. That's how they were identified on their visas: D-TAP spouse. Besides, Giulia did have her own identity. She was a mother.

Diana crossed her fingers in the darkness. God willing, she too would be a mother soon.

25

The sun was rising as they flew over northern Australia—a great dark dull shape against a shining ocean. They descended with a big swoop and landed at their first stop: Brisbane. Out the window, men in shorts and knee socks scurried around, some on foot, some riding bikes, while men in big-brimmed bush hats strolled behind them and chatted.

She heard giggling behind her. It had to be Clarita and Lourdes. She turned around and waved, and the two maids waved back. They looked excited. Neither of them had been abroad before. For them, this was to be a "great adventure." In fact, that was exactly the way Clarita described it when she asked Diana if she could go with them. Clarita had been talking to Lourdes, Abby's maid.

When Abby and Saudur left for Vanuatu, they had assumed they'd hire someone there to help around the house and with the twins. It hadn't worked out, though, so Abby had contacted Lourdes, their Filipino maid, and Lourdes had immediately called Clarita.

"I want to go with you," Clarita blurted out one afternoon while she and Diana were going through the canned goods, deciding which to take and which ones to give away.

Diana looked up, perplexed.

"The maid of Mrs. Rahman is going," Clarita said fixing her gaze on the can of tomato sauce in her hand.

"Lourdes? To Vanuatu?"

"Yes, ma'am."

"But Clarita, you do know it's a long way away, don't you? And we won't be coming back for maybe two years."

"I know, ma'am." She straightened her back and looked directly at Diana. "I want to go with you. It will be a great adventure."

The next day Diana heard from Abby. Lourdes was afraid to travel alone, she said. Could she tag along with Jay and Diana?

Of course she could.

And now, here they were in the Brisbane transit lounge, the two women chattering in Tagalog with a Filipino couple. Diana glanced over her shoulder at them as she and Jay walked around the big airy room. "Will there be any Filipinos in Vanuatu?" she asked.

"A few."

"Still, isn't it going to be a shock for them? They're used to crowds . . . to being surrounded by their own people."

"Don't worry, honey. They'll do fine. Filipinos are good abroad."

Diana looked back again. The two women seemed to be having such a good time with the Filipino couple. She took a deep breath. "Oh, well. Clarita said she was looking for an adventure. I sure hope this one doesn't turn out to be too quiet and peaceful for her."

Halfway around the transit lounge, a group of men in uniform caught Jay's eye. "Be right back," he said, giving Diana's arm a squeeze.

She leaned against a post and watched him. How easily he struck up a conversation with strangers! Soon the men were all talking and gesturing and laughing.

"How did you know they spoke English?" she asked when he finally returned.

He shrugged. "I figured they were Gurkha soldiers recruited by the British. And they were. What I wanted to know was where they were going. They said they'll be on our plane to Fiji. From there, they'll head into the island's interior for a month and a half of jungle training. Then they'll fly back to Hong Kong." His face lit up with the manly excitement of it all. "Gurkhas are the fiercest fighters on the planet," he said.

Diana was puzzled for a moment. Every single one of the men was shorter than she was. And they were so pleasant looking and sturdy, extremely sturdy. "They're from Nepal, aren't they?"

"Right. Mountain men."

The Air Vanuatu plane they flew from Fiji to Port Vila was a Boeing 727 like any other 727. The flight attendants, however, didn't fit the usual mode. They smiled more, and they wore matching dresses in a floral print of pink, yellow, blue, and green. They were the first Melanesians Diana had ever encountered. She'd expected them to look like Polynesians, but they were darker, their hair kinkier.

A couple hours out of Fiji, the flight attendants came back down the aisle with a large basket of cellophane-wrapped candy. The toddler across the aisle plucked one out after careful study, and when urged to take more, blushed like a shy trick-or-treater before taking another. When it was his turn, Jay scooped up a handful.

"For you," he said, dropping them in Diana's lap.

"You're in a good mood," she blurted out as though she suspected him of playacting, which wasn't the case. He'd given her no reason to think he regretted his decision to move.

"Of course I'm in a good mood." He reached across and took back one of the candies he'd given her, unwrapped it, and popped it in his mouth. "I love traveling. Every time I leave headquarters for a mission, I feel like a weight's been lifted off my shoulders."

"But you love working there."

"I do." He sucked in his cheeks. "But it's a pressure cooker. The D-TAP headquarters is like its own self-contained world. It's a kind of mini-United Nations with all the conflicts, jealousies, alliances, and rivalries you'd expect to see there."

Diana nodded. Even from the outside looking in, she could see how self-contained D-TAP was. Even the wives, like moons around Saturn, were caught up in the D-TAP universe.

"We're all devoted to our work," he said over the steady, comforting roar of the engines. "There's something below the surface though. And it's pervasive. You can't get away from it."

Diana glanced at him, at his full lips—tight now, as though pulled together by strings on either end—and at his pinched brows. It reminded her of a moment at Madeline's dinner when she'd looked up and seen him looking equally angry. He and Paolo Moretti were sitting at the other end of the table. When there was a lull in the conversation, they'd quickly lowered their voices. She turned to ask him about it and then changed her mind. Better to let it be.

She looked down at the candies in her lap. "What am I going to do with all these?"

"Eat them?" he suggested. "Save them?"

She chose a red and white mint and stuffed the rest in her carry-on bag. Then, while Jay went back to his John le Carré novel, she turned and gazed out the window.

They were about two and a half hours out of Fiji by now. The ocean had looked calm the whole way, the water a lustrous blue that reached all the way into the Earth's curve and then melded with the soft blue sky. So beautiful, and yet ... She sucked the too sweet candy and looked for something else in the featureless blue view. An occasional whitecap flashed on the periphery of her vision, always disappearing before she could bring it into focus.

Ever since Fiji she'd been gazing out at the ocean's pretty blue surface as though that were all there was to it. She hadn't given a thought to the real ocean, that deep, deep watery world below her. All those creatures—sharks and turtles, rays and whales and spiky sea urchins—all of them hidden from view. The thought of that huge mysterious world sent a chill up her spine.

Suddenly the plane's engines changed pitch. *Oh my god*, she thought, *we're almost there*. Almost there, and Vanuatu was as much a mystery to her as was the ocean. Somehow in her rush to move, her single-minded focus on this one solution to her problem, she'd neglected to imagine what it would actually feel like to live on a remote little island in the middle of the South Pacific Ocean. She gripped her armrests and stared at the seat in front of her.

"What?" Jay folded a page and put his book away.

"Nothing."

He leaned across her lap. "Look. I see something."

And there it was, a strip of turquoise beyond the ocean's monotonous blue, surf splashing white on a beach, a fringe of green trees. Their plane dropped lower until they were skimming over a plantation of shiny green coconut palms. Then they were on top of the runway, dusty bushes along the side, a few drying puddles. The plane settled onto a blanket of air, resting for a moment in that zone a few feet from the ground where you seem to be speeding up before you touch down, holding your breath before you land.

"Well, honey," Jay said, patting her knee as the plane's wheels hit the tarmac. "Welcome to paradise."

They taxied past a tangle of green, turned toward the terminal, and came to a stop. Diana leaned her shoulder against Jay's and unsnapped her seatbelt. "Looks good," she said. It came out almost as a question.

But it smelled good, too. Clattering down from the plane on an aluminum staircase, she breathed in the warm, moist air—sun-kissed jungle foliage, a hint of jet fuel. Unlike that day almost four years ago when she'd stepped off the plane in Manila for the first time, here she wasn't being assaulted by blistering heat. Instead the warm, soft air settled around her like a gentle caress.

She looked back at Clarita and Lourdes who were trailing behind. Then she took Jay's hand, and together they walked toward the white terminal building. She was ready.

Inside, the long, high-ceilinged room that led to immigration was also white. As they approached the tables at the far end of the room, a tall Polynesian who looked like a sumo wrestler before fattening camp stepped out to greet them. "Siole Ifopo," he said, tapping the photo-ID clipped to his pocket that identified him as a D-TAP technical assistant. "Over there." He directed them past the three tables set aside for tourists to the only table for citizens and residents. "I'll take care of your passports."

Diana wondered why they would need help presenting their passports to the immigration officer. But Jay handed his over without complaint. So Diana collected Clarita and Lourdes's passports and handed them together with her own to Siole.

He leafed through them, marked a couple of pages and handed them to the immigration officer, a dark-skinned young man who looked exceedingly proper and colonial in his stiff white uniform.

"Hm." The man frowned. "Two years?"

"Until 1992."

He nodded and adjusted some numbers before stamping their passports and handing them back.

In an easy minute they were at baggage claim, waiting for the carousel to start. "The chief's wife came along," Siole said. "Carole Anne. She's waiting in the lobby. I told her I could get her an official badge." He shrugged. "She didn't think it was proper."

Diana tried to picture Carole Anne Charbonneau. She hadn't seen her for a few years, not since before Marshall was transferred to Vanuatu. Wasn't she tall and blond? Somewhat stand-offish? Whatever. Abby was the one person Diana was waiting to see. They hadn't made arrangements, but if she knew Abby, she'd be at the airport to greet them.

The belt jerked, and bags started tumbling out. Seeing her suitcase, Diana stepped forward. Just as she was about to grab it, though, Siole's meaty hand closed around the handle. When he had all four of their suitcases, he tucked two under his arms and carried the other two by their handles. Motioning for Clarita and

Lourdes to follow close behind carrying their own bags, he walked up to the customs officer and quickly arranged for all of them to be waved through. A scary-looking guy like Siole with a gift for making friends was always useful, even for an influential institution like the Development Trust for Asia and the Pacific.

Leaving customs, they passed through a doorway and out into yet another expansive white space, sunlight streaming in through high windows and glass doors. Something about the offbeat mix of people in the airport lobby sent a thrill up Diana's spine and simultaneously left her feeling more than a little off-balance. Catching up with Jay, her mind wove them all together—the Europeans in shorts and sandals chatting with bearded government officials in safari suits, the couples at small tables sipping cappuccinos, the tourists in flip-flops and bush hats, the smiling ni-Vanuatu women wearing missionary-inspired calico dresses.

Carole Anne Charbonneau was standing off to one side, hands clasped in front of her, her blue-and-white dress and white flats looking conspicuously clean and crisp.

Abby was nowhere in sight.

Vanuatu

1990

26

"Welcome to Vanuatu." Carole Anne threw her arms out as though to hug them all at once. "I know y'all are just going to love it here."

Ah, yes, Diana remembered. Carole Anne was from Georgia.

They exchanged quick double-cheeked pecks. Then they all followed Siole through the door, which he somehow managed to shoulder through with his arms still full of suitcases. Diana scanned the lot across the street for Abby. Maybe she hadn't realized how fast they would get through immigration and customs with Siole's help.

"The parking lot is right over there," Carole Anne said with a little wave of her fingers. Siole will be back before y'all know it."

Leaving their suitcases on the curb, Siole hurried off. A minute or two later, he pulled up in a white Toyota.

"You see, here he is," Carole Anne said. "Don't y'all just love small airports?"

"It was good of you to meet us," Jay said. "Big airports or small, it's always nice to see a familiar face."

Carole Anne clicked her tongue and blushed. Jay's good looks always made women blush or smile too broadly and stand too close. Carole Anne was a blusher. "I . . . we . . . Marshall and I wouldn't

be able to forgive ourselves if no one had been here to meet y'all."
She smiled at Jay. "Y'all are part of the family now." A blusher
and a smiler.

"Excuse me," Jay said, turning away so he could help with
the suitcases.

"No, no. Siole can handle that."

Jay shook his head and swung a suitcase into the trunk.

"Men," Carole Anne sighed. Leaning closer to Diana while
the men rearranged the suitcases to make room for Clarita and
Lourdes's bags, she whispered, "Be sure you tell him to order a
white car."

As was the case in Manila, D-TAP officers here were allowed
to order a duty-free car. The office always did the paperwork, but
no one had ever told them what to order. "White?"

"Yes. A Toyota. It's what we all have. Port Vila is such a small
town. Y'all don't want to stand out. Please," she said, gesturing
toward the back seat. "Are all four of y'all going to fit back there?"

"Yes, ma'am," Clarita said. "Lourdes can sit on my lap."

The ride into town—only seven minutes according to Carole
Anne—led them first through an agricultural area, scruffy little
fields on either side of the road with cattle grazing under spindly
coconut palms. The still-alive fence posts sprouted leaves and beach
hibiscus flowers. A man walking along the side of the road glared
at them under his heavy brow. Then as their car passed, he broke
into a toothy smile that totally transformed his face.

"You came right in the middle of a government crisis," Siole
said, glancing at them in the rearview mirror. "Watch out for the
prime minister. He has a special relationship with a rich Vietnamese
copra trader. Plus, he made the mistake of throwing some of his
rivals out of the country. Now members of Parliament are calling
for his resignation."

And you call that a government crisis? Diana thought, remembering the People Power Revolution in the Philippines and the
many armed coup attempts.

Carole Anne turned back and smiled. "Siole loves politics."

They wheeled around a small roundabout. When the road straightened, the wild countryside gave way to driveways and huts and concrete block buildings with cars and pickup trucks parked at odd angles. The whole area, neither country nor town, looked ragged and confused, as though it couldn't decide what it wanted to be. Not a particularly beautiful sight. But then, you couldn't expect an entire country to be picturesque. Diana glanced at Jay, who was nodding and commenting and asking questions as Siole plied them with stories of the various factions in the country—the ni-Vanuatu from Tanna and Santo, the ranchers and plantation owners and shopkeepers, the French-speaking Vietnamese, and the rich Chinese, some of whom spoke English and some French.

Diana caught Jay's eye and pointed off to their right where the land dropped down to a small shallow bay, resplendent in cream and lavender and turquoise.

A minute later they were entering Port Vila, past the Rossi Hotel, Fung Kuei's, Goodies, Proud's Duty Free. From the look of it—the simple mostly one- or two-story buildings with glimpses of ocean between them, the sidewalk café with its white tables and red-and-white awning, the casually dressed people, and slow-moving pedestrians—it was a charming little town.

"What do you think?" Jay whispered over Clarita's head.

Diana opened her mouth to answer. Was she ready to say? A jeep pulled out in front of them and then slowed in mid-turn so the driver could wave at a lanky young man ambling down the sidewalk with a boom box on his shoulder. What *did* she think? They rolled past a bank and a travel bureau. Was there anything she could conclude from a glimpse of downtown Port Vila, anything that would tell her whether this place would provide the peace and quiet she needed so she could relax enough to conceive a child?

"It's charming," she whispered back. Cute and charming. And, at the same time, well, chilling. When you get exactly what you asked for, who's left to guarantee that it will actually make you happy?

~~~~~~~~~

D-TAP had made reservations for them at Le Lagon Resort Hotel. The rooms there were scattered across the grounds in small groupings. Theirs was on the bottom floor of a four-room unit.

Before leaving, Carole Anne handed Diana a sack of "essentials": cold cereal, juice, bananas, and milk. "For your first morning," she said. She gave Siole a meaningful look, and he pulled a set of car keys out of his pocket and handed them to Jay. One of the officers, Tom Appleby, was letting them use his car while he was on home leave.

"It's the dull gray Toyota at the edge of the parking lot," Siole said.

Carole Anne winced, wrinkling her nose. "Appleby smokes. You'll have to drive with the windows open."

Carole Anne and Siole hadn't been gone more than five or ten minutes when Diana caught sight of a red-haired woman prancing across the grass toward their bungalow. "You found us," she cried as she and Abby crashed together in a big bear hug. "I thought you weren't coming."

"Sorry." Abby stepped back, a pained look on her face. "I wanted to pick you up at the airport. I'm so bummed out that I couldn't. But Carole Anne would have had a conniption fit. She thinks the airport hospitality run is her duty. Her privilege really. And . . . she is the boss's wife. Hey, Jay." She gave him a big smile and a quick hug. "Welcome to Vanuatu."

Behind him, Clarita and Lourdes stood at the edge of the small patio, hands clasped in front of them, shy, expectant looks on their faces.

"Ladies," Abby said, breaking away from Jay and Diana and hurrying over to the two maids. "I'll bet you're glad to see me." She gestured toward the queen-size bed inside the room. "Unless you were hoping to sleep four to a bed."

"No ma'am," they giggled in chorus, blushing like school girls.

"Lourdes's room has two beds." Abby turned back to Diana and Jay. "Clarita can stay there until you find a house. If Lourdes doesn't mind."

"No, ma'am." Lourdes grinned and wrapped her arm around Clarita's waist.

"In the meantime, I think we can find something to keep her busy."

Clarita straightened her shoulders. "I like to work, ma'am."

No matter how glad Diana was to see her friend, she was tired after their flight. "I saw that yawn," Abby teased. "I reckon you need a day to settle in. See you on Friday? Lunch?"

Before Abby left with Lourdes, Clarita, and their bags, she reached under her front seat, pulled a bottle of wine out by its neck, and handed it to Diana. Then she leaned over and fished under the seat again until she found two big Cadbury's chocolate bars. "Here. I don't imagine there was any wine or chocolate in Carole Anne's hospitality bag."

Diana shook her head.

"Cheerios, right?"

"Cheerios, bananas, milk, tea, and plastic bowls."

Abby gave a knowing nod and turned to the maids. "Pile in, ladies. See you on Friday, Diana," she said, leaning out the window and waving as she backed up.

27

This is the life, Diana thought as she looked out on the thatch-roofed bungalows and emerald lagoon. This was what morning in the South Pacific should look like. She cracked open a banana and looked over her shoulder. Jay was inside running water and clanging hangers. She peeled the banana, sliced it over her Cheerios with a plastic knife, and poured milk over it all. "Honey," she called, "the juice and cereal are outside on the patio. It's lovely out here. Why don't you come and join me?"

On the lagoon, a man was paddling toward shore in a dugout canoe with a single outrigger. Watching him, Diana found herself crunching her cereal in rhythm with the dip of his paddle. Dr. Feliciano would be pleased. Here she was on her first morning in Vanuatu, sitting outside, serenaded by birds in a banyan tree, watching a canoe glide toward the shore while she ate sweet, toasted O's, and just relaxing her heart out.

The man tucked his paddle away and coasted onto the sandy bottom. He stepped in the water, dragged his canoe up on the beach and tied it to a log. Then he picked a hibiscus—red, to match his shorts—stuck it behind his ear, and walked down the beach to the boathouse where another man in red shorts was pulling a Jet Ski out of the water and lining it up with a row of small sailboats.

"Hey, look at you," Jay said from the doorway. "Don't you look comfy?"

She looked down at the shorts and tank top she'd slept in and smiled. "Cheerios?"

"I've gotta run."

"It's only eight o'clock." She had to smile at his shiny-clean face and neat schoolboy look—black leather shoes, slacks, a white short-sleeved shirt.

"I've gotta be there by eight thirty." His eyes flitted across the landscape—the lawn sloping down to the lagoon, the bungalows and trees.

"And . . ." She shook the cereal box. "We're only five minutes from town."

"Oh, my god!" Jay shouted. "Look at that sailboat."

Several hundred feet from shore, a small boat with a pink-and-blue-striped sail rested in mid-fall, one leg of the fiberglass catamaran poised at forty-five degrees. When it fell, it was like a slow-motion scene from a TV commercial, one that Diana could see ending with the tourists playfully hanging over one side to tip it back up. The sail would lift skyward and shudder to a stop, and the man and woman would clamber back on board, laughing at their small holiday mishap.

She was still imagining the sight when Jay leapt over the row of coleus at the edge of their patio and ran down the hill, sliding on the wet grass even as one of the boatmen, whose job it was to rescue tourists and account for the hotel's boats, pulled the Jet Ski into the water and started the engine. Throwing it into gear, he roared away from shore, only to make a quick loop in the lagoon, cut the engine and jump back out. The tourists had already righted their boat, just as Diana had suspected they would. Now they were throwing their shimmering pink limbs over the side. The woman tugged at her bikini. The man flipped water off his strawberry blond hair.

"I hope you weren't going to save them in your work clothes," Diana teased when Jay reached the top of the hill and stepped back over the coleus.

"Course not." He winked. "I was going to strip naked. I hope I kept that little shoeshine kit from Philippines Airlines," he added, frowning at his shoes.

"It's probably in your hand-carry bag." Diana shook her head. Why would Jay have even considered trying to swim out to that sailboat? He was a lousy swimmer—skilled at tennis and soccer, but a lousy swimmer.

She ate a few more spoonfuls of Cheerios and took a gulp of orange juice. Then she carried the breakfast tray back inside. "You'll be hungry," she said. "How about a banana?"

He tilted his knee inward so he could buff the outside of his shoe. "Okay. I'll eat it in the car."

A moment later, he was out the door, crunching up the gravel path with his attaché case and banana. She stood at the back door and waved. *Don't worry*, she wanted to shout after him. *You'll like it.* It was a hope more than a prediction.

Leaning against the doorframe, her toes curled over the threshold, she watched his back until all she could see was his dark head and white shirt above the hibiscus. He turned toward the tennis courts and disappeared, and she went inside.

The air conditioner's rattle reverberated between the block walls of the empty room. It clicked off, and the little sticking noises her bare feet made as she padded across the tile floor filled up the emptiness. She stopped beside the bed, and the room was silent again. She switched on the clock radio, and it responded with a song from her childhood. "Tiny bubbles in the wine . . ." She laughed, picking up the shoe polish and cloth and tucking them in Jay's bag. ". . . make me feel happy," she sang along with the radio, "make me feel fine." She rinsed out her juice glass and the plastic bowl from Carole Anne's hospitality package. It had been a thoughtful gesture, she had to admit, even if Cheerios and bananas weren't exactly what she would have imagined eating on her first morning in Vanuatu.

She looked around the bare room. Time to start the day— whatever that meant in this new life of hers. She stared at the clothes she'd hung in the closet last night. What does one wear on a day when you haven't even decided what you're going to do? No, she corrected herself: Today she was going to wander and explore. She settled on a cotton dress in swirling ocean colors, one she'd had for a year or two but seldom worn. Sandals, some lipstick, the room key, and she was ready to go.

The obvious place to begin was the seaward end of Erakor Lagoon. She locked the door, dropped the key into the nearly empty little bag she wore over her shoulder, and started across the still-damp grass.

At the edge of the hotel property, she found a sign for the free ferry that carried tourists and locals to and from Erakor Island. A family, complete with beach bags and mats, was waiting at the far end of the dock: the man with his arm around his wife, the woman tilting her floppy hat to adjust the neck flap on her son's billed cap. Diana leaned on the dock's wooden rail and watched small pale fish swim in twos and threes through the transparent water below her. Jay would be at work by now in the gaudy lime-green building they'd passed yesterday. She'd known the regional office would be small, but actually seeing it yesterday made her want to cry for him. It didn't even have a sign. Back in Manila, he'd gone to work in a landmark building, the flags of fifty-some nations flying out front, officers and staff bustling in and out. He wasn't one to care about appearances, but still . . . Oh, well. She wasn't going to feel guilty about Jay's office. After all, he'd agreed to come.

She heard an engine shift into neutral and looked up to see their ferry—an oversized metal lasagna pan with a blue canopy and an outboard motor. It glided up to the dock and stopped.

Once on board, Diana kicked off her sandals and put her feet up on the bench. Soon they were passing over clumps of coral that looked close enough to touch—cream and white and yellow ochre, round like heads of cauliflower. She leaned over, dipped her forearm into the water and reached toward them. Their boat crossed over a stretch of white sand, the water as clear as an undisturbed swimming pool, the pebbles like spots where the pool's paint had peeled away. Beyond the sand was a forest of thin, brittle coral branches, white with neon blue tips. It was all so beautiful. And, unlike her failed experiment with goldfish back in Manila, this viewing experience didn't require an ounce of effort on her part.

A handful of people were lounging on the island's small beach, and below the water dozens of plump orangey-red starfish with dark brown bumps rested on the sand. At this moment, on this lovely little beach, she felt that all this serenity that surrounded her was bound to rub off. She and Jay would find a house, and, after they'd arranged the furniture and unpacked all the boxes, she would sit on the porch—as peaceful as a starfish—and wait for Vanuatu to change her.

28

They'd probably never use this Jacuzzi at the foot of their queen-sized bed—not together anyway, not if Jay wanted to keep his sperm count up. And the tub was way too big for just one person. She frowned and thought about it again. Oh, what the heck! She might just fill it up to the top tomorrow while Jay was at work and have herself a delicious, relaxing soak.

Sitting on the edge of the tub now, she dangled her feet into the empty Jacuzzi, took a deep breath, and let the air out in what sounded very much like a sigh. It couldn't have been a sigh, though, since she'd had such a nice relaxing day. No doubt about it. Walking around Erakor Island, swimming in the hotel pool, writing letters to Mom and Andrew, making quick sketches of people, trees, and flowers. Her first day in Vanuatu had definitely been pleasant. Of course, she'd spent the day in and around the hotel like a tourist. Tomorrow after lunch with Abby, she'd explore the town and get a better idea what her life would be like here in Vanuatu.

She straightened her knees and pointed her toes. Hurry, sweetheart, she whispered, arching her feet harder before letting them fall back and bump against the wall of the tub. Sweet anticipation.

Waiting for Jay reminded her of all those late afternoons waiting for her father under the maple tree, swinging and twirling. She'd always started out swinging as high as she could, pushing back on the packed dirt with the soles of her sneakers and then stretching her legs up, up toward the branches, challenging herself to swing so high that the rope would suddenly slacken. Only then, when she was afraid she was about to go over the top, would she allow herself to coast to a stop and twirl. She'd tilt her head back and watch the spinning maple leaves and listen for her dad's car. When he was late, Mom would bring her a sweater, and they'd wait for him together. Diana frowned, remembering how her mom would scold him. "You work too hard," she'd say with a worried look on her face, as though working late were the thing that would kill him, not his cigarettes.

She hugged her knees. Outside, the birds were chirping like a mob of politicians in a parliamentary dispute. Fighting for a perch in the banyan tree, she supposed.

And still no Jay.

Moments later she heard his footsteps crunching up the gravel path from the parking lot. "It's unlocked," she shouted, jumping down from the Jacuzzi.

The door opened, framing him against a pale, streaked sky, a familiar strand of dark, wavy hair across his forehead.

"Sweetheart, hi." She hugged him, kissed his cheek. "How was your first day in the South Pacific office?"

He rolled his eyes. "Strange."

"Oh?" She took his attaché case and set it down beside the bed.

"A real small-town vibe. And then there was my meeting with Marshall." He sat down on the bed and leaned over to untie his shoe. "I went in expecting him to discuss the work or his philosophy of development in the South Pacific. Office procedures even."

"So, what did he talk about?"

"Said we should enjoy our three nights in the hotel since that was all D-TAP would reimburse us for." He shook his head. "That's Marshall's brand of humor for you. He likes to needle people. I wasn't in the least bit surprised that he teased me about 'the little woman getting her way.'"

"What?" She frowned, arms akimbo. "He called me 'the little woman'?"

"The only surprise was that he didn't razz me about Hoffmann's promotion. He must not have heard about it yet." Jay pulled his sock off and gave it a shake. "Then he wanted to talk about golf." Jay pulled his other sock off and dropped it—a little black heap on the white tile floor. "Would you believe it? Port Vila has four golf courses."

Diana sat down beside him on the bed. When he finished talking, she'd tell him about the little ferry and about Erakor Island—although she wasn't sure how she'd phrase it. Her island walk, like everything else today, was just a set of impressions—colors and scents and feelings.

"I told Marshall I didn't play golf, but he insisted that all officers played. The green fees are only a thousand vatu he said, as though that clinched it."

She ran her toes over his bare foot. "That's only about eight dollars."

"Huh?" He raised one eyebrow.

"I'm not saying you need to play golf because it's cheap." Outside, the sky was nearly drained of color except for a rosy hue cast on the bulge of land on the other side of the lagoon. The water had a mother-of-pearl texture interrupted by mottled streaks of ripples and currents.

Enough talk about the office. "Look," she said, jumping up. "The sun's setting over the lagoon."

"Ah," he said, giving her a squeeze. "With the setting of the sun, a man's fancy turns to food."

~⁄

They'd barely left the hotel when they saw a huge sign with a big yellow arrow pointing the way to the Golden Dragon Restaurant. They turned off and drove down a narrow road with untended fields on either side.

"I guess this is it," Jay said of the two-story house at the end of the road.

Diana wasn't so sure, but she climbed out anyway. In the twilight, the cleared area around their car was shrouded in shadows. The jungle at its edge vibrated with the one-note trill of a thousand excited cicadas. "Shouldn't there be another sign?" she asked as they walked past a dimly lit ping-pong table in a covered patio.

"Come on. It must be up these stairs."

When they reached the landing, they found a door around the corner that was propped open with a chair. An older Chinese woman who might have been the owner's wife greeted them with a smile. "Lucky you come today," she said. "Monday, Wednesday night we have *guchin* musician. A beautiful lady." She picked up a couple of menus and led them across the spacious open-air dining area to a small round table covered with a white cloth.

Authentic Chinese food from the mainland, the menu proclaimed. The specialties of the house were coconut crab, eight ingredients duck, and crispy fish. "You order, honey," Diana said, turning her chair toward the guchin player. "Something with seafood and vegetables."

The musician was, indeed, beautiful—young with silky, powdered skin and red painted lips, her hair pulled back from the perfect oval of her face. She was kneeling on a raised platform, her turquoise-and-gold silk gown spread around her like ripples in a pond as she plucked the strings of a large, boxy instrument, kind of a zither. She swayed as she played, her elbows, torso, and neck dancing to music that flowed like ribbons from quivering strings. Diana was wasn't well-versed in traditional Chinese music, but it was obvious that this woman was no amateur. In any city, a musician like her would be playing in a high-class restaurant or club crowded with diners. Diana looked over her shoulder at the three other tables that were occupied. "I wonder what she's doing *here*," she whispered.

"The musician?" Jay lowered his menu. "Maybe she knows someone. Thought she could make some money, have an adventure, find a husband. Who knows? Dreams of paradise, perhaps?"

When their crispy fish arrived, it was sizzling, its tail raised in one last swish.

"I walked around Erakor Island today," Diana said as Jay lifted a diamond-shaped chunk of flesh from the fish's side and placed it on her rice. "It was nice." What could you say about a perfect little island at the mouth of a large lagoon? "Small. If I hadn't dawdled, I could have walked around it in half an hour."

She spooned out some sweet chili sauce and dipped the fish in it. "I had a swim in the hotel pool," she said. "Then I sat in the lobby, sketching people who passed by and writing to Mom and Andrew." Separate letters. Pastel, flowered paper for Mom, and wheat-colored linen-look stationery for Andrew.

She picked up another bite of fish with her chopsticks. "I came across some missionary graves on the island. A pastor, his wife and children, and their Samoan assistants. I thought Andrew would be interested. Did I tell you he was still calling Vanuatu the New Hebrides? I wrote, reminding him they changed the name when it became independent ten years ago, and he wrote back that ten years was such a brief span of time. We should wait and see if the name sticks and the country lasts."

"Historians," Jay agreed. "They live in another world."

She nodded, crunching the sweet, crispy fish as she stared out at the night sky. An upside-down slice of moon hung over the lagoon leaving a soft tracing on its surface. If any place could be described as "another world," this would be it.

She'd felt that other-worldliness that afternoon while she was sitting in the lobby, ukulele music playing over the intercom, palm fronds rattling beside her. Looking out the open, windowless sides of the lobby, she hadn't seen a single reminder of the world beyond Vanuatu. The quiet hotel grounds, the hibiscus flowers, big as children's faces, the Indian mynahs whose wings seemed to trace circles in the air when they flew . . . this was her new reality.

When they got back to their room, Jay patted the rim of the Jacuzzi. "A nice soak in the Jacuzzi would sure feel good about now," he sighed, switching on the light.

She smiled. "Warm water up to our chins, bubbles rolling up our backs."

"And between our legs," he said.

He was teasing, of course. She didn't have to remind Jay about the hot water. By this time Dr. Feliciano's fertility rules were permanently inscribed in their brains.

In the beginning, when they believed following a long list of rules, all of them based on research, would quickly solve their problem, they joked around and talked about them. It wasn't long, though, before they began to resent having the rules intrude into their thoughts and lives, especially those rules that regulated their lovemaking. And the calendar. That loveless calendar with its starred days that shouted, *You must have sex today,* and its empty squares that whispered, *Don't bother.* Eventually she started hiding the calendar. If Jay wanted to know if it was a fertile day or not, he had to peek when she wasn't around.

Rules? What rules? It was better to pretend that everything they did was natural and spontaneous and that the outcome would just naturally be for her to get pregnant.

So now, on their second night in Vanuatu, they turned Jay's comment about a soak in the Jacuzzi into a joke. Instead, they took a shower together. Once they were clean, they dried each other's backs. She wiped his chest; he patted her face and shoulders. Then, in unison, they stepped back and dried their own limbs. Just in case she was fertile tonight, it wouldn't do to have sex in the shower, standing. Both of them knew the optimal position for achieving fertilization. Neither of them was about to mention it.

29

*A*bby arrived humming and jingling her car keys. In the sunshine, her red hair was a vivid complement to her lime green sundress and chunky coral beads. "Ready?" she asked.

"Yeah," Diana said. "Let's go." She skipped ahead of Abby, and yet, somehow they both climbed into the car and slammed their doors at the same time. They looked at each other and burst out laughing. "You look bright and sparkly today," Diana said.

"And you look . . ." Abby gave Diana a quick head-to-toe inspection. "Light as air, as though at any moment you might fly away."

"I just might." Diana laughed. But it was true. Heading off to lunch with her best friend made her feel like a kid skipping to the ice cream parlor, carefree and light-footed, coins clinking in her pocket.

"Well," Abby said, "wha'd'ya fancy?" Her accent of the moment was more Michael Caine than Queen Elizabeth. "You keen to try flying fox?"

"For lunch?" Diana was an adventurous eater, but she wasn't ready quite yet to eat a fruit bat, certainly not this early in the day.

Abby backed up, throwing a shower of gravel in her wake. "Just joking," she said with a wink. "We could join the yachties and beer drinkers for steak and seafood at Waterfront Café. They have a hearty salad bar. Or . . ." She raised her eyebrows and grinned. "If you like people-watching, fresh-baked croissants, and strong French-roast coffee, we could go to La Tentation."

"*Oui*," Diana said. "Let us be tempted."

"Did I mention the cream cakes and Napoleons?"

Diana rolled her window all the way down to match Abby's and reached out to feel the breeze. She hadn't felt so carefree for . . . well, for a long, long time.

"Hey," Abby said. "You're messing up my aerodynamic flow."

Diana slapped the side of the Toyota. "Hey, yourself." Finally she pulled her hand back in, grinning. "By the way, what are you doing with a bronze-colored car?"

Abby snorted. "You mean instead of the unobtrusive white favored by Carole Anne?"

"Exactly."

"I told Saudur I had to have red. He was relieved to settle for bronze." She pulled into a parking place at the edge of the open-air market and cut the engine. "This way." Abby locked her arm around Diana's elbow to guide her over the puddles in the parking lot and led her to a large covered terrace adjoining the sidewalk.

Squeezing between chattering diners, they made their way through shafts of light that slipped through the vines growing through the mesh roof. At the edge of the terrace, they found a free table beside a row of potted plants. The room smelled of coffee, fresh bread, and the sea. "Nice," Diana said. "I like this place."

A pale, balding man near the entrance to the adjoining patisserie tipped his head and fluttered his fingers in their direction.

"My dentist," Abby said. She leaned across the table and added in a whisper, "He left the drudgery and boredom of his practice in Marseille, bought a vanilla plantation, and brought his wife out here to enjoy the simple life. Come to find out, growing vanilla wasn't so simple. The plants take two or three years to mature, and pollinating the flowers with a bamboo splinter the size of a toothpick turned out to be more tedious than drilling teeth. The enterprise lost money, his partner backed out of the deal, and his wife divorced him." She sat back in her chair. "These are the stories he tells after he's made me mute with Novocain."

"What a sad tale!"

Abby nodded.

Glancing around the room at the other diners, Diana noted that most of them were white, a few Asians, even fewer ni-Vanuatu. And they all seemed to be enjoying themselves. Whether or not that meant they were in the process of realizing their dreams, it was impossible to say.

"So," Abby said after they'd placed their orders—a spinach quiche for Diana, a *croque madame* for herself, and coffee for both of them—"what do you think so far?"

"I think I'm going to like it here."

Abby nodded. "As you know, I started out hating it. I thought I was Napoleon, exiled to my own little Saint Helena. But Saudur likes the projects he gets here, and the twins couldn't be happier, so . . ." She raised her palms. "What could I do? I had to succumb to the charms of this quirky little country. And now you're here. I was afraid you wouldn't be able to talk Jay into moving. And then, just in the nick of time, that Hoffmann thing happened. Perfect timing, huh?"

Diana was caught by surprise. "You heard about that?"

"Of course. Ye olde D-TAP tittle-tattle."

"Right. But that's not why he decided."

"It couldn't have hurt."

"I guess not. But . . ."

"Hey. People make decisions for multiple motives. Nothing wrong with that. And you're here. That's what matters."

"Yes." Diana nodded. "We're here."

The waitress came up from behind Diana and placed her quiche on the table, a nice looking salad on the side.

"When I was a kid," Abby said, plucking a new subject out of mid-air. "I loved to ride my bike." She sliced off a bit of her croque madame, cutting through the ham and cheese and fried egg. "Did I ever tell you about our village?"

"I don't think so."

"The village was surrounded with green fields." Abby stirred the yolk of her egg in with the béchamel sauce. "I could bike for miles without running into heavy traffic."

It was a picture Diana couldn't resist: the little red-headed girl pedaling down the tree-lined English country road. "We had a hill in our neighborhood," Diana said with the hint of a smile. "Being brave enough to ride down that hill was a rite of passage for us."

As they ate, they talked about baking fiascos and ugly childhood haircuts.

"My parents were rich enough," Abby said with a sad little smirk, "to behave like snobs but too poor and untraveled to have a cosmopolitan outlook ... which was why they objected to Saudur." She tossed her curls. "I don't care. Let them leave the old manor house to my brother. It's so dilapidated; he'll have to spend a fortune fixing it up." They were silent for a moment. Then Abby added: "I reckon your mum loves Jay. Right?"

"Yeah." Diana looked down at her salad. "Everyone loves Jay. Everyone loves Saudur too," she added quickly.

Abby chuckled. "Indubitably. Even my parents like him. Just not for me."

"They'll come around."

Abby made a face and changed the subject.

They were almost finished eating when Diana noticed an Asian woman entering the restaurant. She was unusually beautiful. Graceful as a dancer in her high-heeled sandals, her short white dress dancing around her thighs. "Do you know that woman over by the pastry counter? She looks familiar."

Abby turned around. "Sure. That's Suling Chao."

"How do I know her?"

"Didn't you say you ate at the Golden Dragon last night? She plays there twice a week. Wait. I'll go get her."

She ran off, and by the time Diana had pulled another chair over, Abby was back, her arm firmly locked around Suling's elbow.

"I come here to buy a Napoleon for Alexi," Suling said as she slid into the chair. "But there is no more." She set a white box on the table in front of her. "I buy chocolate meringues instead."

For a moment Diana felt tongue-tied by Suling's beauty. The famous beauties in the movies and on magazine covers really were different from everyone else.

"Well," Abby said. "How 'bout a beer?"

Suling made a face.

"Okay, wine then. No more coffee. You know how I go bonkers when I'm over-caffeinated."

"Maybe I can drink small glass." Suling glanced apologetically from one to the other. "My face is gonna turn red."

Abby shrugged. "We can handle that."

They ordered the house white, and though Suling took small, cautious sips, it wasn't long before she was glowing pink—not a totally unbecoming look on her smooth, pale skin. Aside from the intimidating effect of her beauty, Suling was easy to be around. She was funny and straightforward. And though her English didn't always come out right, it was more than passable.

"Oh-oh." Abby frowned at her watch. "I've gotta pick up the twins soon."

Suling sighed. "You are so lucky. That's what I want, twins. Then I and Alexi can have big family quick."

"Me," Diana said, "I'd be satisfied if I could have just one baby."

"Oh, Diana, you want baby, too? We are same. I want baby sooo much. Sometimes I think I cannot wait one more day." She slumped back in her chair and stared at the vine and iron mesh over their heads. "In two weeks, I am thirty years old."

"Ha," Abby laughed. "You're just a youngster."

Diana nodded, although in fact, she was surprised to hear that she was that old. Suling was right to be anxious. "Before long," Diana said with all the conviction she could muster, "both of us will be walking around with big bellies."

"You think so?" Suling asked.

"Uh huh." Diana swirled her wine. "Here we are on this peaceful, pristine little island. Willing husbands. What's there to stop us?"

30

"*G*'day, miss."

Diana squinted, looking past the racks of dresses to where a freckle-shouldered young woman with honey-colored hair was perched on a high stool. "Good afternoon."

After the sunny openness of the street, Frangipani Boutique felt like a jungle—blouses and dresses climbing the walls like so many orchids, spots of light slipping through the side windows, wide-brimmed hats fluttering like butterflies in the path of a rotating fan.

This afternoon she was exploring the town. She had to pick Jay up at five o'clock so they could drive out and take a look at the house Johnny Gamboa would soon be leaving. Until then, the day was hers. She'd already spent a couple hours walking up and down Port Vila's main street checking out the video store and the drug store, the Vanuatu Museum of Culture and the musty little library. Outside the library, she'd stood puzzling over the sidewalk exhibit of an enormous kettle purported to have been used by cannibals. Then, leaving behind for the time being the question of why the ni-Vanuatu would choose to display their bloody past so prominently, she continued exploring. She poked around souvenir shops filled with wooden masks and T-shirts emblazoned with

funny or obscene phrases. She stopped at a store that sold everything from spools of thread and bolts of calico to televisions and
air conditioners.

She liked this stylish little boutique, she thought, as she
browsed through the dresses. It was the clerk, though—flipping
her hair and filing her nails—who piqued Diana's curiosity. What
was she doing here? It was the same question that had been running through her mind all afternoon. Who were these people?
Not the ni-Vanuatu; they belonged here. Not the Chinese and
Vietnamese whose grandfathers were brought to Vanuatu by the
English and French. No, the others. All those white people who
walked down the streets and stood behind the counters as though
they, too, belonged in this little out-of-the-way place.

"Those are the twos and fours." The young woman crossed one
thin, shapely knee over the other. "The sixes and eights are over there."

"Thank you."

The girl raised her eyebrows in acknowledgement.

Was she bored? Diana wondered, as she smoothed her fingers
over the size sixes, the cottons and rayons and the occasional silk.
Maybe her friends were all in college or working abroad while
she was here, working for her mother or her aunt—someone with
enough money to own a boutique. Someone who, as anyone could
see, had an eye for colors that evoked tropical beaches and sunsets.
Diana took a pink-and-white sundress off the rack and held it up.

"The mirror's over there." The young woman pointed with her
chin. A chummy sort of nonchalance.

It wasn't Diana's kind of dress, but she brought it over anyway.

"Hm," the girl said. "Pretty."

Diana chuckled. "Maybe if I were still in high school . . ."
She draped the girlish pink dress over her arm. Starting to turn
away, she caught a glimpse of herself—her plain white blouse and
navy knee-length shorts, her straight hair and pale blue eyes. The
woman in the mirror looked like an accountant. "I need something
colorful," she said.

The girl might have laughed since all the dresses in the store seemed plucked from a flower garden. Instead, she put the cap back on her nail polish. Then, casually displaying her long legs again, she jumped down from the stool. "Six?"

Diana nodded.

In a matter of minutes, she found herself in a small changing room with a selection of dresses that would brighten anyone's garden. She tried on a sunny yellow dress with blue and white daisies down the front and a sophisticated plum-colored sheath. When she stepped into the blue, green, and purple print sundress, her blue eyes sparkled. The fitted bodice hugged her waist, and the full skirt revealed flashes of coral when she moved. She stepped back and struck a pose. Someday she and her little girl would have matching dresses. She smiled and turned sideways. Even with her bra straps showing, she looked fantastic. Snatching up the filmy fabric, she swished it around like a Spanish dancer. Then she opened the curtain and came out to look in the larger mirror.

"There we go!" the girl exclaimed.

"I'd need a strapless bra."

"Seduction Lingerie. It's across the street, in Pilioko House. All their apparel comes straight from Paris."

Diana turned to get a sideways view of herself in the mirror. "I love this dress." She smoothed the silky skirt over her hips. "I'll take it."

Before she left, the young woman had one more suggestion. "If you want some highlights," she said, "my boyfriend's salon is the best in town. Jean-Philippe's. Tell him Kate sent you. And come back soon. I have plans for your wardrobe."

Crossing over to Seduction Lingerie, Diana thought of the strapless bra she'd worn to her high school prom. White and utilitarian, it had only one purpose: support. Not that she'd needed much in those days. She opened the door to the jingling of a bell and stepped into a cloud of jasmine and lavender. Looking around, she saw displays of silk and lace lingerie in pale pink and green, aqua and gold.

A delicate-boned woman in a mini-skirt and pearl earrings asked her something in French. "Thirty-two B," she said, guessing. "Strapless."

The woman gathered an armful of bras and matching panties and led Diana to a curtained room with hooks on the walls between posters of Notre Dame Cathedral and the vineyards of Bordeaux. On first glance, the bras looked too flimsy to do the job. They were cleverly designed, though. Trying them on, one after the other, Diana couldn't help admiring the feminine curve of her body, the creamy tone of her skin next to pale blue or set dramatically against midnight black. Best of all was the pastel apricot bra and panties set.

~

She laughed softly as she got into the car they were borrowing from Tom Appleby. She'd paid more for the lingerie than she had for the dress, and somehow that didn't bother her. Not today. Not in Vanuatu. She looked up at Jay's lime green office building, and that made her laugh, too.

She took her sketch pad and pencils out of the glove compartment. So many images fluttered through her head, and all of them made her smile. She might as well capture a few of them on paper while she waited for Jay. She could start with the little Chinese girl sitting by herself on the curb across the street, building a tower with spools of thread. Or Kate on her high stool, crossing her long legs and filing her nails. But no. She couldn't resist starting with the Aussie tourist in the floppy hat who had climbed inside the cannibal kettle and smiled for her husband to take her picture.

"Hey," Jay said sliding into the passenger's seat. "What were you drawing?"

She held her sketch up for him to see.

He grinned and nodded. Then he took a sheet of yellow lined paper out of his shirt pocket and unfolded it. "My secretary drew a map to the Gamboas' house. Just keep on this street, past the police station and then up the hill on Rue du Condominium."

"I hope we like the house," she said, considering for the first time that the opposite might also be possible. Gamboa had sent them a copy of the floor plan. And from Manila, everything about it had seemed fine. It was all on one floor, the master bedroom across the hall from a smaller room that would be perfect for guests and later for a nursery. In her mind's eye, Diana saw hardwood floors in the bedrooms, a shade tree in the yard, an expansive view of the ocean or the lagoon. "It has a view, doesn't it?"

"I don't know," Jay said, tapping the window. "Turn this way. De Gueiros Street."

"I mean, just look at all these hills." She turned the wheel and started up de Gueiros. The scene in her rear-view mirror was like a postcard, the bay and the little offshore island with its rows of native style tourist bungalows framed in the brilliant red of a flame tree. "All the houses in Port Vila must have a water view, don't you think?" They rounded another corner and drove up a small hill until suddenly they were leaving the town behind and entering a jungle—the bush, as they called it here. Huge rubber trees and acacias shaded the road. Then, as soon as her eyes were used to the shade, they were back in the sunshine again.

Jay smoothed out his map. "We veer right here at the circle," he said. For another half mile or so, the road was almost flat. As it started uphill again, Jay told her to slow down.

"There," he said. "That's their driveway."

She pulled in behind Gamboa's car and stopped. "Are you sure?" A bit of wild grass and bushes not much wider than a parking strip was all that separated the house and the smallish front yard from the road.

"Yeah, this is it."

She frowned and opened her door, only to be assaulted by exhaust fumes and the sound of a vehicle rumbling past. She ran to catch up with Jay and tapped his arm, but he gave a little not-now shake of his head and rang the bell. The sound of the buzzer briefly obliterated the growl of an old truck straining to make it up the hill.

Maritess Gamboa answered the door. She frowned into the light, ignoring the tabby that was rubbing against her leg. "Oh, Mr. McIntosh." She nodded at Diana. "Come in, please."

For a moment Diana was taken aback by Maritess's terse greeting and pinched face. She looked so different from the lively, happy woman Diana knew from D-TAP parties.

They stepped out of the sunshine into a darkened entry, blinds still closed, a neglected philodendron sitting limp in the corner. Maritess led them through an arched passageway. "Johnny insisted on getting up," she said over her shoulder. "I told him I could show you around."

All grace and speed and cool indifference, the cat ran ahead of them, bounding across the living room floor and coming to a stop beside his master's footstool. He gave the stool a perfunctory rub and then wrapped his tail around his body in a pose designed to look elegant.

Johnny Gamboa's chair was situated in front of a window, the curtains drawn, an array of jars and small bottles on the table beside him. He lifted his right leg off the rattan footstool with both hands and pushed himself up. "Jay," he said, smiling crookedly. "Good, ah . . . good to see you."

"You remember Diana."

"Welcome," Gamboa said, offering Diana his left hand. He used to be a good-looking man, dark eyes, thick black hair. Now his face drooped on one side and a wide stripe of silver hair ran from his right temple to the back of his head.

"Sit down. Please. Maritess, um, some tea . . . and ah . . . cookies."

Diana sat down and then popped back up again. "I'll go with her."

Compared to the simplicity of the floor plan, the décor was a riot of details—crocheted doilies and faded brown drapes, curio shelves, magazine racks, a knitting basket. The menthol odor of Tiger Balm mixed with coconut oil and garlic was hard to ignore. The living and dining rooms, separated by a buffet and a planter, were every bit as spacious as she'd envisioned. She hadn't expected the tile to be so dark, though. Despite flecks of white and gray, it was basically a black floor.

Maritess pushed open a swinging door, and they stepped into the kitchen. At least it was brighter—lime green counter tops, white cabinets, flowered valances on all the windows.

The smell of hot coconut oil was thick in the air. "May I help?" Diana asked from the doorway.

"We're waiting for the tea water to boil. Jasmine is making cheese *lumpia*. You like?"

"Yes, I do."

The woman who was deep-frying the lumpia smiled a greeting, and Diana smiled back.

"I'm so sorry, Maritess," Diana said, "about your husband's illness."

"Stroke." Her voice broke. "A massive stroke," she said, collapsing into a kitchen chair and staring at the table. "Only fifty-one years old. In perfect health. Played golf. Went swimming at the beach. Everything. Better than me."

The kettle whistled, and she hurried over to snatch it from the flame. "Jasmine," she said, "be sure to drain the lumpia on some paper towels. And don't forget the napkins." She filled the teapot and put it in the middle of a tray already heavy with cups and saucers, sugar bowl and creamer. Then she picked up the tray, and before Diana had a chance to help, she elbowed the door open and strode toward the living room.

The perfect hostess, Maritess set the tray on the coffee table. She knelt beside it, checked the color of the tea, and poured, adding warmed milk and the requested number of sugar cubes to each cup. Then she rose, straight-backed as a nun genuflecting before the altar, and presented each cup and saucer to her guests and husband.

Diana stood behind her, still trying to find a way to be useful. Finally, she gave up and sat down beside Jay. She crossed her legs, and, as they ate warm, cheese-filled lumpia, they listened to Gamboa as he struggled to describe his rehab. It was going well, he said. Good progress. He tried to smile, and she and Jay nodded and did their best to encourage him.

By the time the maid brought in a fresh pot of tea, Gamboa's mouth was drooping badly, his cup rattling on its saucer. Maritess slid a pillow behind his neck and lifted his feet onto the stool. He lay back and gave them a crooked little smile. "I'll just ... wait here," he said to his wife, "while you ... uh, show them ... uh ..." She squeezed his shoulders and bent down and kissed his good cheek. Then she opened the French doors that led to the patio and waved Diana and Jay ahead of her.

The moment she stepped outside, Diana felt a stab of disappointment. The curved slab of concrete had pebbles imbedded along the edge. It was everything the floor plan had promised. So why had she been picturing herself on a veranda, leaning on a rail, looking down on a grassy yard and a blue lagoon?

Maritess paused in the doorway, waiting for the cat. "Make up your mind," she told him. "Is it out or in?" He looked both ways and sniffed. Finally, he strolled onto the patio, and she slid the door shut. "Johnny still likes to eat breakfast out here," she said. "We used to sit out after dinner, take in the view, drink a brandy. For our health," she added with a sarcastic shake of her head as they walked to the edge of the patio. In the distance, beyond a large scraggly field that ended in bushes, trees, and a handful of houses, a sliver of water flashed silvery-white. "The second lagoon," Maritess said, pointing. "Very pretty."

"Yes," Jay agreed. "It's a beautiful view."

The cat rubbed against Diana's leg, and she reached down

to pet him. Closing her fingers softly around his tail, she opened her mouth to say a word or two in praise of the fresh air and got instead a nose full of diesel from another truck struggling up the hill. "What's your cat's name?" she asked, raising her voice over the cough and roar of the truck.

"Jasper. We got him from the Van Winckels."

Continuing the tour, Diana followed Maritess through the bedrooms and bathrooms, nodding and making polite comments, even though she'd already made up her mind. In Manila, she'd gone along with Jay's suggestion that they leave the house they were renting in Makati and move into the apartment on Roxas Boulevard far away from all her friends. She'd never lived in an apartment before, and she hadn't foreseen how frustrated she'd feel being cooped up in a box sixteen stories above the ground. She wasn't going to let him talk her into something she didn't like this time.

When they were ready to go, Jasper followed Maritess to the front door. She picked him up and draped him across her shoulder. "Poor Jasper. He has to stay here in Vanuatu." She scratched him behind the ears. "Yes, you do," she crooned. As she swiveled around, Jasper raised his chin from her shoulder and blinked at Diana. "I think he likes you. I haven't promised him to anyone yet, you know."

As soon as they were back in the car, Diana was sorry she hadn't at least asked to hold him. She imagined the pleasure of his weight in her arms, his fur, the warm, fluid drape of his body. She got in the car and fastened her seatbelt.

"Well?" Jay asked. "What do you think?"

"I think we should take him."

"I mean the house."

"The house? No way. It's too close to the road, the floor is too dark, and the lagoon's so far away you have to squint to see it."

"If you don't like it," he said, patting her hand as they backed down the driveway, "we'll find something else."

They'd barely left the Gamboas' house when the sun sank below the horizon, changing the look of everything. Now the fence posts seemed to have sprouted not branches but arms and legs, as though at any moment they would run off in search of their heads. The huge banyan tree beside the road rose up, dripping tangled vines and casting great elliptical blue shadows over the road.

There was still a modicum of light as they circled the roundabout, but a moment later they were enveloped in darkness, heading down a road choked on both sides and over their heads by the tree limbs. "Where the heck are we going?"

"The same way we came. Back to town."

She heard a smile in his voice. And then they were out of it—looking over a landscape of silhouetted trees and a scattering of houses, yellow lights winking from their windows, and Diana relaxed again.

31

"*H*urry, honey." Diana leaned out the door watching for the real estate agent, hoping she'd be early so they could unwrap the houses. That's how she imagined it, as though the houses were tied up in wrapping paper with bows on top—mysterious and wonderful. You'd think from the way she felt about this imagined house that they'd be buying it, not just renting. Regardless, the house would be theirs for the next two years. She'd been an expat long enough to know that a rented space was as close as she would come to a home away from home.

She jingled her keys and stepped outside. They were living at Cloud Nine Apartments now, in a garden apartment. The patio looked out on a lawn edged with a flowerbed and small frangipani trees. No water view, but it was only temporary.

"Hey, Jay. It's almost nine o'clock." *Come on, come on,* she whispered, shifting her weight, tapping one heel and then the other. She was wired this morning. She touched her cheeks. Happy. And beautiful. That's what Jay told her last night. *You're so beautiful.*

Bette Ferguson was waiting for them in the parking lot, one elbow hanging out the window of her weathered white Mercedes. "Over here," she called. The car door swung open, and her foot dropped to the pavement—slim ankle, high-heeled sandal, coral-painted toenails. "You must be Mr. and Mrs. McIntosh," she said, jangling her bracelets as she extended her hand. "May I call you Jay and Diana?"

"Please."

"We'll go to Seaside first," she said as soon as they were settled, Diana in the front, Jay in back. "Contrary to its name, Seaside is not by the sea. It's on the lagoon side of town." She turned around, lifting her oversized sunglasses, and smiled at Jay. "In Port Vila, things are seldom what they seem."

They rode east, away from the bay. Even with the windows open and a pine-scented deodorizer hanging from the mirror, the car smelled of tanning lotion, perspiration, and forgotten sandwiches. The lagoon was a large body of aqua water, probably two miles long, half a mile wide. It was sheltered and serene. Not a bad place to live.

"So, Bette," Jay said, leaning forward. "What brought you to Port Vila?"

The real estate agent made a face. "My former husband. The big investment counselor. Vanuatu's a tax haven, you know."

"Yes," Jay said. "So I'm told."

"The scumbag brought me out here and left me, sailed away with a skinny blonde on her ex-boyfriend's yacht. Now he's back in L.A., looking for another meal ticket. And I'm out here selling and renting real estate. Which I love," she added.

They rode in silence for a few minutes. Then Bette did a sharp right onto Captain Cook Avenue, drove a few hundred feet, and jerked to a stop in front of a wood-framed bungalow nestled between a giant mango tree and two Norfolk Island pines. "Here we are," she said.

Nice. Diana smiled over her shoulder at Jay.

"Just wait till you see the garden." Bette jumped out and waved for them to follow her around the side of the house.

The yard facing the lagoon was rimmed with flowers. In the corner, dozens of orchids hung from a big acacia tree. "And now, for the best part: Erakor Lagoon." She took off across the grass, somehow managing to walk normally despite wearing high-heeled sandals that sank into the sod. "Only a few steps down to your own private beach." She opened a wooden gate in the concrete block wall. "Follow me." Her heels were already clicking down the stairs. "You're gonna like this."

The lagoon was calm as a lake, not a single boat or swimmer in sight.

"It's a fabulous property for swimming and water skiing. Don't you think so?" Bette took Diana's hand. "You do ski, don't you?"

"Water ski?" Diana looked at the motorboat tied to the dock. She'd never even considered the possibility. "Not yet," she said. "I suppose I could learn."

"That's the spirit," Bette said. "How about you, Jay?"

"Yeah. When I was in high school. My friend had an eighteen-foot Chris Craft. Twin Evinrudes." He started up the dock toward the speedboat. "It could pull two skiers at once. We skied a little bit in college too. My, uh . . ." He cleared his throat. "My um . . . friend's friend had a nice little boat."

Oh god, Diana thought as she watched him bend over the boat as though there were something fascinating between its curved sides. He must have gone water skiing with his first wife. Twenty-year-old, bikini-clad Celeste.

The image stayed with her as they toured the house—a nice enough house, cozy with a restful colonial air. She had the feeling that Jay was avoiding her eyes. He lingered behind her as they walked into the kitchen. Then he ducked into the pantry, leaving Diana as the target of Bette's sales pitch.

"Just look at all these cupboards." Bette threw some doors open in the upper cabinet, slammed them shut, and pulled out a drawer. "I wish I had this many in *my* kitchen." She glanced at the pantry. When Jay didn't come out, she turned and pranced into the dining room. "Ceiling fans in every room." Her rings glittered over her head. "Romantic, don't you think?"

"Yes," Diana said. "Very romantic." She was picturing Celeste jumping the wake behind a speeding boat, her suntanned body sparkling with spray, blond hair flying.

"High ceilings, an elegant parquet floor." Bette's eyes followed the sound of banging cupboard doors and knuckles knocking on walls. "He's very thorough, isn't he?"

They were about to look at the bedrooms when Jay caught up with them. "We have a problem," he said. "Termites." Dusting off his hands, he led Diana back to the pantry. "See." He knocked on a wall. Knocked again in another place. "Hear the difference? See these little piles of fine sawdust?"

"Well," Bette said on their way out the door, "sometimes these charming wood-frame houses do succumb to the exuberance of tropical life." She closed the door with exquisite delicacy, gave it a pat, and turned around, ready to go. "Now, this next house we're going to see is brand new. Concrete and masonry construction throughout. A very creative design."

The houses in Nambatri, the area developed after Nambatu—"Number Two," Bette translated in case they hadn't caught it—were scattered. In the morning sun, the newer ones looked starkly naked. The rental they'd come to see was situated atop a small hill, not so much *for* the view, it seemed, but to *be* the view. Its Romanesque pillars and oversized double purple doors screamed pretension and bad taste. The inside was equally overdone—an entry dominated by a large empty koi pond, planters, and a carved floor-to-ceiling wooden screen. On the other side of the screen was an enormous space—a combination living area, master bedroom, and bath without a single wall or privacy partition between them.

"Doesn't it just take your breath away?" Bette said.

Diana wanted to like it, but she had to agree with the look on Jay's face. "It's very dramatic," she said, "but I can't see how anyone could actually live here."

"A rock star and his groupies maybe," Jay said. "Fill this big open space with cushions and futons." He shook his head. "Sorry, Bette. Not this house."

Bette chuckled and started for the door. "Cushions and

futons. You're absolutely right. I'll have to find a client who likes to throw parties. Orgies," she added, cackling and tripping on the purple threshold.

~~~~~

"This is crazy." Diana threw her handbag on the table. "Only two houses and neither of them worth considering."

Jay raised one shoulder as if to say, "What can you do?"

"Termites, a bedroom without walls." She kicked her sandals off and flopped down on the sofa.

"I'll call her Monday, tell her to let us know as soon as she finds something." Jay leaned close and kissed her cheek. "Port Vila is a small market, honey. We just have to be patient."

Jasper bent his tail into a question mark and peeped a small meow. "Come on up," Diana said, patting her knee. She hadn't thought Maritess would give up her cat so soon, but she'd gone along with Diana's request without complaint. And now here Jasper was, purring and warm and soft on her lap.

If she could just stop thinking about Celeste. Sometimes— when Diana was busy with her own life or feeling confident, content to just live in the moment—she could forget about her for months at a time.

"Juice?" Jay poked his head around the corner and held up a can of pineapple-orange.

"No thanks."

He disappeared into the kitchen, and she heard the rising tone of his juice filling a glass, the suck and rattle of the refrigerator opening, the cushioned thud of it closing. Celeste must have learned to water ski when she and Jay were young, when she could jump a wake as effortlessly as a cat jumps onto a chair.

Stop. She had to stop thinking about her. *That's exactly what brings her back. Transforms her from a will-o-the-wisp into* . . . Diana pressed her lips together. *A pebble in my shoe, a burr in my bra.*

Who would have thought the memory of Celeste would turn out to be such a torment? Hearing about her that first time had been a shock, but Diana didn't make the connection then between Celeste's one-time existence and her own. She groaned. A first wife, young and beautiful? How could she have assumed that wouldn't matter?

Suddenly she remembered one thing Jay had said that day at the Emerald City Café. It was about one of the women he had dated before he met Diana. He said she'd dropped him because she didn't want to compete with his dead-but-ever-present first love. At the time Diana had scoffed at the woman's concerns. And yet, here she was, seven years later, still competing with Celeste's memory.

She scratched Jasper behind the ears. Then she twisted around so she could watch Jay from behind as he ducked to look in the fridge. In the beginning, the fact that Celeste had been pregnant when she died had been just one more sad thing. But as time passed, the significance of that unborn baby—the baby who would have been Jay's first child—had grown ever larger in Diana's mind. And yet, after that day at the Emerald City Café, Jay had never again mentioned the child that might have been. Nor had she.

"Jay," she said.

"Yeah?" He bumped the door shut with his elbow and walked toward her.

"Do you ever . . .?"

He opened his eyes wide as though ready to take in anything she might say.

"Do you . . .?" But it wouldn't come out. Years of silence had made Celeste and the baby she'd carried a taboo subject. "I mean," she said, quickly recovering, "that thing with Hoffmann, was that a big disappointment for you?"

He shrugged. "Those things happen."

For some reason, his shrug annoyed her. He didn't mean it. She could tell from the look on his face. "That should have been your job," she said, persisting. She wasn't sure why she didn't just let it go.

"Yeah." He smiled. "That's what I thought at the time. But, hey, we're here now. It doesn't matter anymore."

"Really?"

"Of course not."

She nodded. Yes. She had got what she wanted. So what did it matter whether his motives for moving here were pure or, as Abby suggested, mixed? She let the cat down and stood up. "You know," she said. "It's still early. Why don't we go drive around? Get acquainted with the neighborhoods."

"Good idea." He threw back his head and finished his juice in one big gulp. "Sure you don't want some?"

32

*C*eleste was still in her thoughts as they walked to the car. Jay must have changed by the time Diana met him. Otherwise, wouldn't he have found a second wife more like his first? But then, what did she really know about Celeste? She'd seen photos of her, so she knew Celeste was blond and petite. And she'd seen the way she smiled when she leaned up against Jay. But all the rest . . . wasn't that just Diana's imagination? What made her think that Celeste was idealistic, that she always knew the right thing to say, that children loved her? How did she know that Celeste had no trouble at all finding her place in the world or that she'd never had second thoughts about her chosen profession as a teacher of small children?

She got in the car and immediately opened the window. This car they'd borrowed would probably always smell of cigarettes and beer. She pulled out a tissue and tried to wipe a stubborn spot off the dashboard. "I'll be glad when we get our own car."

"I have the duty-free form now," Jay said as he backed out. "I can place our order on Monday."

"Carole Anne told me we should order a white car." Diana smiled and shook her head as they turned onto the side street. "She says Port Vila is a small town and we don't want to stand out. What do you think that's all about?"

Jay chuckled. "I suppose if you were married to Marshall, you might not want everyone checking up on his comings and goings either. Or maybe she's just a very private person."

"Maybe. But I'd rather not fall in line on this one. I love color." She *did* love color, she thought. It was one of the great pleasures of life: color and form and everything beautiful. And, if she was going to admit it, there was something else behind her opposition. Car color was a small choice, but shouldn't this small decision be theirs?

"Fine. I understand we could order silver, white, bronze, black, or sea mist."

"Sea mist," she said without hesitation.

He grinned and patted her knee.

There was something else, too, she thought as they rode through Seaside and then up into the French Quarter. She didn't like being the kind of person who tried to hide her actions from the world. It felt sneaky. They passed a baby blue church with Vietnamese lettering now. A moment later they reached the Cathedral of the Sacred Heart. It was a mixed neighborhood, modest concrete block bungalows next to old colonial-style houses with wooden louvered windows. Nothing was extravagant, but even the smallest dwelling was brightened by the sunshine and softened by the foliage that surrounded it.

At a high point above the commercial center, Jay pulled over, and they got out. From the side of the road, a stand of African tulip trees covered with brilliant red blooms framed the town's variously shaped roofs and winding roads. In the curve of the bay, a boat sailed over turquoise water on its way to the Pacific. "If it weren't for the cars," Diana said, "this could be 1790 instead of 1990. I almost expect to see an old sailing ship out there by Iririki Island, a seaman scurrying up its mast, whipping out a spyglass to look for friendly natives."

"A peg-legged captain with a parrot on his shoulder?" Jay joked.

They got back in the car and continued exploring, this time in Tassiriki, an area east of town where mostly new houses looked out on the upper reaches of the first lagoon. It looked like a nice neighborhood, but there weren't any "for rent" signs. The only unoccupied houses were still under construction. Jay pulled over in front of one of them and stopped. "Do you want to look?"

The house was all empty spaces and concrete blocks—a great gray ship on a grassy green sea. It looked intriguing, though. "Sure," she said. "Why not?"

The roughed-in driveway was steep, wrapping around to the back of the house where it flattened out. Jay parked next to a maroon pickup and they both got out. Then, in the way of men at construction sites, Jay walked over to the Asian guy who was supervising a parade of ni-Vanuatu workers. The two men stood side-by-side for several minutes watching the workers unload stacks of tile from a flatbed before they exchanged a "hello" and a "*bonjour.*"

The man pointed at the tile. "*Blong Italia,*" he said, switching to Bislama. "*Emi gud tumas.*"

Diana walked away, leaving them on their own to supervise the workers and discuss the "very good Italian tile." She wanted to check out the view. It was hard going, though. The ground was littered with the jagged, cream-colored rock that had been blasted out to make room for the house's foundation. She edged around chunks of coral rock that were as big as a child and as sharp as sharks' teeth. She climbed over and around them. Then she waded through clumps of grass and weeds to the side of the house. The view from there was gentle—the land sloping down to one lagoon, a strip of jungle separating it from another, vines and grass and bushes covering every rock and strip of dirt.

"It looks like a nice place," Diana said as they drove away. "Too bad it's not finished yet."

"Yeah. It would have been a good house for us. Even if it were finished, though, it wouldn't be available."

"What do you mean?"

"Henri is building it for himself, his wife, his son, and the son's girlfriend."

That night as she climbed into bed, Diana thought about the ancient land hidden beneath the grass and vines. Ni-Vanuatu land, even now. The foreigners who lived there and paid rent for it felt as though it belonged to them, but it didn't and never would. Pulling the blanket up under her chin, she turned off the light and listened to the soft steady sound of Jay's shower.

The water stopped, and the shower door clicked open. His feet padded across the tiles. She heard the towel rack rattle and the whisper of the towel rubbing against his skin. He switched off the light, and as he opened the bathroom door, her heart fell. *He doesn't belong to you,* a voice seemed to be saying. *You're the renter, the interloper. The wife who came too late to bear fruit.*

33

The Cathedral of the Sacred Heart looked like a Catholic Church should—carved pillars, statues, stained glass windows. It had a French priest and even a bishop from Quebec. The one thing it lacked was an English-language mass. If you didn't speak French, you had to drive to the other side of town where the Anglophone Catholic community gathered on Sunday mornings in a small rectangular cinderblock chapel called Paray.

Mass was at nine. Diana and Jay arrived at 8:52.

"We're early this time," Jay whispered as they slid into a pew.

Diana nodded. Last week, for some reason she couldn't recall, they'd been late.

She tucked in her feet so Jay could pull the kneeler down and looked around the chapel. All the basics were there—the altar and crucifix, a small plaster statue of the Virgin Mary, votive candles, windows to let in the breeze. And butterflies, she noted as one fluttered through an unscreened open window. She dropped to her knees beside Jay and watched the butterfly zigzag across the side aisle. *Dear Lord,* she prayed, *please bless . . .* It lit on a white carnation in front of Mary's statue, a touch of brilliant yellow in a skimpy pink-and-white bouquet.

Dear Lord, she prayed, trying again, *forgive me . . .* She couldn't think how to continue, but she did seem to need forgiveness. *Forgive me, Lord for . . . pretending to sleep when. . . .*

Sighing, she sat back in the pew and crossed her legs. Whatever opportunity she wasted last night, God wasn't the one she hurt. Of course . . . She pressed her fingers into her temples. A sin against oneself was still a sin. There was no ready-made word, though, for what she'd done, or rather, what she had failed to do. Wasting a fertile day wasn't exactly on any list of sins she'd ever read. Her thoughts wandered as she sat not praying but mulling over any possible connection between her convictions and God's will. If she felt so strongly that she needed to have a child, wasn't that some kind of moral imperative? Didn't God also want the same thing for her, and . . .?

Suddenly the overhead projector lit up a screen. Someone straightened the transparency. The song leader's husband strummed a chord. And as the congregation stood to sing "Gather Us In," a delicate shadow fluttered over the hand-printed words on the screen.

During the readings, the butterfly drifted between the carnations and the altar, dipping its filmy yellow wings at one point dangerously close to the balding head of the old Australian priest. During the homily, when the priest stepped down from the altar, the little creature fluttered ahead, making his disjointed sermon even harder to follow. Finally, during the Eucharistic Prayer, she stopped watching her little yellow friend and let the familiar prayers take over.

"Father, it is our duty . . . always and everywhere to give you thanks."

Most Sundays Diana felt the beauty of the mass prayers lifting her beyond whatever blind alley her mind was stuck in. *Always. Everywhere.* It was like taking a deep breath and discovering more space in your lungs than you felt possible. Like looking up on a starry night, thrilling at the immensity of the universe.

The priest raised his arms. "We join with the angels and saints," he said, "in proclaiming God's glory."

They prayed for the pope and the bishop and all God's people, for their friends and relatives and for those who had "gone to their rest in the hope of rising again." *My father,* Diana prayed, *and Grandpa Walker. Also Celeste,* she added suddenly. *Celeste and her unborn baby. May they rest in peace.*

After mass, walking out the door and into the sunshine, Diana felt somehow lighter than when she entered.

"I liked your homily," Jay told Father Nolan. "Very thoughtful."

"The ageless wisdom of the Church," Diana murmured, smiling and squeezing Jay's hand. She was thinking of the mass prayers, how sensible it was to pray for the "faithful departed," the disembodied souls up there in heaven with "the angels and saints." She should have put Celeste on her prayer list a long time ago.

Walking across the grassy parking lot, Diana wrapped her arm around Jay's waist. "Love you," she whispered.

"I love you, too, honey."

34

"They should have a big bell for us to ring," Jay said. They were standing at the edge of the water waiting for a boat to take them across to the little offshore island tucked inside Mele Bay. The beach on Hideaway Island faced another side of the bay, though. It was a wonder the speedboat operator ever noticed people waiting to be ferried across from the pickup spot.

"Someone will see us before long." Diana swished her foot in the water. You couldn't really complain about waiting for the speedboat when Hideaway Island was only a nine-minute drive from town, so close they'd gone snorkeling there three times in the past month.

Their first trip to Hideaway Island had been with Carole Anne. Marshall should have been with her, but he'd been at a golf tournament. "He really did want to come," she'd assured them when they climbed into her car, "but this is an important tournament, one he's determined to win. Y'all know Marshall. Losing is not an option. Anyway," she said, as she pulled away from their apartment, "y'all are just gonna love the beaches here." She raised her hand from the steering wheel and counted them off on her fingers: "White Sand Beach, Black Sand Beach, Iririki Island, British Beach, Erakor Island. Oh, and Eton Beach," she said, changing hands. "Absolutely gorgeous, and super safe for the kids. We simply must have an office picnic there sometime. Hideaway, of course is much better for snorkeling. And so close—only nine minutes from town."

Nine minutes can be an eternity when you're getting a sales pitch all the way. Carole Anne rhapsodized about the "incredibly" calm, clear water in Mele Bay, the "fantastic" coral reefs, the fish, "every kind you can imagine," the dive shop and restaurant, the grass-roofed picnic tables on the beach. "And," she said, "it's never crowded. Y'all can always find a thatched-roofed beach hut with a table. *Fales* we call them."

Diana had been fully prepared to be disappointed. In her experience, a hard sell meant an inferior product. Hideaway Island, however, turned out to be everything Carole Anne promised.

"A simple bell," Jay said, "a frame to hang it on, that's all they'd need. They could even hang it from a tree."

Diana smiled. "Yeah, appropriate technology." With all the out-of-the-way places Jay visited, you'd think he'd be used to the inadequate infrastructure one routinely found in developing countries. Wherever he went, though, his first instinct was to find a problem and then figure out how to solve it. That was his job, finding ways to make life better for whole populations. Sometimes Diana wished he'd take a break from trying to improve the world. Especially on a day like this.

She reached out with her foot to stir the water, and a school of fingerlings scattered like silver sparks. *This is my life now*, she thought, filling her chest with clean, warm air. *My life in paradise.* Ever since that day in church when she'd prayed for Celeste and her baby, she'd felt something inside her loosening up. Fear, jealousy—whatever it was, it seemed to be fading away. And Diana was grateful for that. *Rest in peace, dear Celeste.*

A boat was leaving the island now, its back end spraying white as it curved away from shore.

"Here he comes," Jay said.

They picked up their bags and edged forward as the boat raced toward them. The young ni-Vanuatu boatman waited until he was seconds from crashing into shore before shifting into neutral. While Diana and Jay waded out knee-deep and climbed aboard, the boatman revved his motor and gazed into the distance. Then they were on their way, planing over the flat water. It was a short, exhilarating ride—the rush of air, the thrum of waves against the boat, the scatter-shot of spray flung up when you least expected it.

Their friends were already there—Saudur, Abby, and the twins, and Alexi and Suling. A glorious day at the beach lay ahead; warm sun and sand, cold beer and lemonade, tasty sandwiches. And snorkeling. Diana loved to snorkel. In the water, she was a fish, a silent observer in a strange undersea world.

Saudur and the boys were already in the water. Diana was quick to join them. Strapping on her snorkel and mask, she put on her fins and waded into the water. Soon she was swimming over coral that looked like blue-tipped trees, crystallized cauliflower, and bouquets of delicate pink flowers. She watched parrot fish, clownfish, and those tiny fish that dart out from the coral like electric blue sparks.

Snorkeling again after lunch, she spied one of the most fantastic fish in the ocean, a red and white lionfish in full display. It was hovering in the clear open water, his poisonous dorsal spines splayed around him like the ribbons and silk fans of a Chinese dancing girl. Since he didn't appear to be going anywhere, she took a chance and stayed for a while, bobbing over him like a jellyfish to admire his otherworldly beauty. It was a monster's beauty, drawing her in with the bright colors and the grace and transparency of his fins. They were like wings. An angel's wings and a devil's face. She found herself floating close enough to see that he had red stripes in his eyeballs. It frightened her, then, how close she'd let herself get, and she quickly breast-stroked away without kicking, holding her torso and legs high in the water and flat. She didn't get out of the water, though, not yet.

The only ones who stayed in longer than she did were Saudur and the twins. "Those daffy fellows," Abby said when Diana finally spread her beach towel in the sand beside hers. Suling was snoozing on a towel to their left. Jay and Alexi were drinking beer at the table a few yards behind them. Abby shaded her eyes with one hand and scanned the water for snorkels. "Those boys will grow gills before they get out. Saudur's just as bad. He thinks a beach trip is a research and teaching opportunity."

Diana bent at the waist and shook the excess water out of her hair. "It must be nice for the twins," she said, dropping onto her towel beside Abby.

"Yeah. Every picnic's a bloomin' oceanography lesson. And they still haven't eaten lunch." Abby stood up. "Enough," she said, teetering as she stepped into her flip flops. "Mama to the rescue."

Diana lay back on her towel. The breeze in the pandanus palms was just a whisper, the waves gentle as they sloshed in and rattled out through the broken coral. Jay and Alexi's voices murmuring softly over their beers barely came through. She really should have washed the salt off her face and applied some sunscreen, but she felt immobilized, sun-drugged, lulled by the deep slow tune of Suling's breathing. Tomorrow she would sketch the fish she saw today. The lionfish would be a challenge, but now, with her eyes closed, she could see him clearly, his spines and fins, the stripes in his eyes.

"Got 'em." Abby plopped down on her towel.

Diana raised her head and looked around. "Who?"

"My blokes." Abby pointed with her chin to where Saudur was walking, mask in hand, two child-sized snorkels plowing through the shallow water at his side.

"Good for you." Diana sat up. She pulled her straw hat out of her bag, and as she sat, one knee bent, straightening the brim, she glanced over her shoulder at Jay and Alexi. Slivers of light slipped through the palm-thatched roof of the fale, turning their black hair a dark mahogany and dancing on Jay's broad back. Across the table from him, Alexi fidgeted, his attention scattered like a distracted puppy. An irresistibly attractive puppy, she had to admit. In a Kung Fu movie—she'd seen enough of them in Manila—they would cast him as the cute boyfriend, not the sober hero. But then, Alexi wasn't the actor in the family.

Lying back, she covered her face with the hat and inhaled the sweet straw smell. She wondered if Suling missed the life she'd lived before Alexi whisked her away from her acting career. Diana imagined her on screen with a sword, leaping and twirling.

Soon, overcome by warmth radiating down from the sun and up from the sand, she sank into a sun-dazed lethargy. Before she dropped off completely, she felt Jay at the edge of the towel, urging her to scoot over so he could cuddle up next to her. She was vaguely aware of Alexi and Suling whispering and gathering up their snorkels and fins. Then, nothing.

She was still sleeping when she felt Jay jerk violently away from her and spring to his feet. He sprinted away, electrifying the air with alarm and kicking sand on her. Her immediate reaction was annoyance.

Later, it struck her how wrong it was that Jay and Alexi had been the first to respond. It should have been Saudur. He was the diver, the fisheries expert. He would have known exactly how to save Suling. But Saudur was up in the café chowing down on sandwiches and soda when she panicked.

And what about her and Abby? They should have been right there watching Suling every time she dipped her toe in the water. *You'll love snorkeling,* they'd told her on Thursday at their Scrabble game. *It's easy. We'll show you how.* And when she wouldn't stop frowning and chewing her pretty scarlet fingernail, Abby had reached across the tiles and squeezed her other hand. "Listen, luv," she said, "if you so much as swallow a mouthful of salty water, I'll drag you back to shore myself."

"Or I will," Diana had said, bragging that she was a good swimmer and mentioning the "A" she got in lifesaving. She'd laughed then, thinking of her high school swimming class, the make-believe rescues of fellow classmates.

But when the time came, when a friend actually did need to be rescued, Diana and Abby were sleeping. Which left Alexi and Jay.

By the time Diana opened her eyes, Jay had already raced across the sand and razor-sharp broken coral and was high-stepping through the shallow water. He was in deep water now, swimming, his arms revolving like Quixote's windmill in a storm.

She must have wasted a second or two trying to make sense of it, and then she too was running barefoot over the broken coral, high-stepping the waves, instinctively calculating the relative advantage of running vs. swimming in the shallow water as she strained to see what was happening.

Beyond Jay, she saw an arm break the surface, then a head. The water was churning in a way that brought only one thing to mind: sharks. She imagined a shark shaking its victim, its smooth animal body writhing as the struggling swimmer fought back. Suling or Alexi. Then Jay. And her. She winced at the thought of the shark's teeth, its evil beady eyes. Sharks, always the first thing you thought of. Not barracudas or sting rays or . . . She pushed off the bottom in a shallow dive.

Ah, my god! Her heart leapt to her throat. How could she have forgotten? The lionfish! She should have warned them about that small dangerous fish.

Reaching long with every stroke, she kept her fingers tight together and kicked as hard and fast as she could. Head to the side and breathe.

A wave forced water down her throat, and she coughed it back up. Easy enough to breathe in a swimming pool. Easy when you weren't scared to death about your husband.

Kick and stroke. Stroke. Breathe.

All those fins on a lionfish, those beautiful, poisonous, porcupine spines. Just how poisonous were they? How fast acting? Was there an antitoxin? And if there was, who would have it?

By the time she reached them, her chest was burning. Her arms felt like sunken logs. Suling's mask and snorkel bobbed on the waves. No shark fin, but the water was swirling with the struggle. Suling rose head and shoulders out of the water and twirled like a swordsman, her arms slashing, her face, a Chinese terror mask. But where were Jay and Alexi? All she could see was an arm and then a dark head.

In a split second she understood. She'd seen this very same scenario before. A swimmer cries out for help. Someone jumps in to save her, but the panicked swimmer, fighting for air, climbs on top of the would-be-rescuer. And now two people are fighting for their lives, kicking, clutching, gasping. Another Good Samaritan jumps in. The woman and the first rescuer grab for him, and soon the Good Samaritan has become the bottom man on their underwater totem pole. If not for the third rescuer who comes at them from behind and below, they might all drown.

And that was exactly what Diana had to do—get them from behind and below. She circled around, and suddenly Alexi's head broke the surface, and then Suling's. She clawed at him, and they both went under. Who the hell was she supposed to save first? And where in the name of God was Jay?

She dove below the surface, pulling herself down. Without a mask, everything was milky, a mass of foam and bubbles and . . . there, that was Jay's foot, his leg, the hem of his blue trunks lifting over the white lining. She came at him from behind. Bending her knees, she coiled her body and struck, kicking Alexi away as she grabbed Jay's hair and reached diagonally across his chest and under his arm. Even as she freed him, her mind was racing, figuring out her next move. Alexi and Suling had been there longer, probably swallowed more water. Suling might at this moment be suffering from the effects of a lionfish sting. True, all of it true.

But Jay was the one she loved.

Scissor-kicking to the surface, her arm wrapped tight across his shoulder and chest, she swam one-armed toward the shore.

"Su . . . ling," he coughed, gasping for air.

"Don't . . . struggle. I'll get her."

"No. Too . . . late."

She tightened her grip and kicked harder. The density of his body made it hard to keep both their heads above water and still make much forward progress. When she looked up, there was Abby swimming toward her.

"I'll take him," she said.

Diana shook her head. Why couldn't Abby just go get the others?

Abby kept coming, though—her clumsy stroke, her hair hanging like corkscrews around her head. "Hand him over. Go." She raised her chin toward Alexi and Suling. "You swim better."

It was true, but . . .

"Here." Abby reached out.

And Diana handed him over, realizing—too late—how heavy he'd become. "Don't let go," she begged. "Please."

"I've got him." Abby grabbed hold of Jay and started towing him away.

"Abby . . ." He looked limp, almost lifeless. "Abby, is he . . . ?"

"Go."

And she did, trusting him to Abby as she swam in the opposite direction.

In the distance, the water near where she'd last seen Alexi and Suling was roiling. A head popped up and then disappeared. She'd get Alexi first, she decided, come at him from below and behind. She swam a little closer and then slipped below the surface. On her left, a cliff of hazy pink, blue, and white coral soaked up the light. On her right was open water. A triggerfish flashed past. She was stroking toward the twisting bodies and pumping legs, bright blue fins on two of the four feet, when she saw the lionfish. It was only yards away, a mass of orangey-red stripes, tantalizing and confusing—stripes on its body showing through stripes that cut across its filmy fins. She stopped, and as it swam in front of her, she could see the stripes on its gnarled face and in its eyes.

She had to come up for air. A gasping breath and she was down again, directly behind Alexi. Unless her stinging eyes deceived her, his back was marked with red stripes. She didn't see blood, but if there was some, wouldn't sharks be close behind? Suling was grasping his upper arm. In a single motion, Diana grabbed both of their arms, pushing Alexi down and Suling up and away. By some miracle, Suling let go. Even the death grip of fear eventually tires and loosens.

Diana was losing focus. As she reached across Alexi's chest, she saw Suling, slipping below the surface. How could she save them both? Her heart was pounding. She had to hurry. "Stop struggling." She gripped Alexi's arm.

He tried to twist away from her. "No," he cried. "No-o-o."

She dug her fingers into his flesh. Then she put her head down and started swimming. Where was everyone? Why didn't somebody come and help her?

When she looked up again, she saw a head, two arms slicing neatly through the water. "Saudur, is that you?"

He waved and kept coming.

Hurry, she thought, and when he was almost there, she released her grip on Alexi and gave him a push. "Take him," she shouted. "I have to get Suling."

She flipped over and swam back. With her head down and eyes open, she followed the now-familiar underwater landscape toward the spot she remembered seeing Suling go under. When she raised her head to breathe, there was nothing breaking the surface. No one.

Daddy, she prayed. *Help me.*

She saw bubbles. Suddenly Suling's head bobbed up, and Diana was looking into the eyes not of her friend but of a wild, dangerous adversary. Quickly she made a surface dive. *Behind and below. Behind and below.* As she started up, Suling turned, and Diana changed course. Maybe she should surface and start again. Her lungs were crying for air. And she was afraid. Suling was the better athlete—a dancer and a martial arts expert. For the first time that day, Diana realized this might not end well. She could die trying to save her friend.

She hesitated a moment. Then she pulled herself up through the turquoise water. "I've got you," she gasped, catching Suling across the chest. "You're going to be all right. Yes, yes," she crooned in Suling's ear. "You're okay now." She felt Suling go limp, her head resting on Diana's shoulder. Thank goodness! She wouldn't have had the strength to fight her.

Even so, it was hard to keep them both above water and still make any progress toward shore. The waves, which Diana had barely noticed before, splashed over her head now and into her mouth. They made her stomach turn with their sudden lifts and drops.

When she saw Saudur, his strong, easy strokes cutting through the waves, she stopped swimming and wept from sheer weariness and relief.

"I'll take her," he said.

"Jay?" she asked as Saudur placed Suling over his shoulder. "Is he all right?"

But Saudur had turned and was already swimming away. If he answered, she couldn't hear it. She started after him, but she couldn't lift her arms above the water. She was too exhausted. So she laid her head to one side and propelled herself forward with a clumsy sidestroke. It was all she could manage.

She was in shallow water when she heard Jay's voice. She tried to stand and come to him, but her legs collapsed under her.

"Honey," he shouted again. And he was running and falling and running again. "Diana. Sweetheart."

35

It was embarrassing—Alexi and Suling thanking her, apologizing, Jay getting all dramatic. Not that the situation didn't call for a little drama, some tearful hugs maybe, some exclamations of *Thank God you're safe!* But Jay didn't stop there. On their way back to shore, he paused several times to hold her, his eyes so soft and soulful that Diana had to look away.

"I was afraid I'd lost my wife again," he said, his voice quavering like an actor in a soap opera. She was too exhausted to grasp exactly what he was saying, too close to drowning right there in three feet of water.

Then the others came, Saudur holding her elbow, Abby helping her lie down. Diana's muscles, responding to the dry, sand-cushioned towel and the promise of rest, simply gave way. She closed her eyes. When she opened them again, she was presented with a jigsaw puzzle of open mouths, dark nostrils, and pinched eyebrows. A chorus of *Diana, Diana, Diana.*

She squinted, trying to focus on their faces. Alexi was hovering over her. "I'm so sorry," he sputtered, his face as pale as bleached coral. "I should have been able to save her. My wife," he sobbed. "I almost lost her. I'm so . . . so . . . sorry."

Sorry? For what? Wasn't Diana the one who kicked him to get Jay loose? "No," she croaked. "*I'm* . . . sor . . . ry." But he turned away, coughing, and Suling took over, crying and apologizing. And it was true that Suling had reacted badly, but Diana should have warned her about the lionfish. That beautiful, venomous fish that brushed against Suling. Or maybe just frightened her. Unless she was frightened by something else. Or maybe she just swallowed too much water.

It was all too complicated. Diana's temples were pounding. Her stomach felt queasy. Everyone was looking at her. Finally she curled up on her side and closed her eyes, and they left her alone. But before she fell asleep, she remembered what Jay had said as he was helping her to shore. "Again," he'd said. He'd been afraid of losing Diana to drowning the way he lost Celeste.

When she woke up, Alexi and Suling had already gone, and Abby and Saudur were wading out to the speedboat. "Bye-bye," Abby shouted as Saudur herded the twins ahead of him. Jay brought Diana a bottle of lemon squash, and she sat sucking the sweet, carbonated liquid through a straw while he took the snorkeling gear to a faucet to wash off the salt. When the boat came back, Jay helped her walk out to it and lifted her over the side. At Mele Beach, he lifted her out again. That Jay had recovered so quickly, that he could shoulder her weight on the way to the car and still carry both bags, didn't really surprise her. Jay was the strong one. On land anyway.

Nine minutes later they were back at Cloud Nine, Jay unpacking the car while Diana stood in the dining room thinking she had to cook something for dinner. She gripped the back of a chair and stared at the refrigerator, trying to remember what was inside. Green beans, she thought, tomatoes. Maybe a cucumber.

"We could skip dinner," she said.

"Are you kidding?" Jay's head snapped around. "I'm starved."

She knew that look, the unreasoning, angry look of his hunger. "But I can't think of anything to cook."

"Let's eat out then."

She groaned. "I'd have to clean up."

"This is Vanuatu. You don't have to dress up. You can just take a quick shower. Come on. I'll help."

He turned on the shower. Then he laid out a towel and helped her pull her T-shirt over her head.

"Now," she groaned as she peeled off her bathing suit and stepped into the shower. "I have to decide what to wear."

"Don't worry. I'll take care of it."

And he did. When she finished with her shower, she found a soft, easy-to-wear sundress on the bed.

The logical place to eat, the closest, was Jenny's Terrace, "good food in a casual setting." The restaurant, part of Cloud Nine Apartments, was on the other side of the building above the office. Only one flight up, but still, Diana's legs shook with the effort.

"You'll feel better after you eat," Jay assured her.

The ni-Vanuatu waiter who escorted them to their table was formal in a white shirt and tie. He pulled Diana's chair out and asked if the table would be satisfactory, courtesies that added a touch of class to a smallish restaurant in a middle-of-the-road apartment building. The menu offered burgers, sandwiches, and spaghetti, but also leg of lamb, spicy coconut crab, and veal paupiettes.

When Diana's curried grouper arrived, she pushed the plate back and closed her eyes. It was just too much—all that fish and rice, the spicy fragrance of the coconut sauce.

Jay stuffed a piece of steak into his mouth. "You need to eat," he said.

She took a deep breath. Reluctantly she picked up her fork and tried a small bite of rice and then a small sample of rice and fish. Jay was right. With every bite, she felt that much better. When she finished the rice and grouper, she started on the salad. It was small and colorful, papaya and red onions with thinly sliced ginger, capers, and oil and vinegar on a bed of lettuce. She started to say that they should grow papaya trees at their house—as soon as they found one. But Jay was staring at her, a strange smile on his lips. "What?" she asked.

"Nothing." He reached across and took her hand. "I was just thinking how lucky I was to be rescued from almost certain death by such a beautiful woman."

"You weren't about to die." She pulled her hand away. The picture he painted wasn't her. The Diana she knew was as ordinary as white rice. "It was luck," she said.

He shook his head. "More than that. You were brilliant, honey. And strong. I didn't know you were so strong."

"I'm not particularly strong. I just knew what to do." She stabbed a bite of papaya and onion. "You can thank my dad for that."

"Your dad?"

"Yeah. It's funny, I hadn't thought about it for years. For decades. But when I saw the way Suling was fighting and pulling you and Alexi under, I remembered something that happened when I was a kid." She paused to savor the ginger. It was pickled, just the right complement to the papaya's sweetness.

"So," he said, leaning closer, his elbows on the table. "What happened?"

"We were at this little lake, Lake Surprise. Daddy and I were swimming. Mom and Andrew . . . I don't know." She shrugged. "They were probably sitting under a tree, sketching and reading, unless Andrew was cannonballing off the high dive." She took another bite of fish, crunching through its crispy crust and licking the coconut curry sauce off her lips.

"And?" Jay sliced off a piece of steak and popped it in his mouth.

"Anyway, there was a commotion on the other side of the dock. Some woman thought she was drowning—even though she was only five or six good strokes from the dock. It seemed to me—in my childish arrogance—that I could dogpaddle farther than that."

Diana cleared her throat and looked away. "Naturally," she said, "the woman's friend and another person, some good Samaritan, thought it would be simple to pull her out. A perfectly reasonable expectation." She glanced quickly at Jay. "I mean, who would think the person you're trying to help would turn on you? But the woman was out of her mind with fear, so pumped up with adrenaline and frantic to keep her head above water that she climbed on top of her would-be rescuers and just about drowned them."

Jay looked at the scraps of meat on his plate and nodded.

"Anyway . . ." Diana put her knife down. "I assume that's what happened. All I knew was, people were shouting, everyone heading in the same direction. I dogpaddled over and waited my turn to climb the ladder. Daddy was way ahead of me." She smiled, remembering his pale body as he hoisted himself onto the dock, ran toward the other end of it, water streaming off his body, and dove. A perfect racer's dive. "He came at them from below and behind," she said, "catching them unawares."

"Smart."

"Mmm." She smiled, pleased. Jay and her dad would have liked each other. "I heard people talk about it as I stood on the dock."

"How did he know what to do?"

She shrugged. "I never asked. In fact, I don't remember that we ever talked about what happened." Afterwards Daddy would have plopped down on their beach blanket. Mom would have handed him a towel to dry off. Then he'd lean back on his elbows. "Hey, Linda," he'd say to her, "how 'bout one of those tuna sandwiches you have in the basket?"

"How old were you?" Jay asked. "Eight, nine?"

She thought for a moment. It must have been the summer after first grade. "Seven," she said.

"Amazing! And you remembered all this time."

"I guess so." It did seem strange that she'd have a vivid memory of something that happened so long ago. "Maybe I dreamed it."

He laughed and patted her arm. "That would be even more amazing, a dream manufactured for the express purpose of one day saving your husband's life."

"No, it really happened." She stabbed the last bite of papaya. "I'm sure it did."

The waiter took their plates and returned moments later with a dessert trolley. They made their choices, coconut pie and soursop a la crème, and then retired to the open-air terrace.

"I'm feeling better," Diana said as she licked the rich, fruity dessert off her spoon. "Almost energetic."

"Saved by dessert."

"And coffee." She *was* feeling better—still a little embarrassed by Jay's praise, and yet enjoying that, too. She'd forgotten what a pleasant little jolt something like this could give to her self-worth.

She reached across the table for his hand. In the muted candlelight—one squat candle inside a darkened holder—his features flickered on and off. In and out like waves. Behind him, darkness extended out across the terrace and the parking lot and the edge of town all the way to the ocean. The endless, deep, dangerous ocean.

He squeezed her hand. "My lifesaver," he said, as though he'd read her thoughts.

The moon that night was nearly full. On their way back to the apartment, they paused and watched its reflection quiver on the surface of the swimming pool.

Later, cuddling in bed, Diana's thoughts strayed for an instant to Celeste. She would always be young and beautiful, but she would never be the one who saved Jay's life.

36

*D*iana wasn't stupid. She didn't expect Vanuatu to turn her into a totally different person. No place can do that. But now, after two and a half months in this quiet, beautiful place, she was beginning to feel different. She felt it in her shoulders and neck. She felt it in the comfortable looseness of her muscles as she walked in the mornings exploring the town and countryside. She felt it in the ease of her laughter when she was with Abby and Suling.

Yes, it was true; she was beginning to feel less stressed. But at this point, it was all just provisional. After two and a half months, they still hadn't found a house; they still hadn't been able to unpack their furniture and dishes and the personal belongings that waited at the port in a shipping container. And until they did find a house and settled into it, she wouldn't truly be able to relax. Until then, their existence in Vanuatu would feel as fragile and vulnerable as a spider web on the wheel of a bicycle.

Bette was losing interest, though, starting to take subtle jabs at them for being too picky. But really! She hadn't shown them a single house in the past eight weeks that she could possibly have believed they'd like.

To cheer themselves up after disappointing outings with her, they often dropped by the house in Tassiriki that was under construction. Jay liked chatting with Henri—although how they communicated in their crazy mix of French, English, and Bislama was a mystery. Diana left them to "supervise" the work while she walked around the grounds, gazing at the view and watching the house take shape. As time went by, she and Jay stopped by at odd moments, sometimes two or three times a week. That was their problem. They'd allowed the Tassiriki house to become the model for the kind of house they wanted Bette to show them.

Without intending to, they'd fallen in love with the house, at least Diana had. Which was foolish. Even if they were willing to wait for it to be finished, it would never be available. Henri was building it for his own family, his wife, his only son, his son's French girlfriend, and their future children. It would be his masterpiece. He wasn't about to rent it out to them, no matter how many times they stopped by to look at it.

Be reasonable, Diana told herself now as she stood waiting for Jay's plane to land. They needed to stay away from Henri's house and set their sights on the available options. As she turned her head toward the far end of the runway, a plane taxied toward them. An Air Calédonie 737. She let go of her musings and allowed herself to enjoy the drama of return—children pounding on the chain link barrier that ran along one side of the open-air deck, women giggling their anticipation. Diana, her chest rising and falling, edged forward, maneuvering into a spot between a solitary white woman and a bevy of small ni-Vanuatu children.

She'd wanted to go with Jay on this trip, but he'd convinced her that Kiribati was the worst possible place he could take her. "Believe me," he said, "you'd hate it. I'll take you on my next mission. I promise."

"There it is," somebody shouted.

A child grabbed Diana's skirt and quickly released it, embarrassed.

The plane was unmistakable, large and white, a red hibiscus prominent on its tail. Curling her fingers through the metal links, Diana willed it to move quickly into position.

The first person down the steps was a ni-Vanuatu government type in a safari suit, serious until he recognized his son's voice and broke into a big white-toothed smile. Next came a tourist family and then a group of Melanesians buried to the ears in leis and greeted by a mini-riot of shouts and laughter from the observation deck. Tourists, business travelers, and families clattered down the stairway.

"Mom, Dad." The woman next to Diana pounded on the mesh. "Up here." An older couple in matching purple and green Hawaiian shirts frowned and then, seeing her, smiled and waved furiously. The woman left in a flurry of lemony-sweet perfume and perspiration, the heavy metal door sucking shut behind her.

Diana leaned her forehead against the mesh and watched a couple of stragglers stride across the tarmac and disappear into the terminal. Then no one. Even the wind stopped blowing. It wasn't like Jay to be so slow. She stared into the arched opening in the plane's bright white side.

Finally he appeared, smiling good-bye to the flight attendant. Not so very late after all, other passengers right behind him. He jogged down the stairs and took off across the pavement, his heavy shoulder bag bouncing on his hip. Diana watched for him to raise his eyes, and when he didn't, she called down to him. "Hey, Jay."

Without breaking his step, he looked up, waved, and smiled. A distracted smile that flashed and disappeared. As she pulled open the heavy door and hurried downstairs to meet him, Diana had a sinking feeling that Vanuatu wasn't working out for Jay the way it was for her.

When he came out of immigration, she was waiting at the baggage carousel knowing what to expect. The warm hug, the slightly distracted look in his eyes. She knew. It was never easy for him to shake off everything that had been occupying his mind for the past week or two in the space of a single flight. He would want to talk about it.

"So," she said. "How was Kiribati?"

"Oh, lord!" He shook his head. "I've never seen a place with so little margin for error."

"Oh? What do you mean?"

The belt hadn't started yet, but they were both focused on the little door at the end of it, watching for suitcases to emerge.

"Even if they do absolutely everything right," Jay said, slicing the air with his hands, "it's questionable whether thirty-three scattered atolls can support life for so many people."

She raised her eyebrows. "How many people live there?"

"About seventy-five thousand."

"That's all? In the whole country?"

"That's plenty," he said with a sad little laugh, "when the people are all crowded onto thin strips of land no more than a meter or two above sea level, when their main source of water is captured rain, and when the soil is so thin and chalky they can hardly grow anything except coconuts."

The baggage carousel groaned to a start, and everyone moved a step closer.

"They must have fish," Diana said, her eyes automatically tracking the first few suitcases making their way around the carousel.

"An ocean full. But they depend on the lagoons and reefs, and they're becoming more polluted every day."

Diana nodded and waited for him to tell her what D-TAP was going to do about it.

"We're giving them an interest-free loan to rehabilitate and expand what is at present a totally inadequate sewerage and sanitation system." He swung his suitcase off the carousel and turned to Diana. "How's everything here?"

"Good. Except I haven't heard a word from Bette all week."

"We can call her tomorrow." He pulled out the handle on his suitcase and started for the exit.

The rich aroma of espresso and warmed croissants filled the air as they passed the café in the lobby. Suddenly the chatter of passengers and their friends was interrupted by the loud scraping of an iron chair against the floor tiles. "Hey, Jay."

Diana turned to see Alexi brushing past the potted plants that marked the edge of the café area.

"Oh, Diana, hi." Dropping his hand-carry, Alexi turned away from her and grabbed Jay's elbow. "You're not going to like this." He frowned and lowered his voice. "They hired that consultant." He looked over his shoulder. "The guy from Melbourne."

"What?! He was the only one with no background in sanitation systems."

Alexi threw his hands up and rolled his eyes in an appeal to the god of the ceiling. "That's the way it goes."

"Son of a bitch!"

Diana backed away and pretended to be interested in the couple pushing three oversized suitcases up to the counter.

"I can't believe it."

Alexi snorted and leaned close. "Now you understand what I've been telling you."

Diana turned back just in time to see Jay's slow eye-blink and the disappointed look on his face, as though he couldn't get over expecting the world to be better than it was—as though he couldn't stop tilting at windmills.

Alexi just shrugged and tossed his hand-carry over his shoulder. "I'm off to Fiji." He took a few steps and turned back. "Hey, do me a favor, will you? Look in on my wife. She's in the family way, you know." He raised his eyebrows, beaming.

~⁓⟋

What? Suling was pregnant? That was great news! Really it was. And yet Diana sighed as she looked out the car window at the spindly, wind-blown palm trees and the dun-colored cattle, staring and chewing. They rounded a corner and drove into a spray of raindrops—a rainbow-making mist, except there was no rainbow.

Time to turn the wipers on. She glanced at the speedometer. Time to slow down.

It may have been just seven minutes from the airport to town, but the way Jay was driving, they'd make it in five. He squealed around a corner, past a group of huts and small, square concrete block buildings. The mist became rain, and finally he switched on the wipers.

She shifted her weight as they approached the turn to Cloud Nine. But when he didn't turn, she had to grab the armrest to keep her balance. "Hey! Where are you going?"

He was clutching the steering wheel with both hands, leaning forward as though he could barely see through the rain-splashed window. "Just driving," he said without inflection.

Giving him a sideways glance, she shook her head and sat back to wait for him to calm down. When she was a kid, sometimes her mom would get cabin fever. Then she'd tell Diana and Andrew to pile into the car. "We're going for a ride," she'd say, "just for the fun of it." And it was fun. When you live in a small town surrounded by fields and forests, rivers and streams, you can just drive and drive, watching the world go by. But where could you go on a small island like this? And why go on a drive when you're obviously still angry about that consultant?

Within a couple of minutes, the main part of town was behind them. They crested a hill and turned. Oh, great! He wasn't heading for the Tassiriki house, was he? "Jay, where are you going? Why don't we just go home?"

"Just give me some time, honey. I need to unwind."

"But if you think the consultant is unqualified . . ."

"There's not a damn thing I can do about it. Let's just drop it."

Even if he hadn't been planning on visiting the Tassiriki house, his muscles remembered, and he turned into the driveway, kicking gravel all the way up the hill. Before she could say anything else, he was out of the car, dashing through the rain, balancing on the boards that served as a makeshift sidewalk to the back door. Oh, well. Maybe standing with Henri and watching the guys work would help him get his mind off things that were beyond his control.

Through the rain-streaked windshield, you could imagine the house as it would look when it was finished—the walkway leading to a wide entrance door, the white walls, the kitchen window. Though she'd told herself to stay away from this house, she was here now. And she was curious. Pocketing the car keys, she jumped out and ran through the warm tropical rain, careful not to slip on the boards.

She paused in the doorway, struck by how much the interior had changed since the last time she'd seen it. When Jay was away she'd driven by almost every day, but she hadn't gone inside. Now, instead of the dull gray of concrete, the house sparkled with the white Italian tile they'd seen the men unload that first day. Perfect squares of white covered the entry, marched down three steps, and spread over most of the dining room where more stacks of tile waited to finish the job.

Diana wiped her feet on a mat and wiped them again. Then she turned into the kitchen. Oh my gosh! The cabinets were already up. A ni-Vanuatu workman was kneeling on the counter concentrating on laying a perfectly even coat of varnish on an upper cabinet. Completing a stroke, he turned and greeted her. "*Moning, misis.*"

"*Moning.*" She took a moment to stand where the kitchen sink would be and looked out the window. It was a comforting scene, a flat cleared area bordered by two huge false rubber trees on the right and a strip of jungle climbing the hill behind. A small area outside the window was set off with a low circular curb. If this were her house, she'd turn that space into an herb garden.

Escaping the cutting pungent smell of varnish, she gave a little wave to the worker and left. He really should have a protective mask, she thought.

Jay and Henri were standing in the dining room watching a couple of workers. They weren't talking. And when they greeted her, both their faces looked drawn. Rainy-day faces. Construction-problem faces. Money-problem faces. Despite their sour mood, she stayed for a while, watching the men work. They were building the stairway to the upper suite, the man below, measuring and cutting the treads and risers; the man above, fitting and hammering them into place. It was an amazing feat, building a stairway in the air.

The living room floor was still unfinished, but the windows were in. One whole side of the room was floor-to-ceiling windows and sliding glass doors facing the terrace and the lagoons. She hoped Henri's son appreciated all the care his father had put into designing and building this house for their family.

Rain fell in Vanuatu on a whim, Diana thought as they rolled down the driveway and away from the Tassiriki house. No big build-up, just a playful splattering of moisture, and then . . . poof. It was all over and the sky was blue again. At least that's the way it had been since they arrived. "Henri seemed to be having a bad day." She glanced at Jay, wishing his mood would blow over as quickly as a Vanuatu rainstorm.

"Yeah. He's down in the dumps all right. Last night he got a call from his son, Antoine. The kid announced he wasn't coming back to Vanuatu. His French girlfriend wants to stay in the French territory of New Caledonia, or better yet, move to Paris."

"Oh!" Diana felt a surge of anger that a child could discard his parents so easily.

Jay sighed. "That's love for you. Or the result of having a bossy girlfriend. Either way, he turned down a suite in the biggest, most beautiful house Henri ever built. That has to hurt."

She patted Jay's knee, as though he were the one who needed comforting.

"I get the feeling," Jay said, "that Henri considers the house more than a milestone in his career. I think he sees it as a symbol of his plans for his family, for its growth and continuation and its expanding prominence in Port Vila society."

They stared at the road ahead. She too had left her country with little thought for her mom, half a world away and living alone. Like lightning on a far horizon, the thought flashed past her and was gone. She had something more urgent in mind. She looked at Jay, raising her eyebrows in a silent question.

"Henri and his wife aren't going to move into the house," he answered. "He thinks it's too big for the two of them."

She frowned. "Did he actually say that?" Every time she saw Jay and the builder together, long silent stretches of time passed between them. They spoke in gestures and half sentences of French, English, and Bislama.

"Yeah. That's exactly what he said." He smiled for the first time since he got off the plane. "My high school French is coming back. Better yet, my ear is getting attuned to Bislama."

Diana nodded. In the past two months, she too was beginning to get the hang of Bislama. "So, Henri isn't going to move into his house."

"He's not." Jay turned onto the road that led back to their apartment. "The house may now be available, and yes, we both love it. But, no, I didn't bring up the subject of renting it. How could I? He and I are friends. I wouldn't feel right jumping in to take advantage of his misfortune."

37

She supposed it wasn't surprising that Henri had been the first one to bring it up. His son may have spoiled his plans and broken his heart, but Henri was a businessman. And he liked Jay. A few days later on their next visit, he came right out and asked if they wanted to rent the house.

Still, Diana could hardly believe her ears. They hadn't had to convince or cajole or even ask him. She wanted to stretch her arms out and twirl, to run up and throw her arms around Henri Nguyen's neck.

Jay warned her off with a look. "We'll have to think about it," he said.

"What?" she whisper-shouted on their way back to the car.

"We should be sure about this, honey, before we sign. That's all."

"I'm sure. Aren't you?" Why did he have to be so deliberate? Some things were just right. No need to think about it.

"Remember," he said as they drove away, "the house won't be done for at least another two or three months. If we sign the lease, we'll be stuck in the apartment until after Christmas."

It didn't take long for them to agree that they were willing to wait. And by the end of the week, the lease had been drawn up and signed by all parties.

Diana suggested they celebrate with a dinner at Le Pandanus. She'd been saving the restaurant, said to be the most romantic in Port Vila, for a special occasion. An occasion exactly like this one.

Daylight was fading and the cicadas were already in full chorus when they arrived. "Something smells good," Jay said, wrapping an arm around her as they crunched up the walkway.

"Jasmine." She peered into the garden beyond the torch-lit coral path. "Jasmine and rosemary."

"*Bonsoir, madame, monsieur.*" A woman with a sophisticated smattering of white in her dark brown chignon greeted them at the reception desk. "*Deux?*"

"*Oui,*" Jay said, "two of us."

She slipped some menus under her arm and turned, her black dress flashing rich aubergine undertones.

The dining room she led them through was dimly lit with flickering candles. It was still early by European standards, so it wasn't surprising that most of the tables stood empty. Diana squeezed Jay's hand and followed the woman out another door onto a patio with only two tables, one on either end. The woman motioned to a table that was close enough to the floodlit lagoon that they could almost dangle their feet in it.

"Cocktails?" she asked when they were seated. "Madame?"

Over the lagoon, the purplish-blue sky was receding, and the moon, still a pale slice of reflected light, was starting to claim its nighttime dominance. "Sangria," she said, as somewhere in the world a bullfighter twirled and snapped his cape and the crowd yelled, "*Olé!*"

"I'll have a scotch," Jay said. "On the rocks."

Le Pandanus straddled two great lagoons. The placid, mysterious waters ran for miles to the east and south of town before emptying into the Pacific. Despite the floodlight on the water, their table sat in near darkness, walled off by potted plants on two sides and a canopy of tree branches and hanging vines, so quiet and private they might have been all alone in the world.

"You know," Diana said when the woman was gone, "this is exactly what I imagined Vanuatu would be like."

"Eating out at Le Pandanus?"

"This spot, being here with you . . . I don't know how to explain it. It feels like a scene from an old movie." Their chairs were on the same side of the round wrought iron and glass table, placed there so they could both enjoy the view. When they turned to face each other, Diana noticed a softness in Jay's eyes. "It *does* matter," she said.

"What matters?" He traced her eyebrow with his finger.

"Our surroundings. The way they make us feel." She looked up at the white moon, a ghostly cradle rocking above its reflected twin floating serenely on the water below.

Jay smiled and looked away.

"Dr. Feliciano was right. I was way too tense."

He moaned, a tiny murmur of complaint.

She patted his hand. "The point is, feeling this way has given me hope. It means I'm capable of relaxing." She paused, waiting for a response. When there was none, she curled her fingers around his hand and squeezed. "When we move into our house. . . ."

He pulled his hand away and sighed, loud and unequivocal this time. "Sweetheart," he said, shaking his head. "When are you going to stop hanging your hopes on something outside yourself?" In the candlelight, his expression seemed to flicker from sympathetic to annoyed and back again. "It's just a house. It won't turn you into a different person." He looked down and sighed again. "It can't make you pregnant," he said finally.

Her mouth fell open. "Why . . . why are you doing this? I thought we were supposed to be celebrating tonight."

"Absolutely." He leaned toward her. "But," he said like a teacher instructing a dull-witted student, "we're celebrating the signing of a rental contract, not the triumph of all our dreams."

"I know that."

"Do you?" Another sigh. "Sometimes, Diana, you scare me."

"What?" she demanded. "I scare you because I'm happy? Because I have hope?"

"Because you're obsessed with getting pregnant, because nothing else seems to matter to you."

"That's not true."

He raised his palms in a gesture of disbelief. "Just a few minutes ago you described the house we're going to move into as though it were a prescription written by your dear Dr. Feliciano, as though it's nothing but a means to an end, some kind of magic elixir of baby-making."

The sarcasm in his voice startled her. She sat back in her chair and tried to breathe. Of course she was concerned about getting pregnant. Concerned, not obsessed. And what if she were obsessed? She was thirty-five years old, almost thirty-six. What woman nearing the end of her fertile years wouldn't be concerned?

"In case you haven't noticed," she said, "I seldom mention getting pregnant."

"That's just it. You don't talk about it, but I know what you're thinking, and you think about it all the time."

"And . . ." She felt the tears starting. "You don't think about it at all."

"You don't know what I'm thinking."

She pushed her chair back.

"Diana . . ."

She had to get out of there. She grabbed the armrests, and even as she was rising off the chair, she saw herself running—hair flying, heels clicking on the tiles, barely touching the ground, past the woman at the front desk where she'd call a taxi. And then . . . at the thought of going back to Cloud Nine by herself, she sank down in her seat.

"Your sangria, madame."

She caught her breath as a silvery-white hand reached past her shoulder with a little paper doily and a chilled drink. "May I take your order?" the woman asked.

For a moment Diana's mind went blank. Then she picked up the menu and ran her finger down the list of items. "Smoked chicken salad," she said. "No soup. Just the salad." She handed the menu back and waited for the woman to leave.

"Beef Wellington," Jay said. "Medium rare."

"Ah, *bon.*"

Diana frowned at her sangria as the woman whirled away in a brief flash of aubergine. Then they were alone, avoiding each other's eyes and staring at the lagoon. She plucked up the arrogant little straw that had been standing, all rigid and male, in the middle of her sangria, and stirred, beating the ice into a scarlet-tinged froth.

There were people in the next room now. Their voices intruded through the doorway, rumbling and then piercing, a man's self-satisfied baritone followed by a woman's annoying waterfall laugh. Diana wished they'd shut up so she could think. Or, better yet, not think. She filled her mouth again and again with the icy sangria, ignoring the freeze that penetrated the roof of her mouth and moved into her brain.

Why the hell didn't Jay put his scotch down and apologize? She took a quick glance at his profile—the unblinking eyes and jutting jaw. If he didn't say something soon, she was leaving. She braced her hands against the edge of the table. She needed to get out of there—to run and run and never stop. No taxi, no destination. Circle the island and just keep going.

She sighed and settled back in her chair. It was a satisfying fantasy, but it wasn't in Diana's nature to walk in circles, and she knew it. Her life had been all about getting somewhere—to college and then grad school, a good job, a promotion, marriage. And right now she was directed toward one and only one destination: getting pregnant.

She wished he'd stop shaking his ice cubes and look at her. She gurgled air up her straw along with the last of her sangria, and still he stared at the lagoon. Who was this man?

A current of cool air brushed across the back of her neck and over her chest and shoulders. She put a hand up to her neck to warm it, but her hand was cold from holding her drink. She rubbed both hands together. The once-picturesque lagoon was deeply black now, nothing but wild bush on the other side, that and, she supposed, a few natives, descendants of cannibals. She felt her foreign-ness as she hadn't since they arrived. Without Jay, she was all alone on this strange little island. If he didn't love her . . . or she didn't love him . . . and how could she know? She hunched forward and crossed her hands over her chest. How could she conjure up loving feelings when the only things that came to mind were his rants and his devotion to work and the way his eyes glazed over when she talked to him? This was the man she was supposed to be in love with?

Stop, she told herself. Enough. She *did* love him. She had to.

Oh my god! She took a deep breath. She couldn't . . . absolutely could not think of him that way. She looked at Jay and then lowered her eyes when he turned to her and smiled. Thank goodness he didn't know where her mind had been heading. She'd been moments away from casting him as the necessary means of achieving her goal. Maybe he was right to call her desire for a baby an obsession. She couldn't let go of it, though, not even for a minute. She needed to make it happen.

Over the lagoon, a sinister little cloud floated sideways, its forward end poised to pierce the moon's perfect curve.

The food arrived. French bread. Sliced tomatoes and garden fresh greens. Diana's smoked chicken and Jay's beef Wellington, both of them elegantly presented. Jay picked up a knife. Diana broke off a chunk of baguette.

"Want a bite?" Jay stabbed some beef he'd sliced off and held it out to her. The meat was wrapped in a flaky pastry with a layer of pate that smelled of garlic and buttery mushrooms.

She shook her head. Don't try to pretend we're not in the middle of a fight, she thought.

He tried to strike up a conversation about the origin of beef Wellington, who it was named after, and whether or not it was originally a French dish. And all she could do was nod. She didn't care a fig about the history of his food. He tried again, this time something about Vanuatu's cattle industry. But she was shaking inside, wondering why she was still sitting there toying with her salad. Wondering how she'd convinced herself that she still loved him. Eventually he gave up trying to engage her in conversation, and they lapsed into silence until they were done eating.

Then Jay pushed his plate back and pointed at the sky. "See that cloud on top of the moon?" It was the same sinister little cloud she'd seen before, but by now it had morphed and moved until it was balanced on top of the moon. He smiled as though everything should be all right by now. "It looks like a visor on a baseball cap," he said.

Wasn't it just like him, blind to the cloud earlier when it was poised to pierce the moon and seeing it now as the visor on a baseball cap? You'd think they lived in two different worlds. Maybe they did.

~

She couldn't imagine what had possessed him to be so negative at a time like this when they should have been celebrating. And why the hell had he chosen this evening to accuse her of being obsessive? As soon as he'd paid the bill, she pressed her lips together and hurried to the car—which only meant she had to wait for him to open her door.

Once inside the car, he just sat in the driver's seat, key in the ignition, staring straight ahead. Then he let go of the key and rested his hands on the steering wheel like someone waiting for the light to change. "All I want," he said finally, "is for you to be happy. For both of us to be happy."

At that point, she still wasn't ready to look at him.

"I dream of us having our own child," he said, as though he were repeating someone else's lines. "I really do. It would be the most wonderful thing in the world. But, sweetheart . . ."

Although she could feel him turning toward her, though she was aware of the pleading in his voice, she continued staring at the windshield, noting in detail the evidence of the earlier rain and the demise of one tiny, unfortunate bug.

And still he kept at it. "I can only do my part," he argued. "And I can hope, and I can pray. But that's all I can do." He paused as though waiting for her to say something. When she wouldn't even nod, he kept going. "This island and the Tassiriki house might be just what we need to tip the scales. And it might not. That's what I'm afraid of, that we'll care too much about something we can't control."

She opened her mouth to object, to tell him she hadn't said the house would change everything. That's just how invested she was in her version of things.

Before she could plead her case, though, he knocked the air out of her anger. "I'm so sorry, honey," he said. "When you talked about the house and how it was going to change everything, I overreacted. I spoiled our evening. I'm really sorry." He laid his hand on the seat next to her, palm up. "We have each other," he said. "The way I look at it, we're already a family."

He seemed to be asking her to go along with the idea of the family they could be for each other, and she wanted to say yes. But there was still a hard edge on her heart that wasn't satisfied. She laid her hand on his, but only loosely without squeezing it.

He must not have noticed the message she thought she was conveying, though, because he lifted her hand and kissed it. "You're the one I love," he said. "And you're enough for me."

She tried to speak, to tell him she loved him. Instead she swallowed and let the tears flow.

Vanuatu

1991

38

She unwrapped another wine glass and held it up to the light. Twirling it between her fingers, she watched sunlight dance across the facets. This house was all space and light—the ceiling over the living and dining room, so high; the floor as cool and shiny as an ice-skating rink. From where she stood in the dining room, the sparkling white tile stretched all the way across the living room and out the sliding glass doors onto the veranda.

But it didn't end there. The space—the sense of possibility— swept out across the lawn and the low picket fence and the treetops down the hill at the Radisson. It skimmed the surfaces of both lagoons and just kept going, over the green hills and into the boundless blue sky.

Diana smiled at the extravagance of her thoughts. And yet, that was exactly the way the house made her feel—extravagantly sheltered and thoroughly free. A woman finally, at the age of thirty-five, poised to find her place in the world.

She reached into the packing box for another glass. Who could say why one place and not another could make a person feel good? She thought about the fight she and Jay had a few months earlier at Le Pandanus. Maybe if she'd made a better case for why she was so convinced the house would help her relax, maybe that would have been the end of it.

At the thought of her anger that night, she felt a chill up her spine. If he hadn't talked to her in the car, who could tell how long she'd have held onto it, or what dark paths it would have led her down. She'd been prepared to let her anger simmer all the way back to their apartment and with no end in sight.

"Ma'am." It was Clarita, flip-flops slapping down the three steps from the back entry. Her cheeks were flushed, her hair tied back in a ponytail. Diana quickly wiped away a lonely tear. It pleased her that Clarita was so enthusiastic about the new house. But then, who wouldn't be? Especially after being given her own bedroom suite at the top of the stairs.

"Look, ma'am." Clarita hefted a crowbar over her head. "Mr. Nguyen give it."

"Good." Diana frowned trying to imagine why Clarita might need a crowbar.

"For the wooden box," Clarita said, pointing with the screwdriver and hammer in her left hand toward a flat wooden crate tucked under the coffee table.

"Why don't you ask one of Mr. Nguyen's men to help?" Diana, Jay, and Clarita had moved in three days ago, and yet the workers were still there. Each morning as Jay was about to leave for work, Henri Nguyen and his men would appear at the back door, tools in hand. "Always a few details to finish," Henri explained the first day in his trademark combination of French, English, Vietnamese, and Bislama. At least that's what Diana thought he said.

"I don't need no man to help." Clarita straightened her back at the thought. "I can open that box myself." She squatted and tugged on the heavy box, grunting as she pulled it, scraping across the tile, out from under the coffee table.

"Wait," Diana said. "Let me help."

"No, ma'am. I can do it."

Diana grabbed a cloth the painter had left. "Here. We can set the box on this. Then you can slide it."

Clarita didn't object. She pulled the box across the floor,

and when she reached the doorway, she gave Diana a quick look of triumph. Then she dragged it out onto the veranda and set to work.

Diana went back to unpacking glasses, crumpling sheets of wrapping paper, and tossing them into an empty box. Behind her, a worker whistled as he pressed putty into screw holes on the banister. Down the hall, a handsaw scraped, a hammer tapped. Outside, men who were pushing another wheelbarrow filled with wet concrete up the steep driveway hooted and hollered like teenagers at a basketball game. She'd have thought the constant presence of workmen these past few days would have driven her crazy. On the contrary, she found she liked having them around. They made the house hum with a kind of cheerful, relaxed industry.

She pulled another wine glass from its padded nest and was starting to unwrap it when she heard tires crunching up the driveway. A car stopped. A door closed, and a woman's voice—spirited, loud and decidedly British—shouted, "Hey-ho! Where's the mistress of the house?" Diana set the wine glass on the table and ran outside and down the veranda steps. Abby, her freckled arms showing under an orange-and-pink tie-dyed T-shirt, lifted a large plastic bag brimming with leaves from her trunk and plunked it on the sidewalk. "Your future garden."

Suling picked up a smaller bag. "Plants from our yards," she said. "This one is jasmine." She sniffed the small white blossoms before placing her bundle on the grass. As she straightened up, a breeze pressed the filmy apricot fabric of her dress flat against the curve of her belly.

"Oh, Suling," Diana said, touching her arm. "You look lovelier every day." Suling's skin had always been smooth and beautiful, but today it glowed.

"Thank you." Suling squeezed Diana's hand until it hurt. "I'm so happy," she said, resting one hand on her tiny tummy bulge. "And I wish the same thing for you."

Diana hugged her—a gentle hug that wouldn't squeeze too hard on the baby.

Abby's Toyota was a jungle packed with bougainvillea, hibiscus, yellow bell, gloriosa lilies, and a half-grown banana plant. "Thank you," Diana said when they'd finished unloading everything from the trunk and back seat. "Thank you so much. Now, come on in. I'll show you around."

The house was large—three bedrooms and two bathrooms plus Clarita's room, an upstairs suite that had been designed for Henri's son and girlfriend. "See," Diana said after they'd toured the house. "It's roomy, but not as big as it looks from the road."

Abby chuckled. "Big enough to make Marshall jealous."

~

For the next few weeks Diana concentrated on setting up the new house. She finished unpacking and ordered curtains and a table for the kitchen. She hung pictures, mirrors, and clocks; she bought furniture for the veranda and seeds for a vegetable garden.

Then, as the house began to take shape, she fell into a pleasant routine of morning walks or outings to the market and afternoons sketching or painting or walking along the beach. She taught Clarita some favorite recipes and drove Jay to work and back. When she and Jay sat on the veranda, looking down on the ever more familiar landscape, when they walked around the yard at night, smelling the damp earth and gazing up at the swarms of stars, she felt the most comforting sense of belonging—not in Tassiriki or Port Vila or Vanuatu, but on the Earth.

Everything was coming together for them. She had the feeling that it wouldn't be long now.

By the first week of February, the house was basically ready for its formal presentation. At Henri's urging, they'd arranged to have a house-blessing party on Saturday morning. Their house-warming party, a larger affair, would follow on Sunday night. In preparation for both events, Henri sent his men over to slash brush around the perimeter, mow the grass, and hang the new chandelier-fan from the impossibly high living room ceiling.

It was raining early Saturday morning when Henri's wife delivered her favorite tablecloths and some Vietnamese finger-food. By the time the guests arrived at eleven, the grass was dry and the blue sky speckled with a mere handful of benign little white clouds.

Henri picked up Father Jean Pierre, a French-speaking ni-Vanuatu priest, and drove him to the house. Meeting them at the back door, Diana and Jay guided the priest into the kitchen— his makeshift sacristy. He poured the holy water he brought into a silver bucket and draped his shoulders with a white stole. Then he stepped out onto the raised platform of the entry and raised his arms.

A hush fell over the crowd gathered in the dining room below. Even the children stood with heads bowed and hands clasped. They were all Catholics—people Jay and Diana knew from the little English-language church and a larger group of Vietnamese invited by Henri and his wife. This house had been Henri's most ambitious project to date, his crowning glory, and it was obvious he wanted his friends and extended family to see and admire it.

"*In nomine Patris et Filii et Spiritus Sancti,*" the priest intoned, making the sign of the cross.

"Amen," the people answered.

"*Seigneur Jesus.*" The young priest's brown skin and pink-tipped fingers glistened as he spread his arms to encompass both house and people in his plea.

His prayer began in French and ended in Bislama, and though much of it was lost on Diana, the meaning was clear. The priest was praying for her house, hers and Jay's. And all these friendly people were praying for them, too. She squeezed Jay's hand, and for a moment she felt overcome by the kindness directed their way, by the sense that their fortunes were just beginning to change.

The priest finished, and everyone made the sign of the cross. Then they looked around, smiling at each other and checking out the spring rolls and open-face sandwiches displayed on a row of folding tables. The children ran out through the open doors, giggling, their feet pattering across the veranda and down the stairs as they raced each other to the trampoline Diana had borrowed from Abby.

Then all eyes turned back to the priest who was gathering up his stainless steel sprinkler and bucket of holy water. This was what the adults had been waiting for—the actual sprinkling of holy water. Henri's nephew, a handsome Melanesian-Vietnamese, held the bucket as the priest dipped the sprinkler. Flicking his wrist to gain more distance, he tossed holy water high up the wall. Those standing closest felt the cool sacred drops on their arms and later on their ankles as he dipped the sprinkler again and sprayed water across the floor.

Blessing the living room and dining room, the kitchen cabinets, the back porch and carport, he was a baseball pitcher, a thrower of Frisbees. The Vietnamese contingent followed him to the laundry room and all the bedrooms and bathrooms, even up to Clarita's room and onto her balcony. They nodded their heads and commented in hushed tones. Their grandfathers and great-grandfathers had come to Vanuatu to work as laborers on the copra plantations, and now, finally, this generation of Vietnamese was making good.

~~~~~

A day later, taking a break from housewarming preparations, Diana and Jay stepped onto the veranda. Behind them, stacks of bowls, plates, and napkins were already set out on the buffet, glasses lined up on the bar. Satay was marinating in the fridge, and the chili was ready to warm. They sank onto a couple of deck chairs and breathed the fresh, grassy air.

"You know," Diana said, "I really liked the house blessing."

"Me, too." Jay put his feet up on the planter and closed his eyes. "Well," he said, "now that the house is officially blessed, are you ready for a wild housewarming party tonight?"

"I'd settle for something more along the lines of a cordial gathering." Diana stood up. "We still have salads to put together," she said. "Pies, cupcakes, and corn bread for Clarita and me to bake. And you've gotta take that trampoline back. We don't want any drunken revelers breaking their legs on it."

A dragonfly dipped low over the tissue-thin bougainvillea petals, its luminous aqua body shimmering in the sunlight. Diana smiled. Her skin tingled with the news she had for him . . . the possible news. Fifteen days late. That had to mean something. "Jay," she said, "I'm . . ."

He opened his eyes. "Hm?"

"I'm . . ." No, not yet. Better to wait until this evening after she had time to do the test. "I'm . . . ah . . . really glad Henri insisted on having the house blessed."

Before Dr. Feliciano and the fertility tests, when Diana still assumed that conceiving a baby would be easy, she'd used up pregnancy tests like bags of candy, ripping one open every time she was two or three days late, setting herself up over and over again for the inevitable letdown. These days she waited longer.

Tonight after the housewarming she'd find out for sure. She pressed her lips together. This time she wouldn't be disappointed. This time the test stick would change color.

39

"I love your house." Jennifer Carson nodded at Jay and Diana and then, tilting her head back, grimaced at the cathedral ceiling. "I'd be lost with all this space, though."

"Jen likes the wide-open spaces of the ocean," her husband Keith said. "But when it comes to living quarters . . ."

"Yeah. I prefer our boat."

Diana gave her a skeptical look. She couldn't imagine living in such a small space. "You must be incredibly neat and organized."

"Obsessive is more like it." Keith winked at his wife.

Diana had met the Carsons just a few weeks earlier at a garden party Abby'd thrown for the twins' sixth birthday. Jennifer was their teacher. Keith worked at one of Port Vila's off-shore investment houses. It intrigued Diana that they'd sailed all the way from Alaska to Vanuatu and that, two years later, here they were, still living on that same small boat.

Port Vila's expat community was small and sociable. It didn't take long to meet interesting people. Tonight, even though Jay's co-workers made up the bulk of the guest list for the housewarming, they'd also invited a colorful hodgepodge of shopkeepers, farmers, artists, and diplomats. Altogether, it was the largest party they'd ever given. And their new house was the perfect setting.

"We eat out a lot," Jennifer was saying. "I blame it on our tiny stove."

Jay chuckled. "Having the Waterfront Bar and Grill only steps from the end of your dock could be a factor."

"Big time," Keith said.

Diana glanced around the room. Clarita was pouring fresh salad into a bowl on the buffet table. Alexi was behind the bar, mixing drinks so Jay could circulate among the guests. She was about to conclude that everyone was having a good time when she noticed Jay's secretary. Elizabeth was standing with another D-TAP secretary, both of them looking small and lost.

"Elizabeth, Grace," Diana called, waving them over, "I want you to meet some friends." Diana had never seen herself as the hostess-type. She still thought of herself as the career woman who entertained guests in a restaurant. Tonight, though, she was enjoying her role. She waved again, and when the two ni-Vanuatu women came over, she put her arms around their shoulders and introduced them to the Carsons. It was something her mother would have done.

Soon they were talking about food, the salads and chicken satay Diana and Clarita had made that morning, the *laplap* they all liked, and the salad bar at the Waterfront Bar and Grill.

"My mother's chicken . . ." Grace started to say.

"Hey, Jay." Marshall elbowed his way into their circle. "Quite a shindig you have here." He put his arm around Elizabeth and grinned down at her, his mustache twitching.

The poor girl didn't move a muscle, but it was clear to Diana that she wanted to swat his hand off her shoulder. Elizabeth was young and smart, but she had no natural defense against this big, obnoxious white man who was also her boss.

"So," Marshall said, "what's up there?" He swung his glass toward the room at the top of the stairs, oblivious to the whiskey he was spilling on Elizabeth.

"That's our helper's room," Jay said.

"What a deal!" Marshall let Elizabeth go and turned to his buddies standing behind him. "In the McIntosh house, the maid gets the upstairs suite and the master sleeps downstairs."

"Downstairs in the master suite," Diana said, raising her voice above the cackles of Marshall's faithful trio: McCurdy, Fabrizio, and Siole.

"I tell you, McIntosh." Marshall clasped Jay's arm. "You'll never get anywhere until you learn to assert your authority. You're such a hippie," he said, shaking his head.

"You mean drugs and free love?" Jay raised his eyebrows and clamped his hand around Marshall's wrist. "No such luck."

"I'd settle for another whisky." Marshall looked at his wrist and waited for Jay to let go.

"Who was that?" Jennifer Carson asked when Jay and Marshall were gone.

Diana glanced at the bald spot on the back of Marshall's head. "That was Jay's boss."

Jennifer gave her husband a knowing look. "Reminds me of a boss I had once."

There was an awkward silence, and then Elizabeth turned to Diana. "I think I should go now," she said. "Your party was delightful. It was kind of you to invite me." She turned away and made a zigzagging exit, keeping as far as possible from both Carole Anne and Marshall. On her way out the door, she cast a quick glance over her shoulder before hurrying across the veranda and down the stairs.

That's right, girl, Diana thought. Keep your distance. That man is trouble. Especially when he's had a few drinks under his belt. Despite Marshall's tendency to stray, he was usually careful around his wife. Tonight, though, he and Carole Anne had come to the party separately, Marshall arriving a good hour before her. And when Carole Anne showed up, she looked as brittle as a sunbaked crab shell.

Jumpy as a sand flea, Diana thought a little later as she carried an empty dessert tray into the kitchen. "You know," she said to

Clarita, setting the tray on the counter. "Mrs. Charbonneau doesn't look well tonight."

"No, ma'am." Clarita peeled aluminum foil off the nearest apple pie. "Pilar says sir and ma'am fighting every day."

"Mr. and Mrs. Charbonneau?"

"Very bad fights. So much shouting. It hurts Pilar's ears."

"Mmm." It was tempting to use Clarita's friendship with the Charbonneaus' maid to tap into their secret lives, but she restrained herself. Everyone deserved some privacy at home, even Marshall Charbonneau.

With forty-five guests to entertain, Diana had little time that evening to think about the Charbonneaus' marital problems. But every so often she would notice Carole Anne across the room. She seemed such a lonely figure—that prim blue-and-white dress, those wrinkles etched at the corners of her mouth. An aging woman with no children and a philandering husband.

It was no surprise that she chose to leave early and without Marshall. "Thank you so much," she said with a flash of southern charm. "It was a fabulous party." Diana was out on the veranda taking a quiet moment with Abby and Suling. Suddenly Carole Anne's smile faded. "Oh, my goodness! Just look at that." She pointed down the hill, beyond their yard. "Y'all can see the Radisson from here, the lobby and all those taxis lined up on the driveway. Oh, lordy." She swallowed. "I hope to god your bedroom curtains are lined."

Normally, Diana would have bristled at Carole Anne's coercive fearfulness. Tonight she simply reached out and squeezed her hand. "Don't worry," she said. "I ordered the thickest curtains in the shop."

"I could give you some fast-growing shrubs to plant in front of the window," Carole Anne added. "If you want them, that is."

"Of course. Thank you."

"That was nice of her," Abby said as Carole Anne's white Toyota rolled down the driveway. "But that woman is obsessed with privacy. Contrariwise, her husband doesn't give a fig. Just listen to him." On cue, Marshall's voice rose above the sociable rumble inside the house. "And McCurdy." Abby snorted. "Cackling like a goose in a henhouse. Trying to keep up with the boss when Marshall could easily drink him under the table."

Suling crossed her arms over her pregnant belly and scowled. "He drinks so much, I don't know why he doesn't fall on his face."

Abby patted her shoulder. "Alcoholics, my dear, don't feel the effects like you and me."

Diana took her friends' hands. Here they were on the veranda, looking out on this tremendous view—the jewel in the crown of Diana's new house—and they were talking about Marshall. "Enough about Marshall," she said. "Now tell me, what did you think of my apple pies? I made them a couple days ago. The New Zealand apples weren't tart enough, but . . ."

"They were scrumptious," Abby said, squeezing her hand.

———~———

By midnight, most of the guests had said their good-byes. The secretaries and all the TAs except Siole were gone. Siole had been buzzing around Marshall all night, matching him drink for drink. At close to three hundred pounds, Diana supposed, the Samoan could easily handle as much liquor as his boss.

She glanced across the room to where Peg McCurdy and Greta Fabrizio sat with their purses on their laps, crossing and recrossing their legs and shooting time-to-leave messages at their husbands. Marshall was still making jokes, McCurdy and Fabrizio still laughing, their chuckles half-hearted at best. Only Siole was still capable of a belly laugh.

Diana stifled a yawn. She was ready for the party to be over. Already her mind had jumped ahead to the pregnancy test waiting for her in the back of a drawer. The bottom drawer beside the bathroom sink.

40

As soon as they said good-bye to their last guest, Diana dashed away. "Sorry," she said without explanation as she rushed off, leaving Jay and Clarita to put the leftover food away and clean up the spills and dirty dishes. She had a good reason, though—a very good reason.

Her heart was pounding as she slipped into the bathroom. She closed the door behind her and turned on the light. The bottom drawer on the left side of the sink was her drawer, filled with sanitary napkins and tampons, hair curlers, and an extra jar of her favorite moisturizer. The sack filled with pregnancy tests was in the back, hidden, the way you might hide a diary or a bloody knife. An object of shame—which, until now, is what the tests had been.

Until now.

Her certainty thrilled her, and it terrified her.

She pulled out a test kit and fished inside for the instruction sheet. She'd read the instructions dozens of times, but she wasn't taking any chances. Unfolding the paper, she read the precautions and contraindications—the medical-eze that drained away the romance even before you peed on a stick. Then she sat on the toilet and read it all again. If diligence and hard work were the main requirements, she would have succeeded in getting pregnant a long time ago.

Pulling open the shiny silver packaging, she removed the test stick. The test was said to be most accurate first thing in the morning, but she couldn't stand to wait any longer. She held it between her legs and urinated. For five seconds, the instructions said. Afterwards she had to wait for five minutes to see the results. She held the wand in the air and concentrated on the slender rod of the second hand jerking its way around the face of her watch. A minute passed. Two minutes. Two minutes forty-five seconds, forty-six seconds, forty-seven.

She was almost certain she was pregnant this time. Her period was fifteen days late. Besides, she was feeling strange. Her breasts were a little tender, and she was almost sure that the flutters she'd been feeling the last two mornings were nausea.

Four minutes forty seconds, Fifty. Fifty-five.

Five minutes. She took a deep breath, her heart beating like a race horse. This was the moment she'd been waiting for. Hungry to look and shaking with fear, she closed her eyes for a second. Then she opened them and looked at the wand.

There it was, in front of her eyes: two pink lines.

Tears streaming down her cheeks, she blinked hard. And they were still there—the two beautiful bright pink lines. She was pregnant! She, Diana Harris McIntosh, was pregnant at last.

For years she'd been imagining what she would do when this day came. In one scenario, she ran to Jay screaming and twirled him around in a circle. In another, she played coy. She held the wand behind her back and asked him to guess what she had. Or, better yet, she waited until they were in bed, climbed on top of him, and whispered in his ear.

Now, though, when the time came, she was in a daze. She made her way to him down the hall and into the dining room. When Jay proposed, he'd dropped down on one knee and opened the little box that contained an engagement ring. He hadn't needed to speak. But an announcement of pregnancy has no script, no agreed-upon posture, no ring. Only the words.

"I'm pregnant," she said. Two simple words, but to her ears, they were a trumpet blast that reached to the ceiling and bounced off the walls.

He stopped sweeping. "You're what?"

For a moment she couldn't tell whether he was confused or simply caught off guard. She couldn't tell whether he was pleased. "I'm pregnant," she said again.

He dropped the broom and threw his arms around her, kissing her and hugging her so fiercely that she couldn't possibly doubt his happiness.

Clarita, who must have wondered what all the commotion was, peeked out of the kitchen.

"It's all right," Diana said, laughing. "We're fine."

"Ma'am is going to have a baby," Jay blurted with a big goofy grin.

———

That night, Diana hadn't been concerned that Jay told Clarita she was pregnant. In fact, she'd wanted the world to know. For days, she was caught up in her happiness and in Jay's. She'd never seen him smile and laugh so much, never known him to touch her as often and as ... well, reverently as he did now. But there had to be a reason that women traditionally kept their pregnancies secret for the first couple of months. They must know—and why didn't she realize it?—that lots of pregnancies just didn't "take." Lots of women lost their babies early while they were still not much more than a cluster of cells.

It worried her that she didn't feel more pregnant. Even the small flutters she felt in her stomach early on hadn't returned. She wasn't nauseated; she didn't vomit; she had no craving for pickles and ice cream or anything else. And yet, when she took out another pregnancy test and tried again, the register still showed two pink lines.

Three weeks after her missed period she called Dr. Granville's office and made an appointment for that afternoon. Even though Port Vila lacked an obstetrician, the two doctors favored by the town's expats, Dr. Granville and Dr. Garae, handled everything. Diana and Jay had gone to Dr. Granville's office when they were new in town to ask about medicine for malaria control. He'd surprised them by advising that they should simply avoid mosquitoes and find a house in a breezy part of town.

Now, as she was about to open the door to his office, she wondered about that advice. At the time she'd thought it was sensible. Now she wondered if he might turn out to be too casual in the way he approached her pregnancy. Oh, well. She took a deep breath and opened the door. When you move to a casual, relaxed country, you can expect to find casual, relaxed doctors.

She remembered the receptionist, a perky dark-haired woman with enormous brown eyes made even more prominent today with eyeliner, mascara, and sparkling coppery eye shadow. The sly, knowing smile she flashed when Diana identified herself reminded her of Abby's warning. "He's a good doctor," she'd said, "if you're not particular about privacy. The receptionist knows everything that's worth knowing about his patients." Her name was Gwendolyn, Abby said, adding that she was Dr. Granville's fourth and youngest wife. Oh well, Diana told herself for the second time in two minutes. Thanks to Jay and Clarita, everyone already knew she was pregnant. She filled out the exceedingly brief form Gwendolyn handed her and waited for Dr. Granville to call her in.

He was a charming older man, which made it even harder for her to undress from the waist down and arrange her feet on the stirrups.

Afterwards, when she picked Jay up from work, she skipped the details of the exam and jumped ahead to the bottom line. "He confirmed that I'm pregnant," she said. And Jay smiled his new silly smile and leaned across the gearshift to kiss her. Then the happy, not-so-young couple drove home to their idyllic house overlooking two shimmering South Pacific lagoons.

41

The Scrabble games were Suling's idea. Or rather her request. She'd asked if Diana and Abby would help her build her English vocabulary, and they'd decided the best way would be over the Scrabble board. They'd been playing weekly now for three and a half months, almost as long as Diana had been pregnant.

It was hard to believe that Diana had completed the first trimester of her pregnancy, that so-called dangerous period, the time when many women—other women—suffered from morning sickness, fatigue, and headaches. Diana's only symptom, even now, partway through the second trimester, was tender breasts, and—she was proud to say—her weight gain was right on track: three pounds, one pound each month. "You were made for this," Jay told her. And she had to agree. She felt just fine. Better than fine.

Today the three women were playing at Abby's house. As they sat around the whitewood table on her lanai, Diana scanned the board looking for a place to use her *x* while Suling made little kittenish sounds and frowned at her tiles.

Suddenly Suling laughed in high-toned triumph as she slapped her tiles onto the board. *Piano.* She'd spelled it down from the *p* in *escape*, leaving a perfect opening for Diana. If Abby didn't spoil things, when it was Diana's turn, she could get some good numbers by spelling *pox* across Suling's *o*.

"Before we start our batik classes next week," Abby said without taking her eyes off the board, "I want to learn to draw." She shuffled some tiles on her tray. "I've been entertaining the thought that my artistic friend here might help me out." She raised her head and smiled at Diana.

"Sure. Why don't we do a sketching trip together tomorrow? I'll drive. Suling, do you want to join us?"

"No, thank you. My students come tomorrow. Chinese song and dance."

"Cha-cha-cha," Abby crowed, snapping down the tiles for *samba* at the top of the board, a move that earned her a double word score but left the *o* in *piano* wide open for Diana.

When they quit for the day, Abby had the high score. Again. They were getting used to it. Not only did she have a wide-ranging vocabulary, she had a fantastically quick mind that saw all the angles.

⁓

The next afternoon, as soon as Diana pulled into her friend's driveway, the front door swung open, and Abby stepped out, bangles jingling, curls escaping from her baseball cap. "What do I need to bring?" she asked.

Diana opened the car door and stepped halfway out. "Just yourself," she said. "I have our art pencils and sketch books in the trunk along with a couple of folding chairs and some snacks."

"Oh, you."

"Come on. Hop in."

"Where are you taking me?" Abby said it like a joke, and yet she hesitated outside the car, her hand clutching the door handle.

Diana had been thinking of a spot out by Black Sand Beach. On a whim, though, she changed her mind. "The road to Montmartre," she said, feeling that the road would be okay for them as long as they went together.

"Montmartre?" Abby bit her lip as she slid in beside Diana. "You don't expect me to draw schoolboys on my very first sketching trip, do you?"

"Don't worry. We won't drive all the way up to the school. We can stop along the way and sketch the flora."

Montmartre was on the other side of town from Abby and Saudur's house in Malapoa. Before she was pregnant, Diana had walked a mile or so up the lonely road, but she'd never been all the way to the top where the Catholic mission and boarding school were located. The quiet and isolation of the road had made her uneasy that day. And these past few months, with Jay constantly advising caution, she'd become more timid. Right from the start, he'd made her promise she wouldn't go to the beach unless he was with her. When they went together, he didn't let her out of his sight. His fear was annoying sometimes. She understood and respected it, but at the same time she was frustrated that the ghost of Celeste's death was still haunting them.

"You know," Abby said, "I stopped drawing when I was in grammar school." She gazed out the car window at the tennis club and then Cercle Sportif. "I figured I was better with my mouth than with my hand."

"Everyone can draw. It just takes patience."

Abby snorted. "That's not me."

"Drawing ability or patience?"

"Both. Anyway . . ." She lifted her baseball cap and ran her fingers through her curls. "Here I am, ready to learn."

They were passing the prison now, a squat concrete block building set back from the road, too large for a racquetball court, too small for a gym. "Strange," Diana said, "that they'd build the prison right next to the town stadium."

Abby chuckled. "A lucky stroke for the prisoners, that. Last year during the playoff with Fiji, their minders let them climb on the roof and watch the game."

"You're kidding! Didn't any of the prisoners run away?"

"And miss the football match? Not on your life."

Diana smiled. Port Vila was nothing like Manila, where people constantly worried about crime. They expected it. Their houses had walls, some of them with broken glass on top. Armed guards were stationed at the entrances to residential villages. Port Vila, on the other hand, was a tourist mecca that billed itself as a paradise on Earth. Its not-so-distant history of cannibalism was celebrated on T-shirts sold to tourists. The crime stories people passed around were the quirky ones.

One of the best, told over and over, was the one about the ni-Vanuatu thief who broke into the house of the British woman whose husband was traveling. No one remembers what he took, or if he stole anything at all. The notable fact was that he was naked except for his black hooded mask.

And now there was this story about inmates sitting on the prison roof to watch a soccer match. Who knew whether Port Vila was in fact a safe place, but people here definitely preferred looking on the bright side—and having a good laugh.

Diana and Abby rode past the university and a row of houses and kept going until they reached the turn.

Once on Montmartre Road, they were alone in a world of trees and green fields. If they drove all the way up to the school, they'd have a view of the whole south end of Efate Island. But Diana had promised simple subjects for their sketches.

"How about this spot?" she asked, pulling over when they were a couple miles up the road.

"You're the artist."

Diana gave her head a little shake. She wasn't an artist. True, she'd always loved to sketch things, to find the beauty and humor in what she saw. But that didn't make her an artist, did it? Her mom was the artist in the family. She painted and sold marvelous unique pictures. There were times growing up, though, when Diana had thought of an artist's work as silly. Her mom didn't go to the office each day like Daddy did; she just fooled around at home in a room she called her studio. To Diana in those days, art didn't seem like a serious job. Besides, she wasn't that talented. She just liked to play around with art. She was an accountant.

"We can sit right there," Diana said, indicating a patch of weeds at the side of the road.

They set up folding stools in the patchy shade of some spindly trees. Then Diana handed Abby a sketchbook and a variety of graphite artist's pencils and demonstrated how to use them to achieve different effects.

"Okay. But what do I do now?" Abby stared at the scene—at the tall green grass and spindly fence directly in front of her and beyond that, the abandoned field leading to a jumble of trees and bushes in the fields going all the way back to a row of hills. "What am I supposed to draw?"

Diana understood her perplexity. On first sight, there was no traditional scene here. And yet, on closer look, the scene was impossibly complex. "You don't have to draw everything. Just look for something that takes your fancy."

Following her own advice, Diana focused in on the fence. Ever since her first day in Vanuatu, she'd been intrigued by the fence posts made from beach hibiscus that were allowed to keep growing, branches and leaves sprouting from the tops and sides of the posts.

She moved her stool closer and fingered a heart-shaped leaf. And though she was tempted to touch the large coral-colored blossom above it, she refrained. It was the only flower on the fence. Its ruffled petals, delicate as butterfly wings, spread out around the long red stamen. She cupped her hand over the flower, and it lifted in an invisible current of air and left a smudge of pollen on her palm.

They were silent for a while, both of them concentrating on their drawings, the only sounds the scratch of their pencils and the occasional rustle of leaves high in the trees.

The heart-shaped leaves growing out of the fence posts had been eaten away, and yet their form remained. Diana tried several times before finding a technique to capture the delicate lacey look.

A cloud passed over, and for a moment it seemed that they'd have to fold up and go. Luckily the rain, which pattered on the leaves over their heads, barely touched their sketchpads before moving on.

They made small talk while they sketched, but they were too focused on their drawing to say much. At one point, Abby stopped drawing. She looked around as though maybe she'd heard something. Then she frowned at Diana.

"They have witchdoctors in Vanuatu," she said. "In the villages."

"What made you think about witchdoctors?"

"This morning Lourdes told me about a woman who hired one to put a spell on her husband's mistress. The poor girl developed a disgusting rash that no one was able to cure." Abby shivered. "Lourdes says the best witchdoctors are from Ambrim. *Clevas*, they call them. Their power comes from fire and brimstone. The island of Ambrim has more than its share of Vanuatu's active volcanoes." She laughed and tossed her head as though to dismiss the craziness of witchdoctors and spells. Then she stood up and stretched. She held her sketch at arm's length and smiled.

"Let's see," Diana said.

Abby had every right to smile. It was a brilliant drawing. She'd chosen to sketch the huge banyan tree to the right of them. The banyan was a tangle of branches and air roots and leaves. But somehow Abby had found a pattern in all the confusion. And then, making use of the different grades of pencils, she'd highlighted the chosen patterns and allowed the rest to sink into the shadows.

"I love it," Diana said, handing it back.

Abby smiled at her drawing. Then, remembering, she looked at her watch. "Lordy," she shouted. "It's almost time to pick up the twins." She folded her stool and started toward the car. "I can't believe how late it is. The time just fl—"

She stopped, and without another word dropped beside the wheel, waving both her arms at Diana and pointing frantically.

He was like a gigantic attack bird, swooping down on her, leaves flapping from his dreadlocks and around his neck and arms.

42

*I*f a wolf or a tiger had jumped out at her, Diana would have turned on a dime. *Fight or flight. Get the hell out of here.* But he wasn't a wolf: he was a man, and so she hesitated. Gave herself a split second to override the prejudice one might feel against a black man who leaps out from somewhere behind your car. A man who's nearly naked, though? Leaves in his hair? A string around his waist holding up—she didn't want to look down—some kind of woven straw thing around his penis? She dropped her stool, but it was too late. He already had her by the arm.

"*Mi wantem trak blong yu,*" he demanded, his tone immediately comprehensible even if his words weren't. "*Kwicktaem.*"

Quick-time? Truck? He wants my what? Diana struggled to yank her arm away. *Quick-time* what? How could she reason with this man when she didn't know what he wanted? "I don't understand."

He flexed his arm, and as he drew her closer, she saw a glint of something in his other hand and felt the rough edge of his penis wrapper against her stomach.

"*Ki blong trak wea?*" He snatched the sketchbook out of her hand and threw it in the weeds. "*Mi wantem ki.*"

Her car key. That's what he wanted. "Oh," she said, edging away as she reached into her pocket. "The key."

She didn't look directly at her friend, but she saw her. Abby had crept around the passenger side of the car, and now she was out in the open, behind the man. Suddenly she ran forward, carrying a fat branch. She swung it over her shoulder like a baseball bat. "Knee him!" she shouted. "Now!"

With the branch already in motion heading for the man's back, there was no time to think. Diana did exactly as she was told. Fast and tight as a piston she swung her knee back and then forward, plunging it hard into the man's crotch—through the softness of his testicles and the thin layer of scratchy woven straw and into the bone and muscle of his body.

He released his grip on her arm, dropped something—a knife?—and fell forward, howling and clutching his genitals.

"Let's get outa here," Abby said.

Diana ran to the car and threw open the door. The man was right behind her. She tried to climb into the driver's seat, but he grabbed her wrist.

"Start the car," Abby screamed.

"I can't." The more she struggled, the deeper his fingers dug into her flesh.

"Throw me the keys." Abby shoved the branch at her. "Here, use this. I'll start the bloody car."

In the cramped space between the car door and the steering wheel, Diana could only jab at the man.

"*Woman*," he said, frightening her with the intensity of his scowl and the crazy glint in his bloodshot eyes. "*Yu nogud woman. Yu kilim me tumas.*" He dropped her wrist, caught hold of the branch and yanked so hard he almost pulled her arm out of the socket before she let go.

"Ready?" Abby slid into the crevice between the driver's and the passenger's seats. She wrapped her arm around Diana's waist and jammed her left foot down on the accelerator. "Hold on." She shifted into drive, and the car jerked forward. Not fast enough, though. As the wheels spun and spit gravel, the man ran alongside.

Diana kicked, and he grabbed her ankle. "Damn it!" she shouted. "Let go." No matter what she did, this crazy wild man would not give up. He was stronger than she was, and he knew how to fight. Why hadn't she just given him the car? Suddenly she felt her hips sliding. "Abby," she screamed, "hold onto me." She twisted and kicked, using her last ounce of strength in an effort to free herself.

The man stumbled, and she reached for the steering wheel . . . for anything.

"Got you." Abby grunted, and with an enormous heave she pulled Diana back into the car. "Now," she said, "let's get the hell outa here. *Kwiktaem.*"

Diana slammed the door shut and stomped on the gas. She imagined him chasing after them, making up ground. But when she looked in the rearview mirror, he was standing still. Her Toyota was new and powerful, and even though the wheels spun in the loose gravel, he couldn't keep up. He shook his fist and grimaced, clutching his crotch.

"Oh, Lord." She tried to catch her breath. "What . . .?" Her heart was pounding so loudly she couldn't think. "I mean, where in blazes did he come from?"

Abby fanned her face with her fingers, her cheeks almost as red as her hair. "Don't ask *me.*"

"Unbelievable." Diana looked in the mirror again. All she could see now was the road and a cloud of dust. "I guess he gave up."

Abby snickered. "Poor pathetic bugger."

Diana took a deep breath and let it out in a giggle that was half-wail. "Pathetic. Leaves in his hair and the crazy . . ."

". . . penis wrapper. The sorriest example of one I've ever seen."

"Oh, so you're an expert on fashionable . . ."

". . . penis wrappers."

They exploded in laughter. *Penis wrapper.* "And," Diana sputtered, wiping her eyes, "he forgot his gun. What kind of carjacker shows up without a gun?"

"Sadly," Abby affected a mock frown, "the poor man lacked pockets."

It was hilarious. "No pants, no pockets."

"No gun . . ." Abby pounded the dashboard. "No car."

"Darn right." Diana fell over on the steering wheel choking with laughter and sending the car into a rut. They were headed up the hill toward the mission school at Montmartre. It was the wrong direction if they wanted to get back home, but they kept going anyway. Give the man time to slink off into the bush before they turned around.

Diana's car was the only one on the road, and there were no turnoffs, only a couple of gated driveways leading into messy fields of grass and overgrown coconut palms where a few cattle grazed.

The entrance to Montmartre was at the top of the hill. Through its open gate you could see a large expanse of parched grass and packed dirt surrounded by dormitories and classrooms in low wood-framed buildings. Skinny ni-Vanuatu boys in white shirts and long pants lounged on the steps while teenage girls in navy blue jumpers held hands and giggled as they paraded past.

Diana backed up and parked under a tree. Her appetite for laughter was gone now. Her shoulder ached, and as she climbed out of the car, her legs felt as wobbly as the lianas that hung from the trees. They walked a few steps to the edge of the hill and gazed out over a coconut plantation and the second lagoon.

"Who do you think he was?" she asked. She remembered a picture she'd seen of people from a village on another island performing a ritual dance before they jumped off a rickety tower with nothing but a vine tied around one ankle. The original bungee jumpers. "He looked like a villager from one of the outer islands, don't you think?"

Abby nodded. "Exactly. From Tanna or Pentecost, not here near the capital. It doesn't make sense." She pursed her lips and considered. "And why would he want to steal a car in the first place? He wouldn't be able to drive it anywhere on this little island without getting caught." She looked at her watch. "Good Lord. I should have picked the twins up ten minutes ago." She clicked her tongue against the roof of her mouth as they piled back into the car. "Their poor dear teacher. She's the one I worry about."

Diana started the car and turned it around. Her mind was as tired as her legs and arms. "Who?"

"The twins' kindergarten teacher. I dare say, my laddies manufacture their most spectacular mischief when I'm late. It's Simon who starts it every time. Causes trouble just to punish me." She threw her hands in the air and frowned. "Tell me, what's so important in a six-year-old's life that he can't wait a few minutes for his old mum?"

Diana smiled. Did mothers know how loving and proud their complaints about their children sounded to the rest of the world?

You couldn't miss the section of the road where they'd struggled with the man. Skid marks and thrown gravel, a discarded branch. Diana had been planning on driving right on past until she remembered the drawings. "Looks like our carjacker's gone," she said, pulling to the side of the road.

"No, keep going. He might still be nearby."

"I want to get our things." She was starting to shift into park when Abby clamped her hand around her arm.

"Are you insane?! If we have to tangle with him a second time, we may not be so lucky."

Glancing across the road, Diana winced at the thought of leaving the sketches behind. They were good, both of them.

"Come on, Diana. Let's go. *Kwicktaem.* Simon and Jeremy are waiting."

She took a deep breath and nodded. "Okay." She put the car in gear and started down the hill.

There were more shadows in the banyan tree now, more hiding places in its air roots for the spirits that would inhabit it after dark. *Nabanga* they called the tree here in Vanuatu. If it didn't rain, she thought, she'd come back tomorrow for their sketch books.

After picking up the twins and dropping them all back home, Diana headed back to her own house in Tassiriki. Just as she was turning onto the little side road that led to her driveway, another car pulled out.

"Hey, Diana." Alexi leaned out the window and waved. "I brought your hubby home to you." He waved again and drove off.

What? She looked at her watch. It was later than she thought. She'd expected to have time to shower before picking Jay up. She drove up their steep driveway and parked. Wondering if she looked like someone who'd just been in a fight, she glanced in the rearview mirror. Not too bad. She took a moment to straighten her hair and went on in. She was still tucking one last stray lock behind her ear when Jay stepped out of the kitchen.

"You're home," she said feigning surprise.

"Yeah. Alexi gave me a ride. He wanted to talk privately about the Fiji project."

They walked side-by-side through the shadowy entry and into the sunlight that flooded the dining room.

"Oh, my god!" He lifted her arm. "What the hell is this?"

The bruises on her forearm were already turning purple and red, blue on the inside where the man's thumb had pressed. She touched one of the bruises lightly. It seemed that she shouldn't have focused her concern on her messy hair. "It doesn't hurt," she said, moving away. A little sympathy would have been nice . . . "Abby and I were sketching on Montmartre Road, and a ni-Vanuatu man jumped out of the bush. He tried to steal our car. But don't worry, honey. The car is fine. Abby and I fought him off."

"You what? The car's insured, you know."

"I know."

"Wait." He knelt on one knee beside her and examined the scratches and bruises on her ankle, his back rising and falling with the expansion of his anger. "What kind of man does this to a woman?" He looked up, his nostrils flaring. "And what the hell were you thinking, going out there alone?"

"I wasn't alone. Abby was with me."

"I just don't understand why you would put yourself at risk. You're pregnant, for god's sake. And then you go out and do this."

"*I* do this?" An angry flood of tears burst loose. "I didn't ask to be attacked."

"And yet, you and Abby went out there alone on a deserted road. You must have known that wasn't safe."

She pressed her lips together. No one could have guessed that a man dressed in leaves and a penis-wrapper would jump out of the bush and try to steal her car. *No one!*

"Don't you understand, sweetheart?" he said, hugging her as though she might suddenly disappear. "That man could have been carrying a knife or a machete. He could have wanted something else from you besides the car."

She shook free of him. "He wanted the car," she said. "That's all. He called it a truck," she added with the hint of a smile. She didn't dare tell Jay what she thought she'd seen in the man's other hand. It may not even have been a knife. Besides, he'd dropped it.

He stood looking at her. Then he hugged her again. "I'm sorry," he said. "It's just . . . It's just that . . ." He choked out the words. "I worry about you, honey, you and our . . . Oh, my god, Diana. You're so pale. Let me feel your forehead."

"I don't have a fever."

"Of course not. You're in shock." He wiped her forehead. "Cold sweat."

"I'm not in shock. I mean, this guy pops out of nowhere and demands my car keys." She tried to laugh. "He surprised me. That's all." Suddenly she remembered they had a dinner invitation for that evening. "I've gotta go. I want to wash up and then rest for a while before we go to the party."

"I'll get some ice and some disinfectant for those wounds."

"Scratches."

43

It was dark when they arrived at Harbour View Restaurant. Diana took a deep breath and swung the car door open. She would have preferred staying home, but she didn't want Jay to think she wasn't up to it. And really, she was just fine. A little shaky, that was all.

They ducked under the bougainvillea-draped trellis and were starting toward the front door when suddenly she felt a wave of vertigo and grabbed Jay's elbow to steady herself.

"You all right?" he asked.

"Yeah," she said, loosening her grip. "I'm fine. They could sure use some better lighting here, though, don't you think?"

He placed his hand over hers, but as they continued through the open door to the reception desk, she suspected he wasn't convinced.

"The D-TAP party," he said.

An Asian woman half-hidden behind an arrangement of bird-of-paradise flowers frowned. "Dee-what?"

"Development Trust for Asia and the Pacific. Mr. Charbonneau's party."

"Ah, yes. This way please." The woman led them through what must have been the living room before the house became a restaurant and out onto a patio where tables were arranged along one side of a swimming pool.

"Mr. Charbonneau's party," the hostess announced, opening the door onto a narrow room with one long table down the middle.

"Hey, McIntoshes," Alexi said, waving. "Glad you could make it."

"Diana, how are you?" Suling asked with a sympathetic squint.

"I told them about our little mishap," Abby said.

"*Near* mishap," Diana countered. "A small adventure at the end of a pleasant afternoon."

"Too many adventures." Suling jabbed Alexi. "Before we married, you said Port Vila is so safe. I don't even need to lock my car, you said."

Alexi put his arm around her shoulder and squeezed. "Still, I'd wager it's safer than Shanghai. Anyway, until tonight, did you ever hear of anyone stealing a car in Port Vila?"

"Lincoln Toms," Saudur said.

Jay pulled out a chair and motioned for Diana to sit in it. "Where is everyone?" he asked, looking at the half-empty table.

"They'll trickle in when it's time to eat." Alexi turned back to Saudur. "Lincoln Toms? Oh, yeah. The guy who escaped from prison last year."

"Vanuatu's most notorious criminal." Saudur gave Abby a disapproving glance. "Something my wife doesn't seem to appreciate. He's escaped from prison more than once. Steals cars and whiskey. Uses the cars to stash the whiskey in the bush, and then, when he's had enough to drink, he drives around and gets caught. I guess he assumes no one will find his stash of booze and he can go back next time he breaks out of prison." Again the sideways glance, the pinched lips.

"And," Abby said, "for all we know Lincoln Toms is still in prison."

Alexi leaned forward. "The way I heard it, this Toms character drove his stolen car past the prison last year so he could wave at his buddies." He laughed. "Wanted to show them he knew how to drive a car."

"Wasn't our bloke," Abby said. She reached across in front of Saudur and scooped up a handful of peanuts. "Unless . . ." She considered the nuts in her hand. "Unless he ditched his prison garb."

Of course. The man was an escapee with nothing to wear but striped pants or an orange jumpsuit—whatever they wore in prison here. Hence the homemade penis wrapper. Diana shivered. Perhaps, despite his leafy necklace, their thwarted carjacker was not so comical after all. Frightening, she thought, remembering his expression as he dug his fingers into her arm, but not stupid.

"We don't need another description of your bloke's improvised outfit," Saudur said. He reached into the peanut bowl and came up empty.

Alexi raised another bowl to show Saudur that it too was empty.

It was past seven thirty, and they were all getting hungry. It wouldn't be right, though, Diana supposed, to order the food until Marshall arrived. Still . . . She looked at Jay and then at the kitchen.

He nodded and waved at the waiter. "Could we have the appetizer plate please," he said, "and some tea."

They nibbled on a sampling of Chinese appetizers and sipped tea for another twenty minutes. By the time the Fabrizios arrived, the Ifopos and McCurdys close behind, the barbecued pork and shrimp toast were gone.

"What's this?" McCurdy glared at the picked-over platters with open-mouthed disbelief. "You're eating without us?" He was a tall, husky man, towering over the table. But Leo McCurdy's hair was turning gray and his skin sagged. Height and aggression were his only advantages, leveraged now by the fact that most of the guests were seated.

"You're late," Jay said.

"Hey, there's still some pickled jellyfish." Alexi pinched up a cluster of semi-transparent strips with his chopsticks, allowing them to shake like a bunch of wriggling albino worms. "Very tender tonight."

McCurdy's face reddened. "Where's the chief?" he demanded.

Abby shrugged. "Who knows."

Ignoring her, McCurdy ushered his wife to the far end of the table. "Sea jelly," he grumbled. "You call that food?"

Food or not, even the jelly fish was gone before Marshall and Carole Anne showed up.

"Hey, chief," McCurdy said the moment the door opened. "We waited for ya."

Marshall paused in the ill-lit doorway. Then he put his arm around Carole Anne and squeezed her shoulder. "We ran into a little trouble," he said at last.

"A *little* trouble?" Carole Anne pulled away from him. There was a suppressed gasp as she stepped into the light where everyone could see the bruise on her neck, a splotchy purplish red from ear to ear.

"We were carjacked," Marshall said. "Late this afternoon on our way home from tennis. The company car."

"You, too?" Alexi asked.

Marshall ignored both Alexi and the knowing looks that were ricocheting around the table. He crossed his arms and uncrossed them as though he were an actor unsure how to play an unfamiliar role. "The guy was a well-known criminal," he said. "Lincoln Toms, a repeat offender. He escaped from jail late last night."

Saudur raised his eyebrows. "You see," he mouthed at Abby.

"They'll catch him soon enough," Marshall said. "No place to hide on a little island like this."

Carole Anne glared at him. "That's not the point." She turned toward the rows of sympathetic eyes on both sides of the dinner table. "Y'all don't know what it's like."

Jay squeezed Diana's hand.

"That naked man had his hands all over me." Carole Anne flapped her hands beside her head like someone fighting off a swarm of insects. She dropped her head and let her arms fall limp at her sides. "I don't know how I'll ever get over this," she sobbed.

Diana winced. She had to hold her hand over her mouth to keep from sobbing. Why did the attack seem worse now when Carole Anne was telling about it?

"Now, now," Marshall said. "It's all over, baby. You're safe now. Come on." He led her to a chair and sat her down. Positioning himself behind her, he rested his weight on her chair and addressed his audience. "This guy was a real wild man—crazy, matted hair, desperate eyes, dried blood on his neck. I could tell that he was capable of anything. And he was armed. These criminals can make a weapon out of anything. A shank they call it. He could have killed Carole Anne."

The image of a homemade knife—there all along, in the man's other hand—sent a cold shock up Diana's spine. The attack had happened so fast, and the sunlight . . . wasn't the light spotted under the trees or slanted or . . .? Her face went cold and then hot, and her stomach felt queasy. Too much tea. Or peanuts and jellyfish. If Marshall would just stop talking, they could eat.

"Sir." The waiter, who must have been as eager as the rest of them to get the meal started, came up behind Marshall. "Sir, may we . . .?"

"Scotch on the rocks."

"Sir, um . . ."

Marshall waved him away and sat down. "The guy had leaves around his neck. Leaves, for Christ's sake. And . . . well, since there are ladies present . . ." He smirked. "I won't describe the contraption that held his penis aloft. Armed and ready, so to speak." He broke into a big smile.

Bastard. Diana thought. Everything's fodder for his dirty jokes.

"Hey!" Jay said.

"Pardon me." Marshall bowed his head, but he looked more pleased than sorry. "Anyway, this guy was standing in the middle of the road, blocking it, and when I stopped the car, he ordered us out. That's when he grabbed Carole Anne and threatened to slit her throat."

Several women gasped.

"Oh, my lord," Peg McCurdy said.

If she interrupted right now, Diana realized, she could spoil Marshall's story by telling her own. She took a breath and leaned forward. She looked at Jay and then at Carole Anne.

"Nothing I could do," Marshall continued. "I had to give him the car keys."

"No question," McCurdy said to an enthusiastic chorus of agreement from his wife, Siole, and Fabrizio. "Absolutely! You did the right thing."

"He ordered me to lie flat on the ground," Marshall continued, "nose in the dirt. When I tried to see what he was doing, he said something like, '*You wantum me killum woman blong yu?*'"

Carole Anne whimpered.

"So I buried my nose in the weeds. Didn't look up until I heard him rev up the engine and dig out. God! I shudder to think what he did to my gears. Ground them getting into second, never did shift into third that I could hear."

Diana and Abby glanced at each other with barely disguised looks of triumph. Let Marshall finish his story first. Soon enough they would tell how they were successful in fighting off Lincoln Toms.

"Poor Carole Anne," Marshall patted her shoulder and tossed down a gulp of scotch. "She was hysterical by the time I got to her."

"I was the one with a knife at my throat."

"A shank, dear."

Diana wondered if there'd actually been a shank. Carole Anne's neck was bruised, but the skin wasn't broken. Unless the supposed shank was extremely dull, it may have been a figment of the Charbonneaus' imagination.

"Where's my gin and tonic?" Carole Anne turned frantically from side to side looking for the waiter. "You ordered one for me, didn't you?"

"Hey, calm down, baby." Marshall patted her shoulder.

She glared at him. "Mrs. Pettyjohn understood how I felt. She said I was in shock."

"The Australian High Commissioner's wife," Marshall said for the benefit of the socially unconnected. "She was coming from a doubles match with the Finance Minister's wife when she found us and graciously offered to take us to the police station herself."

"All I wanted was to go home and take a shower. Damn it, Marshall. I was still in shock." Carole Anne looked from face to face. "Y'all can't imagine how something like this absolutely turns your legs to jelly. I could hardly stand up. And still they expected me to remember what happened. It was all up to me, since Marshall had his head in the sand."

"Anyway, the authorities assured us they'll have the car back within a week."

"The car, the car. Who the hell cares about the car? I can't stop shaking." Carole Anne held out her hands to demonstrate how shaky they were. "I told Marshall I needed to go home." She scanned the table, assuring herself that everyone understood. "He ignored me and told the officer to bring us here."

Peg McCurdy grabbed Carole Anne's hand and squeezed it. "Poor dear," she said. "We're just glad you're all right."

Abby nodded sympathetically. Her eyes and Diana's met, and they both understood that they'd keep quiet for now about their own encounter with Lincoln Toms.

"Hey," Marshall said as he scanned the table—the smeared, empty appetizer plates, peanut bowls, and wine glasses. "Looks like it's time to eat."

A waiter hurried away. Moments later he returned with large serving bowls of hot and sour soup. Placing them on each of the two lazy Susans, he quickly ladled the soup into individual bowls. The salt and pepper squid came next and then the beef and broccoli followed by coconut crab, honey chicken, chili prawns, and fried rice.

Diana had thought she was hungry, but after the soup, she started feeling queasy. She served herself bite-sized servings of the squid and the beef and broccoli. When Jay gave her more coconut crab than she wanted, she pinched part of it up with her chopsticks and put it on his plate, smiling and shrugging at his raised eyebrows.

It was after the fried rice that she felt it, something damp between her legs. For a moment she couldn't move. A hot–cold flash numbed her face and the back of her neck. *No no no,* she cried inside. *Not this.* The voices and faces and plates of food fell away, and for a moment, time stopped and she was alone. She took a breath and blinked. Then she leaned across the table. "Abby," she whispered, trying to hide her panic, "can you come with me?"

All the way to the ladies' room, she was gripping Abby's hand and pulling her along.

"Are you all right?"

"Just wait here." Diana dropped Abby's hand and hurried into the stall.

"I'm bleeding," she said through the door in a stage whisper.

"Do you need help?"

"I don't think so." Diana pulled her panties up and unlatched the stall door.

"How much is it?"

"Just a stain."

"What color?"

"Brownish, like at the start or ending of a period."

Abby let her breath out and smiled. "You're just spotting. That's all. It's normal. It happened to me a time or two." She put her arms around Diana and held her until she stopped shaking.

"You really think it's all right?"

"I do."

As they started back to the table, Diana realized the queasiness she'd had at the table was gone. Still, she couldn't shake the feeling of dread. Jay was right. She should have been more careful. She and Abby could have gone anywhere to sketch. Why in the world had she chosen the road to Montmartre? And when Lincoln Toms demanded her keys, why in the name of God didn't she just hand them over? If anything happened to their baby, she'd have no one to blame but herself.

44

Maybe Abby was right, Diana thought as she climbed into bed that night. Maybe the stain on her underpants was an ordinary occurrence for a pregnant woman. Nothing to worry about. Diana hadn't dared mention it to Jay. After Carole Anne's overly dramatic rendition of the carjacking incident, he was already rattled enough. She pulled the sheet up under her chin and tried to suppress a little shiver. Carole Anne might be prone to hyperbole, but her story made it clearer than ever that the nearly naked man Diana and Abby encountered on Montmartre Road had been dangerous. Far from being just some weird and crazy guy, Lincoln Toms was Vanuatu's most notorious criminal.

After making excuses so they could leave the dinner early, she and Jay had hurried out to the car, Jay holding onto her as though she might disappear. After learning who her attacker was and how he'd treated Carole Anne, Jay was bound to accuse her of downplaying the incident. And he was right. She had. They sat in the front seat for a few minutes without speaking. Finally, he turned to her. In the moonlight she caught the glint of a tear in his eye. "When I think what could have happened to you . . ." He dropped his head and wiped his eye.

What could she have said?

Even later when they were at home, she'd felt too fragile to speak without bursting into tears. She'd taken as long as she could in the bathroom so that when she climbed into bed, Jay was already falling asleep. Without disturbing him, she slipped one hand under the sheet and rested it on her belly. *Baby*, she whispered, *sweet baby, take care of yourself. I love you so much.*

They'd already decided on a name for the baby if it turned out to be a girl: Noelle. They couldn't decide on a boy's name, though. Many an early evening they had sat out on the veranda gazing at the lagoon, drinking lemonade and trying out names: Justin, Shaun, Jason, Micah, Alex, Ryan. Diana liked Luke. Jay preferred something like Michael or Christopher. Whatever name they chose, they wouldn't know the baby's gender for another six months.

Through the open window Diana could see hazy shapes in the pale moonlight—a papaya tree, the downhill tilt of the land, a smooth sheen where the lagoon was. She imagined Lincoln Toms somewhere out there in his crown of leaves and penis wrapper parked beside a banyan tree stretched out on top of Marshall's car drinking whiskey, a slice of moon reflecting off the shiny white paint of the hood. As she was falling asleep, Jasper jumped up on the bed and arranged himself inside the curve of her body.

Later in one of her dreams, she found herself in a strange foreign town with a young man, someone with unruly blond curls whom she knew from other dreams. She raised her wine glass to toast something, and he reached across to steady her hand.

"Careful," he said. But a deep scarlet drop of wine had already spilled on the skirt of her white dress. Ignoring the spreading stain, the young man took her hand, and together they wandered among the stalls in an outdoor market. A vendor with long black braids held up a fat, red tomato for them to see. Suddenly, glaring at Diana, she squeezed it, digging her fingers into the flesh. No! Diana opened her mouth in a silent scream as the juice ran down the woman's arm. Then, doubling over in pain, Diana hobbled away.

She could already feel the flow, hot and wet between her legs, cold on the back of her dress. She turned to the young man.

But no, this was her responsibility. Her blood.

Her blood. The realization woke her. By the time she shuffled into the bathroom, knees together like a geisha, her nightgown was already stained. Jay was right behind her. "What's wrong?" he asked, rubbing his eyes.

He flicked on the light. Blood was trickling down her thighs, past her knees and down her calves.

"Oh, my god, Diana. Here. Sit down." He took her arm.

"What's happening?" she demanded. This wasn't a dream anymore. And this wasn't merely spotting.

"I don't know," Jay said. "I'll call Dr. Granville."

She nodded through her tears. While he was calling the doctor, she sat on the toilet. It didn't seem right to sit there though. Whatever was coming out of her, it wasn't waste. It was . . . Well, she didn't know exactly what it was, but how could she just let it fall into the toilet and be flushed down the drain?

A moment later Jay stood in the doorway, his face drained of color, his hands at his sides. "Dr. Granville is sending his wife. He said she's a midwife." For a moment he seemed frozen in place.

Diana was still sitting on the toilet, trapped there, and she needed to go someplace else. "Could you . . . um . . ." She looked around the room. She could sit in the shower. But, no. "Could you put something on our bed, honey. Something for me to sit on. Towels maybe, lots of towels."

He opened the closet door and threw a stack of towels over his arm.

"And could you bring me . . . some, uh, clean underpants," she said, struggling to get the words out.

The cramps had stopped, so she made her way on shaky legs to the sink to wet a washcloth. She was sitting again on the toilet seat, wiping blood off her legs when Jay returned with the underpants. "I'll need a heavy-days pad," she said, concentrating so the words would come out right. "They're in the bottom right drawer." The washcloth in her hand smelled metallic, like blood. It didn't remind her of the smell of menstrual flow. She wanted to consider whether that was a good sign, but it was hard to think. The bleeding had stopped, though. She hoped that was the end of it, that her body would repair whatever had happened and the baby would be all right.

Jay helped her to the bed. She was just getting settled on the towels, arranging pillows behind her back when the doorbell rang announcing Gwendolyn's arrival.

From then on, Diana's pain and bleeding stopped being private. Gwendolyn, who arrived with a serious-looking medical bag and none of her usual makeup, took charge of Diana and Jay's bedroom. "We'll keep watch," she said, setting down her bag. "Try to sleep." Clarita, who always heard the bell, came rushing down the stairs. She was quick to bring a chair and some water for the doctor's wife/receptionist/nurse/midwife, who crossed her legs and settled in for what could turn out to be a long night.

"Isn't there something I can do?" Diana asked. It was her body, her baby. She must be able to have some effect on what was happening to her.

"Just relax."

Oh, my god! That word again! How many times had she heard it? She didn't want to relax. She wanted to *do* something. But what they were all telling her, what Dr. Feliciano had been saying all along, was, "It's out of your control. Live with it. Smile. Breathe. You're helpless." She clamped her teeth together and glanced from one to the other. They looked as helpless as she felt—Jay and Clarita, scared; Gwendolyn, professionally noncommittal. Diana sighed and fell back on the pillows. Who in the world would help her?

It was three in the morning when she looked at the clock beside the bed. She'd felt too jittery to sleep. Besides, whether she could influence the course of events or not, still, she felt the duty to keep watch, to monitor her body. To pray for her baby. Eventually, Clarita nodded off in the chair she'd brought in, then Gwendolyn, then Jay, who had insisted on climbing into bed beside her. Then, just before dawn, Diana, too, fell asleep.

With the first rays of light sneaking in between the curtains and a mismatched chorus of birds chirping, cheeping, and warbling to greet the day, Diana was jolted awake by intense pain. It came in waves, low in her belly. And then in her back. She tried biting her lip, but she couldn't keep from crying out. This time the blood gushed out, filling her pad and spilling over onto the towel.

"Diana. Honey." Jay crawled back onto the bed and knelt over her, his face a portrait of agony.

"Mr. McIntosh," Gwendolyn said in the no-nonsense voice of a medical professional in charge of sickness and health, life and death. "Please wait outside."

He squeezed Diana's hand and kissed her cheek.

"Go," Diana said. Right now she couldn't think about him and whatever it was he was feeling.

"Mr. McIntosh, please."

Reluctantly, Jay stood up and backed away from the bed.

The contractions continued off and on for the rest of the morning. Sometimes clots and bits and lumps came out with the discharged blood. Sometimes nothing. The contractions would begin and build and continue as though they would never finish. She moaned through the pain; and when the contractions hit her hard, she screamed. She couldn't help it.

Then, just before noon, the contractions stopped. Diana sat up and looked around the room. At Jay, standing in the doorway looking bedraggled as he tried to muster a closed-mouth smile. At Gwendolyn, who, with her dark hair and big brown eyes, looked striking even without her makeup. At Clarita, who stood faithfully beside the bed looking anxious.

When she swung her legs over the side of the bed and stood up, everyone smiled and asked if she was feeling better. No one mentioned the baby. No one said, "It looks like the baby will be okay now." Or, "That's it. The baby is gone." But Diana knew. It was over. All that was left was to finish the painful, melancholy work of giving birth—either naturally or in the hospital—to a dead baby.

The afternoon sun was casting a scarlet glow on the bedcovers when the pain began to intensify again. This time she didn't fight it. She let it happen, the blood and clots and tissue slowly working its way out of her. She was too tired to stop it, too disheartened. Clarita brought clean towels and took the stained ones away.

She didn't cry as she was losing bits of the lining of her uterus. But then as the pain strengthened, strange animal sounds she didn't recognize came out of her. She felt too confused to think, but her body knew exactly what to do. Without her willing it, she pushed out a clot bigger than all the others.

Gwendolyn leaned over and picked it up. "Do you want to hold it?" she asked.

Diana held out her hands. It was tiny and warm, curled up in her hands like the pictures of fetuses she'd seen in magazines. And it wasn't moving.

Jay sobbed beside her, his hand on her shoulder. The way he stood there beside her struck Diana as being a cruel parody of a *crèche* scene, Joseph with his hand on Mary's shoulder and Mary holding Jesus. Except in this manger scene, Diana and Jay's baby was dead.

45

*D*iana ran her hand down Jasper's back, taking what comfort she could from his warm fur and vibrating body. "You're a good kitty," she whispered. He raised his head and squeaked a tiny meow. Ever since the miscarriage, as though he knew she needed him, Jasper had stayed close to her. Now, making room for the book in her lap, he stayed snuggled up beside her leg.

She rubbed her fingers over the cover of the old corner-curled paperback as if it had something to tell her. And heaven knows, she did need some direction.

The first few days after the miscarriage, she was a basket case, too tired and weak to do anything. All she'd wanted was to be left alone to cry. For a while, crying had felt good. Only for a while, though. After that, it just made her chest ache and her eyes puff up, reminding her and everyone else that the pregnancy she'd waited so long for had failed. That her baby, the baby that never became more than a fetus, was dead and buried.

That was just one more thing that haunted her: the burial. She bit her lip. Maybe they should have pretended the fetus was just another blood clot and flushed it down the toilet. There'd been nothing particularly right and solemn about what they did. It was more like the "funeral" she and the neighbor kids performed on a summer's day for a dead bird than a real burial service. Jay had wrapped the fetus in an embroidered handkerchief and placed it in a lacquer box. Then, with his arm holding her up, they'd taken the box out to the backyard to the hole he'd prepared. After he covered the box with dirt, neither of them could think of a prayer suitable for a fetus, so they simply stood in silence for a moment looking down at the bit of disturbed earth. And then they left. No one else was there except Clarita, watching from the kitchen window.

Now, five weeks after the miscarriage, Diana's sadness was impervious to crying. With every passing day her grief burrowed deeper and spread wider into everything she saw and touched. This baby had been her hope. And now it was gone. Without that hope, nothing else mattered.

Jay went to work every day, carrying on. When he returned home, they smiled tiny smiles and made the smallest of small talk. Neither of them wanted to discuss the miscarriage, but they couldn't maintain interest in anything else. After dinner the prior night, Jay had suggested they listen to music.

"Okay," Diana said. "What do you want to hear?"

He shrugged. "You choose."

She popped a Whitney Houston cassette into the player and sat down beside him on the sofa. The first song was okay. She even forced herself to hum along now and then. Only a few bars into the second song, though, she had to jump up and stop it before she drowned in a tsunami of musical drama and sorrow. She tried a few more cassettes, but the loud upbeat songs grated on her nerves, and even Beethoven stirred up emotions she wasn't ready to contend with.

Maybe, she'd decided the following morning, reading would be something she could handle.

Port Vila didn't have a bookstore, but it did have a small library. She'd peeked in one day months ago and found nothing but a colorless room that looked more like a storage space for a used-book store, so she'd turned right around and left. This morning, though, she'd needed a book. Opening the door and venturing inside, she passed through a thin shaft of light dancing with dust motes and began looking for the fiction section. What she found was two small shelves marked fiction, most of which appeared to be hundred-year-old novels and cheap supermarket romances. Finally on the lower shelf she found *The Trembling of a Leaf,* a book of short stories about the South Seas by Somerset Maugham.

It should have been a good choice. And yet, here she was, still sliding her fingers over the cover. It occurred to her that the Tahitian woman smiling out at her was the standard image of a South Pacific Paradise—a beautiful woman in a sarong with flowers in her hair sitting on the grass stringing frangipani flowers into leis. She was a white man's image of Paradise that somehow everyone else had been conditioned to adopt.

Jasper looked up at her and meowed his tiny squeak. This was her Paradise, she supposed—this perfect house, this veranda that ended in planters filled with bright pink bougainvillea. The view of the lagoons was as lovely as anyone could hope for. And though the pleasure it brought Diana these days was muted, the breeze was indeed pleasant and the plastic-slatted lounge chair she sat in was comfortable. She sighed and opened the book to the first story.

It began with a long paragraph about a man swimming in the sea, showering, drying himself, and then dressing for breakfast. In the second paragraph, which was even longer, the man complained about the mosquitoes, the heat, and the constant roar of the breakers on the reef. It was obvious already that the man, who coincidentally was named Macintosh, hated his situation. Everything about the beautiful island seemed to be driving him crazy. To find out why, she'd have to keep reading. Her mind kept wandering, though. Even when she succeeded in reading a whole page, she found that by the time she reached the end of it, she had no idea what she'd just read.

Folding back her page, she closed the book and looked out at the grassy, downhill slope of their front yard. *I won't forget you,* she whispered. Everyone else wanted her to move on, to forget about her baby, the small promise of life that had seemed so real to her when it lived inside her womb. At lunch yesterday, Suling had tried to encourage her by telling her not to worry. She would surely get pregnant again soon. Suling hadn't meant to call attention to her own bulging belly, but her hand just naturally fell there.

She and Abby had dragged Diana out to lunch at La Terrasse to cheer her up, and for a while it seemed to be working. When you were surrounded by Port Vila, you couldn't ignore its distinctive enthusiasm for life—the chatter and clatter of expats and locals inside the little café and outside at the sidewalk tables, the traffic on the street, the ocean-scented breeze. As time went on, though, the invisible shape of what wasn't said cast an ever larger shadow. Why didn't either of her friends mention the baby she lost? Okay, the fetus, but it was on its way to becoming a baby. And why couldn't Diana bring herself to talk about it?

She wiped her eyes and stood up, dropping the book on the chair next to Jasper. He meowed his little peep, and she leaned over and scratched him behind the ears. "I'm going to take a walk," she told him. She would walk down the hill, maybe turn into the Radisson, walk through its lobby, past the swimming pool and out onto the little island with the path along its shore and the back nine holes of a golf course in the center. She wouldn't think. She'd just walk. And maybe, for just a little while, she'd forget.

46

Walking was one way Diana got through her days. Sketching was another. When she wielded a pencil or paintbrush, she didn't have to think about herself. She didn't have to plan and make sense of her life. She could just wander around, a sketchbook under her arm, a pencil in her pocket. And when something caught her eye, she could simply sit down and make a quick sketch of it. If drawing involved making choices—emphasizing one pattern or shape over another, choosing which leaf or tree or person to accentuate, which to heighten or soften—they came naturally to her. She'd been sketching what she saw all her life.

Most mornings after breakfast, she walked down to the Radisson Hotel, through the grounds, and around the little island, where tourists hit golf balls and walkers like her listened to waves lap against the shore and watched shorebirds wade and fly.

She took the little lasagna-pan-shaped ferry to Erakor Island where she swam in the lagoon and walked on the trail. She sketched Aussie children on the beach and the ni-Vanuatu waitress in the little café. She walked out to the end of the island where Erakor Lagoon met the Pacific Ocean and sketched the waves and the graceful, tangled mangroves.

When she got back to the house, she elaborated on the sketches with colored pencils or watercolor.

Thus she got through the days and weeks without crying too much. During the dark and silent hours of night, however, her thoughts inevitably sank into a morass of sadness and defeat.

It took a month for her to finish reading the first story in Somerset Maugham's book of short stories. Each time she sat down to read it, her mind wandered. Sometimes she paced back and forth on the veranda as she read. It was not a happy story. Despite being set on a beautiful little island in Samoa, it was all about the clashing personalities of two men, the British administrator of the island and his assistant, Macintosh. On page after page, Macintosh found more reasons to hate his boss until he was obsessed with his hatred. The ending came fast. Reading it, she could only gasp and slam the book shut.

That night in bed, she told Jay she was going to take the book back to the library without reading the other stories.

"Why?" He rose up on his elbow and looked at her. "He's a great writer."

"Maybe so, but his stories are too dark, at least the first one was. A murder and a suicide? The main character walking out into the ocean and blowing his brains out? You can't get much darker than that."

"Hm. Did he have a good reason?"

"You could say so. He was implicated in the death of the other man."

Jay nodded and fell back on his pillow.

In the past, they would have had a longer discussion. They used to enjoy talking about the books they were reading. Now neither of them had the heart to talk about difficult topics.

"Night," Jay said.

"Goodnight, honey."

What woke her from a more-or-less sound sleep she couldn't say. It might have been a noise . . . maybe a feeling. All she knew was, something was wrong somewhere. She reached for Jay and blinked her eyes open. The sheet on his side of the bed retained his shape, but it was flattened, as though he'd melted into the bed.

"Jay," she called softly, throwing off the sheet. "Where are you?" She hurried to the bathroom. She was going to feel foolish if he'd just gone there to pee.

He wasn't in the bathroom, though.

She started down the hallway, poking her head into the nursery that was now just a study. "Jay?" she called, her voice just above a whisper in deference to the secret quiet of the night.

She peeked in the laundry room. Then she walked into the kitchen where pale moonlight fell silently on the breakfast table and the counters and floor. The view out the window—the jagged shadows and complicated patterns of dark and darker in the jungle-like area behind the house—made her shiver.

"Jay." She stood at the top of the three steps that led down to the combined dining and living room. With the large windows across the front of the house and shiny white tile floor, you didn't need a full moon to see that Jay wasn't there. She clasped her hands together and tried to think where he might be. He couldn't just disappear. Their car was still in the carport. She'd seen it there when she looked out the kitchen window.

The house was so still and quiet that she felt a momentary sensation of unreality. Then, suddenly, the silence was broken by a strange noise. She ran down the stairs and across the dining room, her bare feet barely touching the white Italian tile.

There it was again. It sounded like someone choking. She dashed across the living room and yanked open the sliding door to the veranda. And there he was, sitting on one of the plastic chairs, his head between his knees, his back heaving, as though he couldn't breathe.

"Jay!" She hit his back. "What is it?" Was he crying? She'd never seen him actually cry. Tear up maybe, but nothing like this. "Jay." She rubbed his back and the back of his neck.

A wail escaped from his throat followed by more shaking.

"Honey. What's wrong?" She rubbed up and down his back. His muscles felt tight enough to snap. She ran her fingers through his hair, massaging the back of his head until he stopped panting. His breathing was still ragged though. Now and then little high sounds escaped from his throat. She continued massaging his shoulders and waited.

Finally he was still, his elbows resting on his pale white knees. He raised his head and wiped his eyes and nose on his T-shirt.

She pulled up a chair, and they sat together side by side, looking out at the starry sky and the crescent moon. The occasional fruit bat flitting from tree to tree. "Do you want to talk about it?" she asked.

He wiped his nose again. Then he stood up and walked away, stopping at the far end of the veranda, his back to Diana. "I can't stop thinking about her," he said finally, turning to face her. "I held her in my hand—our child . . . not quite a child. And now she's gone." He wiped his eye. "Touching her," he said, "she seemed so real. She *was* real."

Diana nodded. She walked toward him, and they stood looking out at the lagoons, Jay's arm on her shoulders, her arm around his waist.

"He might have been a boy," she said.

"No," he said. She thought she heard the hint of a smile in his voice. "I think she was a girl."

47

Their papaya surplus reminded Diana of tomato season back home when you had so many tomatoes coming ripe all at once that you had to give them away to friends and neighbors. The main difference was that papayas grow and ripen all year long. Diana and Jay figured their embarrassment of papaya riches was due to the lunch habits of Henri's workers. They must have grabbed papayas on the way to work, sliced them open for lunch, and then tossed the seeds into the yard. By the time Diana and Jay moved in, small papaya trees were growing everywhere. They'd pulled many of them out, leaving only those trees that grew at the edge of the yard. Now they were all bearing fruit—big juicy papayas, some as fat as your head; others as long as a celery stalk.

Jay's solution to the oversupply was to take a couple baskets of papayas to work every Friday morning and share them with the secretaries and officers. And today was Friday.

Diana left her coffee on the table, slipped into her sandals, and hurried outside to help. Peeking into the open trunk of the car, she saw that he'd already filled the first basket.

It didn't take long for her to find a long, fat papaya blushing orange through the green. Such amazing trees, she thought as she carried the papaya over to the car. She did love the trees' exuberant rush to life, even though—she had to admit it—at times she'd resented their effortless fertility. You couldn't be jealous of trees, though.

She smiled at herself and placed the papaya in the second basket.

Jay was making his way up from the front yard now, his arms overloaded with fruit. "Let me help," she called, hurrying down the still uneven surface of their side yard. As she reached for the big papaya he was balancing precariously in his arms, she felt the urge to hug him instead. Something about seeing him cry the night before had made her love him more than ever. Men should cry more often, she thought as they walked side by side to the car.

"It must be hard," she said.

"What?" Jay stowed his papayas and straightened up.

"I mean, men don't give themselves permission to cry. That must be hard."

He shrugged. "I never thought of it that way." He closed the trunk and fished in his pocket for the keys. "Do you need the car today?"

"Yeah. Abby and I are going to discuss Suling's baby shower over lunch at La Terrasse."

Jay gave her a good-for-you smile and squeezed her shoulder.

She smiled back. It felt as though they were starting to heal. Seeing him cry last night had changed things, made her realize the miscarriage wasn't just hers to bear; it was theirs. They were in this together.

"Ready?"

"Just let me grab my purse."

It was a lovely morning, blue sky, fluffy white clouds. Diana commented on it as she drove down their driveway. And Jay agreed, even though most mornings in Vanuatu were every bit as nice as this one.

As they started up the hill, he rested his hand on her bare knee. "Shall we try again?" he asked.

She knew what he meant, but something about the phrase "try again" hit her wrong. "I don't want to think about it like that. *Try.*" She scrunched up her face. "It's such a brittle, weak word. Why the hell do people talk about it that way? It's like saying I'll try to climb Mt. Everest when you don't believe you can do it. Like making tight fists and gritting your teeth."

"Wow! Sounds like I hit a nerve."

"Yeah," she said, wrinkling her brow. "I guess so."

"So how shall we talk about it?"

"I don't know, honey." She sucked her breath in through her teeth. "Suddenly I just hate that word. *Try.*" She spit it out as though it were poison. They were coming over the crest of the hill now, looking down on the town and the bay. Soon they'd be at Jay's office. She wanted to answer him before they arrived. "How shall we talk about it? Well . . . let's just say we're going to live our lives. There's nothing physically wrong with either of us. Right? So let's just assume that we'll eventually have children. Or not." It wasn't lost on her that this was what Jay had been saying for a long time. She hadn't been able to accept it, though. Hadn't been able to give up control, a control she never actually had.

He squeezed her knee. "And not worry about it? Sounds good to me."

She turned onto the side street and pulled up to the curb behind a midnight blue Toyota.

"The new office car," Jay said.

Diana smiled. "Yeah. I heard Carole Anne refused to ride in the old white Toyota. Said Lincoln Toms sullied it by his 'dirty, criminal' presence."

Jay leaned over for a kiss-the-wife-good-bye peck. His lips were soft and warm, and they lingered longer than usual before he hopped out and disappeared into the building.

Back to work, she thought, remembering how alone she'd felt and, yes, resentful when he went back so soon after the miscarriage. She hadn't stopped to think how hard it might have been for him.

She knew the people he worked with. Except for the secretaries and a couple of technical assistants, they were all men, and none of them would have approved of him taking time off to grieve for his wife's miscarriage. Men don't cry, and miscarriages are women's business. They might have said a word or two of sympathy, and then it was back to work.

As she pulled out onto the street, Diana felt a wave of compassion for him. He'd had to stuff it all down, as though losing the promise of a child meant nothing to him.

Stiff upper lip, she thought as she backed away from the midnight blue Toyota. It wasn't only men, though. After the carjacking, Carole Anne had given rein to her emotions, but she was the only one. The rest of them, men and women alike, were smirking inside, thinking her reaction was way over the top. Even Diana and Abby were imagining themselves braver and tougher than Carole Anne was.

Everyone wants to be macho, she thought as she drove up the hill and around the bend. Starting down the other side, the road curved and quickly fell into shadow. The steep hillside on her left and the huge overhanging trees from the jungle on her right combined to block out the light.

Moments later, she was out of the shadows, looking down on their Tassiriki house and the lagoons, the prospect of another day stretching out before her.

Seattle

1996

48

The crowd was beginning to thin out. Finally, Diana could catch her breath and look around. Mom seemed pleased with the turnout, and the gallery owner had sidled up to Diana a couple of times to whisper that sales were going well. She hadn't had a chance to see for herself, though.

She was headed toward a wall of her favorite paintings when a waiter swooped in beside her, an ironic smile on his lips. He raised one eyebrow and offered her the last flute of champagne on his tray. Returning his ironic smile, she couldn't resist a tiny head shake at his perfection as she took the champagne. He was so quintessentially artsy—hair smoothed back in a ponytail, features chiseled to reflect subtleties of light, and a practiced manner that was simultaneously flirty and reserved. Mom sure knew how to pick them. But then, Mom knew all there was to know about arranging an art exhibit.

She'd been planning this one ever since Diana first let it slip in one of her Sunday letters that someone at the University of Washington was talking to Jay about a job prospect. Even before he accepted the offer, Mom had started talking to gallery owners, showing them samples of Diana's art, inquiring about how far out each of them were scheduled. She ignored Diana's objections about jumping the gun. By then, they all knew that if Jay didn't accept this offer, he'd accept the next one or the next. He still liked his work with D-TAP, but in the past seven years he'd experienced international development in every corner of Asia. He'd done it all. Besides, now things were different for them.

Wandering over to a quiet spot along the wall, Diana stopped in front of *Firewood Parade*. It had been her first serious painting. Until then, she'd only been fooling around with art, considering it more of a hobby. After her miscarriage it was a good distraction.

Then one morning, coming back from her usual walk down to the Radisson and around the golf course island, she happened upon a stunning sight: three ni-Vanuatu women and two girls cutting across the field carrying firewood on their heads—enormous headdresses of tangled branches. Their feet were hidden by tall grass, so they seemed to be sailing across the landscape. She'd stood there, open-mouthed, struck by the way the thin morning light outlined their faces and the graceful curves of their necks and shoulders, turning them into a painting. It was, she realized, a painting she needed to create.

She'd worked on that painting for two weeks and still wasn't satisfied with the results. She knew how to sketch, but she didn't yet have the technical ability to create a work of art that did justice to the image of those three women and two girls that she carried around in her head. What she needed was a crash course in painting techniques—several courses, in fact. And she needed to create the course of study for herself.

That realization, she remembered, had thrown her into a whirlwind of activity. She'd signed up for an intensive watercolor class in Suva, and she'd traveled to Sydney to study oil painting. Thanks to a letter of recommendation from her mom, she'd been accepted into a small class taught by a well-known Australian artist.

And it all started with the graceful parade of these three women and two girls with firewood on their heads. They'd changed her life. She smiled at them, these ladies who'd helped her find something she really cared about and, with hard work, was able to make happen.

She was so caught up in her thoughts that she didn't notice Jay coming up behind her until she felt his arm around her waist.

"Congratulations, honey," he said, kissing her cheek. "Looks like your exhibit is a huge success." He pointed at the red sticker on the card below *Firewood Parade*. "Another sale, I see."

"Uh huh."

"Uh huh? That's all? You don't sound sufficiently pleased."

She sucked in her breath and let it out in a big whoosh. "I know. I'm glad it sold. It's just that . . ." She pressed her lips together. "I hate to let go of this painting."

"That's the nature of the business, honey."

She elbowed him in the ribs. "So when did you become such a businessman?" She was still getting used to his new role as a professor—still an international development expert, but now he taught at the University of Washington and lectured around the country.

He grinned. "I was trying to convince myself not to shed a tear over the Samoan band painting. It has a red dot, too."

She wasn't surprised that that one sold. It was a real crowd-pleaser. Taken from a sketch she made in Apia Western Samoa when she accompanied Jay on one of his missions, it depicted a parade band that had passed below their balcony at Aggie Gray's. All men and all husky, the band members wore white military jackets, black sandals, and *lava lavas*, those ubiquitous wrap-around skirts that leave the men's muscular brown legs bare. As the band passed, she remembered, they'd been playing "Semper Fidelis." It seemed that all around the world people love a John Philip Sousa march.

She felt a light tap on her shoulder and turned to see a tall slim young woman in a sophisticated black dress trying not to teeter on her spiky high heels. Beside her stood a definitely-ready-to-leave young man in faded jeans and a T-shirt.

"I adore your paintings," the woman gushed. "Absolutely adore them. The way you capture light is so masterful. And such exotic subjects."

"Thank you."

"I wish I could afford this one." She made sad eyes at *Firewood Parade.*

"It's already sold," the young man said, jabbing his finger at the red sticker. "Thanks for inviting us." And with that, he clamped onto his girlfriend's arm and led her away.

Diana smiled and glanced around the room. She was about to ask about Noelle when she saw her and Mom heading their way.

"Somebody's sleepy," Mom said. It was an understatement. Even though Noelle's Cinderella dress was perky as ever, her eyes were only a millimeter above closed for the night.

"Poor baby." Diana knelt and opened her arms to the little girl. "Come here, kitten."

"I'll take her home." Jay said. "You and your mom can wrap things up and meet us there."

Diana kissed Noelle's cheek. "Okay," she said, hugging her tight for a long minute before letting go so Jay could put their darling sleepy daughter to bed.

End

Acknowledgments

*M*y husband, Eugene, died twenty-one years ago, and yet I still find myself thanking him—this time for all the adventures, trials, and delights of our life together. As a young woman, I was determined not to marry someone who was dull and boring. Eugene turned out to be the perfect choice.

For this novel, I needed only a smattering of internet research. For the most part, I relied on my journals to fill in the many details about life in the Philippines during the December 1989 coup attempt and in Vanuatu during the early 1990s.

Throughout the long process of writing the book, I had the support, advice, and friendship of my critique group. Over coffee (and if we stayed long enough, baked potatoes with sour cream, bacon, and cheese), we read and critiqued our work. The suggestions I received from these talented ladies were invaluable. Thank you Gretchen Houser, Katie Johnson, Dianne Forth, and Maureen Rogers. Thank you also to Paddy Eger, Emily Hill, and Sandra Walker who helped me earlier in the process.

Finding Susan Meyer, my developmental editor, was a lucky break. I loved working with her.

She Writes Press was another lucky find. Thank you to Brooke Warner, the publisher, Shannon Green, my editorial manager,

Jennifer Caven, and to everyone at She Writes Press who helped to make the publication of my novel possible.

A big thank you to Lucinda Dyer and Bryan Azorsky of Nodebud for guiding me through the creation of my magnificent new website. I wouldn't have had the patience or skill to do all the work required without their cheerful coaching and expertise. And finally, I'm indebted to Caitlin Hamilton Summie and Rick Summie, my publicists, for helping me get the word out. Caitlin has been unfailingly kind and understanding, and her background and hard work have been invaluable.

About the Author

*N*icki Chen is the author of the award-winning novel *Tiger Tail Soup*. She was born in Sedro-Woolley, Washington, and spent nearly twenty years abroad, in the Philippines and then Vanuatu. While living in Vanuatu, she earned her MFA in creative writing from Vermont College of Fine Arts. She now lives in Edmonds, Washington.

Author photo © Lifetouch

SELECTED TITLES FROM SHE WRITES PRESS

She Writes Press is an independent publishing
company founded to serve women writers everywhere.
Visit us at www.shewritespress.com.

As Long As It's Perfect by Lisa Tognola. $16.95, 978-1-63152-624-4.
What happens when you ignore the signs that you're living beyond
your means? When married mother of three Janie Margolis's house
lust gets the best of her, she is catapulted into a years-long quest for
domicile perfection—one that nearly ruins her marriage.

The Moon Always Rising by Alice C. Early. $16.95, 978-1-63152-
683-1. When Eleanor "Els" Gordon's life cracks apart, she exiles
herself to a derelict plantation house on the Caribbean island of
Nevis—and discovers, with the help of her resident ghost, that only
through love and forgiveness can she untangle years-old family
secrets and set herself free to love again.

Center Ring by Nicole Waggoner. $17.95, 978-1-63152-034-1.
When a startling confession rattles a group of tightly knit women
to its core, the friends are left analyzing their own roads not taken
and the vastly different choices they've made in life and love.

Play for Me by Céline Keating. $16.95, 978-1-63152-972-6. Middle-
aged Lily impulsively joins a touring folk-rock band, leaving her job
and marriage behind in an attempt to find a second chance at life,
passion, and art.

Magic Flute by Patricia Minger. $16.95, 978-1-63152-093-8. When
a car accident puts an end to ambitious flutist Liz Morgan's dreams,
she returns to her childhood hometown in Wales in an effort to
reinvent her path.

Peregrine Island by Diane B. Saxton. $16.95, 978-1-63152-151-5. The
Peregrine family's lives are turned upside-down one summer when
so-called "art experts" appear on the doorstep of their Connecticut
island home to appraise a favorite heirloom painting—and
incriminating papers are discovered behind the painting in question.